keeping Kate

Praise for *Keeping Kate*

"Suspense and unusually vivid characters—people as complex and surprising as anyone you might know—distinguish this debut novel about horrifying family secrets. An engrossing read from a young writer to watch. Farnsworth weaves a familiar tale with a vibrant modern twist."

—ANNETTE HAWS, author of *The Accidental Marriage* and *Waiting for the Light to Change*

"A story with a lot of heart, *Keeping Kate* took me to beautiful locations and introduced me to interesting characters. It's a sweet LDS romance that's appropriate for even the most sensitive readers."

—REBECCA H. JAMISON, author of *Persuasion: A Latter-day Tale*, *Emma: A Latter-day Tale*, and *Sense and Sensibility: A Latter-day Tale*

"If you're as enchanted by *Jane Eyre* as I, *Keeping Kate* will have you mesmerized from the first page. Lauren Winder Farnsworth weaves a tale of promise, heartache, and redemption. Just as the lead character, Kate Evans, is on the cusp of her happily ever after, circumstances toss her into turmoil. The grace with which she moves through these challenges is truly endearing. The supporting characters advance the story in ways that are at once charming and maddening. *Keeping Kate* will keep you turning pages, gasping, and cheering. Farnsworth's debut novel is certain to become a modern classic."

—CAROLYN STEELE, author of *Willow Springs*

LAUREN WINDER FARNSWORTH

keeping Kate

BONNEVILLE BOOKS™
An Imprint of Cedar Fort, Inc.
Springville, Utah

This is a work of fiction. The characters, names, incidents, places, and dialogue are products of the author's imagination and are not to be construed as real. The opinions and views expressed herein belong solely to the author and do not necessarily represent the opinions or views of Cedar Fort, Inc. Permission for the use of sources, graphics, and photos is also solely the responsibility of the author.

ISBN 13: 978-1-4621-1563-1

Published by Bonneville Books, an imprint of Cedar Fort, Inc.
2373 W. 700 S., Springville, UT 84663
Distributed by Cedar Fort, Inc., www.cedarfort.com

LIBRARY OF CONGRESS CATALOGING-IN-PUBLICATION DATA

Farnsworth, Lauren Winder, 1986-
Keeping Kate / Lauren Winder Farnsworth.
pages cm
ISBN 978-1-4621-1563-1 (perfect : alk. paper)
1. Single women--Fiction. 2. Man-woman relationships--Fiction. I. Title.
PS3606.A7262K44 2015
813'.6--dc23
2014033314

Cover design by Michelle May
Cover design © 2015 by Lyle Mortimer
Edited and typeset by Melissa J. Caldwell

Printed in the United States of America

10 9 8 7 6 5 4 3 2 1

For Ali—you know what you did. Thank you for ensuring that I don't make a complete idiot of myself. My "appreciation cup" runneth over. I love you to bits!

Also for Bryan, my very own beautifully imperfect fairy tale. I'm so blessed to get to write my forever with you. I love you.

prologue

"Cam, I'm home!" Tyler Thorne called as he closed the front door to the one-bedroom apartment behind him. He heard rapid footsteps almost immediately, and his dark-haired wife rounded the corner into the entry and threw herself toward him, her brown eyes snapping with excitement. Tyler eagerly enfolded her in his arms, picking her up easily off the floor as he kissed her soundly.

"You're late!" Camille Vance Thorne said resentfully, but the animation on her face belied her indignant tone.

"The train was late . . . again," he said sheepishly, rubbing a hand along his six o'clock shadow.

"You already know how I'm going to respond to that," Camille said, her smile tightening ever so slightly.

Tyler did indeed. The old model BMW that Tyler had driven in his high school days was currently their only mode of transportation. He left it at home with Camille while he took the train to his MBA classes at Northwestern University every morning. Camille disliked the arrangement and couldn't understand why, with literally millions of dollars sitting in a trust fund waiting for his use, he wouldn't just buy himself a new car. Then he could stop depending on the unreliable mass transit system, and she could stop worrying about his safety on a daily basis. But Tyler couldn't do it. He wouldn't give Harrison Thorne the satisfaction of knowing that his son couldn't make it on his own. Camille refused to condone the forced physical and emotional separation from Tyler's father, but Tyler wouldn't budge. Other than the annual visit to the Utah ranch where the center of Harrison's lucrative horse-breeding enterprise resided, Tyler's relationship with his father would remain cold and distant. That was how it had always been, dating from the death of Tyler's mother nearly fifteen years earlier. And now, that was how he preferred it.

Tyler decided to ignore Camille's veiled jab at his stubbornness and smiled as he followed her into the kitchen. He noted immediately that the table had been set with candles and their more formal dinnerware. He watched as Camille pulled a pork roast from the oven and set dishes of potatoes and green beans on the table.

"It looks amazing," Tyler said warmly. "You must have been working all day on this. What's the occasion?"

Camille's face fell as she looked up at him. "Don't tell me you forgot! I reminded you this morning!"

"You did?" Tyler asked, feigning confusion and trying not to smile. "About what?"

Camille sank dejectedly into a chair. "Nothing. Never mind."

Tyler couldn't stand to see that look on her face. He immediately dropped the façade. Pulling her up from the chair, he drew her close. "I'm kidding, Cam, I promise. Of course I remember. Happy anniversary."

Relief flooded her eyes as she gazed up at him. "Rude," she said in mock indignation, but a smile lit her face. She hugged him tightly. "Happy anniversary! Can you believe it's been five years? We're *veterans* now!" Laughing as she let him go, she put a basket of steaming rolls in front of his plate. "And achieving veteran status warrants a decent home-cooked meal. Besides, you know how much I *love* cooking for you."

Tyler chuckled and rolled his eyes. Camille loathed cooking, which made the fact that she'd put so much effort into this dinner all the more precious to him.

They ate slowly, talking over their day as they always did. Tyler laughingly explained how one of his professors had spent weeks building up a guest speaker for his class, only to snore loudly through her entire presentation. Camille updated him on their neighbors' comings and goings. There was plenty to tell, since she often complained that she could hear it through the wall every time one of them blinked too loudly.

When the meal was over and the leftovers stashed in the refrigerator, Tyler suddenly felt a change in the air. He had noticed a strange, restless excitement in Camille's demeanor over the past week but had assumed it was simply her anticipation of their anniversary and had not asked about it. But as her eyes became steadily brighter, he knew he had missed something and his curiosity flared immediately. As they sat close beside each other on the sunken couch, watching the lights of downtown Chicago twinkle from the dark windows, he knew he had to ask.

"So what's going on?" he questioned, smoothing back the silky, chestnut strands from around her face and tucking them behind her ear. "You've had this irritatingly secretive look for days now. Are you going to let me in on it?"

"Eventually." Camille smiled up at him. "I didn't think you'd even noticed. It sure took you long enough to say something. Your forbearance is impressive."

"Gee, thanks," Tyler said sarcastically. "You've been torturing me on purpose. I appreciate it."

"You bet." She smiled and kissed the underside of his chin.

"So spill," Tyler prodded, poking her gently in the side. "What's up?"

"Well . . . ," Camille hedged, biting her lip. Her look changed from playful to slightly nervous. "I . . . um . . ."

"What is it?" Tyler asked, suddenly alarmed by her expression and not sure why. He gently moved Camille from her lounging position against his chest and turned her to face him. "Tell me," he said firmly.

"You have to promise not to freak out," she pleaded and grasped at his hand. "I mean, I know this isn't the best time, with your MBA and all that student debt we have . . ."

"Best time for what?" Tyler asked through clenched teeth. "What are you talking about, Cam?" He struggled to keep from squeezing her hand too hard, concentrating on keeping his expression relaxed.

He usually kept very tight control of his emotions, and he knew that Camille depended on that control. If he lost his cool, Camille would undoubtedly lose hers in unison.

"Is this about finances?" he asked calmly. He really didn't want to talk about that again. It was old news that they were poor because of his paternal prejudices.

"No, not just finances." Camille chewed on her lip. "I mean, that will play a part in it, but . . . I . . . well . . ." She took a deep breath. "I'm pregnant, Tyler," she said, so quickly that he almost didn't catch the words.

Tyler stared at her, allowing his brain to catch up with her mouth. *Pregnant?* They hadn't even talked about starting a family. That was probably unusual for most couples five years married, but they'd been so happy as they were that adding a child to the mix seemed almost superfluous.

"Are . . . are you sure?" he breathed.

She nodded, a small smile curling the corners of her lips. "I found out last week."

Tyler just continued to stare into her face, dimly lit by the lights of the city shining through the window. He could hear his breathing coming at irregular intervals, and he wondered if he was about to hyperventilate. "I . . . ," he stuttered in astonishment. "We . . . ," he tried again, but stopped.

"Are you . . . mad?" Camille asked quietly, the smile abandoning her flawless face. Tyler could almost hear the tears in her voice. He pulled himself together as quickly as possible, not wanting to upset her.

"No," he said firmly, squeezing her shoulders. "*No.* I think it's wonderful." He pulled Camille against him, hugging her fiercely. "I'm going to be a dad," he whispered to himself, his lips in her hair. The words seemed to make the unexpected news finally sink in. "Camille," he breathed, pulling back to look at her. "I'm going to be a dad!"

Camille smiled at him and nodded, her eyes shining with unshed tears. "You'll be such an amazing father, Tyler. I know you will."

Feeling an almost senseless joy permeate every square inch of his body, he pulled his wife into his arms once again. Could life possibly be any sweeter?

one

My name is Kate, and with such a generic name, it's pretty much inevitable that my life would begin unspectacularly. I was born as the only child to Caroline and Matthew Evans, a young couple who lived in a small house in the suburbs of northern Utah. In the beginning, I was one of the lucky ones—I knew my parents loved me very much, and as proof of it, they showered me with affection and praise. They taught me from a young age that I was a child of God, something that made a profound impression on me. My parents were active members of The Church of Jesus Christ of Latter-day Saints, or "Mormons," to use the popular vernacular. I was baptized into this church when I was eight years old, just like every other Mormon kid in my community. However, *unlike* every other Mormon kid in my community, my parents were killed in a car accident roughly four months after my baptism.

Following the accident, my life veered dramatically from the norm. I was sent away from my home, friends, and everything else familiar to live in California with an aunt and uncle I had never met. John Whitman was my mother's brother, and, though he was a good man, my life with his family was not to be a particularly pleasant one. His wife, Sarah, despised me for reasons that I've never really understood and did her level best to make my life miserable while I lived under her roof. My situation became exponentially worse when my Uncle John suddenly died, around my tenth birthday. I was a lower life-form in the Whitman household from that moment forward. With Uncle John no longer there to play interference, Aunt Sarah had the power to turn my world into a dark place—and she didn't hesitate to do it.

In the two years following my uncle's death, I discovered what hell was like. It's a place where every day you're told how insignificant, stupid, and worthless you are. A place where mistakes are harshly and painfully punished, and successes are simply ignored. A place where you're considered to be a waste of human space who exists just to be an inconvenience and annoyance to others.

As the years passed and my circumstances became increasingly desperate, the memories of my parents that I treasured so much grew faint and somewhat fuzzy around the edges. There was one memory, however—one psychological and spiritual impression they left with me—that I would never forget. In fact, I held onto it even more securely, feeling it was the only piece of them that I could keep with me always. Even when my own personal nightmare began at the age of eight, I didn't feel the despair that many other young children would have. I had a gift from my parents that lived inside of me—a secret talisman that gave me the strength I needed to carry on without them. My parents taught me that I had a loving Father in Heaven who was always with me. Even though I couldn't see Him, He could hear my every prayer and would listen to the cries of my heart. And hearing those cries, He would lead me where I needed to go, even if the way seemed impossible. This knowledge was unbelievably comforting.

Looking back, I have no doubt that I was led by His hand, albeit sometimes kicking and screaming like a toddler, along every step of my journey. And that journey, dear reader, begins here . . .

two

Micah?" I spoke hopefully into the phone, praying the agent from Signal Hill Nannies had something worthwhile to report.

"Yep. How you doing?" she asked, obviously not really wanting to know.

"Good. What's up?" I asked, breathless. *Please, please, please* . . . the words reverberated desperately in my mind.

"Well, I have good news for you," she said.

My spirits hit the ceiling.

"Really?" I replied. "You actually got something?"

"Kate, I don't know why you were so worried," Micah said, popping her gum in my ear. "You were probably the easiest nanny I've ever placed. Most clients would *kill* for someone with degrees in elementary education *and* child psychology."

"So, what did you find?" I asked, disregarding the compliment. "What is it?"

"Okay, this offer is for just one eight-year-old girl, so it should be a snap. Her name's Addie. She's the child of the CEO and managing partner of a successful brokerage firm in New York. His name is Tyler Thorne, and he's loaded. I'm talking billionaire here, Kate."

"The job's in *New York*?" I squealed. As a twenty-two-year-old recent college graduate, formerly oppressed and constantly destitute, I had always wanted to go to New York but had never had the time or the resources to manage it.

"Uh . . . no, actually," Micah answered, sounding nervous all of a sudden. "His firm is in New York, but this offer is actually in a little town in Utah called Oakley."

"His firm is headquartered in New York, and this Thorne guy lives in *Utah*?"

"Well, naturally, he has several houses." Micah spoke to me as if I were somehow being slow. "From what I understand, he spends most of his time in New York. He's originally from Utah, but he rarely visits his residence there. I think he keeps his daughter tucked away in a ranch house in Oakley while he lives in Manhattan and manages his business. That's just a guess though; I've actually never spoken to him personally. My main contact has been an employee of his, a Charlotte Fairview."

"Hang on—*he* lives in New York, but his daughter's in Utah?" I clarified. "What's up with that? What about her mother?"

"I'm not really sure what the story is there," Micah answered. "As far as I can tell, her mother is out of the picture. I don't know whether she died or just took off, but she's not around."

I was quiet for a minute, processing the information. My weakness for small, abandoned creatures was softening my reluctance to move to a small town in Utah—it wasn't exactly the exotic locale I had been hoping for. But how sad that this poor little girl was separated from her father by thousands of miles and her mother by something even more insurmountable than distance! At that moment, I knew I would take the job.

But my silence seemed to be making Micah anxious because she turned on the persuasion. "It's a really great offer, Kate. Way better than anything you would find for a schoolteacher. He's offering eighty thousand dollars a year, plus a vehicle, and medical and dental insurance."

I gasped in amazement. I had never expected my first offer to be so extravagant. How could I even consider turning it down? And the fact that I already felt a connection to the abandoned little girl made it a done deal.

"I'll take it," I answered, immediately feeling good about my decision. I could hear Micah's sigh on the other end of the line.

"Excellent," she said, her voice once again easy and relaxed. "I'll get you the details immediately. Ms. Fairview said that Mr. Thorne wants someone in place by next Monday, so you've only got a week or so to pack up and get to Utah. I'd start right away if I were you. Talk to you soon, Kate!"

As I hung up the phone, I contemplated my new position. Granted, Utah wasn't the most glamorous spot, but I was never one to fit in with glamour anyway. Pale, petite, and thin, with shoulder-length, dark brown hair, I was as ordinary as it was possible to be.

That's why a career as a nanny is meant for me, I told myself whenever I began to feel doubtful about my chosen career path. The purpose of a nanny was to control and care for children without being conspicuous in the process. I was exceptional at fading into the background.

Fighting the urge to skip as I headed to my room to begin packing, I wondered what my new home would be like. It seemed strange that Mr. Thorne would keep his eight-year-old daughter nearly a continent away from his own home in New York. I wondered how often he visited and why he had entrusted the employment of a nanny for his child to another employee instead of taking the trouble himself.

Shrugging off the questions, I threw open my closet door and pulled out the boxes I had used to move my few belongings from the home of my former guardians, the Brooks, to my dorm room four years earlier. Looking around my room, I contemplated the turns my life had taken to deposit me at that point.

My aunt Sarah had finally managed to shrug me off once I hit the ripe old age of twelve. She had off-loaded me to a friend of hers, a Mrs. Brook, who was a bored, wealthy socialite that maintained a rigorous calendar of events involving the other bored, wealthy ladies in her Santa Monica neighborhood. Given her almost constant preoccupation with her societal events, she required two things: a maid for her hosted society parties and a babysitter for her two young daughters. As a championless pre-teen, I fit the bill for both. So, despite my underage status, I entered into my first employment arrangement out of necessity. In return for my service, Mrs. Brook provided me room and board and paid for my education at an upscale private academy.

My years with the Brooks were not as miserable as they might have been, and they were nowhere near as horrific as my time with the Whitmans. My new school was prestigious, and the instruction I received there made a profound impact on me. It instilled in me a love of learning and a desire to someday use that learning to teach others. Unfortunately, as I quickly discovered upon college graduation, the life of a teacher is a meager one. So when the option of becoming an "educated nanny" for the children of high-ranking business executives was presented to me by an old school friend, I lunged at it. Hence, my current good fortune.

My life hadn't exactly been a picnic to this point, but as I felt the fluttering fingers of excitement playing in my middle, I couldn't find anything but gratitude for where my path had led me. So I packed up my belongings, threw a few old boxes and bits of furniture I wouldn't need into a miniscule storage unit in L.A., and within a few days was on my way to Utah.

Although I hadn't been back to Utah since I had originally left at age eight, I felt a sense of recognition as I drove along the Wasatch Front. However, once I turned onto Interstate 80 through Parley's Canyon, everything became unfamiliar once again. Passing through Park City and exiting toward Kamas, it seemed I was leaving all civilization behind. I knew that the area was decidedly rural, but I was unprepared for the discomfort I felt at the long stretches of highway with no sign of humanity.

Finally, entering the tiny community of Oakley, population 948, I was astonished at the size of the homes I passed. I had been expecting mountain shanties with a few scattered campers. Wasn't that what a mountain town was supposed to look like? Instead, I found a small but obviously very wealthy community consisting of sprawling ranch-style homes tucked against mountainsides or nestled among pine trees. Most of them were surrounded by acres and acres of prime real estate that I was sure had cost a fortune.

My new home was several miles beyond Oakley, and passing the city limits, I found myself in open, mountainous country. Following the directions emailed to me earlier that week by Charlotte Fairview, the head of command at this particular residence of Mr. Thorne's, I pulled off the highway onto an unpaved dirt road that twisted and turned through wooded hills.

Jostling up and down, I clenched my hands on the steering wheel so tightly that my knuckles turned white and the veins stood out blue and spidery. I suddenly understood why Charlotte had insisted I get a four-wheel-drive vehicle when she had called to provide a list of approved car dealerships for me to browse. I had never had the experience of choosing a new car off the lot for my very own, especially with the knowledge that I wasn't paying for it. Looking at the prices, I had felt almost guilty at the time. Now, bumping unceremoniously over a rocky, mountain dirt road, I was immensely glad I had chosen the silver, late-model jeep.

After what seemed like hours of headache-inducing jars and bumps, I finally turned onto a level road of loose gravel. Looking around, I realized I was in a little valley, hidden away in the cradling shadow of several small mountains. The view was breathtaking, especially with the brilliant oranges, reds, and yellows covering the mountainsides. No one had ever told me that fall in Utah could be every bit as breathtaking as fall in New England.

Not that I've ever been to New England, I thought, smiling to myself.

The flat gravel road stretched out straight in front of me, and on the opposite side of the small valley, I could see an impossibly huge structure nestled up to the largest of the surrounding mountains.

I drove through a stone archway that proclaimed my entrance to Thorne Field Ranch. The road led straight to the rounded driveway in front of the main house, but I could see several smaller houses off to the left, farther back toward the tree line. To the right of the imposing structure was a large stable built of what looked like white pine. I made a mental note to give the place a wide berth. I was not overly fond of horses.

The main house itself was a charming combination of brick, wood, and stone, with gabled roofs and large windows. It reminded me of a French chateau with a western twist. I was immediately in love with it.

I pulled up and parked in front of the large garage to the left of the house, grabbing for my purse as I looked around. I took a deep breath of the fresh mountain air as I exited the jeep, noting the blessed change from the smoggy closeness of L.A. Walking resolutely to the front door of the main house, I knocked with purpose. A few seconds later, the door swung open and an attractive woman who looked to be in her late forties stood there, a welcoming smile on her face.

"You must be Kate," she said by way of greeting, her smile widening. At my affirmative nod, she took my hand, shaking it and pulling me through the door at the same time. "I'm Charlotte. I am *so* glad to see you," she said warmly. At my surprised expression, she explained. "Women are few and far between in this area. It's a little too remote to be popular with the brunching and shopping crowds." She winked at me. "Addie and I have been the only females on the ranch for quite some time. But to have some *adult* female company is more welcome than I can possibly describe."

Buoyed by her enthusiastic reception, I smiled back at her.

"I'm very happy to meet you," I said. "I can't believe how beautiful it is here. So much space . . . it's very different than what I'm used to."

"After Los Angeles, I'm sure you're ready for some peace and quiet," Charlotte agreed. She took my purse from my arm and set it on a hall table. "Now, let me show you around."

Charlotte led me to a massive staircase, directly ahead from the front door across the entrance hall. She began the tour on the second floor, showing me the north wing (which she referred to as the "guest wing") with all its expertly decorated guest suites. On our way back to the stairs, we tiptoed past a door with a colorful wooden name board proclaiming "Addie." Charlotte whispered that my young charge was asleep and would meet me later. As we approached the stairs, Charlotte pointed beyond them to the south wing of the house, indicating that Mr. Thorne's bedroom, the largest and grandest in the house, and a few more guest suites were in that direction.

As we stood at the top of the stairs, I looked around the elegant landing. It ran around the entire perimeter of the entrance hall below and culminated in a spacious alcove at the far end, with large windows that looked out toward the front gate and the view beyond. As we descended the stairs to the ground floor, I was struck by the airy feel of the residence. Like the country surrounding it, everything was wide-open space.

The ground floor held all the "community" rooms. Charlotte took me quickly through the large common rooms, directly off the entrance hall and on either side of the front door. She walked me down the hallway off the entrance hall to the left, which contained Mr. Thorne's office and the library, ending in large French doors out the back of the house.

"Tyler rarely uses the office," Charlotte explained. "He prefers to do his work in the library."

When she opened the door to the library, I couldn't suppress a gasp. In a house of seemingly countless rooms, this was one room I knew I would remember. It was large, just like every other room I had seen thus far, and decorated in rich, dark woods and muted colors. There were more books than I would ever be able to read, but I was willing to try.

"Good grief," I said as we left the library behind. "Who keeps all this clean? You must have an army of cleaning staff."

"Well, I do the touch-up stuff," Charlotte said, laughing. "But we have a cleaning service that comes in three times a week to do the basic day-to-day cleaning. There's no way I could keep up on all of this, and Tyler isn't the type to employ full-time maids."

Every comment she made about Mr. Thorne made me that much more curious about the man. She obviously had a great deal of respect for him, but it was more than that. She sounded almost motherly when she spoke of him. But this observation seemed ridiculous to me. Mr. Thorne, successful entrepreneur that he was, was probably in his late forties himself. I found myself wondering when or if I'd get to meet this intriguing man. Given the fact that he had chosen to be separated from his daughter by so much distance, I was already somewhat disposed to think badly of him, but that didn't stem my curiosity.

After showing me the library, Charlotte led me back down the hallway, through the entrance hall, and to the right.

"Through here," she said as I followed her down a hallway with large open doorways, "is the dining room, game room, and the kitchen. Back that way is the laundry room," she said as she reached the end of the hallway and pointed right, toward the front of the house. "Come this way," she said. Charlotte led me down a smaller, darker flight of stairs, just before the entrance to the kitchen.

"These are the only stairs leading to the basement," Charlotte explained as she hit the light switch. "As you saw, the grand staircase only goes between the ground floor and the second floor."

As we descended, the air became chilly. The wood floor gave way to rock and tile floors, and the décor and general ambiance seemed much more modern.

Charlotte led me into a huge room that greatly resembled a high-end movie theater, except that the two rows of movie chairs were instead closely spaced leather recliners. My eyebrows raised automatically. Even at the Brooks' I had never seen such wealth. The back of the room held a few card tables and chairs clustered for socializing.

After I had sufficiently marveled at the room, Charlotte led the way to the room next door to the theater room, which turned out to be a gym. But it was like no private gym I'd ever seen. With a smirk on her face at my dumbfounded expression, Charlotte also presented the indoor pool to me. Finally, I could stand it no longer.

"Why?" I asked, turning to Charlotte. "My agent told me Mr. Thorne is rarely here. Why does he have all this when he doesn't visit often?"

Charlotte nodded knowingly at my question. "I've often asked myself that same question," she said. "Tyler didn't build this house, you know. It was designed and built by his father about ten years before he died. Tyler generally uses the ranch as a retreat for his business partners and associates. And although we rarely see him, he wants all the modern comforts available here that his friends enjoy in New York. And many of them are somewhat particular."

As we headed back through the basement toward the stairs, Charlotte continued to point out other less-significant rooms, but I had stopped listening. I was contemplating the idea that someone would pay for the continuous upkeep of a mountain kingdom, just to satisfy his stuffy New York cronies. It seemed wasteful to me.

"Would you like a tour of the grounds?" Charlotte asked as we climbed the stairs. "Just so you know your way around?"

I nodded, and she led me again past the kitchen, dining room, game room, the large living space, through the entrance hall, and past the grand staircase. Then came the office, the library, a mudroom, and a bathroom. I ticked the rooms off as I passed them, wanting to make sure I had a firm grasp of the floor plan, but once I exited through the massive french doors in the back of the house, I stopped ticking and gasped at the view that met my eyes. It was like stepping into Eden.

A large garden lay directly in front of us. Several pathways, ornamented with small stone statues, wound through the trees and around the flower beds. It looked like something you might see in a fairy tale, and I immediately wanted to get lost in it. Unfortunately, Charlotte had other ideas, and she spent the next half hour showing me tennis courts, putting greens, another pool with an accompanying pool house, sweeping lawns, and a staff village. I was starting to consider the possibility of shin splints when she finally stopped in front of a cheerful little cabin with wilting flowers in the window boxes.

"This will be your cabin," Charlotte said calmly, looking completely at ease as she dropped this bombshell.

I stared at her in disbelief.

At my silence, she turned to face me, taking in my expression with a worried one of her own. "Are you all right, dear?"

"This cabin is mine?" I asked, incredulous. I'd never had more than twelve square feet to myself before, and now here I was, suddenly presented with what looked to be over a thousand.

Charlotte looked confused at my surprise.

"Well, of course it's yours," she said. "Where did you think you would live? Surely you didn't think we would make you stay in a guest suite?" She sounded appalled at the idea. I decided not to mention that that was exactly what I had thought.

"I'm sorry it's so far away from the main house, but the other cabins are currently inhabited by the ranch hands we employ," she informed me as she unlocked the door to the cabin and handed me the key before entering. It was almost a Publishers Clearing House experience, holding that key in my hand. Gesturing around the living room as she walked in, Charlotte assured me, "I know the furniture is a bit sparse, but it and the appliances are all nearly new, since no one has ever used this particular cabin before. You shouldn't have any problems with them." She gave the room a once-over as if to verify that everything was in its place and then turned back to me.

"Well, why don't you get your things and get settled in. You probably want some time to freshen up before meeting Addie."

I nodded, somewhat dazed, and thanked her, watching as she walked back up toward the main house.

As I turned and took in my new home, I couldn't help but think that it was all too good to be true. I expected someone to jump out at any moment and yell, "Smile! You're on *Candid Camera*!"

I jogged the five hundred yards or so back to my jeep and pulled it around the left side of the house, past the large gardens, and through the little village of staff cabins to park in front of my new home.

I was able to bring all my belongings inside in only four trips, and all of my boxes fit on the kitchen table. Looking around the empty cabin, I realized I didn't have enough possessions to fill the excessive space. Shrugging, I went to explore the rest of the house.

On the ground floor was the kitchen, a small living area, a laundry room, a teeny tiny guest room, and a half bathroom. Upstairs, I found a full bathroom with a jetted tub, which excited me beyond all reason, but when I entered the master bedroom I actually squealed in delight.

The room was bright and airy with french doors that led to a private balcony in the back of the cabin. The room held a vanity, a large wooden wardrobe instead of a closet, and a huge bed with a carved wooden headboard.

Sitting on the edge of the bed and sinking into its softness, I felt the need to pinch myself to make sure I wasn't dreaming. I felt even more like I was staying at a luxury resort now, instead of settling in to a new job. Did things like this actually happen in real life? Knowing that this was indeed reality, I followed my second impulse, which was to fall to my knees beside my new bed and pour out my gratitude in prayer.

Pulling the cabin door shut behind me an hour later, I took the opportunity to look around and take a deep breath of mountain air before heading back down to the main house. In the light of the setting sun, the fall colors on the mountain peaks blazed brilliantly. Feeling again that sense of dreamlike good fortune, I began the walk back to the ranch house. My cabin was the closest to the tree line and the furthest from the main house, so the walk took several minutes.

Letting myself in through the back doors, I walked past the huge library and Mr. Thorne's office, finally coming to the entrance hall and grand staircase. My footsteps echoed loudly in the excessive space, but I heard nothing from any of the nearby rooms. I wasn't sure whether I should call out Charlotte's name or physically go searching for her. By the time I had decided to just forget politeness and yell, I heard the sound of pounding feet. Turning around, I saw a small child with dark, curly hair racing down the staircase toward me. She came to a screeching halt right in front of me, her huge brown eyes full of eagerness as she took in my presence.

"Are you Kate?" she asked, out of breath from her quick descent.

I smiled at the adorable child. "Yes, I am," I said. "And you must be Addie. Am I right?"

She nodded excitedly, obviously thrilled that I managed to guess right on the first try.

"Did you know that I have my own pony?" she asked conspiratorially. "And I have twelve pink dresses too."

Not quite sure how to respond to this incredibly exciting information, I just smiled at her and tried to look impressed. It was difficult, especially since I had no idea why any eight-year-old would require twelve dresses of any color. Addie suddenly grabbed my hand and hauled me toward the stairs with every bit of strength she possessed.

"Come on, I'll *show* you," she cried, yanking my arm helplessly as if convinced I didn't believe her.

"Is pink your favorite color?" I asked as I followed her up the stairs to the second floor.

She looked back at me like I was nutty. "Of course!" she cried. "Isn't it yours?"

I again suppressed a smile and nodded. "I do like pink," I answered.

Finally, after a walk that felt like it approximated a 5K, we arrived at Addie's bedroom. My eyes widened as I entered the lavishly decorated room. Every surface seemed to be covered with something pink and frilly. This room alone was easily half the size of my whole cabin, and apparently there was more to it, because Addie was pulling me through the room toward another doorway.

The doorway led to a room almost as large as the bedroom, completely stuffed with every kind of toy imaginable. One wall seemed to be devoted to Barbie and another to American Girl paraphernalia.

Addie began stuffing random things in my arms, explaining what they were as she went. She introduced me to every single one of her dolls (she had names for all of them, and I was astonished she could actually remember what they were) and gave me a grand tour of all of her six (yes, *six*) Barbie houses.

Although Addie was, without a doubt, one of the most beautiful children I had ever seen, it became clear to me very quickly that she was also spoiled. Apparently the father who could spend so little time with her in person thought his money could keep her company in his absence. My disapproval of the man I had never met increased tenfold.

"So, do you like to read?" I asked Addie, praying for something I could relate to. I had no memory of ever actually owning a doll. By the time I was Addie's age, I was already an inmate of Whitman Purgatory.

She wrinkled her nose at the question. "Read?" she asked. "Read what?"

"Anything, really," I answered. "Stories, poems . . ."

She looked unenthusiastically up at me.

"Reading's boring," she said, turning to pull out some new toy to show me.

"Well, we're going to be doing a lot of it now that I'm here, so I hope I'll be able to change your mind," I said.

She turned to look at me with an expression of horror twisting her little features.

I squatted down to be level with her.

"Addie, did you know that I've actually met a princess?"

Addie looked appropriately impressed. "A princess?" she repeated in delight.

"Yep," I answered. "And a pirate too. I've also been to Mars. And to the bottom of the sea to swim with mermaids."

By this time Addie was looking skeptical. "How?" she asked simply.

"In books I've read. Reading takes you to places you'd never be able to go in real life," I explained, praying I could make this child enthusiastic about expanding her horizons beyond blonde, anatomically incorrect, plastic people.

"I can go anywhere," she answered matter-of-factly. "Tyler will buy me whatever I want."

Hmm. Not exactly the response I had expected. I may need to have a conversation with the elusive Mr. Thorne. The first order of business with this child was some serious toy deprivation.

It wasn't lost on me that Addie referred to her father by his first name. This didn't surprise me as much as it probably should have. If she saw him as infrequently as I had been told, and everyone around her referred to him as "Tyler" or "Mr. Thorne," Addie would undoubtedly refer to him in the same way.

He doesn't even seem deserving of the title "Father" anyway, I thought a little cynically.

"Well, why don't we go see if dinner is ready?" I asked, changing the subject. "I'm starving."

Addie nodded and grabbed my hand. "I'll show you the way," she said, pulling me as hard as she could yet again through her bedroom and through the maze of hallways to the stairs. I was beginning to doubt whether the girl believed I could get anywhere under my own steam.

On our way down the stairs, we met Charlotte, who was on her way up to get us for dinner.

"Oh, I'm so glad you two have met," she said, smiling at me. "And how are you getting along?"

"Great," I answered, smiling back at her. However, I took the opportunity to pull her aside as Addie ran full throttle into the dining room, which was large enough to double as an indoor football field if needed.

"Is there any way I could speak with Mr. Thorne?" I asked.

Charlotte looked perplexed. "Tyler? What for?" she asked.

"Well I'm just a little . . . concerned about Addie," I answered, choosing my words carefully. "She's been showing me all of her toys.

I don't mean to shove my nose where it doesn't belong, but I'm wondering if it might not be a good idea to hold off on any toy purchases for a little while. It's a little difficult to encourage the kid to spend time with her books if all she wants to do is play with her dolls." I felt like I was being pushy, but I couldn't stop myself from adding, "It's just that reading is such an important part of childhood, and Addie seems to hate it already."

Charlotte studied me silently for a moment. "You know," she finally said, her expression thoughtful, "Addie does have a tutor. But I won't deny that it's crossed my mind that she isn't as encouraged in her schoolwork as she ought to be. I wonder . . ." She looked away for a second. Then, seeming to make up her mind, she squared her shoulders and turned back to me. "Technically, this isn't my call to make, but I wonder if you might consider doubling as Addie's tutor. I know you have a degree in elementary education, and Addie's education already seems to be more important to you than to her current tutor. I think you may be exactly what she needs."

"I . . . ," I began hesitantly. I hadn't been expecting my concerns to translate into an automatic teaching job. The idea made me nervous for some reason. I didn't feel ready. Was I prepared to have the responsibility of a child's education, something I deemed more important than almost anything else, heaped onto my shoulders? I bit my lip, uncertain.

Charlotte misunderstood my hesitancy. "Oh, there'd be a definite raise in pay, you understand," she said, persuasively.

I smiled. "That's not necessary," I assured her. "I'm not worried about the money. I've just never really taught anyone unsupervised. My only real teaching experience was a few months as a student teacher, and it was for a very small kindergarten class. I don't know, for some reason I just don't feel qualified."

"Nonsense." Charlotte smiled, patting my arm. "You're just the woman for the job. What do you say?"

Her confidence in me felt somewhat misplaced, especially given the fact that she hardly knew me. But teaching *was* what I had originally planned to do with my life. How could I turn down this opportunity? Finally, I nodded.

"I'll do my best," I said resolutely.

"Wonderful!" Charlotte exclaimed. "I'll notify Tyler immediately and get back to you with the details. You'll probably need to meet with her current tutor so he can brief you on what he and Addie have covered so far."

She turned and swept into the dining room, leaving me in the doorway, wondering if, perhaps, I had bitten off more than I could chew.

three

All in all, teaching Addie turned out to be much easier than I expected. She didn't seem to be a particularly bright child, but she was willing—which made all the difference in the world. The only problem I continued to face was her resistance to reading. She worked hard at math, science, and even history, but when I tried to get to her to appreciate the subject that I valued most of all, she dug in her heels and pulled back with fierce determination.

The first time I attempted to have her read aloud, she refused to even try. Eventually, however, as I pushed and prodded, she began to make an effort. I was astonished to find that her reading skills were absolutely abysmal. The simplest words were difficult for her, and I wondered how her former tutors had dealt with the roadblock. Or had they addressed it at all? She knew her letters well enough, but when it came to actually putting them together, she was completely lost.

Determined to succeed, I decided to start at the beginning and work upwards, but after three months of lessons, Addie still showed little improvement. My frustration growing, I wondered if she had some kind of learning disability that I hadn't been told about.

Despite the aggravating reading lessons, Addie and I became very fond of each other. I began to notice that the smiles and laughs I had kept so well hidden during the past several years were beginning to emerge more frequently. Charlotte and I became close as well, although we had few interests in common. I began to look upon her almost as a mother figure, something I missed more than I had supposed. I felt myself becoming increasingly attached to Thorne Field Ranch. A sense of home resided there that had never existed anywhere else for me.

Although I was much closer to a happy home life than I could ever remember being before, it was not perfect. Addie's lack of progress in her studies caused me great disappointment, and I often needed time away from her to evaluate and adjust my strategies. On days when my frustrations seemed especially close to the surface, I found that a brisk walk around the garden did wonders for me. However, I soon became curious about the surrounding area and began to wander outside the confines of the ranch itself.

One such day, after a particularly trying reading lesson, I was walking aimlessly along a heavily forested stretch of gravel road leading to the ranch. Although it was early December and absolutely freezing, the beauty of the area took my breath away more effectively than the cold temperatures and exercise.

The snow crunched beneath my feet, and my breath came in warm, steamy puffs. I looked around, feeling as though I were inside one of the Christmas cards from Mrs. Brook's society friends.

After spending about an hour walking through the frosted trees, I noticed that the snow was falling more rapidly than before. Knowing how quickly the weather could change in Utah and not wanting to get stuck in a mountain blizzard, I turned around and hurriedly made my way back toward the ranch.

I was so focused on staying upright on the slick road that my ears barely registered the roar of an approaching vehicle until it was almost, quite literally, on top of me. Turning to find the source of the growling noise, I threw myself immediately off the road and against a tree, in an attempt to avoid the huge truck that came dangerously close to turning me into a human pancake.

The driver apparently hadn't been expecting to see me any more than I had him. In his efforts to avoid me, he swerved violently on the narrow road, slipping and sliding until he finally came to rest in a shallow ditch, inches away from a huge pine tree.

As I pulled myself cautiously to my feet and brushed the snow from my pants, I heard the truck door slam and footsteps crunching angrily in my direction. Glancing up, I saw a large figure bearing down on me, muttering all the way.

"What the—what exactly do you think you're doing?" a deep, unfamiliar voice demanded.

Squinting through the thickly falling flakes, I realized that I didn't recognize the face of the irate man in front of me. I was familiar with everyone on the ranch, so I knew he was not one of the eight ranch hands employed there. I stepped closer, and his features came into sharper focus, assuring me that this man was indeed a stranger. He looked to be in his early to mid-thirties, not handsome necessarily, but with strong, decided features. He was large—several inches over six feet tall—and broad through the shoulders. His most distinguishing feature however, was the large cut on his forehead, which was presently gushing blood.

"You're bleeding!" I exclaimed.

He ignored my concern and took an irritated swipe at the gash, wincing slightly. "Who are you?" he demanded rudely.

I didn't particularly like being addressed in this manner when my only crime was to be on the road at the same moment as his monster truck. I straightened, squaring my shoulders and meeting his eyes unflinchingly.

"My name is Kate Evans," I said, my voice strong and confident. "And who are you?"

"I don't believe that's any of your business," he said coldly. "What're you thinking, being out alone, at night, in a snowstorm? Are you crazy?!"

"No more than you," I protested. "I was out for a walk."

"A walk?" he repeated with disdainful incredulity, glancing around him at the weather conditions.

I immediately decided that I didn't like this man.

"Yes, a walk," I snapped defensively.

He stepped closer to me, scrutinizing my features. "I've never seen you before," he said accusingly, as if it were my fault we'd never been introduced. "What are you doing on this road?"

I stared at him. What was his problem? Just because he didn't know me, I suddenly wasn't allowed to be on the road? Who did he think he was, anyway?

"Well, there aren't exactly many to choose from around here," I returned, my voice as cold as the moisture I wiped from my face. "I figured walking along this road probably made a bit more sense than breaking a new one across the countryside."

He rolled his eyes. "No, I mean, why are you even *here*?" he said, gesturing widely to the area around him. "This land all belongs to Thorne Field Ranch. I know Thorne Field Ranch very well, and I've never seen you there before."

"I work at Thorne Field," I defended.

"As what?" he demanded.

Resisting the temptation to tell him exactly where he could put his prying questions, I sighed in irritation.

"I'm the nanny for the Thornes," I said, my voice betraying an extreme degree of annoyance. "Now if you'll excuse me, it's snowing, I'm miles from home, and I need to get back."

As I moved to step around him, he blocked my way.

"Excuse me?" he snarled. "You realize you just made me crash my truck into a ditch, and you're just going to walk away?"

"Yes," I said, every ounce of indignation I felt pulsing in my gaze. I was surprised he didn't shrivel in the intensity of it. "Because I didn't make you crash your truck into a ditch. *You* crashed your own truck into a ditch when you realized that you were sharing the road with a *pedestrian*. Who, for your information, had the right of way. Now excuse me. I'd like to get back up to the ranch house before I freeze to death. Good night."

I attempted again to walk around him. He blocked me yet again. Unease began to prickle subtly beneath my skin. Why wouldn't he let me go?

"You're going to walk two miles in this?" he asked, incredulously, gesturing to the heavy snow falling all around us.

"Well, I don't exactly have a choice, now do I?" I said rudely.

The man sighed in exasperation. "Well, if my truck will still *move*,

I'll drive you to the ranch. I'm headed there anyway, and you'll end up with frostbite if you walk that far in this weather."

Suspicious at his sudden hospitality, I resolutely shook my head.

"Thank you, but I prefer to walk," I said firmly.

"Don't be stupid."

I bristled at his offensive tone, even more determined to walk every step of the two miles back to the ranch.

"Again, thanks but no thanks," I said, finally succeeding in walking around him and starting down the road. I heard him mutter something about brainless females, but he didn't attempt to stop me.

Shortly afterward, I heard the truck's engine roar to life and it came speeding past me, spraying me (deliberately, I'm sure) with dirty snow and slush. About twenty steps further down the road, I was already regretting my obstinate refusal to ride with him to the ranch. I was freezing and soaked, neither condition being particularly conducive to making good time along a frozen mountain road in deepening darkness.

About an hour later, I finally pulled my exhausted feet up the stairs to the door of the main ranch house. The cursed truck was parked directly in front of the house. It irritated me that the stranger felt he was important enough to block the steps to the porch, but I bit back any comment as Charlotte came rushing up to me, worry evident on her face.

"I was just about to send someone out to look for you!" she exclaimed. "You're soaked! Let's get you into some dry things."

I protested that I would really rather just continue on to my cabin, but Charlotte was adamant. She provided me with some sweats of her own (which completely drowned me) and made sure I had a hot meal when I was finally warm and dry. She clucked over me like a mother hen, and as she pulled a blanket securely around my shoulders, I felt a surge of warmth toward her. But the next words out of her mouth immediately chased away any traces of contentment.

"Tyler's here, dear," she said as she cleared dishes from the table. "He had a bit of an accident on the way, with the roads being so bad, and he's having a cut stitched right now, but afterwards, he'd like to meet you."

My breath caught painfully in my chest and I felt a little light-headed.

Tyler Thorne is here? Now? Was it just a coincidence that a man I'd never seen before had arrived at the ranch the same night the mysterious owner had returned? And both of them needed a cut stitched? I knew coincidence had nothing to do with it and that I'd unknowingly offended and irritated my employer. Not good.

But how could I have guessed such a thing? How could I have known that Tyler Thorne wasn't the graying, distinguished, middle-aged executive I'd expected, but was instead a young, bad-tempered, reckless driver?

"I really think I should wait until tomorrow," I protested at Charlotte's warning that Mr. Thorne wanted to meet with me. "I mean, it's late and I'm in your sweats and he probably has a headache, so I think I should just go back to my cabin—"

"How did you know the cut was on his head?" Charlotte asked, looking at me strangely.

Oops.

"Oh, is it?" I asked, feigning innocence. "I just assumed that driving all that way in this weather would, uh, give him a headache. I know it would me." I smiled at her, feeling like an idiot.

Charlotte looked at me funny for a minute and then shrugged. "You can run back to your cabin and freshen up if you want, but he was pretty insistent that he see you tonight, so you'd better hurry back."

I sighed resignedly and stood. Pulling on my coat and boots, I braced myself against the cold and exited the house via the back door. I mounted one of the snowmobiles used for shuttling back and forth between the staff village and main house. Turning the key, I gunned the engine much more forcefully than was necessary and shot toward my cabin at high speed, muttering under my breath all the way.

I took extra time with my appearance, hoping a sense of professionalism would make up for my earlier rudeness. Pulling my straight, dark brown hair back into a smooth ponytail, I slipped into tan slacks and a cream sweater. Finally smearing some clear lip gloss on my lips, I studied my reflection. *Not great, but better than usual,* I thought. I slipped back into my parka and boarded the snowmobile, taking care not to muss my hair with my hood.

Once back at the main house, I found myself pacing the entrance hall nervously, sure I was about to be fired from a job I'd had for barely three months. Charlotte exited the library with Robert, the ranch's resident veterinarian, who was wiping his hands on a towel. Mr. Thorne had been stitched up by a vet? I supposed stitching a cut was the same operation whether the patient was an animal or a human, but something about being stitched up by someone who had never attended medical school seemed risky to me.

Robert nodded cheerily to me as he passed, and I muttered something that sounded rather strangled, because at that moment, I heard a familiar voice shout from the dark recesses of the library.

"Charlotte, where's the dang nanny? I don't have all night!"

Hmmm, not particularly friendly. Shuddering, I stepped forward into the room.

Attempting to be the model of confidence (and failing), I saw the imposing figure I had abused earlier that evening hunched in a chair next to the fireplace. The room was dark except for the blazing fire, and the shadows made Tyler Thorne's presence even more alarming.

He had a large bandage covering the right side of his forehead, and I winced at the sight of the blood-soaked gauze in a bowl beside his chair. Regardless of his condition, however, Mr. Thorne rose as I crossed the threshold of the room. Whether it was an ingrained gesture of politeness or an attempt to intimidate me, I couldn't say, but intimidation was its result. I was determined to meet his wrath with courage, and I kept my head up and my eyes focused on his shadowed face.

"So," said Thorne, his tone mildly threatening, "we meet again, Miss Evans."

"Yes." My voice was surprisingly steady. "How are you feeling, Mr. Thorne?" I asked, attempting to be polite. I immediately regretted it when he snorted derisively.

"Do you care?"

Deciding silence was the best policy in this particular situation, I simply met his gaze.

"I didn't think so," he said darkly. "Seeing as how you are

responsible for my unbelievable headache, I'm sure you won't mind if I sit down in your presence, correct?" Not waiting for my response, he sank back into his chair and turned his face toward the fire.

"I'm sorry for your discomfort, but I was *not* responsible for your accident," I insisted again, surprised by my smooth address. Still, I wondered why I couldn't, for once, manage to keep my mouth shut. "I was simply walking along the road, Mr. Thorne. Perhaps it was your speed that caused your truck to slide," I suggested.

He glared at me for a few seconds, then returned his gaze to the fireplace. He stared fixedly into the flames, saying nothing for several minutes. I stood motionless until my nervousness peaked and I could stand the silence no longer.

"Was there something in particular you needed to discuss with me, Mr. Thorne?" I asked.

"Sit," he said shortly, gesturing to the chair across from him. "I need a better look at you."

Feeling like a naughty child obeying an angry parent, I approached the large man and sat across from him. He studied me thoroughly from head to toe, apparently disliking the view, because his expression showed an interesting mixture of incredulity and distaste.

"How old are you?" he finally asked.

Biting back a comment on the impropriety of such a question, I decided to answer, but only in an effort to keep my job.

"Twenty-two," I said clearly.

His eyes showed a glimmer of surprise, which he quickly masked.

"So old?" he asked. "You seem much younger. I would have guessed seventeen at the most."

I knew he was trying to offend me, but as I had often been told I looked younger than my years, I met his gaze without flinching. Letting my disdain at his attempted insult show in my eyes, I answered, "Well, you would be mistaken, sir."

He snorted, and I tried not to cringe. *Sir?* I groaned to myself. I actually called him *sir.* If I wanted to make myself seem instantly ten years younger, I had just succeeded.

Mr. Thorne studied me for a moment more before continuing his questioning. "And what is your background?"

Irritated at his aggressively condescending tone, I had to struggle not to roll my eyes. I knew he was aware of my background, because Charlotte had mentioned that she had cleared my credentials with him before offering me the position. But I managed to remain impassive as I answered the inquiry. "I graduated earlier this year from UCLA, with degrees in elementary education and child psychology. Before college, I was responsible for the daily care of the children of my guardian, Mrs. Brook."

"Hmm," he said, not sounding impressed. "And with your experience and lofty education, you chose to become a nanny."

Trying not to take offense at his blatant sarcasm, I simply nodded once. "I felt I could do some good, and it pays much better than teaching." I hated the feeling that I was defending myself.

"Oh, so it's money you're after," he answered. He seemed strangely delighted at this revelation.

"I'm conscious of my financial needs. That's called being responsible." I felt my professional tone slipping.

"Not being out in the middle of the road in a snowstorm," Thorne pointed out mockingly. "Now *that* would have been responsible." I glared at him, wanting to argue, but weary of the circular conversation.

"Mr. Thorne, I am very tired. If you have nothing else to speak to me about, I'll say good night."

Cold amusement evident in the lines of his face as he took in my distressed expression, he gestured lazily toward the door with his hand. "Good night," he said, turning back to the fire.

Not bothering to answer, I strode quickly from the room, tears smarting in my eyes. I never thought I could feel such loathing for someone I didn't know. How could anyone be so needlessly confrontational? All my curiosity surrounding the mysterious Tyler Thorne had given way to dislike and a strong desire for him to vacate the house he so rarely visited.

four

"Kate! Kate!" I heard the excited squeals and sharp pounding from far away. "Kate, wake up!"

Rubbing the sleep from my eyes, I recognized the youthful voice of my pupil. Sighing, I pulled myself from the warm blankets and wrapped a thick flannel robe around me.

"Coming, Addie. I'm coming," I called, descending the stairs toward the front door of my cabin. The second I opened it, the eight-year-old came whirling in, bringing way too much cold air with her. Her eyes were bright, and her little frame positively shook with excitement.

"Tyler's home!" she crowed, clapping her hands. "He got here last night!"

Memories from the unpleasant evening before invaded my mind, and a sick feeling rose up inside me.

"Kate? Kate, did you hear me?" Addie was tugging on my arm, trying to get my attention. "Tyler's back! You have to hurry! We always eat breakfast together when he's here. Charlotte says to be in the dining room in ten minutes."

"What?" I gasped. The last thing I wanted to do was face, yet again, the cruel man I had met the day before, especially with so little time to prepare for it.

"Hurry!" Addie said, not appearing to have heard my exclamation. Without a backward glance, she raced from the cabin, slamming the door behind her. Kicking into high gear, I brushed my teeth and ran a quick comb through my hair before pulling it up into a simple ponytail. I changed into jeans and a long-sleeved shirt, hoping breakfast wasn't a formal affair to my lord and master. You never knew with these crabby rich types.

Realizing I was already late, I raced outside and jumped on my snowmobile, praying Mr. Thorne wasn't too much of a stickler about mealtimes. Arriving three minutes after the established time, I entered the dining room under his stormy gaze.

"Miss Evans, I am admittedly ignorant of your usual morning routine, but in this house, breakfast is served promptly at seven. This is the last time we will wait for you."

Geez, it's just breakfast! I was tempted to protest. However, showing impressive and unexpected self-control, I kept my mouth shut and simply nodded once.

Mr. Thorne seemed almost disappointed that I didn't argue. He continued to glare at me for a minute more, as if waiting for something disrespectful to suddenly burst unrestrained from my lips. When it became clear that I was going to maintain my silence, he promptly started on his breakfast as if no one else were present in the room.

"Tyler, we haven't said the blessing yet," Addie protested, poking him in the arm.

He looked at her silently for a second, his face expressionless. "Excuse me?" he finally said, glancing up at Charlotte and then back to Addie. "Blessing? Since when do we bless the food around here?"

"It's so we won't get sick," Addie explained earnestly. "Kate showed me how to do it."

She folded her arms and looked at me, seeking permission with her eyes. I nodded and bowed my head and noticed Charlotte, suppressing a smile, do the same.

"Dear Heavenly Father," Addie began. "Thank you for this food. Thank you that Tyler could be here. Please bless the food that it will be healthy. And please bless that Tyler won't get sick from the food he already ate. Name of Jesus Christ, Amen."

I raised my head and saw Mr. Thorne studying me, his look speculative. His eyes flicked between my face and the CTR ring prominently displayed on my right hand ring finger. "You're religious," he said. It wasn't a question, and his look, amazingly enough, wasn't accusing. He actually looked intrigued.

"Yes, I am," I answered, meeting his gaze. "I'm a member of The Church of Jesus Christ of Latter-day Saints." I cringed inwardly, waiting for some kind of derisive remark related to my religious beliefs to be hurled in my direction.

But it didn't come. Mr. Thorne didn't even seem surprised at my declaration. He smirked ironically down at his plate and returned to his breakfast. When it became apparent he would make no answer to my admission, I began eating as well, musing at the strange exchange.

Soon after, Mr. Thorne excused himself, fixing me with one last contemplative glance before leaving the room.

Over the next few days, I managed to avoid Mr. Thorne whenever possible. It was impossible to miss him at mealtimes, however. He was adamant that Charlotte, Addie, and I be present at every breakfast, lunch, and dinner, promptly on time. His insistence that we all gather for meals confused me, since he really seemed to detest company—especially mine. In fact, he never seemed to even notice that we were in the room with him. Most of the time, he would appear in the dining room with some kind of reading material in hand (usually a magazine or newspaper with microscopic writing) to occupy him. I found that if I focused on making as little noise as possible, so as not to distract him from his financial literature, I was usually able to avoid conversation with him. However, on the occasions where he felt the desire to torture me a little, it was unavoidable.

"So, Miss Evans," he said one day at breakfast, about five days after his arrival. "Where are you from originally?"

Up until that point, Mr. Thorne had, as usual, been present only physically. Engrossed in the *Wall Street Journal*, his eyes had never once left the page, even when Charlotte had asked if he'd like more french toast. In like fashion, those intense blue eyes didn't deviate in the slightest from their concentrated perusing as his lips had formed the unexpectedly civil question. I wasn't sure if I was more surprised by his complete lack of calculated enmity or his ability to read and make conversation at the same time.

"Uh, I was born here, actually," I answered after a pregnant pause. "Well, in Utah anyway. I grew up in Salt Lake."

"So how did you end up in California?" he inquired, still not bothering to look at me. If it weren't for the question's relevancy to the conversation, I would have thought he was following some random psychological script.

"My parents died when I was eight and I went to live with some relatives there," I answered. The fact that he wasn't even glancing up from his newspaper really irritated me. It was like talking to one of those department store dummies. Why bother asking questions if you weren't willing to invest your attention in the conversation?

"You lost them very young," he replied in exactly the same tone of voice with which he might have commented on the state of the NASDAQ. The idea that my parents' death might be a tender subject didn't even seem to occur to him.

"Yes," I said simply.

"You were lucky," he said coldly. The sudden steel in his voice was the only indication I had that he was even aware that he was actually speaking to me.

Excuse me?" I said with a little more force than I meant to. "Losing both of my parents—all the family I had ever known—at the age of eight makes me lucky? How so?"

"It's simple, really," he said, finally lifting his eyes to meet mine, but only for a split second. "You were lucky to lose your parents before you were old enough to become disillusioned with the idea that parental love is somehow perfect and unconditional."

"What are you talking about?" I said heatedly. "My parents' love for me *was* unconditional! And losing them was one of the worst things I've ever been through. I still miss them every single day, and their memory is one of the most important parts of who I am." I was breathing hard by this point, feeling an equal measure of fury and confusion at the turn this discussion had taken.

"Please," he scoffed unconcernedly. "All forms of love are conditional. And the fact that your parents' memory is such a defining characteristic of your own personality only illustrates your immaturity. Maturity comes as we make our own choices without reference to anyone else's opinions or influence. Your parents' memory is nothing more than a crutch—an excuse to keep you from making the difficult decisions that taking charge of your own life would require. Why bother trying to earn their approval now? They aren't here, and chances are, they wouldn't care even if they were."

He was back to staring at his stupid newspaper, but his eyes were no longer racing over the tiny words. I knew the conversation had finally captured his complete attention. But I couldn't come up with a single thing to say. What did you say to a person who straight-forwardly insulted not only the memory of your parents, but their very character? And yours along with it?

"I . . . ," I began, but my mind was a black mass of rage and indignation, and I couldn't think of a single coherent response. I pressed my lips tightly closed, afraid that if I allowed them to remain in their relaxed position, emotion would take control of my mouth, resulting in a stream of insults fired from my general direction.

I'd already noticed that, despite the fact that I was intimidated by Mr. Thorne, I couldn't seem to keep a measure of civility in my address when speaking to him. I'd never been particularly good at being a doormat, but generally I could manage at least *some* control over my temper and sharp tongue. But how could I maintain my silence in the face of such bold-faced unkindness? What had happened to this man to make him so cold?

"That's what I thought," Mr. Thorne said in response to my shocked silence. His tone held a hard finality, and his eyes once again began their determined skimming of his newspaper. "It's time to grow up, Miss Evans. Welcome to adulthood and to the real world."

I had always hated that phrase. It was intensely condescending, as if I had been living in some kind of fairy-tale existence up to this point. As if losing the two people I loved most and then enduring years of abuse and loneliness didn't qualify as living in the "real world." I was tempted to launch myself across the table, claws unsheathed, and make him sorry he'd ever thought to ask about my origins. Instead,

I rose to my feet and walked toward the door with jaw clenched, determined to keep my thoughts to myself. I could feel Charlotte's and Addie's eyes on me, but I didn't bother to glance back at them.

I escaped to the garden, hoping the harsh winter winds would cool my temper. It unnerved me that Mr. Thorne seemed to get under my skin so easily. I strengthened my resolve, determined that although he seemed bent on making my life miserable, I would not give him the satisfaction of seeing me upset. Charlotte had told me that he rarely stayed at the ranch for longer than a few weeks at a time, unless he brought business associates and friends with him, so I assumed he would soon be gone.

I could bite my tongue for another week.

But Tyler Thorne didn't stay for just a week. Other than a few short trips back to New York for board meetings, my employer stayed at Thorne Field for *months*. Granted, his concentrated abuse fell off dramatically a few weeks into his visit, and he rarely spoke to me directly (which suited me), but our association was anything but easy.

While I did not exactly relish Mr. Thorne's company, for Addie's sake I was glad he stayed. She thrived in his presence, despite the fact that he seemed to want nothing to do with her. I often found myself choking back heated words of reproach when he shook off her efforts to get close to him. How could a father be so cruel to his only child? I could freely admit that thoughts of my own unhappy childhood with the Whitmans colored my perception of Tyler Thorne's character, but it was precisely those personal experiences that made my opinion worth something.

Despite the awkwardness between Mr. Thorne and myself, my first Christmas at Thorne Field was wonderful—by far the most pleasant I had ever known. The house sparkled with holiday magic: banisters woven with pine boughs and twinkling lights, spicy candles shining from every table, and sleigh bells ringing with each opening of the front door. I felt as though I were living an Irving Berlin Christmas song each time I walked through the house. A general feeling of goodwill seemed to permeate everything and everyone in the house. Even Mr. Thorne seemed to soften, albeit slightly.

Although I despised him, I felt a strange curiosity about Tyler Thorne. I never sought his company, but when we were forced together, I found myself studying him, trying to form some kind of concrete impression of his character. As I observed him over the holidays, I noted especially his communications with other staff members on the ranch. I was continually surprised by the level of respect they seemed to have for him. His rough communication style seemed to be accepted as a normal character trait, and his associates and employees continued to hold him in the highest regard. Still, I didn't realize just how devoted Mr. Thorne's employees were to him until I made a derisive comment about him to Carl, one of the younger ranch hands. Mr. Thorne had publicly rebuked him for his care of some of the brood mares, and I was indignant, feeling the scolding was much too harsh.

"Don't let it get to you," I said to a mortified Carl after Mr. Thorne had stormed from the room. "It wasn't fair of him to treat you like that, although I can't say I'm surprised he handled it that way. Everyone knows what a *jerk* he is."

Carl's eyes had snapped up to meet mine. "Don't, Kate," he said firmly. "I appreciate what you're trying to do, but Tyler wasn't being harsh—he was being honest. He's right. I shouldn't have given the mares their shots without talking to Robert first, even if it is standard procedure." Carl bit his lip as if trying to make up his mind about something. Finally he shook his head almost imperceptibly and said, "You don't understand Tyler. You don't know him. He's a good guy, and I trust him. I know he would never dress me down publicly unless I deserved it. You shouldn't be so hard on him." With that, Carl turned and left the room.

This conversation puzzled me, since I had never felt the need to take any of Mr. Thorne's public criticisms so graciously. In fact, I felt most of them were completely unwarranted. As a result, I spent much of my time attempting to avoid the man, hoping that that would enable me to avoid his brusque comments as well. Why did everyone else seem to admire him? Trying to appease my burning curiosity, I continued to scrutinize Tyler Thorne from beneath lowered eyelashes throughout the remainder of the winter months, noting everything from his mannerisms to his favorite pair of jeans. What was it about this man that inspired such respect from those that knew him better than I did?

Except for the rare moments when his dark sense of humor made an appearance, I could only manage to feel dislike for Thorne. He treated everyone, including his daughter, as an irritant, yet they all seemed to reverence him. How could someone so coarse be so respected? It was a matter of endless frustration to me, and I began to feel that he was keeping his true nature elusive just to irritate me. It made me all the more determined to search it out. However, it did prove difficult since we rarely saw each other except at mealtimes, and even then we seldom conversed directly. It seemed that if he wasn't torturing me, he had nothing to say to me. I should have been grateful for the absence of his needling conversation, but instead I felt only unreasonable resentment. I was beginning to feel that no matter how much time I spent around Tyler Thorne, I would never get to know exactly who he was.

Around the beginning of March, however, the winds finally seemed to be changing. One cold night, I received an unexpected summons from Mr. Thorne by way of Charlotte.

"Tyler needs to speak with you, dear," she said to me in passing, as I closed the door quietly to Addie's room. "He's in the library." Her look of sympathy was tinged with amusement. My general dislike for Mr. Thorne was well-known by all the staff, and apparently Charlotte found our uncomfortable association funny.

I ground my teeth as I watched her turn the corner. I was in no mood to deal with Tyler Thorne. I had finally managed to put Addie to bed after what seemed like hours of arguing about it. I was anxious to get back to my cabin, since it had been a very trying day overall, but apparently it wasn't over. Mr. Thorne wanted to try me a bit more.

I sighed and headed toward the stairs. *What now?* I thought, feeling the exhaustion settle in, bone-deep.

Pausing outside the library door, I took a deep breath. This had become my habit before I did anything that involved Tyler Thorne. Although things had been relatively uneventful between us since Christmas, our relationship was one of tolerance and nothing more. I sincerely hoped he wasn't looking for a fight.

I knocked softly.

"Come in," said the deep voice on the other side.

I entered, nervously smoothing my long shirt over my jean-clad hips and attempting to look self-assured. "You wanted to see me, Mr. Thorne?"

He was seated behind the heavy oak desk, his laptop open in front of him and paperwork covering every square inch of the large surface. Glancing up as I entered, he immediately put down the expensive-looking pen in his hand.

"Hello, Kate," he said pleasantly.

I blinked, surprised at both his friendly tone and his use of my first name. I attempted to mask my shock, but it was a fruitless exercise. He was exceptionally observant—something I had noted in my determined efforts to study him.

"Does it bother you if I call you Kate?" he asked, raising an eyebrow.

I shook my head. "No, that's fine. I'm just not used to hearing you say it, I guess."

"Well, I figure since you've been here for quite some time, the appropriate period for formal name-calling has ceased," he said. And then he smiled.

I had seen Tyler Thorne smile only once before. The attempt had been so pathetic that I was immediately convinced that a weak lift at the corners of his mouth was all he was physically capable of. But I had been wrong. *This* was the genuine article. His expression of open friendliness and humor was so striking that I lost my train of thought for a second.

"And since I'm going to call you Kate from now on, I would prefer that you call me Tyler," he continued, not seeming to notice the fact that I was ogling him. "Everyone else does, and I'm tired of remembering to answer to 'Mr. Thorne.'"

I quickly pulled my thoughts back in line and nodded, remaining silent.

He watched me for a minute before gesturing to the chair across from him on the other side of the desk. I sat down, watching him carefully. I felt off-balance, as though I were existing in some kind of alternate reality. What exactly was happening here? Where was this friendliness coming from? I had become so used to our uneasy coexistence, that I wasn't quite sure how to react to this new, and much improved, Tyler Thorne. For the life of me, I couldn't fathom why he wasn't glaring at me . . . or at least pretending that I wasn't actually in the room. What change had occurred to shift our relationship so drastically?

"Um, so . . . did you need something?" I asked hesitantly when he didn't say anything.

He shook his head. "Not really. I've been reviewing this valuation report all day, and I could use a break. I just needed some . . . well, distraction."

I stared at him. "So you asked me to come in here so I could, what, *entertain* you?" The fact that he knew me as little as I knew him was apparent in his statement. There were few people alive less entertaining than myself. "I'm pretty sure I'll be a huge disappointment," I said, smiling self-consciously. "I'm really not much of a performer, unless you count my rousing rendition of 'The Wheels on the Bus.' "

Tyler laughed. He *laughed.* It was a deep, pleasant sound that I immediately wanted to hear again. I couldn't help myself from smiling in return and immediately wondered what was wrong with me. I had never even been *tempted* to smile in his presence before. But even more worrisome was the fact that I seemed to be struggling to find enough air to fill my lungs. Was it me, or did the room contain only a fraction of the oxygen it had a moment before?

Tyler stood, and I stared up at him, noticing his impressive height. My senses seemed to be in sharper focus than usual, and I observed for the first time as he walked around the desk to lean against it, that he was sort of . . . graceful. He stood, arms folded, facing me for several seconds without saying anything. I looked down at my hands as he studied me, feeling strangely shy all of a sudden. I glanced up at him when the silence seemed a little oppressive. He looked suddenly serious and I found it difficult to tear my eyes away from his somber baby blues.

"Actually, Kate," he began, his tone almost hesitant. "While I have you in here, I suppose I should take care of something."

A thousand dramatic scenarios were suddenly running rampant through my mind—the most prevalent involving me being chucked unceremoniously from the house for my lack of respect for my employer. Had I finally crossed the line? I hadn't been brilliant at hiding my dislike of him, even to his face. Had he finally had enough? Was I about to be fired? To my credit, it even occurred to me that I might deserve it.

Tyler continued, not seeming to notice my internal struggle. "I think I may owe you an apology."

My wild speculating came to a screeching halt, and I stared dumbly up at him.

"An apology?" I repeated. Tyler Thorne and the word *apology* did not seem to belong in the same room together. "Um, why?"

"Charlotte was in here earlier, and she mentioned how, uh, *charming* I've been the past few months—particularly to you," he said with a touch of self-deprecation. "I'm sorry to say, it hadn't occurred to me that I'd been so unpleasant. I really didn't know that I'd made life so uncomfortable for you. I apologize for that."

I nodded at him, not trusting my brain to come up with a sufficient response. I still felt as though I'd been hit by a very determined freight train, and I wasn't sure if my numb lips were capable of speech anyway.

"I don't mean to excuse my actions, but my life and position in New York have not been easy," Tyler continued. "Last December, I reached the end of my rope, and a break became vital to my sanity. There were many people and situations I needed to get away from, at least for a while. I came here to unwind a little, but I'm afraid in the process, I transferred some of my stress to you. Charlotte even went so far as to say I was victimizing you. It was completely unintentional," he said sincerely, and to my surprise, I realized I believed him. Strange, how quickly he had gained my trust. I tucked that thought into the back of my mind to nibble on later. "I should probably warn you now," Tyler said seriously, "that it's in my nature to be brusque, but regardless, I had no right to treat you as I have. I apologize."

I stared at him, trying to formulate an acceptable response.

"Well . . . ," I began and cleared my throat quickly, trying to make my voice stronger. "You've been, um, relatively *non-explosive* enough the past several weeks." I smiled hesitantly up at him. "I think I can find it in my heart to forgive you. Although, if it happens again, I may have to sic Charlotte on you." I widened my smile to show him I was teasing.

Tyler smiled back. "In that case, I'll watch my mouth."

We sat in awkward silence for a few moments before he continued, his tone taking on a little of its usual roughness, "Well, that was my main concern in speaking with you. Unless there's anything you'd like to talk to me about, I'll say good night."

I nodded and stood, recognizing the dismissal. I felt a desperate need to escape the tight awkwardness of his presence and find somewhere quiet to think through the conversation we had just had. I moved quickly toward the door, already replaying it in my head.

"Oh, Kate?"

I turned quickly at the sound of his voice, almost as though it had lassoed my spine and spun me to face its source. "Yes?" I asked.

"I do want you to know how pleased I am with your performance as Addie's tutor. Charlotte has given me a full report, and I'm very impressed with Addie's progress in her schoolwork."

I had the feeling that he was trying to make up for the months of torture, because although Addie had shown a little progress in her schoolwork since I had undertaken her education, it wasn't enough to warrant a positive review from Charlotte. I appreciated the gesture nonetheless.

"Thank you," I said softly. "Good night . . . Tyler."

I turned quickly to leave the room, but not before I glimpsed a small smile on his face as he once more seated himself at his desk.

Over the next few weeks, bits of Tyler's personality started to emerge from the quiet, albeit hardened, shell of a human being he had been since his arrival at the ranch. While still reserved, he began to make an attempt to actually converse with me. What was more, he seemed to be truly interested in my opinions and views, which surprised me. I often told him how unqualified I was to express judgment on the topics of conversation he favored, but he ignored my objections. He would press me until I shared my thoughts, and to my astonishment, would seriously consider them.

As his interaction with me gradually increased, my interest in him skyrocketed. I found that the more I learned about him—whether from himself or from others—the more my opinion of him changed. It wasn't long before it dawned on me that all my former feelings of dislike had completely faded. With this realization, I began to watch Tyler more openly. I found myself eavesdropping on conversations anytime I happened to overhear his name. This strategy proved useful, and I learned more about him in a matter of days than I ever had in the months spent watching him clandestinely.

For example, I discovered that despite his strictly corporate reputation, he was an avid outdoorsman. I was sure I had misunderstood when I heard Jarom, one of the ranch hands, mention this to a member of the cleaning crew. With all the time he spent squinting at his laptop screen and buried in paperwork, I had always assumed that Tyler preferred stock market reports and stuffy board rooms to the great outdoors. However, as spring descended on the ranch, Tyler proved Jarom right, leaving for days at a time on long hikes up through the surrounding mountain range. He also spent countless hours riding, grooming, and caring for a huge, black stallion. I seldom saw him with any other animal. I was always hesitant to ask Tyler personal questions, but one night I finally summoned the courage to inquire about his horse.

"Pilot is my oldest friend," he said with a rare lack of reserve. "I raised him from a colt. He was the last gift my father gave me before he died. Well, actually he was pretty much the only gift my father ever gave me . . . out of sincere affection, anyway."

It was not the first time Tyler had referred to his father in a somewhat derogatory manner, but I didn't question him. Instead, I nodded for him to continue.

"No matter what stupid decisions I've made or idiotic things I've said, Pilot is still happy to see me when I walk into that stable. It may be kind of juvenile to consider an animal a friend, but I guess I prefer Pilot's company to most of the people I know," he said.

Until that moment, I had never considered that perhaps Tyler might be lonely. Was it possible that he felt the friends he had were more attached to his wealth and influence than to him? Could it be that behind that direct and intimidating persona there was a man who was silently hurting? The questions quickly faded however, when his face hardened and he changed the subject, asking for my thoughts on the latest political scandal.

Trying to formulate a somewhat intelligent and informed response, I pushed any suspicions of Tyler's solitude away, convinced that such a powerful and interesting man could never lack for sincere friendship.

"Addie, come on," I said, trying to keep the frustration from my voice. "Come away from the window and concentrate on your math."

When she didn't move, I sighed and pushed myself to my feet, curious to see what had her so fascinated. Tyler was standing in front of the stable, speaking with a few ranch hands. At the sight of his tall frame, I felt an odd leap in the pit of my stomach. Hmmm . . . that was new. I cleared my throat to hide the strange sensation and tore my eyes away from the figure below.

"What is it?" I asked Addie, pretending I could see nothing of interest.

"He'll be leaving soon," she said, her voice morose.

"Who?" I asked, knowing perfectly well.

"Tyler. Charlotte said he's been here for four months," she said, looking up at me, tears in her eyes. "And that he's never been here this long before. That means he'll be going back to New York soon."

"Well, he has a business to run," I explained, running my hand softly over her shining curls. Quite frankly, I had no idea how he had been able to manage his affairs from this remote location over the last four months with only a few trips back to the city. "He can't stay here forever," I said, surprised to be defending him in the one thing that continued to bug me. While I could understand that Tyler needed to be in New York for his company's sake, I could not understand why he didn't take his daughter with him.

Addie leaned against me. "I miss him when he goes away. And he's always gone for such a long time."

I hugged her, patting her shoulder comfortingly. "But he'll be back. And you don't know when he's leaving. He may stay for another week, or even longer. Now, come on. Let's get back to work."

Sighing, Addie followed me back to the table where her schoolbooks were spread and picked up her pencil.

Hours later, I wandered alone through the blossoming garden, thinking back to what Addie had said. In the month since Tyler had called me into the library for his surprise apology, things had become relatively comfortable between us. I respected him and admired the way he naturally exuded confidence and power. One of the by-products of being the CEO of a multibillion-dollar company, I supposed.

Although my opinion of Tyler Thorne had improved drastically, I simply could not excuse his poor treatment of Addie. She seemed to be the ultimate nuisance to him. He sent her away gruffly whenever she tried to get close to him or win his approval in any way. I didn't understand his behavior, and it made me furious! However, given that our relationship had only recently become peaceable, I stewed in silence.

As for Tyler's treatment of me, I had little reason to complain. He was completely cordial, and at times even seemed to seek my company. My mind raced through all the moments we'd spent together, and I felt my heart begin to beat a little faster as strange tingles exploded in my middle. What was happening to me?

I pulled out of my memories with a sigh and reached up to touch the blossoms of a pear tree as I passed it.

"Kate," I heard from behind me. I paused, looking over my shoulder. Tyler was walking through the garden toward me.

"Out for a stroll?" he asked.

I nodded. "It's beautiful. I wish I could spend my whole day out here."

"Sometimes I do," he said, looking around at the touches of green surrounding us. While it was still a little chilly, the trees were blossoming and the tulips were beginning to emerge from the soil. "Thorne Field is nice this time of year, but . . ." He paused. "I just couldn't live here permanently, even if my firm wasn't headquartered in New York."

"Why not?" I asked, curiously. "I think I could be happy to live my whole life at Thorne Field."

A smile touched his lips, but it seemed almost sad.

"Too many reminders," he finally said. "As I'm sure you know, I only inherited this house. It was actually designed and built by my father . . . which explains why it's so large and ostentatious." He turned to me, his tone slightly mocking. "My father was not a humble man, particularly in the last decade or so of his life. Thorne Field was his last and greatest project. And what a legacy," Tyler gestured widely toward the house with sarcasm. He faced me again and explained needlessly, "My dad and I . . . we didn't really get along."

He didn't go any further into detail and, as usual, I didn't ask. We continued walking along the winding pathways, enjoying the fresh air and colors, when Addie came running toward us.

"Tyler!" she cried. "Look!" she twirled, showing how her newest pink dress-up gown flared out around her small frame. "Do I look like Amanda does when you take her to parties?" she asked.

I noticed Tyler stiffen slightly.

Who is Amanda? I wondered, but, again, didn't ask. Watching Addie spin in circles, I considered how long it would take for all of my pent-up curiosity regarding the many aspects of Tyler's life to kill me off.

"No." He answered her question in a needlessly terse fashion. "Addie, take that ridiculous thing off and go find something constructive to do."

I felt the resentment build within me as Addie's face lost its sparkle and she trudged, disappointed, back to the house. Seeing the devastated hunch of those little shoulders, something inside me snapped. That was it. No more.

"That was completely unnecessary," I said, turning to glare up at Tyler. "Why do you do that? Why do you treat her the way you do? She's just a kid! She loves you and she wants your approval. You're her *father*, for heaven's sake. Don't you think you could at least show her a little affection?"

Tyler looked at me in surprise but didn't answer.

"Don't you care for her at all?" I pressed, frustrated by his silence. I couldn't understand it. Addie was so loveable. How could anyone, especially her own parent, resist her?

Tyler looked away, his face twisting momentarily into a look of intense pain. "When I look at Addie, all I see is her mother."

"And that's difficult for you?" I prompted, surprised by my sudden courage in prying into my employer's private affairs, especially right to his face. I had never heard anyone mention Addie's mother, so I assumed the subject was somewhat taboo. Even Charlotte, who was a little prone to gossip, had stayed curiously silent on the matter. Still, as Tyler had been the one to open the topic of conversation, I decided to press my luck. "Why?" I asked.

"I prefer not to think of Camille if I can help it," Tyler said slowly. "Those memories tend to be rather painful, as you can probably imagine."

"What happened to her?" I asked.

Tyler turned to look at me, disbelief written on his face. His expression turned mocking. "You mean Charlotte hasn't entertained you with unsavory tales of my youth?" he said with considerable sarcasm.

I shook my head slowly. "No . . . ," I said in confusion. *Unsavory tales?* "What do you mean?"

Tyler sighed and turned, walking away from the house, further into the garden. I followed, sensing I was about to finally understand the strange and somewhat tragic relationship between my employer and his daughter.

As we walked, I studied Tyler's form. With his broad shoulders slumped in defeat and his head down, he looked almost beaten. It was a striking difference from the confident, proud man I had come to know. It made my curiosity burn all the more intensely.

"I grew up with Camille. We were close friends from childhood. She was beautiful, even then," he explained, sounding as if he were trying to excuse himself. "I fell in love with her as a child, really. Well, as much as a boy that young *can* love, but it wasn't until we were in high school that Camille showed interest in me beyond friendship. I didn't allow myself to question why. I convinced myself that it had just taken longer for her to realize that we were meant for each other. We dated through high school and married very young. Too young. I was . . . ," he trailed off and rubbed a hand over his face, his agitation evident. ". . . an *idiot*," he finally continued. "I wasn't ready to be a husband, and Camille was even less ready to be a wife. But I was crazy about her—so smitten that I was blinded by it. I was terrified that one day she would suddenly wake up and realize that she could do so much better than me. So I pushed hard, convincing her that marriage was the right thing for us, and really, it felt that way for a while.

"Our marriage seemed perfect to me. I woke up every day, marveling at how lucky I was to be so happy. Several years into our marriage, Camille informed me that she was expecting. I've never felt anything like that before. It was like God was confirming to me that I lived a charmed life. We had been married for five years by that point, and though we hadn't been trying to have a baby, the addition to our family just felt right. Logical. I felt like everything was falling into place for us." Tyler sighed and shrugged helplessly. "It still baffles me that I could have been so stupid."

"What happened?" I asked, a little breathlessly. It certainly sounded to me like Tyler and Camille had been the perfect couple. And it was clear that he still held her memory close to him, wherever she was. Just the mere mention of her affected him greatly. He wasn't as put together as usual; his composure seemed to be fraying at the edges.

Tyler squared his shoulders and the muscles along his jawline were tight and pronounced as he continued. "One day, about four months into the pregnancy, I came home early from my classes at Northwestern and found Camille with another man . . . a much better-looking man," he said, with a hint of a wry smile on his face. "The kind that everyone probably expected her to choose, instead of me. Our marriage was supposed to be perfect. I had believed with all my heart that Camille had been as much in love with me as I was with her. Everything she had said and done for the past near decade seemed to confirm it. How could I have been so *blind*?" Tyler seemed to be asking himself this question for the first time. His eyes were far away, focused on some point in the distance. He was silent for a long time, and I wondered if he had forgotten I was there. I touched his arm softly with the tips of my fingers, not really knowing why.

He blinked and continued as if he had never stopped, his voice much stronger now. Resigned. "Well, as a reckless young husband, I naturally did not react well to seeing my pregnant wife with another man." He paused momentarily, obviously reliving the pain of the memory. He turned to look at my face, as if searching for some hint of what I might be thinking. He held my gaze for a moment before looking away. "While it was probably one of the most defining moments of my life, it definitely wasn't my finest," he finally continued. "After throwing the guy out on his ear, I turned on Camille. I told her I was ashamed of her, carrying on with someone else when she was expecting our baby."

Tyler's jaw tensed, and I knew he was clenching his teeth. He straightened his frame as if hardening himself against his next statement.

"In that moment, she became a different woman. A complete stranger. She told me the baby *wasn't* mine, so I shouldn't concern myself. She told me that she'd been seeing this guy for the past year, that she was in love with him, and that the baby was his. She ripped away everything I thought I was in less than ten seconds. She railed at me for several minutes, telling me how unhappy she'd been with me and how we'd married too young. We were poor, you see," Tyler explained, turning again to look at me. "Although my father was wealthy to a ridiculous degree, I'd refused to take any money from him. Anyway, after she finished her ranting, she pulled out a suitcase. It was then that it hit me what she was going to do. I tried to stop her, although to this day, I'm not sure why. I tried to get her to listen to me, to think about what she was doing. She was throwing away our entire life together. She was pregnant, for crying out loud! How could she support herself and the baby without me?" Tyler looked at me, real concern in his voice. "In the end, the only thing she would agree to was my monetary support. I broke my cardinal rule and delved into my limitless trust fund. I handed over enough to support her for a good long while."

Tyler shoved his hands into his pockets and was silent for a few minutes, seeming to relive the horrible experience all over again. Finally he spoke. "It was harder than it should have been to watch her leave. She cheated on me! I should have been *happy* to see the back of her!"

He searched my face, as if waiting for me to confirm that it should be easy to forget an unfaithful spouse. I just looked back, feeling sympathy saturating every corner of my heart. Seeming to sense my pity, he continued, looking past me.

"In a way, it's ironic," he said. "I graduated from Northwestern three months after she left me and came back here to care for my dad, who was very sick at the time. He and I never really reconciled our differences, and our relationship was tenuous to the end, but he must have felt some gratitude, because he left me everything he owned. I suddenly was wealthier than I'd ever dreamed of being. I resisted using any of it at first, as I had for most of my adult life. Finally though, I decided that if I wanted to make something of myself, my dad would have wanted to help me. So I used a good portion of my inheritance to start my brokerage firm, which has made me wealthier than my dad ever was."

Tyler paused for a second and then said, almost conversationally, "You know, it has occurred to me that the only reason Camille ever agreed to marry me was because of my family's wealth. I've thought that maybe she never really did love me, and when she finally realized that I would never take my father's money, staying with me lost all of its appeal. Ironic," he said again and let out a humorless chuckle. "Because nearly as soon as she left, I became richer than Midas, with no qualms about using my wealth." He shook his head, his mouth forming a cheerless smile. Clearing his throat, he went back to the story.

"Well, anyway, for months I practically buried myself here at Thorne Field, foolishly pining away for her, even though she'd shown me exactly what kind of a person she was. It was difficult, attempting to wipe away a lifetime of near obsession. My grief was compounded by the fact that my father passed away six months after Camille left, so, essentially, I was an emotional mess. I felt guilty that my dad and I had never taken the opportunity to reconcile our differences. Actually, it seemed like my life was just one big mass of regrets. I wanted those days of absolute happiness back, even though they were tainted with the knowledge that they had all been a lie. I didn't care. I preferred the lie. I had come to the realization that ignorance really was bliss. I would have given anything to trade in the life experience and truth for blindness, if only it meant that I could have my family back."

It didn't escape me that Tyler still seemed to be mourning the loss of his "perfect" marriage. Despite the fact that it was many years past, he appeared to feel Camille's abandonment as potently as ever. No wonder he was brusque, with such memories haunting him.

"Did you ever divorce her?" I asked hesitantly.

"I considered it, but I never took the steps," Tyler answered. "They turned out to be unnecessary anyway. Right about the time my dad died, an attorney and a social worker showed up on my doorstep with a baby girl and a custody agreement. They informed me that Camille had passed away due to complications during the baby's birth." His voice sounded tighter, as though the muscles in his throat wouldn't quite cooperate. He swallowed convulsively.

"I probably shouldn't admit this, but I completely lost it," he said after a moment. "Despite what she'd done to me, I couldn't imagine a world without Camille in it." His eyes focused again on that far distant something. "I mourned for years. That's a pathetic confession to make, isn't it?" he said, still not bothering to look at me. "Especially considering the fact that she had never even really been in love with me."

Though his words implied it, his face showed no hint of embarrassment, just remembered pain. I wanted to reach out and comfort him, but I kept my hands to myself.

"Camille had listed me on the birth certificate as Addie's father," he continued. "I never found out why Camille didn't list Addie's biological father, whoever he was. In fact, like an idiot, I even hoped that the baby was mine after all, so I had a paternity test done to see. But it confirmed what I think I knew all along—I am not any relation to Addie."

His voice revealed a surprising amount of distress, given his treatment of Addie. Suddenly it dawned on me. I had been operating under the assumption that Tyler was a cruel parent, refusing to show his child any kind of love or affection. But in truth, Tyler was nearer to a saint, providing for a child that was the physical manifestation of his wife's adultery. Having seen how painful it was for him to even think about his wife, I was completely astonished at his goodness. How did he do it? How could he accept responsibility for Addie, knowing where she came from?

As if he had heard my unspoken question, Tyler explained, "With Camille gone and no one to care for Addie, I couldn't just surrender her to social services, especially when I could afford to give her a home. So, although I had no real ability or desire to be a parent to her, I accepted custody of a child that wasn't mine, and . . . here I am."

"I'm sorry," I said, not sure exactly what the established condolence protocol was in a situation like this. I opened my mouth, ready to offer a more substantial form of commiseration, but instead I astonished myself by saying, "I admire you for your choice, and I can't tell you how glad I am that you made it, but I have to say that I disagree with how you've handled things since then."

Even to me, the words sounded callous. Wincing at my tactlessness, I tried to soften them. "Don't get me wrong. I understand that having Addie around must be difficult for you, but I can't help but feel that you've held her responsible for her mother's choices. A child should never feel unloved or unwanted, and unfortunately, for all of her life, Addie has felt both."

Tyler's gaze swung to my face, vehemence plain on his features. "I wanted her plenty when I thought she was mine," he growled at me. "You can judge me if you want, Kate, but you'll have to excuse me if I discount your opinion. You don't know anything. You've never been in love—you have no idea what it is to feel jealousy and betrayal to that degree, and to have a daily reminder of it. I loved Camille! She was my *wife*. And yet Addie is not my daughter. What exactly should my reaction be to that?"

"You *chose* to make Addie a permanent fixture in your life," I reminded him. "Maybe if you *had* given her up for adoption, she would have found a home with someone who actually loves her." I felt immediately guilty for my words. The initial choice he made had been selfless, even if he hadn't handled things perfectly since then.

"I'm not judging you," I said quickly but with firm softness. "I think you did a noble thing by taking in a child that was not your own, especially if her mother was married to you when she was conceived. But I can't help feeling sorry for Addie, suffering the loss of her mother and the neglect of her father . . . guardian," I corrected, wincing again. Tyler raised an eyebrow at me, and I lifted my chin and stared in his eyes, daring him to disagree with my observation.

"Yeah, well," Tyler said, looking away from my gaze. "That's why *you're* here. So she won't be neglected."

"And I'm glad I'm here," I said, not backing down. "But Addie needs *you* too. She loves you, Tyler. At least let her know that she's not completely unwanted."

"Even if she is?"

"You don't mean that."

Tyler glared at me in frustration. "Why don't you just stick to teaching and leave the psychoanalysis to more qualified individuals?"

I glared back but finally decided to drop the subject.

"Speaking of teaching, I need to talk to you about something," I said. Tyler grunted, so I continued. "I've been working with Addie on her reading, but she isn't improving. She can't read even the simplest words, and it's beginning to worry me. I think she might have some kind of learning disability."

Tyler finally met my gaze, surprise evident in his expression. "She's dyslexic," he said.

I was instantly irate. "Well, why didn't anybody tell me before now?! We could have gotten her the help she needed *months* ago!"

"I didn't know before now," Tyler defended himself. "Nobody ever told me she had trouble reading. Her mother was dyslexic, so I'm assuming she passed the disorder down to Addie. We can have her checked to be sure, though."

"When?" I asked, eager to get the problem resolved.

"Whenever. We'll have to take her to Salt Lake, so it will have to be on a day that I have considerable free time," he replied. "Am I right in assuming that you want to come along?"

I nodded in response to his question.

"All right, I'll look into it today and see if I can set up an appointment with a therapist," he said.

"Thank you," I said sincerely, my mind greatly eased.

He nodded and turned, walking toward the house at a brisk pace, as if wanting to put as much distance between us as possible. I wondered briefly if he regretted sharing his personal history with me, a mere employee. As I watched him go, I realized that if I could, I would learn everything there was to know about this intriguing man. I smiled, realizing that I had grown to respect him more in the span of a single conversation than in all our previous encounters combined.

five

Kate?" I heard Tyler's voice from his office as I passed it coming from the veranda a few days later.

Sticking my head in, I smiled when I saw him reclining on a leather couch, his laptop open on his lap. He looked much younger than usual, dressed in sweatpants and a hooded sweatshirt, his thick, dark hair stylishly unkempt.

"Hmmm?" I asked finally, tearing my eyes away from his impressive form.

"I've been in contact with a clinic in Salt Lake. Addie has an appointment this coming Thursday."

"Great!" I said enthusiastically.

Watching him sink back onto the leather cushions, I was again struck by the difference in his appearance. I had never seen him so relaxed, so vulnerable looking. It was strangely appealing.

"What are you staring at?" he asked, his tone curious. Then he smiled as he watched the panicked expression flit across my face. "Think I'm good looking, do you?"

I blanched.

"No," I said automatically. It wasn't really a lie. I wouldn't have described him as handsome—not in the traditional way, but that didn't change the fact that I was still much more drawn to him than was wise for a woman in my situation.

He laughed uproariously at my response, but it seemed to me that his mirth didn't quite reach his eyes.

"Kate, you are without a doubt the most tactless person I have ever met," he said. "You could have at least lied to spare my feelings."

I tried to smile at him but found that I couldn't.

He continued, "But you do tend to be brutally honest, so I would never expect you to lie, even if it would have been kinder."

"I'm sorry," I said, meaning it. "I could have phrased that more delicately. I guess what I mean is that attractiveness involves so much more than just outer beauty. I suppose everyone is *physically* appealing to somebody. I guess I'm just not your kind of 'somebody.'" I attempted to keep my wince inconspicuous. Such a lie.

"And I would have to echo your statement . . . I am not your kind of 'somebody' either," he claimed, taking in my reaction with a calculated look.

"Well, considering that I'm your employee, it's probably a good thing that we aren't attracted to each other," I said, expertly masking the momentary disappointment. I knew I wasn't beautiful, so why did it matter that he was validating it?

"Well, that and the fact that I'm a good twelve years older than you," he said.

Deciding that it was probably best to change the subject from this uncomfortable vein, I motioned to the couch. "You look comfortable. What are you doing?"

"Just damage control," he said, glancing down at his laptop. "One of my larger clients isn't particularly happy with me right now." He closed the computer and looked up at me. "I could use a break, though. You busy for the next few hours?"

For some reason I couldn't identify, my heart skipped a beat.

"No, Addie's asleep. Why, are you in need of *entertainment*?" I spoke the word with heavy sarcasm.

He rolled his eyes and chuckled. "Have you done much horseback riding?" he asked.

"No," I answered quickly. "I've never been, actually."

Tyler jumped to his feet. "Well, you can't live on a ranch and not know how to ride. Give me a second to change into some jeans, and I'll give you your first lesson."

"Oh, you really don't have to—"

But he was already gone, taking the stairs three at a time.

What was I going to do? I had never admitted to anyone that I was afraid of horses, and no one had ever pressured me in such a way that I felt the need to disclose my secret. I was embarrassed to tell a man who had practically been born in the saddle that the idea of mounting a horse had me breaking out in a cold sweat. But I would tell him, if only to save face in the long run. Better to endure a little humiliation now than a full-scale panic attack while six feet off the ground.

However, despite my determination to spill the beans, five minutes later I was following Tyler into the one building on the ranch I had sworn never to enter. The stable was huge, almost as large as the house, and there were so many horses that I wondered how Tyler could keep track of them all. As we walked through the rows of stalls, he explained that his grandfather had actually been the one to begin horse-breeding. He had had a small ranch in Colorado in the early 1930s. His son, Tyler's father, had built Thorne Field in the mid 1990s and had moved the very successful breeding business there. However, after his father's death, Tyler had reduced horse-breeding at Thorne Field to just a lucrative hobby, deciding to focus on his brokerage firm instead.

He led me to the largest stall in the far corner of the stable and stopped. I paused several feet from the stall, refusing to come any closer. Why couldn't I just tell him about my phobia and then get the heck out of there? Unfortunately, Tyler's observant nature seemed to have failed him at the very moment I was counting on it, and he didn't notice my terrified reaction.

"This," he said proudly, "is Pilot."

I studied the familiar animal. I was overcome by his beauty and power, yet my hands still shook when I thought of how easily he could crush me.

"I raised him myself," Tyler continued, running his hand along the horse's neck and winding his fingers in the silky black mane. "That's why you turned out so well, huh?" he spoke affectionately to the animal.

I marveled at how the horse responded to him, as if he knew him. I had never really considered horses to be like dogs, in that they knew their owner's voice and responded to it, but Pilot recognized his friend and caregiver immediately. Pilot affectionately nibbled on Tyler's fingers, and Tyler pulled a carrot from his jacket pocket, feeding it to the horse.

"So," he said, turning to me. "Which horse would you like to ride?"

Suddenly he seemed to notice my deer-in-the-headlights look, because he stepped closer, his expression confused. "Kate?" he asked. "Are you okay?"

"I, uh," I whimpered, my feet itching to get as far away from the building and its inhabitants as possible. "I don't really like horses," I finally admitted.

"What?" Tyler said, raising an eyebrow. He studied my expression for a moment longer before breaking into a huge grin. "I don't believe this," he said, the amusement plain on his face. "The outspoken and opinionated Miss Evans is actually *afraid* of something?"

Tempted to shut his mouth for him, I turned my gaze from the horse to Tyler's face.

"Yes, I'm afraid of horses," I said, defensively. "And if you don't get me out of here in the next thirty seconds, I think I may go ballistic."

Tyler chuckled and escorted me quickly from the stable. Once outside, I took several deep breaths of the clean, mountain air, vowing never to enter the cursed building again.

"So why are you afraid of horses?" Tyler asked, shoving his hands in his pockets and rocking back on his heels. "Did you have some kind of traumatic experience when you were younger?"

"No," I replied, still sucking in air. "I think this probably qualifies as the most traumatic experience I've ever had involving a horse," I breathed.

Tyler rolled his eyes.

"I just have a phobia, okay?" I said aggressively. "I mean, they're so *big*, and the way they move their eyes when they look at you . . ." I shuddered.

Tyler laughed out loud. I did not appreciate it. I glared at him and turned on my heel, stalking toward the house. He called after me, still laughing, as I climbed the porch steps, but I ignored him.

I hate him, I told myself as I went inside, but I knew that regardless of how much he chose to tease me, I would have gladly spent every waking minute in his company.

"But, Kate, I don't *want* to go," Addie whined as I tried desperately to tame her mane of wild curls. "I want to play with my Barbie house."

Thursday had come, and I was attempting to ready Addie for her appointment at the clinic in Salt Lake. I was eager to see if the reading troubles I had observed stemmed from the disorder her mother may have passed on to her. Each day that Addie struggled was just another reminder to me of all she was missing in the world of literature. It was a gift I was determined to give her.

"Addie, you play with your Barbie house every day," I said, gritting my teeth in frustration. She was usually such an agreeable child, but she was seriously trying my patience today. "Don't you want to take a little trip? Go somewhere you've never been before?"

"I've been to Salt Lake before," she protested petulantly, folding her arms across her chest.

"Well, the clinic is in West Jordan, and you've never been there," I said, choosing to omit the fact that West Jordan was technically *in* Salt Lake. "Come on, Addie, it will be fun. I promise!"

She didn't look convinced, but she stopped complaining.

"What's the holdup?" Tyler's impatient voice came from the doorway. "The appointment is at eleven, and it takes an hour and a half to get there."

"Hang on," I said, spraying Addie's hair with hair spray, knowing it would hold the stubborn flyaway strands for about five seconds and no longer. "Okay, we're ready. Let's go."

Tyler huffed and turned, hesitating only for a second when Addie ran to take his hand. I noticed that, for once, he didn't pull away.

Settled in Tyler's large truck with Addie between us, I realized that Tyler and I had never been in a confined space for such a long period of time before. The situation became even more awkward when Addie fell asleep ten minutes into the drive.

I was sure Tyler hadn't even entertained such thoughts, given his insistence that he could never consider me attractive, but the fact that I was feeling any kind of awareness at all disturbed me greatly. Not only was Tyler Thorne thirty-four years old, and therefore much too old for me, but he was also my employer. And if that wasn't sufficient to squelch this strange magnetic pull I felt, I could just focus on the fact that he was the chief executive officer of a multibillion-dollar brokerage firm. We weren't exactly on the same playing field. In fact, our playing fields were pretty much in separate galaxies at this point.

I kept my gaze safely directed out the passenger-side window, but at times I could feel Tyler's eyes on me, and I knew he was wondering why I was so quiet. Lately I couldn't seem to shut up when we were together.

"What's wrong? You carsick?" he finally asked, after a half hour of dead silence.

"No," I said, refusing to look at him. "Just enjoying the scenery."

"Well, then you're missing everything on my side of the road," he said. I could hear the amusement in his voice but decided not to acknowledge it.

I shot a quick glance out the window to his left, but turned my head quickly back to stare out of my own window.

"Not as interesting as what's out your window?" he asked.

"Nope," I said, rolling my eyes at his persistence.

Addie stirred to my left, and I prayed that she would wake up and give me someone to concentrate on besides the man in the driver's seat. However, just as I expected, she snuggled closer to me and continued to snooze.

"Do you mind if I ask you a personal question?" Tyler asked suddenly, startling me enough that I finally looked at him.

"Not at all," I said, curiosity overcoming my resolve to remain aloof.

"You're a Mormon," he stated, and I nodded in confirmation. "Did you grow up in one of those active Mormon families, with scripture study and family prayer and family home evening every Monday night?"

I stared at him, astonished at his knowledge of Mormon culture.

"How do you know all that?" I asked.

"This is Utah, Kate," he answered incredulously. "You can't throw a rock without hitting a Relief Society president." He looked at me expectantly, waiting for an answer to his question.

I contemplated my response for a minute.

"Well, I guess I did. For a while anyway," I said finally. "My dad was a bishop in the Church, and we did all those things when I was little, but my parents both died shortly after my baptism and, as you know, I went to live with my aunt and uncle. They weren't members of the Church."

"Yet you're still active?" he asked.

"As active as possible," I answered. "I attend a ward in Oakley whenever I can, and I still read my scriptures every night and pray, well, almost constantly. I'll bet the Lord is sick of hearing from me, actually." I smiled self-consciously.

"But your aunt and uncle weren't even members, and you continued to go by yourself at such a young age?" He sounded astonished.

I smiled at him, understanding his disbelief.

"My knowledge of the gospel and my dependence on the Savior is the most precious thing my parents gave me," I explained. "After their deaths, it meant more to me than ever. Every time I sat in church or read my scriptures, it was like having them back for a little while. My aunt and uncle didn't understand at all, and I think my aunt was embarrassed to have a practicing Mormon under her roof, but during my growing years, my relationship with the Lord was all that kept me going. I couldn't just abandon Him because my parents weren't there to press me into Church activity."

Tyler looked thoughtful. "Your aunt and uncle didn't appreciate your beliefs?"

"Well, I don't think my uncle really understood why the gospel meant so much to my family, but he didn't try to persuade me otherwise. My aunt, however, is powerfully anti-Mormon. Well, she's powerfully anti-Kate, actually. I think if I had announced I was a Democrat, she would have started financially contributing to the Republican Party—and trust me, that's saying something."

Tyler snorted. "She doesn't like you? Why?"

"Search me," I said, shrugging. "She's never liked me. She made my life absolutely miserable during the years I lived with her. Not as bad as her son, John, though. Here, look."

I showed him the thin scar along my hairline and another on my arm, just above my elbow.

"Both are tokens of my cousin's affectionate nature," I said. "He loved to knock me around. Honestly, it was a tender mercy when my aunt sent me to the Brooks'."

"Wait, your aunt *sent* you away? Why?"

For the next hour I gave him my history, telling him of the years I spent in service at the Brook mansion in exchange for schooling at a private academy. I told him of my lonely years in college and how, through the lucky connection of a school friend, I had come to be Addie's nanny.

He listened without comment.

When I had finally finished, he looked at me in amazement. "And after all of that—after all of the difficult things you've been through, and the cruel treatment you've received—you still believe in a loving God who guides and protects you?" He snorted. "You must be some kind of saint. I know I wouldn't be nearly as faithful as you are if those things had happened to me."

I gave him an understanding smile.

"But the whole reason I made it through those experiences relatively unscathed is *because* I believe," I said. "The Lord never left me alone. I always felt Him near, especially when I had been abandoned and mistreated."

"You talk about Him like you know Him personally," Tyler said, his voice skeptical.

"I *do* know Him." I smiled. "That's the whole point, Tyler. He's there; I *know* He is! I've felt His presence with me just as surely as I feel your presence right now. He loves us so much! That knowledge is what makes everything worth it."

I looked at him, my eyes pleading with him to understand.

He shook his head, the expression on his face looking almost hopeless. "You know, I really wish I felt that way. But I just don't think God cares all that much."

I could tell by his tone that the topic was closed.

I turned and looked again out my window, studying the residential streets of Salt Lake as they flashed by.

Two minutes later, we pulled into the parking lot of the Utah Dyslexia Center. It was a cheerful building with a well-manicured lawn and flower beds. I gently shook Addie, attempting to wake her.

"Addie, come on. We're here," I said softly. Once she was fully roused, I helped her down from the truck, and the three of us made our way to the building.

As we sat in the small waiting room, I noticed a faraway look in Tyler's eyes, as if he were reliving years past. Addie and I had followed the therapist, Dr. Bennett, halfway across the room before he even realized we were no longer seated beside him. I wondered what was preoccupying him to such a degree, but once in Dr. Bennett's office, Tyler had his full attention focused on the matter at hand.

Dr. Bennett looked to be around thirty-five or so, with short, thick, black hair and wire-rimmed glasses. She smiled at Addie and held out her hand to her.

"My name is Marcie Bennett. You must be Addie."

Addie nodded and smiled hesitantly at her, taking her hand for a split second.

"I understand that you're having some trouble reading, Addie," Dr. Bennett continued with a warm smile. "We're going to see if we can figure out why that is, okay?"

Thus began a series of flash cards, writing samples, and computer exercises that Addie, mercifully, seemed to enjoy. After concluding her tests, Dr. Bennett sent Addie to a table in the corner of the room and provided her with coloring books and crayons. She then returned to sit across from me and Tyler. She confirmed our suspicions that Addie was indeed dyslexic and proceeded to give us some ideas on how best to help her begin to associate letters with sounds and from there, construct words. By the end of the session, I was feeling much more confident about Addie's future.

Leaving the clinic a half hour later, Addie's hand clutched tightly in my own, I wondered when I had become so attached to the little girl walking beside me. Her future meant more to me than my own.

I wanted so much for her to have all the opportunities that I could possibly grasp for her.

"So what did you think of Dr. Bennett?" I asked her as she skipped along beside me, bouncing a rubber ball that Dr. Bennett had given her as we left.

"She's nice," Addie said. "Her computer games were pretty fun too."

I smiled and shooed her toward the truck, as I turned to ask Tyler his opinion of Dr. Bennett. The question died in my throat as I saw the expression of horror on his face as he stared past me. I whirled to see Addie chasing her rubber ball directly into the path of a large white sedan that had pulled into the parking lot and appeared to be moving at an unprecedented speed toward the little girl I adored.

"Addie!"

I wasn't sure if the scream came from my lips or Tyler's, but I didn't care. I wasn't aware that I had begun running, but without conscious thought, Addie was suddenly in my arms and I felt the bumper of the white car hit me hard on my hip as I swooped her up and out of the way. I flew forward, suddenly airborne as the motion of the car forced me to the side. I attempted to pivot, to hold Addie to my chest and protect her from hitting the hard asphalt. I felt the jarring jolt as my other hip hit the ground hard, and I slid a few feet along the rocky gravel. I felt no pain, just relief that Addie had not been between me and the ground.

"Kate! Kate!" I heard the fear in Tyler's voice, just as I registered his face above mine. "Kate! Are you all right?"

"Addie," I murmured, my arms holding her tightly against me, praying she was unhurt. I couldn't seem to locate the part of my brain that stimulated movement, so I couldn't check.

"She's fine," Tyler assured me, and I felt her weight disappear from on top of me. Without her body to hold onto, my arms fell to the asphalt. Suddenly, with Addie's safety no longer a concern, the pain crashed over me like a tidal wave. Both hips throbbed, one from contact with the car, the other from contact with the ground. The hip pressed into the ground burned savagely, as did my arm on the same side. I attempted to roll gingerly over to remove the weight of my body from pressing down on them, but Tyler's hands prevented me.

"No, don't move," he insisted. "Not until I make sure nothing's broken."

I felt his hands moving down my arms and legs and feeling the alignment of my neck and shoulders. The irrational part of my brain even managed to resent the fact that because I was in so much pain, I couldn't relish the sensation of him actually touching me. I groaned, as much in self-disgust as in agony.

"I know," Tyler said, his voice still slightly panicked. "I know it hurts, Kate. Just hang on for one more second." He finished running his hands down my sides, feeling for broken ribs, I assumed. "Okay, I'm going to roll you over onto your back, okay?" he said gently, and I nodded.

I could hear other voices, frantic ones, speaking near me, but I focused only on Tyler's voice, needing its calming effect. I felt him slowly roll me off my hip and shoulder, and I gasped as the open wounds hit the air. I heard Tyler's sharp intake of breath as he saw them and watched as he turned toward the owners of the frantic voices.

"How soon can that ambulance be here?" he asked, his voice urgent. Almost in response to his question, I heard sirens growing closer. The fear in Tyler's voice caused a sudden wave of panic to rise in my chest. What could he have seen to make him sound like that? What was wrong with me? I raised my head slightly to look down at my exposed hip and arm. A throbbing pain in my temples required that I set it down again quickly, but not before I got an eyeful of the raw hamburger my skin now resembled. Still, I knew it had been worth it as I glimpsed Addie standing next to a stranger, who appeared to be holding her back as she tried to run to me.

Above me, Tyler conversed with the EMTs who were quickly gathering around.

"The car hit her, but I'm not sure where. I think her worst injuries are where she hit the ground. She slid for several feet, and it looks like it caused a lot of damage."

I felt a surge of warmth inside as I watched him wipe a trembling hand over his face. I was feeling more alert now, the shock of the incident wearing off. I looked around again for Addie, needing to reassure myself once more that she was indeed uninjured, but she was beyond my line of vision. All my attention was suddenly focused on the EMT who had begun cleaning the wounds on my hip. The agonizing burning sensation prompted me to push him away, but knowing he would just come back to finish the job, I simply closed my eyes and pressed my lips together to keep from crying out. As he cleaned, he spoke encouraging words to me, the most comforting being, "It looks worse than it is." He continued to swipe gauze that smelled like alcohol across the open wounds over and over, and though the stinging sensation brought tears to my eyes, I began to get used to it.

"She's really only grazed," the EMT said, looking up at Tyler and smiling reassuringly. "She won't even need stitches. I'll just clean it and bandage it here. Unless there's something broken somewhere, she likely won't need to go to the hospital."

Tyler looked relieved but still didn't take his eyes from my inert form. After my injuries were cleaned and bandaged, the EMTs proceeded to begin moving my limbs, just to verify that nothing had been torn or broken. My hips were both severely bruised but appeared to be in working order. With Tyler on one side and an EMT on the other, I was raised to my feet, my head spinning slightly. Tyler held on to me tightly, however, and my vision soon cleared. The EMT shined an annoying flashlight into my eyes and proclaimed me concussion-free and good to go.

"Are you sure we shouldn't take her to the hospital?" Tyler asked the EMT doubtfully.

"Well, it's up to you," he answered. "She has no serious injuries, just cuts and bruises. But if you'd like her to have a full evaluation, feel free to stop by."

"I don't need a hospital," I insisted, looking around for Addie. "I just want to go home."

"She should be fine," the EMT assured Tyler. He nodded to both of us and turned back to his team to help pack up the medical supplies scattered across the pavement.

"I—" Tyler started, but I cut him off.

"Really, Tyler, let's just go home," I pleaded. "I'll take some ibuprofen and be as good as new." I looked around again. "Where's Addie?" She was, after all, the whole reason for this mess. Fine lookout it would be if she'd been abducted while everyone was hovering over me.

"She's in the truck," Tyler said, and without another word, his hand slid around my waist and he swept me up into his arms.

"Kate," he began as he carried me toward the truck. I was having trouble drawing breath with his arms around me, so I just nodded, trying to look nonchalant. "Thank you," he said simply. "What you did for Addie . . . I—just—thank you."

He glanced at my face and then away before I could translate the look in his eyes. He set me down gingerly on my feet so he could open the passenger door of the truck, and then picked me up again easily to deposit me on the seat. He stood by my side for a second, looking like he wanted to say something else, but then he shook his head slightly and closed the door.

Six

The next day, I woke to aches and pains everywhere. My cuts still burned fiercely with the slightest movement and every muscle in my body screamed in protest as I pulled myself from my bed.

Glancing at the clock, I was appalled to see it was nearly one o'clock in the afternoon, but I was grateful that, for once, Tyler had seen fit to excuse me from breakfast and lunch in the dining room.

He hadn't said much on the drive back from Salt Lake, but occasionally he'd reached over and squeezed my hand, for no apparent reason. My fingers still burned slightly from the contact.

I showered quickly and re-dressed my injuries with gauze that Charlotte had provided me with the day before. Feeling almost human again, I grabbed an apple from my little kitchen and headed toward the main house, relieved to find that walking was much less painful than it had been the day before. In fact, once I'd warmed up my joints a little, I was walking almost normally.

Despite my slightly battered condition, I was in high spirits. I had a picture in my head, a picture that I was sure would be ingrained in my memory forever. A tall, dark-haired man was staring down at me with such distinct tenderness and concern in his eyes that I knew that I would never see another look to match it. Although I knew his worry for me had been based solely on the perceived seriousness of my injuries, it warmed my heart that Tyler could feel something as personal as concern for me. I knew how crazy it was to hold on to any kind of hope with regard to Tyler Thorne, but I couldn't seem to get rid of it. Worse, I wasn't sure I wanted to.

Walking across the deck and through the back door of the ranch house, I almost ran into Charlotte, who was carrying a can of furniture polish and a rag.

"Oh, there you are," she said, smiling in greeting. "I wondered when you would finally grace us with your presence. How did you sleep? I imagine you're pretty sore after what happened yesterday. You should be so proud of yourself."

She put an arm around me as we walked toward the staircase, careful not to touch my injuries.

I shrugged self-consciously and changed the subject, not really wanting to remember the horrific fear of that moment. Instead, I asked where Addie was. I hadn't seen her outside and if she wasn't trailing along after Charlotte, she had to be in her playroom.

"Oh, she's moping around somewhere," Charlotte said, putting the furniture polish in the supply closet as we passed it. "We knew Tyler wouldn't stay much longer, but it came as a shock to Addie all the same."

I froze.

"What do you mean?" Unspeakable dread was welling up inside me and I was terrified at what it might signify. "Tyler's gone?" I asked.

"Yes, he left for New York this morning," Charlotte replied, leading us into the laundry room. I was grateful she didn't seem to notice my distress. But then, she'd never been particularly observant.

"Another board meeting?" I asked, trying to keep my tone casual, but instead sounding strangled. "Will he be back tomorrow as usual?"

"No, I don't think so," Charlotte said, throwing towels in the dryer. "I got the sense that this will be a much more prolonged absence. Not surprising, as he rarely makes it out here more than twice a year under normal circumstances."

My heart felt like it was somewhere around my kneecaps. Twice a *year*?

"And seeing as how he's been here for nearly six months, I wouldn't expect to see him again for another year or more," Charlotte continued. "He never spends so much time with us, and I suspect his business will be suffering for it. It will need all his attention now. And I'm sure he's been missing Amanda."

My heart fell the rest of the way from my knees to my shoes. Amanda. There was that name again. Well, *this* time I would satisfy my curiosity.

"Amanda?" I repeated in a pathetically weak voice.

Finally, Charlotte seemed to notice my low spirits.

"Are you all right, Kate?" she asked. "You look awful. Probably lingering effects from yesterday. Come on, let's get you something to drink." She pulled me by the arm across the hall into the kitchen and sat me on one of the barstools at the marble counter.

"Who is Amanda?" I asked again. I knew it was foolish to pursue the subject so relentlessly, but for some reason, I didn't care.

Charlotte pulled a glass from the cupboard and filled it with ice water.

"Amanda Ives," she clarified. "She's Tyler's girlfriend. They've been together, oh, about two years now. She's the daughter of one of his business associates."

Girlfriend. Excellent. I should have known.

"Is she pretty?" The inappropriate questions continued to spew unchecked from my mouth.

Charlotte didn't seem to think anything of it however, and after setting the ice water in front of me, she commenced wiping off the counters. The woman seemed to always be cleaning something. I wanted to shout at her to stop, to focus on me, to tell me every single detail about this relationship of Tyler's that I had never known about.

"Oh heavens, yes," she answered as she worked. "She is a model, after all."

Of course she is, I thought.

"She and Tyler are a striking pair," Charlotte continued, oblivious to the dismay that was blatantly evident on my face. "I wouldn't be surprised to hear of an engagement in the near future. They've certainly been together long enough." I couldn't help but notice that she didn't seem particularly pleased by the idea. Didn't she like Amanda?

If I hadn't been fighting acute disappointment, I might have asked, but all I wanted now was to get out of the room. Mumbling something about needing to use the bathroom, I stumbled across the kitchen and down the hall to the nearest one. Locking myself in, I stared at my reflection in the mirror. I gazed silently at myself for what felt like a very long time, letting the plainness of the features looking back at me seep into my wounded consciousness.

"You idiot," I said finally to the girl in the mirror. The pain suffused in my voice surprised even me.

Clenching my jaw against any further betrayals of emotion, I took a deep breath and steeled myself. *Never again*, I thought. *Never again will I let myself get carried away like that. He is a thirty-four-year-old business tycoon with a supermodel girlfriend. And I am the nanny.*

Allowing those words to sink in and freeze their way around my heart, I opened the door and went in search of Addie.

As the spring weather turned warmer and began to take on the dry dustiness of summer, I felt the same dryness and dullness inside myself. I seemed to have lost every spark of animation I had, and although I had expected the sharp ache in my middle to fade with time, it seemed determined to take up permanent residence there.

Charlotte and Addie noticed the difference in my demeanor, but, while I knew it puzzled them, neither of them commented on it. I was frustrated with my listlessness, but I couldn't dispel it, no matter how I tried. It felt like the source of all my energy had disappeared.

No, not disappeared, I thought unhappily. *Just gone thousands of miles away . . . to be with his girlfriend.* Every time these thoughts invaded my head, I found activities to engage my mind elsewhere.

I was surprised to learn that despite the existence of two pools at Thorne Field, Addie had never learned to swim. Having taken up the sport as my main source of exercise in college, it had always helped me clear my head when times were especially rough. I relished the opportunity for some stress relief, and I immediately instituted swimming lessons as part of my daily regimen with Addie. I soon found that time spent in the pool with my young charge was time where my mind was occupied with keeping her safe, and not with holding my insides together. Addie was a regular water bug, and while she had no sense of technique, she took to the water like a fish.

Addie's ninth birthday was at the end of June, so more as a desperate attempt to employ myself than anything, I threw her a festive outdoor party, inviting several children from the LDS ward. I had ulterior motives, hoping that if I could introduce her to some children her own age, she might one day be interested in attending church with me on Sundays. The party was the perfect distraction for me and was an absolute hit with Addie and her compatriots. But once the last of the balloons and streamers were taken down, I found myself again in dire need of a project.

It was at times like this when I became increasingly grateful for the many different available activities at the ranch. They helped me keep my mind on things other than Tyler. Besides our regular school lessons and time spent in the pool, Addie and I began venturing up into the mountains along the winding trails surrounding the ranch. Addie began teaching me how to play tennis, having been instructed since she was five years old. Being taught by my pupil was an interesting experience, but I found Addie to be a surprisingly patient teacher. Especially since my lack of coordination was a regular barrier to any kind of real progress.

During one such lesson, as Addie was demonstrating her long-suffering by showing me, yet again, how to execute a backhand, Charlotte came rushing onto the tennis court.

"Kate!" she cried. "I need your help!"

"What is it, Charlotte?" I asked in alarm, dropping my racket squarely on my foot. "What's wrong?"

"I just got a call from Tyler," she said breathlessly. My pulse immediately doubled at the mention of his name. I nearly rolled my eyes at the involuntary physical reaction. "He's going to be here first thing in the morning," Charlotte said as she continued to gasp for air. "And he's bringing more guests than this house has seen in years."

My already-racing heart nearly leapt from my chest at this news. Tyler was coming back! He'd only been away a month, and he was returning already!

"Really?" I asked, feigning nonchalance with great difficulty. "He's certainly not giving you much of a heads-up. How many friends is he bringing? Who are they?"

"Well, he's bringing his partners in the firm, Jonathan Kelly and Joshua Coleman. I would have expected that, but he's also bringing the entire Ives family with him. Amanda, of course, and her father, who does a lot of business with Tyler, and her mother and her younger sister, Ashley. Several more are coming, but he didn't bother to say who. He said overall, there will be about ten of them."

"Do we have enough room?" I asked.

"One can only hope," Charlotte said, looking worried. "We'll have to convince some of them to share. If worse comes to worse, we can always have a few people stay in the pool house. I'm just not sure I have enough time to get all the guest rooms in order," Charlotte fretted, looking toward the setting sun. "Tyler said they'd be here by noon at the latest. I have seven guest rooms with adjoining bathrooms as well as the master suite and master bathroom to clean. Not to mention the pool house!" She put her hands to her face in alarm. "How will I get it all done before they get here?"

"Don't worry," I comforted her. "Addie and I will help you, won't we, Addie?" I smiled at Addie, and she nodded solemnly. Charlotte smiled gratefully at me and mentioned something about a quick dinner before rushing up the path to the house.

My heart felt light and airy as Addie and I gathered up the tennis rackets and tennis balls I had managed to scatter far and wide in my pathetic efforts. We chattered cheerfully about seeing Tyler again, and by the time we stowed our equipment in the closet just inside the back door, I felt my face would split in two with the intensity of my smile.

Then, suddenly, I realized something that hadn't yet registered fully.

Amanda Ives was coming.

I wouldn't have Tyler to myself as I had before. His runway-ready girlfriend would be at his side every waking moment.

"Tell me about Amanda," I said the next morning as I helped Charlotte make the beds in the guest rooms. "What's she like?"

"Well, I don't know her well personally," Charlotte answered. "We've met, but I only know her through what others have told me. She's beautiful, of course, but very particular. She comes from a great deal of wealth, so she likes things done her way, if you get my drift."

"So she's spoiled?" I asked. I could have guessed that one easily.

"That's what I've heard," Charlotte replied. "But she's absolutely head-over-heels for Tyler. Although some say they're a mismatched pair, she's been an almost permanent fixture on his arm for the past couple of years. I have to admit, I thought they would be married long before now, but Tyler has been hesitant to propose, due to the fact that Amanda's not a Mormon. Although to be perfectly honest, I'm not sure why that matters this time around. His first wife wasn't a Mormon either."

I tripped on the trailing bedsheet as my eyes shot to Charlotte's face.

"Why would Tyler care about that?" I asked, astonished. "Is *he* a Mormon?"

"Didn't you know that?" Charlotte asked, seeming surprised at my reaction. "Goodness, he's been a Mormon all his life! Granted, he's not been very active for the past decade or so, but he must still believe in it. He's certainly kept Amanda at arm's length, from an intimacy standpoint anyway, and I believe that's what your church teaches?"

She looked at me for verification and I nodded, numbly. I wondered idly how Charlotte knew so much about Tyler's romantic attachments. Tyler wasn't really the kind of person to volunteer such sensitive information.

"Well, he can't drag it out much longer," she continued. "I predict he'll soon forget about the religion issue and propose regardless of her church membership."

I wasn't really listening. My brain was still several sentences back, fixed on the idea that Tyler had been a member of the Church all his life and he had never mentioned it to me. I was stunned and a little hurt. Why hadn't he told me? Or why hadn't I guessed? I had never even considered the idea that Tyler was a member of the Church. His knowledge of Mormon customs suddenly made perfect sense.

Eventually, the main point of Charlotte's revelation hit me, and an unbidden smile came to my lips. Tyler had put off proposing to

Amanda because she wasn't a member of the Church? That suggested that he was interested in a temple marriage. The thought made me almost giddy. The strength of my reaction to this news scared me a little. I was supposed to be *distancing* myself from my feelings for Tyler. I shook myself mentally and concentrated on tucking the bedsheet under the mattress.

Charlotte and I heard car doors slam just as we were straightening the last fluffy comforter. Addie, who had been halfheartedly dusting the room, flew to the window with an excited shriek.

"They're here!" she squealed. "Look! I can see Tyler! And Jonathan! And there's Josh!"

I looked at Charlotte questioningly.

"She's met all of Tyler's business partners. They've been here several times before," she explained as we walked calmly to the window, my smooth movement belying the tumultuous storm of butterflies raging in my stomach.

We watched as people emerged from several expensive-looking vehicles. My heart sped up to the rate of a hummingbird's wings when a familiar dark head emerged from a black Range Rover and began pulling bags out of the backseat. His features were beautiful to me, despite their ruggedness. Seeing him, I felt as though my lungs could finally expand to their full capacity again. I watched the muscles in his broad shoulders flex as he pulled luggage from the car, and my hands clenched unconsciously on the windowsill.

My attention was thankfully averted from his actions when the passenger door of the same vehicle suddenly opened, and I watched as a pair of long, shapely legs unfolded from their cramped position.

I knew immediately I was looking at Amanda Ives. I examined her while she waited for Tyler to pull her bags from the back of the Range Rover, and I was struck by the immense physical differences between us. She wore a pair of short, fitted denim shorts and a casual designer tee, her perfect figure filling them out beautifully. Even in her sporty attire and glaringly white tennis shoes, she was stunning. Her long, blonde locks were trendily cut but pulled back into a sloppy ponytail, and she wore a pair of large, face-eating sunglasses that obscured her features but emphasized the lovely shape of her face and her clear, tanned skin. I felt my heart sink. In fact, it plummeted so fast that I nearly heard the *plump* of it hitting the floor. How could someone like me ever compete with the image of blonde perfection currently winding her graceful fingers around Tyler's arm?

Hang on a second! I mentally shouted at myself, reining in the crushing self-pity. *Let's not get carried away. You are not expected to compete. You never WILL compete. Because you are not qualified to compete. Remember, Kate? You're not in the running for Tyler's affections. You know why? Because you're the nanny, that's why.*

My nonverbal conversation with myself was interrupted then, because Charlotte began pointing out the different guests as they appeared. She was surprisingly knowledgeable about them and entertained me by explaining little quirks about each.

The tall, shockingly handsome, sandy-haired gentleman in slacks and a sweater, despite the warm weather, was Jonathan Kelly. The shorter but more muscular man with the graying temples was Joshua Coleman. They were Tyler's junior partners in the brokerage firm. Charlotte revealed with a smile that both men were known to be confirmed bachelors and therefore had women clamoring for their attention. They were friendly and sociable, and highly respected in the business world.

The slight, pale, blonde young woman was Amanda's sister, Ashley. She was delicate and quiet, unlike her older sister. The prim and proper couple walking close behind her were her parents, Richard and Marissa Ives. Richard was a senior officer in a prominent investment bank, Charlotte informed me. *He looks every inch the successful banker,* I thought. I noticed the look of approval on his face as he watched Amanda banter playfully with Tyler. Well, why shouldn't he approve? Could he possibly have found a better suitor for his daughter?

Marissa greatly resembled her eldest daughter, but her face showed the obvious strain of attempted age defiance while her daughter's face was naturally fresh and young. Marissa's features were so tight, I wondered if it hurt her to smile, although it didn't look like smiling was something she did very often. I followed her tight-lipped gaze, and then, swallowing, I looked away again as I saw Tyler grin at Amanda and put his arm comfortably around her tiny waist. Taking a deep breath and attempting to ignore the strange ache I felt under my ribs,

I chose instead to focus on the two other gentlemen in the party, both with petite brunettes hanging onto their arms.

"The blond one is Kyle Eshton," explained Charlotte, pointing through the window. "He's a well-known plastic surgeon, ironically enough."

I snickered, noting the prominently crooked nose of the cosmetic surgeon. It looked as though it had been broken at one time and improperly set.

"The girl with him is Marlee Lewis. She's pretty big on Broadway right now," Charlotte explained, smiling at my amusement.

I was beginning to feel a little panicked at the sudden entourage of famous, powerful, and gorgeous people arriving below. Hopefully I wouldn't be expected to converse with them during their stay. I wouldn't have the first idea of what to say to any of them. We existed in completely different spheres.

Charlotte gestured to a distinguished older man walking arm-in-arm with the other brunette. "Calvin Donaldson," she said. "He's a financial consultant in New York and has been like a father to Tyler. Took him under his wing when Tyler first started his brokerage firm. Tyler owes much of his success to Calvin," Charlotte said earnestly. "The woman with him is Marlee's twin sister, Dawn. She's an anchorwoman for a local station in Connecticut."

I studied the girls, noting their resemblance. Both of them were very attractive and very tiny. Their stylish clothing hugged their curves, emphasizing their figures. Confidence seemed to be seeping in copious amounts from every one of their pores. They both appeared to be aware of their blatant appeal, tossing their long, shining chestnut locks as often as possible.

Overcome with delight at the beautiful people below, Addie turned on her heel and raced out of the room. I was hot on her trail, determined to keep her out of the way until Tyler asked for her. I managed to snag her just before she started down the stairs. I dragged her back to her bedroom, telling her to be patient and wait for Tyler to get his guests settled before accosting them.

She pouted for the rest of the afternoon until Charlotte entered the room around five o'clock, declaring that Tyler had requested that Addie join his guests in the theater room after dinner so he could introduce her to them. Just before leaving the room, Charlotte turned to me.

"He wants you to bring her down, Kate. He's expecting both of you to spend the evening with the rest of the group."

I stared at her retreating back, butterflies suddenly rampant in my middle. He wanted me to come too? I wasn't sure whether I was excited or dismayed. On one hand, I would see Tyler in a few hours and possibly even talk to him. But, on the other hand, there was the presence of the model and her entourage of only slightly less dazzling people to consider. Instantly the butterflies became dead weights. How could I appear in my baggy jeans and T-shirt with so many attractive men and women looking on? I was ashamed of myself for thinking it. I told myself that I didn't care how ill fitted I was for Tyler's company, that nobody would judge me by my outward appearance. But I don't think I was stupid enough to believe it. Finally, I was reduced to repeating the nanny's mantra over and over to myself. *Be Invisible.* If I were invisible, no one would notice my plain face and shabby clothes.

It almost worked.

Walking down the stairs to the basement of the ranch house, I had to hold on to the back of Addie's shirt to keep her from sprinting into the theater room at full speed.

The basement of the ranch house had always overwhelmed me, since it housed all of Tyler's toys. I tended to avoid it, knowing that its main purpose was to please the celebrity crowd, not to amuse the nanny. The unfamiliar atmosphere only added to my nervousness as I approached the door to the theater, my finger hooked in the collar of Addie's shirt.

Pausing outside the room, I finally freed Addie, letting her enter the room without me. I took a deep breath and smoothed my hair, telling myself I would only stay long enough for Addie to say hello to those she knew and meet those she didn't, and then I was gone. Tyler would know that I had made an appearance, and I wouldn't be forced to drown in my insignificance for too long.

I entered the room silently and made for the darkest corner where I could observe but not be observed. I watched as Addie ran to Tyler and threw her arms around his waist. He made no move to return the embrace, but he didn't shake her off as he used to. Progress.

"This must be Addie," came a honey-smooth voice from behind Tyler.

He turned to face the attractive blonde and pulled Addie to stand in front of him.

"Addie, this is Amanda Ives," Tyler formally introduced.

Addie pressed shyly back into Tyler but smiled angelically up at Amanda.

"Oh, she's adorable," Amanda gushed. I wasn't sure whether or not I was just looking for reasons to dislike Amanda, but her smile seemed strangely forced to me.

Addie pulled away from Tyler and ran to say hello to Jonathan Kelly and Joshua Coleman. I was surprised when Jonathan Kelly stood at her approach and swung her up into his arms.

"How's my favorite girl?" he asked, giving her a squeeze. "Charlotte tells us you just had a birthday. Nine years old already, huh?"

Addie nodded and smiled proudly.

Joshua Coleman stood and pulled Addie from his friend's arms to give her a hug and a peck on the cheek.

"Hi, Ads," he said, smiling. "You get prettier every time I see you."

Addie blushed but she beamed with the praise. I smiled, grateful that even if Tyler couldn't seem to grasp the idea of parental affection, at least his business partners had it down pat.

Joshua carried her around the room like a princess and introduced her to everyone. I thought Addie handled herself very well and was a perfect little lady, but I could tell that Richard and Marissa Ives wanted nothing more than to have the child out of sight. Marissa's already strained features seemed to tighten impossibly as Addie reached out to shyly shake her hand.

I tried to keep my eyes trained on Addie at all times, but I found my gaze continually floating to Tyler and his blonde shadow.

He sat in one of the overstuffed leather chairs, and she seated herself promptly on the arm of the same chair, eventually sinking onto his lap. She had her arm constantly threaded through his or her fingers clasped tightly in his.

I tried to ignore the twinge of disappointment when Tyler's eyes never even came close to my corner. He made no move to acknowledge me. He was eventually forced to recognize my presence, though, when Amanda picked up the subject of Addie.

"I thought you didn't like kids," she said as she played with his earlobe.

"I don't . . . generally," Tyler replied, smirking ironically up at her.

"Well, then why on earth did you keep Addie?" she asked.

I wished she would lower her voice. Addie had glanced up at the sound of her name and was now watching Tyler with a look of curiosity mingled with something like nervousness.

"Well, she was left in my hands. I couldn't exactly abandon her," Tyler answered quietly. I was grateful that he seemed to be conscious of Addie's attention.

"Why didn't you just put her up for adoption or something?" Amanda continued, ignoring the fact that the nine-year-old's eyes were widening more with each word she spoke. I gritted my teeth. Couldn't the horrible woman see what she was doing? Didn't she care?

"I mean, think of all the trouble you would save yourself if you didn't have to care for her," Amanda's smooth voice continued to carry throughout the room. "Not to mention the money. And what's worse, you've hired a nanny for her, and now you have to pay for her *and* the girl."

Tyler's eyes finally flitted toward my dark corner. I didn't move.

"Kate doesn't cost me much," he answered, staring fixedly ahead, his voice hardening slightly. "And she's probably the best thing that's ever happened to Addie."

The pleasure I felt at his praise was tempered by the fury I felt building inside me at Amanda's continued commentary.

"Oh, I'm sure she is," Amanda said smoothly, but her voice had a slightly sarcastic undertone. "But I can almost guarantee you're paying her more than she's worth. For the life of me I can't figure out what would possess a person to become a nanny." She laughed. "It's not exactly something to aspire to, is it? I'm surprised at you, Tyler, supporting the useless profession by actually *hiring* one," she said, smacking his arm playfully. "Talk about throwing money after worthless pursuits. You'd be much better off just sending Addie to a boarding school somewhere. Then the nanny wouldn't be eating up any of your income, and you wouldn't have to deal with a child underfoot. Problem solved."

I was fuming. Addie had begun making her way toward me, bottom lip trembling, and I gently gathered her in my arms. Smoothing back her hair, I whispered softly to her, trying to get her mind off Amanda's tactless remarks. I smiled gratefully at Jonathan when he succeeded in distracting her with a game on his smartphone.

As soon as Addie was preoccupied, I slid quietly from the room and headed for the staircase, determined to escape from the uncomfortable atmosphere Amanda's comments had created for me. I could feel my hands start to shake in suppressed rage as I recalled the insensitive words she had spoken. I stopped at the foot of the stairs and leaned back against the wall, taking deep breaths to calm myself. *A useless profession*, she had said. Since when was educating a child a worthless pursuit? I wanted to throw my fist through the wall behind me, I was so wound up. Maybe some of the misplaced drywall would hit Amanda square in her irritatingly perfect mouth.

As I was contemplating the great satisfaction that the sight of Amanda with a bloody lip would inspire, I heard footsteps coming down the hall toward me.

"Kate," came the all-too-familiar voice.

I hated the way my heart sped up automatically every time I heard that sound. I turned slowly, fastening my eyes on his feet.

"Where are you going?" he asked.

"I have some things to do," I answered vaguely. "I'm going to go be productive until Addie has finished making her rounds, and then I'll be back to get her and put her to bed."

"You seem a little tense," Tyler observed. "What's wrong?"

What a stupid question, I thought unkindly. As if he hadn't heard every word Amanda had just said. What did he think was wrong?

"Nothing," I answered firmly, squeezing my clenched fists at my sides. "I'm just tired."

"No, you're upset," he insisted.

I looked up at him, not surprised to find his eyes boring into mine. He watched me silently for a moment, and his gaze softened slightly.

"Go ahead," he said finally. "And don't worry about coming back down here. I'm sure Jonathan or Joshua will be happy to tuck Addie in tonight. But, Kate—" His tone stopped my hasty retreat. "I expect to see you and Addie every night at dinner as usual, no excuses."

I glared at him for a few seconds, hoping he could read the mutinous thoughts on my face. If he could, they didn't faze him. His face was carefully expressionless as he nodded a curt good night. Then, spinning on his heel, he left me once more alone in the hallway.

Dread was my constant companion throughout the following day.

I hadn't missed Amanda's unimpressed expression as she appraised me the night before. I had no desire to be confronted with that again. I was well aware I didn't compare with her stunning beauty, and I didn't need to be reminded of it.

Addie, on the other hand, was bouncing off the walls with excitement at the prospect of spending time with the ranch's visitors. She was still wary of Amanda and her parents, but she adored the other guests and talked about them nonstop.

"Did you know that Marlee and Dawn are twins? They told me. They're not identi— identa—" Addie paused in consternation.

"Identical," I provided, gathering up her schoolbooks.

"Yeah, that," she said. "That means they don't look exactly like each other. But they are so nice. Dawn said I have the prettiest hair she's ever seen."

"Did she?" I said, preoccupied with my own thoughts.

I pulled Addie from her chair and steered her toward her bathroom so I could begin getting her ready for dinner. She continued to chatter on as I brushed her hair and pulled it back from her face. Finally, something in her voice caught my attention.

"Amanda is really pretty," Addie began hesitantly. "But I don't like her. Do you think if she marries Tyler she'll put me up for 'doption?" Her eyes held as much worry as it was possible for a nine-year-old to feel.

I pulled her into my arms and stroked her hair.

"Addie, Tyler would never send you away," I answered. "Don't worry about that, okay?"

I kissed the top of her head, and she smiled at me. I left her to play quietly in her playroom while I returned to my cabin to ready myself for dinner.

I was determined that I would not feel as inferior as I had the night before. Plain I might be, but everyone had at least a couple redeeming characteristics, right? I had been told that mine were my eyes, which were large and a luminous blue, and my skin, which, while pale, was very clear. Hopefully I could find some way to use those features to my advantage.

I spent more time on myself than I had in a long time, and when I at last took a look in the mirror at the finished product, I was pleasantly surprised. The deep purple shirt I had chosen made my eyes look almost violet, helped along by my eye shadow. My dark brown hair was getting longer, several inches below my shoulders now, and while not particularly voluminous, it was sleek and shiny. My form was too thin and lacking in curves to be considered attractive, but at least the fitted black slacks I wore accented my negligible hips to some extent. Overall, the effect wasn't bad.

Taking comfort in my satisfactory reflection, I took a deep breath to steady my nerves and headed back up to the ranch house.

Addie and I entered the dining room silently and nobody seemed to notice us. Everyone was congregated in groups around the table, talking loudly and laughing. I caught sight of Tyler speaking to Calvin Donaldson and Richard Ives near the head of the table, with Amanda right next to him, her fingers threaded securely through his as she smiled up at him. Did she *ever* leave Tyler's side?

My attention was thankfully stolen away then by Joshua Coleman, who caught sight of us and came over to harass Addie.

"Here's the curly-headed imp," he said, bending down to kiss her forehead. "I swear, Medusa has nothing on you."

"What's a Medusa?" I heard Addie ask as she followed him around the table to claim a seat beside him. Suddenly I was alone in a room crowded with people and had nowhere to hide. As I searched for a place to sit where I would not be in the middle of the conversation, I heard Tyler call to me.

"Kate, why don't you sit here?"

I turned and saw him motioning to the chair to the left of his own seat at the head of the table, unfortunately across from Amanda but mercifully next to Addie. I saw Amanda eye me coldly as she seated herself.

What's her problem? I wondered silently. *Has she not yet realized that she's got the looks, the fame, the money, and the guy? Why should she bother to even notice me, let alone glare at me?*

I decided to ignore the woman and focused instead on Addie, making sure she behaved herself. Keeping one eye on my charge and the other on my plate, I listened carefully to the conversation taking place at the other end of the table.

Marissa Ives was speaking of the presidential election that was to take place later that year, extolling all the virtues of the candidate I vehemently opposed. I noticed how Tyler remained silent throughout the conversation, allowing others to comment.

"He is precisely what this country needs," Marissa claimed, her tight features looking even more stressed with her enthusiasm. "We can't continue in the way we've been going if we want to remain a world power. It's embarrassing when visitors from other countries come and see how we live here. He will finally instigate the change this country needs so desperately."

I disagreed wholeheartedly but kept my mouth shut. I glanced at Tyler and saw a look of amusement playing in his eyes, tinged with the tiniest amount of disgust. Having had the opportunity to speak with him several times on the topic of the coming election, I knew he had disagreed with just about everything Marissa had said.

"What do you say, Thorne?" Richard Ives looked at Tyler appraisingly, daring him to disagree with his wife's opinion. "I assume William Barton will be fortunate enough to claim your vote."

"I make it a rule never to discuss politics at the table," Tyler responded, lying through his teeth. He had discussed politics often enough with me at mealtimes. We had discussed and argued public policy back and forth until my head spun.

I bit my lip to keep from smiling. Amanda caught my expression and glared at me yet again. I ignored her and turned to help Addie cut her roast chicken.

"How about we decide what the plan is for tonight instead?" Tyler asked, glancing around the table at his guests. "There are several options. We can go for a swim, play some tennis, go horseback riding, watch a movie, play pool, play cards, or we can just split up and everyone can fend for him or herself. I think we should put it to a vote."

In the end, it was declared that everyone was so tired from the day of activity that another relaxing evening in the theater room would be the best idea. As I excused myself to herd Addie upstairs for her bath, Tyler surprised me by catching my arm.

"Why don't you join us?" he said quietly, so no one other than Amanda could have heard. Truthfully, she was always so close by his side that I doubted he got any privacy at all. "Come down to the theater room after you put Addie to bed."

"Oh, I don't think—" I began, but he cut me off.

"I insist." He smiled kindly, and I wondered if he thought he was doing me some kind of favor.

Amanda looked as mutinous as I felt and we both began to object at the same time, but Tyler had already turned his back on us to speak to Jonathan. I groaned under my breath and quickly left the dining room.

After putting Addie to bed that night, I stood at the open window on the upstairs landing and watched the trees at the front of the house swaying in the stiff breeze. The air felt cool and refreshing, and I was content to just stand there and breathe it in, putting off going down to the theater room for as long as possible.

Suddenly I heard soft footsteps behind me on the carpet. Without even turning around, I knew instinctively who stood behind me.

"Shouldn't you be downstairs with your guests?" I asked.

"They'll be fine for a few minutes," he said. I could hear the smile in his voice. "They are grown-ups, you know."

"Unlike me, who apparently needs supervision," I said facetiously. "I told you I'd be down when I could. You felt the need to check on me?"

"No, you said you'd be down when Addie was in bed. Well, I just checked, and Addie's in bed asleep, and yet you are not in the theater room," Tyler responded. "So, naturally, I'm here to find out what happened to you."

"The breeze feels nice," I said simply.

"Yes, it does," Tyler said.

My heart sped up perceptibly as he came to stand beside me at the open window, his arm mere centimeters from mine. He stood slightly in front of me, giving me the opportunity to study him.

In his bare feet, worn baggy jeans, and a pale yellow polo shirt, he looked nothing like the high-powered executive he was. But despite the absence of the power suit and briefcase, I found him completely awe inspiring. I studied him from head to toe, my eyes lingering on his broad shoulders and narrow waist. I mentally shook myself and focused again on the dark tree line, berating myself for my boldness.

"So, what do you think of Amanda?" he asked.

His question threw a heavy bucket of ice-cold water over my heated awareness, and I froze, my muscles tensing with discomfort. How was I supposed to answer that? I felt his gaze shift from the view outside the window to my face. I blinked, willing my mouth to open and sound to issue from it.

"Um, well, she's . . . she's very pretty, isn't she?" I said, stumbling for something positive to say about the woman I spent most of my time actively disliking. She was his girlfriend, after all.

"Yes, she is," Tyler agreed. "One of the prettiest I've ever seen, actually. We aren't a particularly well-matched pair in that respect, are we?" He chuckled a little tensely.

I knew he was remembering the conversation in which I had informed him of his unattractiveness. Little did he know that whatever I had said then was a bold-faced lie. I made no reply to his comment, unwilling to voice my opinion and refusing to agree with his assessment. True, he wasn't as aesthetically blessed as Amanda Ives, but I would rather look at him than at her any day.

"I've been considering surrendering my bachelor status," Tyler said conversationally. "She would make a fine wife, don't you think?" he asked, his eyes still locked on my face.

I almost snorted. *Um, no.* Why was he asking me this? And why was he still so focused on my face?

Look somewhere else! my mind pleaded with him. He was making me seriously nervous. I struggled to hold my limbs still, not wanting to betray the effect he was having on me by fidgeting.

"I mean, I have to marry sometime," Tyler continued when I

didn't speak. "And, really, it only makes sense to marry the woman I've been dating for two years."

"I guess so, but—" I said, then suddenly clamped my lips together as I realized the objection I was about to make.

"Yes?" Tyler asked when I didn't continue. "But what?"

"Uh . . . ," I began, thinking quickly. "Don't you think you should wait and talk to Addie about it first?"

I cringed, knowing the question sounded absolutely ridiculous. If he lived primarily in New York and rarely saw Addie anyway, his marriage would probably be of little consequence to her.

But Tyler once again surprised me with his answer.

"I probably should," he said, seeming to honestly consider it.

My heart warmed even more toward him. No matter how much he tried to convince me that Addie was his ward and nothing more, I knew he really did care for her. I finally met his gaze, and the reply that had been about to escape my lips died away at the look I saw in his eyes as he stared back at me.

Or the look that I *thought* I saw. For as soon as our eyes met, a petulant exclamation sounded loudly from the end of the hallway, behind us. The electric charge between us fizzled immediately as Amanda's svelte form started toward the place where we stood.

"Here you are," she pouted. "I've been looking for you everywhere. This place is a maze; it took me nearly ten minutes just to find the stairs."

They're those big, tall things thirty feet from the front door, I thought unkindly. It was obvious that she had been watching us and had interrupted when she thought things were getting too cozy. I bit my lip to keep from snarling.

Almost as though she could hear my grumbled thoughts, Amanda laughed, the sound tinkling like little Christmas bells. She threaded her arm through Tyler's, drawing him from my side. He didn't give me a backward glance as he smiled down at her and walked away from me, back toward the staircase.

"I would have thought the size of this place would appeal to you," he said, his voice growing fainter as they descended to the ground floor. "You're the one with the massive penthouse on Fifth Avenue."

I closed my eyes as the tinkling laugh sounded again, and I pressed a fist to my mouth, stifling my groan of frustration. I stared out at the moonlight spilling over the flower beds, and it occurred to me that I should be thoroughly enjoying such a spectacle. But I was unable to drown out the reverberating laugh in my head that sounded increasingly triumphant with each echoing repetition.

Over the next few days, I managed to avoid Tyler whenever possible, choosing to take Addie for "nature walks" whenever I heard his voice coming nearer, dragging her outside and escaping into the garden. We spent a lot of time there, watching the bees buzz around the flowers and the wind play with the leaves on the trees. Addie liked to play pretend, and I found myself, more often than not, playing the part of the wicked witch or evil sorcerer while she ran among the trees and flowers, the beautiful damsel in distress. Sometimes I would take a book into the garden and read as Addie pranced around me in her favorite dress-up gowns, the heroine of some imaginary fairy tale.

Our daily school lessons in Addie's playroom were the only times I felt truly safe from the possibility of suddenly running into Tyler, since he never ventured into the room for any reason. I found myself spending longer and longer periods of time working with her on her reading, desperate to avoid the large, dark-haired form that seemed to haunt my thoughts day and night. The reading lessons were becoming much easier due to the methods that Dr. Bennett had recommended—they were working wonders with Addie. Her reading was coming along beautifully, and she seemed to finally look forward to it. It was also interesting to see how her games of pretend became more creative as her reading material became more varied. I was amused and strangely thrilled when I heard Addie exclaim to her imaginary foe that she would not be "intimidated." It was a word we had spent a great deal of time sounding out earlier that day in her lesson. I sent a silent prayer of gratitude heavenward after hearing it and returned to my book, smiling.

One day, about a week after Tyler and his friends arrived at Thorne Field, Addie and I were involved in an active game of pretend in the garden with Addie playing the part of Princess Ariella and me playing the villain, as usual. I was chasing her through the enchanted forest on my dragon when I heard a sudden exclamation. "Watch where you're going, you little brat!" I heard a familiar voice exclaim in fury. "Look what you've done! These are brand new! They're *Prada*, for crying out loud!"

I rounded the corner at a dead sprint and came face-to-face with an irate Amanda, trying desperately to rub the muddy smudges off a pair of expensive-looking white sandals. For once she was Tyler-free, choosing instead to enjoy the garden with her tight-lipped mother.

"Honestly, can't you control that child?" raged Marissa, glaring at me.

Addie rushed to my side and buried her face in my shirt.

"She was only playing," I defended, rubbing her back soothingly. "She didn't mean any harm, and it was my fault, anyway. I was chasing her."

"Well, I hope *you're* prepared to pay for my shoes, then," Amanda shot back, her attractive face twisting in immense irritation. "These are my most expensive pair!"

"And you brought them to a *ranch*?" I asked, incredulously.

Amanda obviously didn't like being told off by someone several years her junior. She stepped forward and I wondered if she was actually about to slap me. She raised her hand menacingly but stopped cold when a voice rang out from behind her.

"Well, this looks like trouble." Tyler's tone was good-natured, so I assumed he had no idea what he'd just stumbled upon. But when Addie raced to him and buried her tear-stained face in his side, his tone became wary.

"What's going on?" he asked, his gaze flicking from Amanda's furious expression to her mother's aggravated one, and finally to my fiercely determined stance.

"Nothing really," Amanda claimed, her voice taut with sarcasm. "I just had my most expensive shoes and a two-hundred-dollar pedicure destroyed by *that* adorable thing." She gestured furiously to Addie's hunched figure.

"Why did you bring your most expensive shoes to Thorne Field?" Tyler asked with his eyebrows raised, unconsciously patting Addie's head.

Amanda let out a furious snort and glanced quickly back at me, as if daring me to say something.

"Addie," Tyler began, with chastisement positively dripping from his tone as he looked down at her.

"She was playing, Tyler," I interrupted, straining to keep my voice under control. "The run-in with designer wear was completely unintentional—and could have easily been avoided had any kind of common sense been attempted." I shot the offending shoes a significant look.

Amanda glared at me, her green eyes shooting daggers directly into mine. She didn't comment on my veiled insult—I wondered if she had caught it. Tyler looked as though he were trying not to smile.

I reached out and took Addie's hand, leading her away from the group. Amanda immediately began hurling verbal darts, loud enough for both of us to hear. I sped up, hurrying Addie from the scene before she was able to register what Amanda was saying about her. I seethed inside, Addie's pain making mine tenfold.

Less than thirty seconds later, Tyler had caught up to us, pulling me to a stop with his hand on my shoulder.

"Kate, are you all right?" he asked, his eyes showing confusion and, to my irritation, a little amusement as well. "You look like you could breathe fire."

I looked up at him, my eyes snapping blue sparks. I gave Addie's shoulder a squeeze and sent her up to the house before turning to face him. "No," I replied tightly once Addie was out of earshot. "I'm not all right." I folded my arms across my chest and looked resolutely up at him. "Didn't you hear what Amanda was saying about Addie? Did you happen to miss that?"

"No," he answered, his eyes tightening slightly. "And I gather you didn't either."

"Yeah, well, she wasn't exactly concerned about volume, was she?" I snapped. "Out of respect for you, since Amanda is likely to become your wife, I won't say exactly what I'm thinking at this moment. However, I would appreciate it if, in the future, you would attempt to keep her out of my way. Because I doubt I can show that kind of self-control twice."

I glared into the rose bushes, my breath coming fast as I steamed inside. It occurred to me after a few seconds that the silence around me seemed charged with something ominous. I looked up at Tyler, taking in his expression in an instant. He looked one part troubled and two parts irritated as he towered over me. I took a step back.

"What's wrong?" I said, racking my brain for the insult in my last statement. I thought it had been rather diplomatic, considering his girlfriend's offenses.

"So," he said, his voice sounding exasperated. "It appears that you've finally formed an opinion on whether or not Amanda and I should get married. That's interesting."

"It is?" I blinked at him in surprise. His look was strangely unsettling. I stammered, wanting to make it go away. "I thought that was already decided. I'm sorry, I just assumed—"

"Don't worry about it, Kate," he said shortly. Without another word, he turned on his heel and walked briskly away, his hands clenched in tight fists inside his pockets.

I sank down onto the planter box and buried my face in my hands. This employer-employee relationship was turning out to be more complicated than anything I had ever encountered before. I never knew what would set him off next! The man was a complete puzzle, and I was fairly certain that if either he or I stayed at the ranch much longer, one of us just might be driven to commit suicide.

Sighing in frustration, I went in search of my young charge.

"I don't like Amanda," Addie sobbed into my shoulder when I found her sprawled dramatically across her bed. "I didn't mean to hurt her shoes."

"I know," I soothed, rubbing her back comfortingly. "Don't worry, Addie. I talked to Tyler about it and we'll take care of everything."

Addie sniffed and nodded, leaning heavily into me.

"She was mean to you," she said, her dripping eyes meeting mine. "I hope Tyler doesn't marry her."

I smiled tiredly at her, not wanting to get into this again. "Well, I'm sure Tyler will make the right choice for himself and for you."

"What about for you?" Addie asked, wiping her eyes with the back of her hand.

"For all of us," I amended, biting my lip. I stood up and pulled her to her feet. "Now, let's go get some lunch. I'm starving."

Addie sniffled and nodded, following me from the room.

As we descended the stairs, we met Jonathan Kelly on his way up. He took one look at Addie's red face and squatted down to her level, no mean feat for a man of his height.

"What's this?" he said, brushing his fingers over her tear-stained cheeks. "What's wrong, Ads?"

He looked up at me questioningly, but I kept silent, not wanting to repeat the story. Addie, however, was all too eager to relate Amanda's despicable behavior. As she imparted the story, Jonathan's features became distorted in disgust. To my irritation, I also detected a bit of amusement on his handsome face, although I could tell he was trying to hide it.

"And then Kate yelled at her and told her she shouldn't have brought her expensivest shoes to a ranch," Addie finished.

"Most expensive, and I didn't yell. Not really," I corrected sheepishly as Jonathan grinned up at me.

"Well, even if you had, she would have deserved it," he said, standing.

I noticed that although he was standing two stairs lower than I was, his head was nearly level with mine. Criminy, he was tall. Good-looking too. A brilliant smile lit his eyes, almost as though a 60-watt bulb burned behind them. "I'm getting the sense you don't care for her much," I said to him, realizing too late the danger in making such an observation.

Jonathan looked at me closely as if trying to guess the motive behind the comment.

"I won't pretend that Amanda and I adore each other, but Tyler is one of my oldest friends," he said. "I would put up with a lot more than an irritating girlfriend for him. So I smile and support him in his relationship with her."

He eyed me carefully as he spoke, making me nervous. Jonathan and I had spoken often since his arrival at the ranch, and over the course of our many conversations, I had noticed that he seemed to have an uncanny knack for predicting my responses. It irritated me a little. I sometimes felt that he could read my mind. Although, because I regularly wore my feelings plainly on my face, I probably gave him more credit for his discernment than he deserved.

"You're a good friend, Jonathan," I said. "Better than I am, it seems."

He smiled at me with a little too much understanding. "Well, I have reason to believe that marriage is in their near future," he said, his eyes seeming almost apologetic. "So I'm more determined than ever to coexist peaceably with Amanda, despite my reservations."

"Oh, well, that's great," I said, forcing all the enthusiasm that I didn't feel into my voice. "I'm sure they'll be very happy."

"I hope so," Jonathan said, still watching me closely.

I forced a smile. "Well, we better get down to lunch. See you later."

I steered Addie around him and down the stairs, safely away from his probing gaze. Unfortunately I steered her a little too quickly because we ran right smack into Tyler and Amanda exiting the dining room together. Amanda demonstrated her immaturity to great effect by looking away and refusing to acknowledge us. Tyler, however, smiled almost tiredly at me and moved to allow us entrance to the room. I smiled back tentatively and continued moving, not wanting to risk any chance for conversation.

"Why don't you and Tyler talk like you used to?" Addie asked a few minutes later as she devoured her sandwich.

I sighed, wishing the child wasn't quite so observant.

"We're just occupied with other things," I fibbed. "He's got guests here, and I'm too busy having fun with you."

Addie smiled at me, her eyes shining. "You like Tyler, don't you?"

I choked on my water, spraying it all over the table. Merciful heavens, if a nine-year-old child could see my weakness for Tyler Thorne, *everyone* must know about it. I vowed right then and there that the entire imaginary affair was done. No more. I would *not* expose myself to pitying stares and smirks. I squared my shoulders subconsciously in my determination.

It was over.

seven

Unfortunately, it was a lot easier to make the commitment than to keep it. I felt as though I was lecturing myself constantly in my cabin every night, having just come from hours in Tyler's company. The more time I spent in the same room with him and Amanda, the more it occurred to me that something was lacking in their relationship. I noticed that while Amanda always seemed to be touching Tyler and praising Tyler and talking about Tyler, I rarely saw her talking *to* him. But this arrangement seemed to work well for Tyler, because he didn't appear to care whether she talked to him or not. He would loop an arm loosely around her waist or bear her distracted toying with his earlobe as he spoke earnestly with one of his business partners. Observing their behavior was really a study in human nature, and if it hadn't been so painful for me, it could have been very interesting.

I began to hear more frequent mention of Tyler's suspected marriage plans, and this distressed me. Would he really marry that woman? I was fairly sure, after watching them together, that they weren't actually in love. Why would anyone willingly marry someone they didn't care for? Was Tyler really only interested in a trophy wife? If so, then my chances had been doomed from the beginning.

Another thought occurred to me as I observed the passionless relationship from a distance. Perhaps Tyler *wanted* a loveless marriage. Maybe he had determined that a marriage without love equaled a marriage without pain. After all, he had invested his heart and soul into his first marriage and emerged with countless scars. But somehow, Tyler didn't strike me as the kind of person who would settle for a life like that. Still, I'd been wrong before, and it wasn't as if I wholly understood Tyler Thorne.

Tyler didn't speak to me often when Amanda was in the room, although he always stopped for a chat if we ran across each other alone in a hallway or somewhere on the grounds. Most of the time, I spent the nightly get-togethers clustered in a corner with Jonathan, Joshua, Marlee, Dawn, and Kyle. The fact that I was several years their junior didn't seem to keep them from including me enthusiastically in the conversation. Sometimes, I even found myself looking forward to their company, an entirely new experience for me in social situations involving large groups.

About a week after the Prada Sandal Disaster, while attempting to coerce Addie into eating her broccoli at dinner, I was startled to find a large male hand suddenly resting on my shoulder. I turned to see the handsome figure of Jonathan Kelly standing behind me.

"Kate, you look fantastic tonight," he said kindly.

I blushed slightly and nodded my thanks, glad the room was loud enough that no one except Addie and possibly Tyler heard the unnecessary compliment.

"It's getting a little stuffy in here; I'm going to step outside for a bit. Care to join me?" he asked.

Hesitant to be under his microscope again, I shook my head. "I really shouldn't leave Addie here by herself," I replied, relieved to have such a reasonable excuse to beg off.

"Josh can keep an eye on her. Right, buddy?" Jonathan said, reaching out to the other side of Addie's chair and clapping Joshua on the shoulder.

His business partner looked up, startled at the sudden contact. He studied Jonathan's face for a moment, then glanced at me quickly.

"No problem," he finally said. He grinned down at Addie. "Nobody can force feed vegetables as effectively as I can," he winked at her, and she giggled.

Stripped of my legitimate defense, I sighed internally. I liked Jonathan, but he made me nervous. He was too observant, and the last thing I needed was to be x-rayed again. But I didn't want to be rude—not when he'd been so kind to me from the start. I finally nodded up at him.

"Um, sure," I said and rose to my feet, catching Tyler's attention as I did so. I imagined that I could feel his eyes on my back as I left the room at Jonathan's side, but glancing back at him, I found that he was still involved in deep conversation with Calvin Donaldson.

I tried not to feel awkward as I walked toward the garden with Jonathan, but the touch of his hand on the small of my back as we descended the deck stairs did not help me. The contact seemed much too personal, and it made me want to squirm with discomfort. Still, because I assumed he was just being a gentleman and ensuring I didn't fall, I didn't protest.

We walked along the winding paths toward the pool in silence. I wondered at Jonathan's lack of conversation. I assumed he had something specific to speak to me about, hence the walk in the deepening twilight.

Finally deciding to let the man broach the subject in his own time, I breathed deeply, letting the fragrance of a thousand different flowers flood my senses. As I looked around at the green peaks surrounding the ranch, a small sigh of contentment escaped my lips.

"It is pretty nice, isn't it?" Jonathan said, smiling down at me. "I love coming here. Feels like life just stops for awhile and lets you catch your breath."

"Then my life has been on hold for a long time." I laughed. "I live here, remember? This is where my whole life *is*."

"Really? Your whole life? Nothing outside of Thorne Field? You don't have family or friends anywhere else?" Jonathan asked, his face showing surprise.

"No, no family that will claim me," I said. "I've been on my own since I was about twelve."

"*Twelve*?" Jonathan exclaimed. "Were you in foster care, or what?"

"Sort of," I said, smiling at his astonishment. "My parents died when I was eight and I was sent to live with some relatives who didn't care for me. They transferred custody to another family who paid for my schooling in exchange for my 'employment.' I was kind of like a maid/nanny for them."

"Is that legal?" Jonathan asked, his expression horrified.

"I don't know, actually," I said thoughtfully. "But who was going to confront them about it? The only people who were related to me didn't care if I lived or died, and the only real friends I had were either close to my age or didn't know the extent of my situation."

Studying his distraught appearance, I attempted to assuage his worry.

"It wasn't much fun, but I was well taken care of. I always had plenty to eat, clothes to wear, and I got a good education. I didn't begrudge the work I had to do to get them. Work's what I'm good at." I smiled at him, trying to convey the sincerity of my feelings. "And look where it's gotten me. Sure, being a nanny isn't a glamorous job, but I honestly love it here. I feel like I make a difference every day. I'm paid well, and I live in a place more beautiful than anything I could have ever dreamed up. I'm actually really blessed."

"Blessed?" Jonathan questioned. "Interesting choice of words. Are you religious?"

"Very much so," I answered. "You?"

"Not really," he replied, tucking his hands into his jeans pockets. "My parents were devout Catholics, but I never really got into it," he said. "If you don't mind me asking, what religion do you claim?"

"I'm a member of The Church of Jesus Christ of Latter-day Saints," I said, ready to clarify.

But Jonathan surprised me.

"You're a Mormon?" he asked, his eyebrows raised. "Like Tyler?"

"Yes," I answered. "Does that surprise you?"

"Well, now that I think about it, not really," he answered. "I see a lot of the same goodness in you that I admire in Tyler. There's something kind of . . . different about you. You both seem to have a purpose that no one else knows about. Like you really know what you're living for."

"Well, I'd like to think so," I said, laughing. "What's the point of living if we don't know what we're living for?"

"I guess that's a poor way to phrase it," Jonathan said, smiling. "I suppose what I mean is, you seem to have a goal in mind. Something that you're reaching for in the grand scheme of things. So many of the people I know just float through life, grabbing whatever they deem to be theirs and a lot of what they know isn't. I think the reason I admire Tyler so much is that he seems to be more concerned with God's view of him than anyone else's."

This description of Tyler confused me. We hadn't spoken of religion at all since the day, months earlier, when we had taken Addie to her appointment in Salt Lake. Though I had wanted to, I hadn't had the nerve to broach the subject with him after Charlotte had informed me of his religious views. Tyler had never seemed particularly religious to me, but Jonathan's description of him disagreed with my analysis.

"I thought Tyler wasn't active in the Church," I asked hesitantly. I shivered slightly in the cool air. The sun was going down and it was getting chilly.

"Well, I'm not sure he goes to church every Sunday, if that's what you mean," Jonathan said, slipping his jacket off and draping it around my quivering shoulders. "But that doesn't necessarily mean he doesn't believe, does it?"

"I guess not," I answered, nodding my thanks to him for his jacket. "I have to admit, though, your description of Tyler surprises me. He's never seemed religious at all to me. He just doesn't seem to want a spiritual presence in his life."

"What makes you say that?" asked Jonathan, raising an eyebrow.

I shrugged weakly. "I don't know. Tyler and I, as a general rule, don't talk about spiritual subjects, but the one time we did, he seemed to dismiss the usefulness of depending on a spiritual being."

Jonathan thought for a moment.

"My judgment of his spiritual status, if you will, is not so much from discussion as from observation. I've seen how he lives his life," he said, shrugging. "I don't think a man lives like that unless he feels he will be accountable to someone for his actions in the next life."

"So you believe in an afterlife?" I asked.

"I don't know," Jonathan answered. "I guess I should say that I hope there is one, because if there isn't, the whole idea of living seems rather pointless. But who knows?"

"I don't know how anyone can go through life without a firm belief in God and in the eternal nature of our spirits," I said. "How could anyone experience the loss of a loved one and not go crazy? The only thing that keeps me going some days is knowing that I'll see my parents again and that I have a loving Father in Heaven who put me on this earth to learn and love and grow. That knowledge is behind everything I do. I—"

I cut off suddenly when I realized I was walking alone. I stopped and turned. Jonathan was standing some five feet back on the garden path, his eyes studying me with a look of surprise.

"What?" I asked.

"Wow," he said, his tone confirming his facial expression. "How can someone so young be so . . . grounded? I've never met anyone with that kind of spiritual conviction. You seem so sure."

"Well, I *am* sure." I laughed. "I've made it a priority since I was young to maintain a personal relationship with God."

"Is that possible?" Jonathan asked. He looked completely baffled.

"I think it is," I answered gently. "In fact, I think it's more than possible. I think it's imperative."

"Why?"

"Because how on earth can we live the way God expects us to, if we don't know Him or His reasons?" I said earnestly. "There would be no purpose, no understanding. Not only that, but there could be no assistance. We can't make it in this world alone. We require the Lord's help. It's a partnership, really. Those who willfully ignore Him try to make it on their own, and many of them don't even realize what they've given up. The whole purpose of this life is completely lost on them. I don't think I could ever live that way. I have this driving need to know everything, but most of all, I need a purpose. And my religion gives me that," I finished with confidence. We continued to walk in silence, lost in our thoughts.

"You amaze me, Kate," Jonathan said suddenly. He turned to smile down at me. "I think I've got the hang of you, but then every time I talk to you, you manage to surprise me."

I started to reply but stopped when I noticed something. The look in his eyes had changed from ten minutes ago. Deepened, somehow. I wasn't sure I liked it. Needing to lighten the mood, I good-naturedly rolled my eyes and turned back toward the house. As I walked, I searched frantically through my thoughts. I remembered back to some of the conversations that Jonathan and I had had during our nightly activities. I realized quite suddenly that out of the group of Tyler's friends I had been associating with for the past few weeks, Jonathan had by far shown the most interest in me. I had never really considered that interest to be anything more than politeness, but now I was reevaluating that view. His look was making me seriously uncomfortable. It was about time we got back to a more populated area.

"Ready to go back in?" Jonathan asked, turning to match my stride.

"Yeah, I'm freezing," I fibbed, quickening my step.

I was immediately punished for the lie by suddenly having Jonathan's arm around me, pulling me into his side as we walked. His hand rubbed vigorously up and down my arm, as though trying to warm it. I walked faster, needing desperately to end this uncomfortable encounter. I hoped in vain that Jonathan would keep his current pace and just let me go on ahead.

Naturally, I was mistaken.

"Kate, wait a second," he said, pausing and pulling me to a stop with him.

In a smooth, practiced movement, he pulled me against him, letting his arms slide all the way around me. I closed my eyes in horror, not knowing what to do. This man was the best friend and business partner of my boss. How could I get him away from me without simultaneously wounding his ego and my employment status?

I was about to open my mouth to say something to the effect of "Get off me now," when suddenly Tyler and Amanda rounded a bend in the garden path, stopping suddenly at the sight of me in Jonathan's arms.

I stifled a groan. I was cursed, plain and simple.

My heart sank even further as I saw the tightness of Tyler's jaw as his eyes ran over the scene. I wished Jonathan would let go, but he just smiled confidently as if he enjoyed being caught in the act of seducing the nanny. Tyler's irritated expression was in direct contrast to his girlfriend, who, for some reason, looked maliciously overjoyed.

"Well, what do we have here?" Amanda exclaimed with a huge, fake smile. "I had no idea you two were having a fling!"

"Amanda," Tyler began in a tone of warning, his eyes still glued to me, but his girlfriend rode right over him.

"Don't they make an *adorable* couple, honey?" she asked, sarcasm dripping from her lips. "Well, don't let us interrupt you . . ."

She tried to lead Tyler off onto an intersecting path, but he didn't budge. His eyes narrowed as he glared disapprovingly at me. Oh help, did he think I was responsible for this?

"Kate, it's late. Shouldn't you be putting Addie to bed right now?" he asked stiffly, his tone oozing displeasure.

Not meeting his furious gaze, I nodded. "Yes, I'll go right away."

Shrugging off Jonathan's embrace and his jacket at the same time, I pushed it into his arms and bolted toward the house.

I rose the next morning to the sound of a ringing telephone. Jumping groggily from bed, I rushed down the stairs to the kitchen and snatched the phone from its cradle.

"Hello?" I croaked, then cleared my throat. "Hello?"

"Yes, I am attempting to get in touch with Kate Evans. I spoke to a Charlotte Fairview at Thorne Field Ranch and she informed me that I could reach Miss Evans at this number. Is there anyone by that name residing there?" came the smooth, professional female voice on the other end of the line.

"This is Kate Evans speaking," I answered hesitantly. Who could be trying to contact me? The only people outside the ranch that I was acquainted with were people I had no desire to ever see again.

"Miss Evans, are you by chance originally from the Los Angeles area and a graduate of Brentwood Academy?" the professional voice pressed.

"Um, yes," I answered. Who was this woman, and how did she know these things about me?

"My name is Cory Daniels. I'm an attorney. My client, Sarah Whitman, has asked me to contact you." The female voice had a distinct air of relief about it now. "I have been searching for you for several weeks now. I'm relieved to have finally located you."

"Sarah Whitman?" I squeaked. I hadn't heard of or from my aunt since the day I left her home at the age of twelve. "What does she want?"

"Miss Evans, I'm sorry to have to tell you this, but your aunt passed away last week. She had some matters she wished to discuss with you before she died, but unfortunately, it took more time than we anticipated to find you."

"What happened to her?" I asked, ashamed at the realization that I felt almost nothing at this news.

"Mrs. Whitman was diagnosed with cancer several years ago. It was in remission for a while, but it returned about three months ago and was no longer treatable. She had very little time to prepare. However, she did dictate to me a letter for you, just in case this eventuality occurred. May I get your address so I can send it to you?"

Nonplussed, I quickly gave my address and hung up. Sinking back on a kitchen chair, I contemplated the conversation. What on earth could my aunt have wanted to say to me so badly that she would dictate a letter on her deathbed? Three days later, I found out.

When the letter finally came, I sat staring at the envelope for a long time. "Kate Evans" was all it said, with the Thorne Field address scrawled below. Biting my lip somewhat nervously, I broke the envelope's seal and pulled out a single sheet of thick paper. I closed my eyes for a moment, trying to push away my anxiety. Finally opening them, I took a breath and began to read.

A letter to Kathryn Marie Evans, daughter of my late husband's sister Caroline, and her husband, Matthew Evans.

Kate:

Knowing as I do that I will soon be dead, I have found my conscience to be greatly disturbed as of late. I feel no hesitancy in admitting that I resented every moment you spent in my home. However, as I reflect on my husband's fondness for you, I suspect that my treatment of you was not in accordance with his wishes. Now knowing that I am going to meet him again, I find myself feeling a measure of guilt for this. I do not ask your pardon or your forgiveness, but I fully acknowledge my failure to respect my husband's desire that I create a loving home for you in his absence.

There is one other matter I feel the need to disclose. I received a phone call soon after you left my household from a Jack Evans, who claimed to be your father's brother. He inquired after you, saying that he had known nothing of your existence until very recently, and he wished to acquaint himself with you. He disclosed to me that he was a wealthy man but without family. Because of this, he wished to care for you, as you are his only living relative. I responded that I knew nothing of you.

I now regret this action, simply because I know I shall be held accountable for injuring you. Do not mistake this regret as concern for your welfare. I remain as indifferent to that as I ever was. However, now you may correct my actions if you so choose. I have no memory of Mr. Evans's contact information, but I do know that at the time, he was the owner of a publishing house in Boston. Now it is up to you to contact him if you wish. With this information, I consider all to be settled between us. I now owe you no further explanation and no further notice. I neither wish you well, nor wish you ill, but pray that life has humbled you, particularly as I could not.

Sarah Whitman

Dictated by Sarah Whitman to her attorney, Cory A. Daniels.

I sat motionless in my kitchen chair, allowing the words I had read to whirl around me. My aunt's loathing for me was nothing new, but an uncle? I had another family member somewhere? Even if they hadn't been particularly close, why hadn't my father ever mentioned his brother? And why had it taken my uncle twelve years to learn of my existence?

The questions spun chaotically through my head. I wasn't as alone as I had thought. I had an uncle who wanted to care for me.

As I walked dazedly back toward the ranch house an hour later, I nearly plowed right into Tyler as he headed from the veranda toward the garage. It was a testament to my state of mind, because I could usually feel his presence long before I actually saw him.

"Kate!" Tyler cried, grabbing my shoulders to keep me from colliding with him. I jumped comically, a hand flying to my chest.

"Oh!" I exclaimed. "Sorry about that, I was just . . . ," I trailed off.

"Sleepwalking?" Tyler grinned, studying my face closely. "Are you okay? You look . . . distracted."

"I am distracted," I agreed. "But it's a good thing, actually, that has me so absorbed."

"Really?" he asked. "What is it? Can I ask?"

"Of course." I smiled up at him. "I received news a few days ago that my aunt had passed away—"

"The aunt who essentially sold you into slavery?" Tyler interrupted, his eyes hardening. "You're right. That *is* good news."

I glared at him pointedly. "Yes, that aunt, but that's not the news I was referring to. She left me a letter informing me that I have an uncle in Boston who has been looking for me," I said happily. "He wants to meet me! He even mentioned having me stay with him." Tyler stared at me silently for several seconds. I couldn't read his expression.

"Well," he finally began, clearing his throat. "That *is* exciting, isn't it? So . . . are you going?"

"Well, I haven't even met him yet." I laughed. "I'll at least need to introduce myself to him before I move into his house."

"Fair point." Tyler chuckled.

"But the thought has occurred to me . . . ," I started, then trailed off again.

"Yes?" Tyler prompted.

"Well, this may turn out to be a good thing for me," I said, a little uncertainly. Given Tyler's last reaction when I brought up this topic, I might be treading on thin ice. "I understand that you and Amanda will likely be married soon," I continued.

"You do, do you?" Tyler said, a little gruffly.

"Yes," I said staunchly, refusing to be cowed. "That's what I've been led to believe. And I think we both can agree that when that happens, it's best I find a new position." I looked at him significantly, knowing he would understand my full meaning. I would not work for Amanda Ives.

Tyler studied me for a long moment. "Yes, you probably should."

Pushing away the sadness that this curt statement caused, I continued. "Well, in that case, at least I know I'll have somewhere to go when the time comes."

"I suppose," Tyler said, continuing to study me. "But there's no reason to worry about that right now. Not for a while."

I tried not to show my relief. "So . . . how much longer is everyone staying, anyway?" I changed the subject smoothly. It was valuable information to me, because I had been expending a great deal of effort attempting to avoid both Amanda and Jonathan Kelly in the past few days.

"Only through tomorrow," Tyler responded, his mouth twitching. "You'll get your solitude back soon, I promise."

"Believe it or not," I said, grinning, "I'll actually be kind of sorry to see everyone go. Well, *mostly* everyone."

Tyler laughed and walked with me back toward the house.

I was tempted to spend the entire following day holed up in my cabin, just so I could be one hundred percent sure that I wouldn't encounter Jonathan Kelly at any point before Thorne Field was free of him. I felt a little guilty for the temptation, since I actually was fond of Jonathan; I just worried that he was a little *too* fond of me. The sensation was a bizarre one—I had never had to worry about such things before.

Even if I had determined on such a course of action, however, it would have been in vain. A knock sounded on my cabin door as I tied my shoes that morning, and, thinking it was probably Addie, I didn't hesitate to answer.

"Hi, Kate." Jonathan smiled at me from my front porch. My heart palpitated unpleasantly as I took in his handsome face. "Long time, no see," he said. "I feel like you've been purposely avoiding me."

Well, yeah, I wanted to say. *Can you blame me?*

"Jonathan," I greeted, trying to keep the dismay out of my voice. "You're up early."

"I've never really gotten off New York time," he offered, smiling. His face suddenly turned serious, and he studied me for a moment. "Kate, can we talk?" he finally asked. "It's my last day out here, and I'd really like to discuss something with you."

"Like what?" I asked straightforwardly.

"Just . . . future possibilities," he replied vaguely.

"Future possibilities with regard to whom?" I pressed.

"Us," he said simply. "I'd like to talk about the potential for us in the future."

"Meaning that you'd like to know if there is potential for an 'us' in the future," I stated for clarification.

"Yes," Jonathan answered with no attempt at pretense. "I'm intrigued by you, Kate. More than intrigued. You've become . . . *important* to me." His look was sincere and open.

"What? Why?" The words burst from my mouth before I could stop them. "Jonathan—" I began again, but he shook his head, silencing me.

"It's fine," he said. "I understand if you don't feel the same way. I didn't come out here to force myself on you, I just wanted to . . . let you know."

"Let me know?" I repeated incredulously. "Why?"

"Because while you may not want me now, that might not always be the case," Jonathan replied. "And I want you to know that if that day comes, I'm all in."

"Jonathan, I'm very uncomfortable right now." My tone pleaded with him to stop talking.

"Why?" he asked, his face twisting in confusion.

"Because there is so much in this idea of 'us' that is incomprehensible to me," I replied.

"Okay," Jonathan said, his face still showcasing his confusion. "How so?"

"Well, first of all, you live in New York. I live in Utah. That's a little prohibitive, wouldn't you say?" I said, raising an eyebrow at him. "Second, you barely know me. I don't see how you can be so sure of yourself after a few weeks of lighthearted conversation. And third, I just don't have the same feelings for you that you seem to have for me," I said, hoping I wouldn't cause him too much pain.

"May I respond?" Jonathan asked respectfully. At my nod, he continued. "Well, to your first point, yes, distance is an issue. However, New York is a wonderful, exciting place. Perhaps you may feel the need to bring Addie out for a visit sometime in the near future and we'll convince you to stay."

I started to open my mouth to protest, but he held up a hand.

"Second, I know you better than you think. I tend to be a pretty observant person, and everything I've seen has convinced me that I want more. And who says that you have to know everything about a person before starting a relationship with them? Isn't that what relationships are for? And as for your last point, I know you don't feel the same way for me. But that doesn't mean you can't or won't if you give us a try."

"I really can't even consider it," I broke in, finally. "I'm . . . kind of attached to someone else."

"Does *he* know about it?" Jonathan asked, with a piercing look.

I had suspected it before, but I sensed immediately that he knew all about my feelings for Tyler.

"No, and he probably never will," I said honestly. "But the feelings are there regardless, and I can't find room for anyone else right now."

Jonathan studied me for a few seconds, his eyes taking in every detail of my face.

"I care about you, Kate," he said slowly. "But I meant it when I said I wouldn't force myself on you. If you would rather that we were just good friends, I won't argue."

Feeling a measure of relief, I smiled gratefully at him and replied, "I can always use another good friend."

"But," he said pointedly, "I'm not going anywhere. I'm not convinced that you're a lost cause to my best friend. I'm going to stay in contact with you. I hope that's all right."

"Jonathan," I began in protest, but he held up a hand.

"Even if it's not, I'm going to do it. You don't have to respond," he said. Leaning forward, he pressed his lips to my forehead. "See you later, Kate." With that, he turned and disappeared.

"So where is everybody?" I asked Charlotte an hour later as I entered the kitchen. I had seen no one as I'd walked toward the ranch house, after taking some time to recover from my encounter with Jonathan.

"Everyone decided to make a stop in Park City on their way to the airport, so they left a little early," Charlotte responded as she cut apple slices for lunch. "But," her voice took on a conspiratorial air as she glanced up at me, "I heard something interesting before they all left. Apparently, Tyler finally proposed to Amanda last night."

My breath caught painfully in my chest. *What?* My mind refused to accept it. Hadn't Tyler just barely informed me that I didn't need to worry about leaving Thorne Field in the immediate future? What had changed his mind?

All the happiness and contentment I had been basking in, knowing that I was free of Jonathan and Amanda, that I would once again have Tyler all to myself, at least for a while, suddenly evaporated. Of course, the engagement had been inevitable, but I had still allowed that last bit of foolish hope to survive. Well, now I was paying for it.

"How do you know?" I managed to choke out.

Charlotte, true to form, didn't seem to notice my strangled tone. "Oh, I had a chat with Marissa before they left this morning. She said that Tyler pulled Amanda into the garden for a long talk last night and that everything was settled between them." Charlotte looked away, an expression that was astonishingly like displeasure on her face. "I guess I'm not surprised. Tyler's been alone for so long, this had to happen sometime. I'm actually rather surprised it didn't happen sooner."

I wanted to ask her why she disliked the idea, but I just didn't have the heart for it. I made an excuse about needing to find Addie and escaped quickly outside. I walked slowly down the gravel drive, my thoughts racing, but feeling strangely heavy as they did so. They dragged through my mind like bags of sand, leaving trails of despair behind.

I had nearly made it to the tree line when I heard the sound of a vehicle approaching. I felt a strange sense of déjà vu as I saw the white truck bearing down on me. I remembered the first time I had seen it, months earlier. I wanted to smile at the memory, but my face refused to obey. Unlike that long ago day, however, the truck slowed as I approached, and stopped. Tyler rolled his window down and smiled at me. "Hello, Kate!" he said jovially.

I nodded numbly up at him and continued walking. I could feel his eyes on me as I moved, but I didn't turn. He called to me once more, but I ignored him. Finally, I heard the truck continue on down the drive.

I walked for hours. I didn't feel them pass. I knew Charlotte would be worried about me. I knew that I was shirking my responsibilities with Addie, but I knew I would have been useless anyway. I needed to let my mind process. To accept.

My days at Thorne Field were now officially numbered. I needed to enjoy every minute I had, because soon it would all be gone. I wanted to cry at the miserable thought, but I knew it wouldn't change a thing.

I dragged myself past the ranch house and to my cabin sometime in the early evening. I walked straight up the stairs to my room and got into bed without even taking my shoes off. Compared to the sudden disaster that was now my life, grubby sheets seemed ridiculously trivial. I closed my eyes and tried to sleep, knowing that the sooner I could surrender to oblivion, the sooner I would forget that my world was crumbling around me.

I woke the following morning with a pounding headache and a dry, scratchy feeling in my throat. It felt strained, and I wondered if I had been crying in my sleep. It took me a second to recall why a tight knot of dread had taken residence in my chest. Once the recollection was clear, I groaned audibly, tucking my knees up to my chest. Tyler was getting married. Addie would be getting a new "mother." The most important people in my world would belong to someone else. I buried my face in my pillow, trying to rein in the misery flooding my mind.

In the midst of my brain-scourging exercise, I heard a firm knock on my door. It wasn't Addie's knock; I knew that for certain. I jumped from my bed and threw my robe around myself, concealing my wrinkled clothes beneath it. I answered the door expecting to see Carl or one of the other ranch hands. They sometimes stopped by to offer to water the plants in my window boxes. But it wasn't Carl standing on my doorstep—it was Tyler. My mouth nearly dropped open, but I stopped it just in time. Tyler had never just shown up on my doorstep before.

"Hi, Kate," he said, smiling warmly. "Got you up, huh?"

I said nothing. How should I react? I couldn't bring myself to address him in my usually affectionate way, not when I knew he was now officially engaged to be married to a woman he didn't love. So I just stared at him, memorizing every feature on that beloved face, knowing I would only have it in front of my eyes for a short time.

"You okay?" he asked when I didn't answer.

I nodded, finally looking away.

He watched me, a puzzled expression on his face. Finally, he shrugged. "Well, I'm taking Addie and Charlotte into town to do some grocery shopping. I just wondered if you wanted to come."

I silently marveled at how many things had changed since Tyler had first arrived at the ranch in December. I remembered his abrupt manner and the aggressive way he communicated with people. Back then, it would have taken some serious convincing to get him to take Charlotte to the hospital with a severed limb, let alone grocery shopping. And to allow Addie to come along? Yes, things were definitely different. Tyler had changed in more ways than I had ever expected in the months since I had met him. But there was no way I would spend more time than I absolutely had to in his company. I would not torture myself.

"No, thank you," I answered softly. "I have some things to do around here this morning." I knew the excuse was painfully weak, but I didn't care. I shut the door without waiting for his reply and went back up to my room, curling into a miserable little ball on my bed.

After about ten minutes of wallowing, I decided to find something constructive to do to distract myself. I pulled out my laptop and began searching for available positions. Despite the fact that my uncle was eager to meet me, I would likely need employment before I had the chance to connect with him. Therefore, employment was my primary concern. The best plan of action would be to call the Signal Hill agency again. I wondered if Micah, the agent I'd had before, could find me another job with a wealthy family. Maybe this time I'd get to go somewhere a little more exotic. Strangely, this thought didn't excite me at all. I didn't care about exotic anymore. All I wanted was to be with Tyler—wherever he was.

Realizing that the job search was not helping my mood at all, I pulled on my swimsuit and cover-up, grabbed a towel, and headed for the pool. Exercise was the only thing I could think of that would rid me of my morose outlook.

I swam hard and fast for as long as I could stand to. My breath came in uneven gasps and my muscles ached with the intensity, but my head remained obstinately focused. Finally unable to swim another stroke,

I collapsed against the pool wall and leaned my head back on the warm cement.

"Wow," I heard from directly behind me. "That was quite a swim. Who were you racing?"

I fought a groan of frustration. It was bad enough that I couldn't rid myself of the memories and fantasies and dreams of him, but the actual physical representation couldn't seem to leave me alone either.

"A ghost," I said cynically. "He won."

Tyler chuckled and came to stand above me, staring down at my face. For some reason, his look felt almost intimate, and I jerked my head up and away from his view. I pulled my goggles back over my eyes and hoped that he would get the hint that I was busy. He did, but instead of leaving the pool area, he settled back on a recliner to watch me.

I rolled my eyes and pushed off the wall. I swam even longer this time, thinking that the longer I took, the more likely he was to get tired of watching me and leave.

He didn't. Every time I turned at the wall, I caught a glimpse of him watching me with a small smile on his face. Why wouldn't he go away? Didn't he have a fiancée he should be cooing to or something?

Finally too tired to continue, I pulled myself from the water and stormed resolutely toward my towel, which had magically transported itself from beside the pool to the recliner next to Tyler. I didn't meet his eyes or speak a word as he watched me dry off and wrap myself securely in my cover-up. I slipped on my flip-flops and headed for the gate to the pool area, listening for the sound of footsteps behind me. I heard them almost immediately. Aggravated beyond measure, I whirled around.

"Can I help you?" I demanded. "Is there any particular reason you're following me around like a lost puppy?" Obviously my ability to treat Tyler as an employee *should* treat her employer had not improved much in the past several months.

Tyler grinned unaffectedly at me. "Well, I did need to talk to you about something, but you seem determined to ignore me today, so I'll postpone the conversation."

I knew what he wanted to talk to me about. He was going to inform me of his engagement and the subsequent necessity of my departure. And judging from the smile on his face, he didn't mind in the least that I would be leaving him. Struggling bitterly against the pangs stabbing from somewhere in my chest cavity, I turned swiftly and headed toward the staff cabins, hearing Tyler's footsteps continue on toward the house.

I showered and dressed quickly and then headed to the main house to find Addie. Knowing now that I was leaving, I was determined to get her ready for either another tutor or to attend school when I left. The idea that I would soon be separated from her was too painful to contemplate, so I didn't. I walked swiftly through the upstairs hallways, keeping a sharp eye out for the tall, broad-shouldered shadow I knew was lurking somewhere. I sighed with relief when I made it to Addie's room without being sighted.

I had to stifle a scream of frustration when I entered the playroom to find Tyler already seated at the table, helping Addie with her reading. He never entered this room! He didn't notice my entrance, and I found my anger and annoyance seeping away as I watched him work through the rows of words with his young charge.

He smiled encouragingly at her as she struggled with a longer word and sounded it out, letter by letter. He praised her when she read it correctly and motioned for her to move on with the next word, before looking up and meeting my eyes. His smile seemed to light the whole room.

I couldn't help but smile back, but it felt limp and lifeless on my face. "What are you doing here?" I asked tightly.

"Well, you see, I *own* this house," he joked but stopped when he noticed my look. "Kate, what exactly is going on with you today? Have I done something to irritate you?"

Yes, you proposed to Amanda.

"No," I said quickly. "I'm just not used to having you in here."

"Oh," Tyler said, his face showing his puzzlement. "Well, I can go if you want."

"No!" Addie cried, grabbing his arm and hugging it to her. "I want Tyler to stay!"

I sighed. "No, you're fine," I said to Tyler. "You were doing great. Just go ahead and finish up that page with Addie."

"Yes, ma'am," Tyler said, smiling at my bossiness.

I ignored him and sat down on the other side of Addie.

Tyler stayed through Addie's reading, history, science, and math lessons. I attempted to avoid his gaze whenever possible, but I couldn't help blinking at him in surprise every time he added some new tidbit to the lesson. Despite the fact that I knew he was engaged to another woman, I could feel myself falling deeper and deeper, and I was helpless to stop it. How was I supposed to get *over* this extraordinary individual?

Tyler was completely oblivious to my struggle and his manners were as friendly and detached as ever. I remembered the way he had smiled down at Amanda, however condescending the smile, the way he used to hold her hand in his, the way she was always at his side or on his lap. What would that feel like? Well, now I would never know.

"What's wrong?" he asked, startling me from my thoughts. Addie was working on a page in her workbook and the room had been silent for several minutes.

"Nothing. What do you mean?" I asked, feigning confusion.

"You just sighed. Like you were sad about something."

"Oh, I was thinking about my Uncle Jack," I lied quickly, surprised at how easily it came. "I just wish I'd been able to get to know him before now. I think it would have made life a bit easier if I'd even just known he was there."

"Have you contacted him?" Tyler asked. "Do you even know where he lives?"

"Boston somewhere," I answered. "He owns a publishing company there. I'm sure I'll have an opportunity to go and see him soon." *When I leave here.* I didn't speak the words, but I could feel them hanging in the air between us, somewhere over Addie's curly head.

Feeling the depressed thoughts creep in again, I turned once again to my pupil to monitor her progress. I could feel Tyler's eyes on me, but I didn't meet his gaze or speak to him for the rest of the afternoon.

I escaped as soon as I could after dinner, retreating to my favorite place on the ranch. The garden was at its most beautiful during sunset, and that was my favorite time to walk and allow my mind to roam freely. Usually my thoughts painted a much more pleasant landscape than tonight, however. The afternoon spent in Tyler's company had made the thought of my imminent separation from him that much more difficult to bear. I had never considered myself an overly emotional person, but I had never been in love before either. I was almost disgusted with my own sentimental reaction to such a condition. Where was that steadiness? That cool acceptance of things I couldn't control? When had I become such a mess of emotions?

I walked for nearly an hour, my heart beating furiously and my legs feeling sluggish and weak. I felt strange, like I was existing in a bizarre dream. I had been on the verge of tears for most of the day, and I could feel my resolve steadily breaking down now.

I wandered silently along the moonlit pathways, and when I felt that my jelly legs finally couldn't hold me up another second, I sank onto a bench underneath a blossoming pear tree in the far corner of the garden. I closed my eyes and breathed in the familiar scent of the mountain air and felt the breeze play with my hair. The sounds of the trees whispering and the crickets chirping gave way to another sound, a familiar one that had me on my feet in an instant.

As Tyler's footsteps came nearer, I looked around frantically, searching for a place to hide. I wasn't fast enough.

"Kate," he said pleasantly as I came into his view.

I had always loved the way my name sounded when it came from his lips. His voice seemed to caress the word, giving it added meaning. I closed my eyes, frozen in my flight, and finally turned to face him.

"Hello," I said, my voice revealing every iota of awkwardness I felt.

"How are you?" he asked. His face took on a concerned look. "You've seemed a little distracted today. Not your usual cheerful self. You barely said a word at dinner."

"I'm fine," I replied, my response hurriedly delivered. I moved to walk past him down the path, but he gestured toward the bench I had just left.

"Sit down," he invited as he seated himself on a planter box across from the bench.

"It's pretty late, I think I'd better head back to my cabin," I said. The protest was weak and Tyler capitalized on it.

"It's not that late, and as you've been either ignoring me or biting my head off all day, I haven't had the chance to talk to you like I wanted to."

I sighed, knowing how pointless it would be to object when I knew how easily he could argue me into a corner. Besides, we'd have to have this conversation sometime. Maybe it was better to get it over with now.

"Okay," I replied and I seated myself once again on the bench.

We were silent for several minutes, Tyler appearing to take in the dark beauty of the garden and I taking in his presence. However, regardless of my peaceful surroundings, I felt tense and ready to spring at the smallest sound. I dreaded the subject I knew would inevitably come up when Tyler finally broke the silence.

"So, I get the feeling you're a little bit irritated with me, Kate," Tyler said, looking pointedly at me. "Care to tell me what I've done? I don't like getting the silent treatment, especially from you."

"I don't know what you're talking about," I said vaguely.

"Oh, come on," Tyler said, his tone amused. "It's not like you've been trying all that hard to hide it. What's going on?"

I looked at him, the determined set of his jaw, and knew that he wasn't going to drop the subject until I explained. I stood, knowing I couldn't be face-to-face with him without his closeness muddying my thought processes. Taking a deep breath as I moved further down the garden path, I finally opened my mouth. "I understand you're finally engaged," I said quickly, hoping that the faster I said it, the firmer and more controlled it would sound. "Congratulations."

Tyler looked faintly surprised at my outburst, but he smiled slightly as he considered it. "Is that why you're so out of spirits? I guess I understand. If I'm going to be married, you'll suddenly be out of a job."

"I can find something," I said, almost defiantly. "I'm not worried about finding another job."

"I have no doubt a woman of your talents would be snapped right up," Tyler replied, his eyebrows raised. "But if you're so sure you can find something, then why are you so depressed?"

I glared at him. What a stupid question.

"Because I don't actually *want* to leave, Tyler," I said, my tone much colder than I intended. It was downright arctic.

Tyler raised his eyebrows and leaned forward, placing his elbows on his knees. "Well, I'm certainly not going to force you," he said casually. "If you don't want to leave, then why are you going?"

"You know why!" I insisted angrily. "I won't work for her! I won't be here if she is!"

Tyler smiled. "Kate," he said, "how often do you expect to see her? I mean, this year has been a bit of an exception, but usually I don't spend much time here. And I can pretty much guarantee you that if Amanda and I were married, it would be even less. She prefers city life."

"But you'd still come!" I said, and I was horrified to hear tears in my voice, even if they hadn't yet reached my eyes. "I'd still have to see you! You and her!"

"Is seeing me so terrible?" Tyler asked, his eyebrows still raised. "I'm a little hurt, Kate. I thought we were good friends."

"We are," I said, and I could feel the burning starting behind my eyelids. "We are good friends, but it's more than that. I can't . . . ," I trailed off, knowing that I was about to change everything. Once I continued and said what was on the tip of my tongue, everything that had ever existed between me and Tyler would be different. But I had to say it. I needed to say it.

Tyler stood, looking concerned, but I turned my back on him. It would be easier to speak if I couldn't actually see his face.

"You can't what?" Tyler prompted from behind me. I could hear the confusion in his voice. "What is it?"

"I can't see you with her. Not like that. It hurts too much." I said it softly, but in the quiet garden it was loud enough. There was nothing but silence surrounding us now. I couldn't even hear Tyler breathing, but I could imagine the look on his face. Surprise. Humor. Maybe even disgust.

"I . . . I'm not sure . . . ," he began. I heard the uncertainty in his voice, and I squeezed my eyes shut, steeling myself for the mortification I was sure was on its way. "Kate," he said, and I jumped. He had moved closer to me without my notice, and he was now directly behind me. I felt his hand on my shoulder, and he softly but firmly turned me to face him. I still did not open my eyes, but I felt his hand under my chin, forcing my face up so he could see it.

"Don't leave," he said, and his voice was so different from its usual confident tone that I opened my eyes and stared at him. "Please?" he said and smiled at me.

"If you're going to marry Amanda Ives," I said, "then I am leaving." My tone left no room for discussion.

"Then I won't marry her," he said.

I stared at him. He wouldn't marry her? Just like that?

"What?" I said, blinking.

"If that's what it takes to keep you, I won't marry her," Tyler repeated.

"But what will you tell her?" I asked. "How can you just take back your proposal like that?"

"What I'd like to know," Tyler said with a pointed look, "is where you got the idea that I had ever proposed in the first place."

"Charlotte said that Marissa said that—" I began but stopped at Tyler's amused expression. "You never even proposed to her? You aren't engaged?" I asked, attempting to keep the sweet relief from my voice.

"No," Tyler said, and I thought I saw him shudder slightly. "No, I never proposed to Amanda. And what's more, I don't even want to talk about her. The subject that I'd like to discuss is why the thought of me marrying her was so distressing to you. *That* is what interests me."

I felt my face redden. "I . . . ," I said, but I couldn't think of a single thing to say. Tyler's fingers were still under my chin, and I felt them slide softly up the side of my face. I nearly gasped at the physical reaction it caused. It was as if trails of flame followed their every movement.

"Yes?" Tyler prompted as his face came within inches of mine. I felt his arm slide around my waist, pulling me tightly against him. I couldn't draw breath, and my knees weakened as I felt his lips graze the skin below my ear. What was happening here?

"Tyler," I breathed, attempting to sound firm. The effort was completely wasted. "What are you do—"

"You know, I think I'm being pretty obvious," Tyler interrupted, his lips brushing against my skin as they moved down my jawbone.

"But what—" I gasped as his lips came within centimeters of mine. The question died as he pressed his lips softly to mine. I stopped breathing, wondering when the dream had started. Because this couldn't possibly be reality. Not my reality, anyway.

Tyler pulled back and studied my face somberly, gauging my reaction.

"What was that?" I asked. My legs felt as though they might give out at any moment and my heart was pounding furiously in my chest.

"That was me telling you why I could never have proposed to Amanda," Tyler said simply.

"Oh, really?" I said breathlessly, still trying to process the past minute and a half. "I must have missed that part."

Tyler smiled. "Well, pay attention and hopefully you won't miss it this time around." He leaned close to me, his lips nearly touching mine again. "I love you," he whispered.

Every one of my muscles seemed to be strangely locked in position. I stared at him, wondering if I had actually heard him correctly. "You—what? Why?" I asked before I could stop myself.

"Beats me," Tyler said with a smile. He began to trace the side of my face with his fingertip, and I closed my eyes, relishing that strange, unfamiliar, wonderful burning sensation as it seared across my skin. The heat made it even harder to breathe than before. I had never felt anything like it.

"You're twelve years younger than me," Tyler said with the air of someone trying to figure out a difficult calculus problem. "You're stubborn and bull-headed, outspoken and impulsive. You rarely think before you act, and you *never* think before you speak. You have no respect for authority, and you never surrender a point without first arguing yourself blue in the face. I don't think I've ever met a person who irritates me as much or as regularly as you do."

"Gee, I sound charming," I muttered, frowning up at him.

"But—" Tyler continued, laughing. "Despite all that, I can't seem to stop thinking about you. I admire every aspect of you. Your tenacity, your courage, your trust, your faith, your loyalty. I can't find a way to be happy without you near me. You seem to be somehow connected to me, and when you're gone, I feel like half of me goes with you." He looked earnestly at me for a few seconds and then smiled. "Do you believe me?"

I said nothing but stared doubtfully up at him. My heart was pounding away joyfully, already convinced of his truthfulness, but my mind couldn't seem to catch up. "I . . . ," I said, not really sure why I had opened my mouth in the first place. My mind was empty of possible responses.

"What can I say to convince you?" he asked me, trailing his fingers down my cheek yet again. I stared into his eyes and saw something in them change. A flash of something hard and intense that sent flames rushing down the entire length of my spine. He slowly bent down, giving me plenty of time to pull away. When I didn't, he took my face gently in one hand, his fingers sliding around my neck beneath my hair. His arm tightened around my waist, pulling me closer. I could feel the tension building toward a breaking point inside me as he softly pressed his lips once again to mine.

Something inside of me erupted. My nerves were a strange mixture of fire and ice as Tyler's lips moved with mine. My eyes closed involuntarily as he pulled me tight against him and my hands, which had been in taut fists at my sides, were suddenly gripping the front of his shirt with all their strength. His lips released mine and I gasped as they moved gently down my jawline to my throat. I clung desperately to him, my eyes closed, shivers running up and down my arms.

Suddenly he pulled back, physically setting me away from him to put space between us. "Convinced?" he asked breathlessly.

"I . . . um . . . yes," I breathed, wondering if my feet would ever actually touch the ground again. As the stars clouding my vision began to clear and I saw Tyler's face swimming above mine, I felt the truth settle in folds around my frantically beating heart. My middle exploded with fierce joy, and I could have sworn I heard strains of the "Hallelujah Chorus" echoing throughout the garden. Happiness that I had never known filled me with indescribable warmth.

Tyler, my hero and my fantasy, the one person I was sure I would love until the end of time, was, by some miracle, telling me that he loved me in return. And I believed him.

"Yes," I repeated and reached up to touch his face. It was rough and smooth in all the right places, and it felt as familiar to my fingers as my own, despite the fact that they had never before touched it. Tyler closed his eyes, and I heard him inhale slowly as my fingers traced his features. He smiled the angelic smile he saved just for me and pulled me again into his arms.

eight

I left my cabin the next morning with a smile on my face, but a part of me wondered if everything I remembered from the night before was actually leftover from my dreams. As I emerged onto the porch, I stopped suddenly.

Tyler was sitting on my front stoop, his elbows resting on his knees as he took in the morning. At my appearance, he rose and pulled me immediately into his arms.

"Finally," he said, breathing in my scent as he buried his face in my hair. "You take forever to get ready in the morning."

"How long have you been sitting there?" I laughed, thrilled that my fantasy showed every sign of being actual truth.

"Since about five," he said, almost sheepishly. "I couldn't sleep, so I decided to take a walk and I ended up here."

"I'm glad," I said happily. "I can't think of a better way to start the day."

Tyler grinned at me and hooked his hands around the back of my neck, pulling my face up to meet his as he pressed his lips to mine.

"Wow," I said a little breathlessly when we broke apart. "That is *so* much better than the way we usually say good morning."

Tyler laughed and threaded his fingers through mine as we began our walk toward the ranch house. "Agreed."

Life at Thorne Field seemed to take on an entirely new charm from that moment onward. I lived for glimpses of the man I loved. It was just like he had said that night in the garden—it was as though we were connected in some strange way. He sought my company daily, even coercing me into moving Addie's lessons into the library so he could watch us while he worked. I didn't mind. I longed to spend every moment with him.

Tyler was discreet in his manner toward me, not showing me any physical affection unless we were alone. All the same, I watched the other ranch employees closely to see if they suspected anything, but nothing appeared to have changed in the way they addressed toward me. I wondered if that meant that they had grown used to seeing me with Tyler long before he had ever proclaimed his feelings. It was true that he had often showed a marked preference for my company in the months since we had become friends, but as I had never wanted to get my hopes up, I had always told myself that his treatment was nothing noteworthy.

As time went on, it became harder and harder to hide our relationship. I often caught him staring at me during mealtimes, and sometimes when he passed me in the hall or on the landing, he would pull me quickly into his arms, his lips immediately finding mine. Charlotte nearly stumbled on us once, causing him to yank me quickly into the library to avoid detection. It was at that moment, huddled breathlessly against the bookshelves with Tyler attempting to stifle his laughter, that I knew I needed to put my foot down.

"This is getting too . . . I don't know, dangerous," I said, blushing slightly. "We're getting carried away."

"I'm in love with you," he said simply. "There's no such thing as carried away." He stopped, considering. "Well, at least not in a public thoroughfare. And that's the only place I ever accost you, you know."

I rolled my eyes at this and pushed him toward his office. "Go work or something," I said. "I think you need to cool off for a bit."

He grinned boyishly at me and left.

However, my words apparently stayed with him, because a week later, Tyler cornered me in Addie's playroom and dragged me out to the garden. The air was crisp and chilly, and I shivered as he pulled me toward the bench where he had made his unexpected declaration a month earlier. Afraid he was attempting to "accost" me in a less public place, and thoroughly ashamed of my hope that he would, I protested strongly that I needed to finish Addie's lessons.

"This will only take a minute," he said, laughing at my objections. He deposited me on the bench and stood silently for a moment, seeming to gather his thoughts. I took the time to appreciate the colors around me. The leaves had long since begun to change to red and gold and the mountains surrounding us were resplendent with fall colors.

"Kate, I love you so much," Tyler suddenly said, pulling my attention back to his face. "You know that, right?"

I nodded, smiling at him. "And I love you," I replied. He waved that away as if it were irrelevant, and I chuckled. He seemed nervous, and while I didn't know why, it was adorable.

"And you also know that I never jump into things without a passably good reason," he said, and I nodded again. He reached into his pocket and pulled out a small leather ring box.

"Um, what are you doing?" I breathed, my throat suddenly tight.

"What does it look like I'm doing?" he said, an eyebrow raised. Without another word, he sank to one knee in front of me. I gasped.

"I didn't think I would ever be ready or willing to do this again," he said. "I never thought I would fall in love with another woman. Especially not so much that the only thing I wanted was to have her beside me for the rest of my life. But I was wrong—because I do want that. I want it so much that the thought of not being with you is physically painful. But I don't just want you next to me for the rest of my life—I want you forever."

I had stopped breathing several sentences back and my lungs were screaming for air by this point. But I couldn't make them pull any oxygen in. I stood suspended, waiting for the words I knew were coming to actually clear his lips.

"Kate, will you marry me?"

I inhaled suddenly in one sharp breath. "Are you sure?" I asked.

"You realize what the reaction to this is going to be, right? The obscenely wealthy CEO engaged to the nanny of his charge?"

"Obscenely?" Tyler raised an eyebrow at me again.

"Whatever," I said. "Are you sure you're ready to deal with that?"

"Trust me, I've put up with worse," he said. "Do you really think that something as trivial as what other people think would influence whether or not I spend the rest of eternity with you? I love you, Kate!" He looked at me as though I were crazy. "Now, do you think you could answer my question? I've been down here for quite a while now and my middle-aged joints can only take so much."

I smiled at him, loving him so much I nearly burst with it. "Of course I'll marry you," I said, sweeping my fingers down his cheek. "Need you ask?"

Tyler chuckled at the ridiculous question as he opened the ring box. I gasped in delight. The ring was a perfect match for me. Simple and elegant, it was a round-cut solitaire in a slender white gold setting.

Tyler smiled at my reaction and slid the ring on my finger as he got to his feet. He took my face in his hands, kissing me with a fervency that made my heart pound and my breath come faster, a reaction I was speedily getting used to. We broke apart in surprise as a voice came from a few feet away.

"Well, this is not really what I expected to find when I came out here, but not all surprises can be pleasant ones." Jonathan leaned languidly against the nearest planter box, watching us with pained curiosity in his gaze.

"Jonathan!" I cried, my heart constricting. This was something I never would have wanted him to witness. Despite his claims that he would, he had never actually contacted me after he had returned to New York. I had hoped that his silence meant he had realized the folly of his choice, but judging from the look on his face . . .

No such luck. His expression was stiff and hard, and I could tell he was gritting his teeth. Though his arms were folded, I could see his hands clenched in fists.

"Jonathan," Tyler greeted uncertainly. I could see his concern as he looked at his friend. I knew he had long suspected that Jonathan had feelings for me, although he had never specifically mentioned it.

Jonathan nodded. "So, when did this happen?" He gestured almost lazily between Tyler and me, and I knew he was making a marked effort to be nonchalant.

"About nine months ago, actually," Tyler smiled. "But it's only been thirty seconds since she agreed to marry me."

Jonathan jerked involuntarily. "You're getting married?" he asked, his voice a little strained as he tried to gain his composure. "Wow . . . congratulations."

Tyler smiled kindly, understanding permeating from his face. "Thank you, Jonathan," he said.

Jonathan's gaze swung to me. "Congratulations, Kate," he said, his face showing his sincerity. "You look really happy."

"Thanks, Jonathan. I am," I assured him. I wished I could take away the pain he was trying so hard to hide, but I knew only time would do that.

Jonathan turned his gaze back to Tyler, and the movement seemed abrupt. "I have a few business-related items to talk through with you, Ty," he said firmly, apparently tired of the subject at hand. "Since I was going to California for a new client meeting anyway, I figured I'd just stop in here on the way and discuss them with you in person. I'll wait in the library." He smiled quickly but stiffly at both of us, then turned on his heel and walked away.

"Poor guy," Tyler said, watching him go. "I know how I would feel if our roles were reversed."

He looked down at me, and his face seemed to be almost glowing. He enfolded me tightly in his arms, his head resting on top of mine. We stood there in silence for several minutes before he pulled away.

"Are you sure?" he asked. "I mean, *really* sure?"

I stared at him. "Sure? About what?" I asked.

"That this is what you want?" He looked earnestly into my face, then raised his eyes to look after Jonathan. "After all, other than a slightly higher salary, I don't have any more to offer you than Jonathan, and he's closer to your age than I am. Much better looking too." He smiled at me.

I did not smile back. It bugged me that he would ruin this nearly perfect moment with doubts about my feelings for him. "Tyler, I can't believe you're saying this," I said, my voice ringing with irritation. "I don't care how much closer to my age Jonathan is or how much better looking you think he is; I am *not interested*." I reached up to cradle Tyler's face between my hands as I spoke, hoping he could feel my sincerity. "This isn't a business transaction. I didn't accept your proposal because you can bring more to the table than Jonathan. I love you. *You*," I emphasized.

Tyler smiled, the relief on his face surprisingly intense. He kissed me quickly and began leading me through the garden back toward the house.

"I have a question," I said hesitantly as we reached the veranda. I looked away, keeping my eyes from his face as he turned to search my expression.

"Yes?" he prompted curiously.

"I was just wondering . . ." I paused, afraid to go on, but knowing that a great deal of my happiness depended on the question I needed to ask.

"Well?" Tyler prompted again at my silence.

"I assume this marriage you speak of . . . that it will take place in the temple?" I asked, hoping this question didn't open a can of worms.

"Naturally," Tyler responded, a serene smile on his face.

I took a deep breath and met his gaze. "Well then, I was wondering if it would be possible for us to adopt Addie after we get married. Maybe be sealed to her?" My voice grew steadily quieter as I watched Tyler's expression change from frank curiosity to dismay. "Please?" I asked, cringing away from the troubled expression on his face.

"Kate, I'm not sure that's such a good idea . . . ," he began.

"Why?" I cried, a mixture of disappointment and irritation flooding through me. I understood his hesitancy, but I couldn't stop myself from being irrationally annoyed that he was feeling it. "You love Addie; I know you do! I've seen it on your face!"

"She's a great kid, but—" Tyler paused, looking frustrated at his inability to convey his feelings. His eyebrows were pulled down low over his eyes and his mouth was an aggravated grimace. "I'm just not sure I want an eternal reminder that the woman I pledged my life to had so little regard for me. Every time I look at Addie that's all I see."

"That's not fair," I protested. "None of that was Addie's fault and she deserves a home with people who love her!"

"And she'll have a home," Tyler reassured me, "But having her live with us and claiming her as my daughter are two different things. The fact is, she *isn't* my daughter, and I don't think I can pretend she is."

"Why?" I asked. "It all happened so long ago! And it really has so little to do with Addie herself. Yes, she's the result of Camille's mistake, but she didn't ask to be born in those circumstances, and we can't hold her responsible or punish her for that."

"Punish her? I don't want . . . ," Tyler began, looking perplexed, but stopped. "You're right," he finally said. "It's not about Addie herself. In actuality, she has nothing to do with it. It's all me. It's just . . . painful to remember." He seemed ashamed to have to admit it. I wanted to reassure him, but I felt certain my reassurances weren't wanted. I stood silently beside him, waiting for him to finish. "And when Addie is around," he finally continued. "Remembering is inevitable. I'm not sure constant remembrance is something I can face at this point."

"Are you really still so consumed by it? By her?" I whispered, and we both knew I was speaking of his deceased wife. "I suppose I should understand, but I have to admit that I don't. Why are you so resistant to letting Addie into your life completely? What Camille did still has that powerful of an effect on you? Even after all these years?"

I had tried thus far to ignore the possibility that Tyler still had lingering feelings for his late wife, but I couldn't any longer. If Tyler couldn't stand to call Addie a daughter simply because her mother had been unfaithful to him, it was a pretty clear indication that he had not yet come to terms with his feelings in that respect. I understood that having a constant reminder of Camille's betrayal was a painful option, but was it too painful to even consider? Especially when it meant so much to me and would mean the world to Addie as well? Or was I just being selfish?

"Kate, I'm not sure you understand the extent of the damage she did," Tyler said, almost apologetically. "My life was in absolute shambles when she left. It would be easy if I could hate her, but I just . . . can't. I'm not sure I ever will stop loving her. Can't you understand why I'd rather start my life with you with a clean slate? No strings attached?"

His eyes were pleading with me, and I looked away so as not to be swayed by them. Staring hard at the back of the ranch house, I attempted to come to terms with the fact that my future husband had just admitted to still being in love with his unfaithful late wife. It was harder than I thought, given the fact that she was dead and therefore not really competition for his affections any longer. So why did I feel like I was competing with Camille Thorne?

"Besides, don't you want to have your own children?" Tyler asked, changing tactics. "I know Addie means a lot to you, but she's not your child. She's not even my child. Do you love her enough to be bound to her forever, even when your own biological children come along?"

"Yes," I said firmly, yanking my mind back to the matter at hand. I turned to look at him to emphasize my meaning. "I love her every bit as much as if she were my own child. And I think you do too."

Tyler didn't deny it, but he didn't meet my gaze either. He sighed, a heavy, burdened sound, and looked forward at the house as we began to climb the stairs to the veranda. "It means that much to you?" he asked.

"More than I can say," I answered, grasping at his hand.

Tyler sighed again. "Then I'll make some inquiries with my attorney and see if it's possible."

I wished he could sound more excited at the prospect, but I was happy enough that I figured it could count for both of us for now. I threw my arms around him and pressed my lips to his cheek.

"Thank you, thank you, thank you!" I said, and my enthusiasm was rewarded with a small smile from him. "I know you don't agree now, but I promise you won't regret it," I enthused.

"I'm not so sure," he sighed. "There goes our chance to be newlyweds. We're starting out with a nine-year-old child."

"We would have had a nine-year-old child whether we agreed to adopt Addie or not," I reminded him.

"Well, we could have pawned her off on Charlotte for a few months out of the year and not felt as guilty about it," Tyler teased.

I smacked him and laughed as we climbed the steps and entered the ranch house, my heart lighter than ever.

Much to Tyler's dismay, I insisted on continuing with my usual schedule, despite the fact that I was the future Mrs. Thorne. I spent my day with Addie, teaching her as I always did. Tyler sat in the room with us while we went over her math and spelling, happy to just watch us together. Every time I happened to catch his eye, both of us would beam blissfully at each other until Addie would again steal my attention away. If anyone with more discernment than a nine-year-old had been in the room, they probably would have thrown up.

The next few days after the proposal were a whirlwind of activity. We had communicated our plans to the ranch residents at large and had been pleasantly surprised, for the most part, at the response. The ranch hands were effusive in their congratulations. But Charlotte was on the opposite end of the spectrum, and I was trying not to think too hard about the reasons behind her disapproval.

Although we didn't really want to wait to marry, I decided a little extra time to let everyone get used to the idea would be beneficial. I was most worried about Addie and Charlotte. We had received word that there were no legal barriers to adopting Addie, but Tyler and I decided to hold off on telling her about our decision to adopt her until she had first grown used to the idea of Tyler and I getting married.

Charlotte's case seemed entirely hopeless. I knew there was a specific reason for her displeasure, but she refused to talk about it. In the meantime, she had withdrawn into herself, barely speaking to me at all. Tyler tried to comfort me by telling me that Charlotte had always been the protective sort, but that just made me feel worse. Did she really believe I wasn't worthy of him? I supposed it wasn't that far-fetched, since I certainly didn't feel worthy of such a man, but it was painful all the same.

In the end, we decided to set the date for early November, a month and a half away. The wedding was constantly on my mind, and although I was nervous about the general response that our announcement would generate in the neighborhood, I chose to ignore that part.

Tyler and I had discussed the idea of moving our little family to New York permanently, but I was hesitant to leave Thorne Field, the place where I had been so happy for so long, even though I had always wanted to travel. I also wasn't entirely sure that New York was the best place to raise an impressionable child like Addie. Thankfully, Tyler agreed that with a few changes, he could operate his company just fine from Thorne Field, for a few months at least, and we had no reason to decide anything permanently yet.

However, with Tyler's already extended absence from New York, the wedding looming ever nearer, and the long honeymoon directly afterward, he decided that he should spend the last month before our marriage in the city. I was dreading being without him, even for that relatively short period of time, but I knew it was necessary.

Breakfast was a quiet affair the morning of Tyler's departure. Addie pouted in her chair and Tyler studied his plate, not bothering to transfer the food from it to his mouth. I just sat and watched him, continuing to recommit every feature to memory.

Finally, when it became evident that Tyler wasn't going to move until I prodded him, I rose from my chair and instructed Addie to run upstairs and brush her teeth, telling her to be back downstairs in five minutes to say good-bye to Tyler. She jumped at my authoritative tone and immediately left the table. I turned back to Tyler, noting how his hands were clasped tightly together and pressed to his mouth, his elbows on the table.

"You should probably do a last-minute check, just to make sure you have everything," I said softly.

He glanced up at me, his face somber.

"It's only a month," I said, more to convince myself than him. "It will fly by."

"Yeah," Tyler said in a dead sort of voice. "Maybe."

I took a deep breath. I suddenly felt close to tears, and I didn't want to cry in front of him. "Come on," I said, taking his hand. "You'll miss your flight if you wait much longer."

"It's my plane," he said incredulously. "How can it leave without me?"

I smiled weakly and bit my lip, blinking quickly. Tyler's fingers squeezed mine reassuringly, and I was sure he could tell I was on the verge of tears.

He slowly rose to his feet and walked past me, out to the entryway where his bags were waiting for him. He methodically checked through his files, ticking them off as he found them.

As he zipped up the last bag, Addie raced down the stairs and launched herself at him. She locked her arms around his trim waist and buried her face in his shirt. "I don't want you to go!" she cried pitifully. "Kate doesn't want you to go either, do you, Kate?" She turned around, her look pleading with me to stop him from leaving.

"No, I don't," I answered honestly. "But he'll be back before we know it, Addie." My attempt to be brave was pathetic, but I kept it up for Addie's sake.

I raised my eyes to Tyler's face, taking a deep breath to steady myself. I was surprised to see that Tyler's eyes looked moist. I had never seen him come anywhere close to tears before. I looked away quickly, afraid that I would lose it completely.

Tyler bent down to kiss the top of Addie's head. "Be good, kid," he croaked. He pried her arms from around him and wiped a tear from her cheek.

She backed up and nodded, sniffling.

He then walked forward and gently took me in his arms. His eyes still seemed a bit watery as he took my face in his hands and kissed me so softly I barely felt it, but still my heart beat furiously.

"I'll call every day," he promised as he pulled away. "And if I don't, then you call me. If you need *anything*, call my cell phone, day or night. If I'm sleeping, I'll wake up. If I'm in a meeting, I'll leave it. Understand?"

I smiled and nodded. "I love you," I said quietly.

"I know," Tyler said, returning my smile. "And I love you."

As I backed up to allow him access to the bags on the floor behind me, I noticed Charlotte standing uncertainly in the doorway of the dining room. She had been a mother figure to Tyler since the death of his own mother when he was ten, and I knew that although she didn't approve of his marriage to me, she loved him dearly. I suddenly felt guilty for putting a barrier between them. I opened my mouth to alert Tyler to her presence, but he didn't need my warning. He looked up at her and nodded, the rough manner he had adopted toward her in the past few weeks completely gone.

"Charlotte," he acknowledged, and his eyes crinkled slightly in a tiny smile. I detected the smallest trace of exasperation, but more noticeable was the warmth and affection.

Charlotte smiled back and gave a small wave.

Turning back to me, he kissed me hard once more and then, picking up his luggage, turned and left the house without looking back.

nine

That first week of Tyler's absence seemed to take about four years to pass. However, it wasn't without its benefits. When Charlotte saw how miserable I was without him, she warmed up considerably until things were almost back to normal. It wasn't until nearly two weeks later, however, that she finally provided me with any kind of explanation for her initial reaction to our engagement.

We were sitting in comfortable silence in the dining room one evening, Addie having already left the table. It finally occurred to me that Charlotte seemed a little fretful. Her hands were clenched on her napkin and her eyes kept flitting from my face to her plate and back.

"What is it, Charlotte?" I asked her, eyebrows raised. "You have something to say, but you're trying to talk yourself out of saying it."

She released the tortured napkin and clasped her hands together as she considered. Turning to face me full-on, the words rushed out of her mouth at top speed. "I realize I never really explained my behavior after learning of your engagement . . . ," she trailed off, looking uncomfortable.

I smiled. "It's all right, Charlotte," I assured her. "It doesn't matter now."

"Yes, dear, it does," she insisted. "I owe you an explanation." She took a deep breath. "You may have noticed that I wasn't particularly keen on the idea of Tyler marrying Amanda either. The truth is, I felt that Tyler wasn't ready for another marriage. He never fully got over Camille, you know. Even to this day, I don't believe he has fully recovered from losing her . . . and I'm not just talking about her death, although that definitely threw him into the twilight zone for a while." She shook her head sadly. "I've never seen a man more in love than Tyler was with Camille. And she put on an astounding show as well. I would have sworn that she was as devoted to him as he was to her. Just goes to show that you can't always tell . . . ," she said.

"But, anyway," she continued after a moment. "I felt he was being unfair to you and to himself to marry you without having sorted out his feelings for Camille. But"—she looked at me pointedly—"that's not to say that I don't think he's in love with you. Having seen Tyler in love before, I know exactly what it looks like. And I have no doubt that he loves you very much." She stared at me earnestly for a few moments, as though afraid I didn't believe her.

"Thank you, Charlotte," I said with a smile, but inside I was suddenly cold. Charlotte didn't believe that Tyler was over Camille either? I'd managed to push any troubling thoughts regarding Tyler's first wife out of my head for weeks now, but hearing Charlotte voice them aloud brought them all flooding back. I hoped it was something that Tyler and I would be able to work through, but I was worried, nevertheless. Would he ever be free of her?

The day before Tyler's return, I began packing my belongings. Our wedding was set for two days after his arrival, and I knew I wouldn't want to spend my time on such tasks when he was finally home. The boxes sat by the door of the cabin, ready for their transfer to the ranch house. The idea that I would soon be living there with my husband still seemed surreal to me.

I spent the morning of Tyler's return pacing from room to room. I couldn't seem to stand still, and the fact that the clocks all seemed to have slowed down was a point of endless frustration. Charlotte laughed every time my impatient feet carried me into the same room that she was occupying.

"I think someone's a little restless," she said to Addie.

"What's restless?" Addie asked in confusion, and Charlotte chuckled.

"That," she said emphatically, pointing at me as I paced almost frantically around the dining room. "*That's* restless."

"Ugh, I *can't* stand it!" I said suddenly. "Why does time always slow down when you need it to speed up?"

"Because the good Lord never misses an opportunity to teach us patience," Charlotte said, her smile growing even wider.

"I'm patient," I said a little sulkily.

Charlotte laughed again and went back to wiping down the dining room table. Just then, I heard the front door open. My heart went into overdrive as I sprinted out of the room and into the entrance hall.

"Whoa!" said Mitch, one of the ranch hands, seeing my hasty approach. "Where's the fire, Kate?"

I slid to a halt. "Sorry," I said, practically choking on my disappointment.

Mitch smiled kindly. "Don't worry. I have a feeling he'll be here any minute."

"Yeah," I said weakly, turning back toward the dining room. The front door opened again. I whirled around in time to see all six feet, five inches of my fiancé walk through the doorway. I squealed like a teenager and ran at him. He barely had time to drop his suitcase before I was in his arms, my lips on his. He kissed me fiercely, his hands cradling my face and knotting in my hair. When we finally broke apart, he beamed at me.

"I think someone's glad to see me," he said, a little breathlessly.

"You have no idea," I said, my voice breaking.

Tyler smiled. "Oh, I think I do," he said, and kissed me again.

That night, I beamed around the dinner table, basking in the presence of those I loved most. Everything was set for our small wedding ceremony, less than two days away. We had just received the papers from Tyler's attorney that would legally make Addie our daughter. And as the cherry on top of our perfect life, Charlotte finally seemed to have decided that maybe our marriage actually was a good idea.

Could life possibly be any sweeter? I thought.

"You know, you really don't have that much stuff," Tyler said as he hefted the last box into the back of the jeep the next morning.

"You say that like it's a *bad* thing," I said, slamming the door shut. My belongings were about to make the journey to their final resting place, the home I would make with Tyler and Addie. The very thought made me feel as though my blood were suddenly carbonated.

"Not at all. I'm exceptionally grateful that you're not a pack rat," said Tyler, kissing the top of my head as he passed. "I'm just astounded that we were able to fit the entire contents of your cabin in the back of this jeep."

"I've always been a fan of packing light," I said, smiling. We climbed into the jeep and drove through the village of staff cabins, past the garden, and around to the front of the ranch house. As we pulled up in front of the porch, I noticed a silver Mercedes parked in front of the garage.

"Did you buy another car and forget to tell me about it?" I asked, pointing to the luxury vehicle. "I've never seen that one before."

"Nope, not mine," Tyler said, squinting at the license plate. "It has Colorado plates."

"No one I know, then," I said. "What about you?"

Tyler smiled at me. "It could be any one of about three thousand people."

I snorted as I climbed out of the jeep. "You can't possibly know that many people from Colorado."

"Take a look at my address book and then say that again."

I laughed as I walked toward the back of the jeep to grab a box.

"I'm starved. Let's grab some lunch before unloading," Tyler said, snagging my hand as I reached for the latch on the back door of the jeep.

We entered the house and headed for the kitchen, arguing good-naturedly about Tyler's tendency toward exaggeration.

"Oh, there you are!" Charlotte said when we entered. "I just sent Addie out to look for you. Lunch is ready."

"I'll grab her," I said. "Which way did she go?"

"Toward the garden, it looked like," Charlotte answered. As I left the kitchen, I heard Tyler start to question her about the silver Mercedes in the driveway.

I hurried out the door onto the veranda, looking around for the small nine-year-old with dark, corkscrew curls. I walked swiftly down all the main paths in the garden, but I couldn't find her. Finally, as I was about to turn and head back to the house to see if she'd returned, I heard voices off to the left. Changing direction, I rounded the corner in the foliage and came upon my charge. She was not alone.

She sat on a concrete bench in her bright pink parka, and beside her was a petite brunette with large, expressive brown eyes and stunning features. I had never seen her before.

"Addie?" I said tentatively. The small girl turned to face me, uncertainty written on her pixie-like face. She moved quickly to my side and put her small hand in mine.

The woman rose to her feet, and I found she was only an inch or so taller than me. She smiled genuinely, and I blinked, marveling at the brilliancy and symmetry of her features. I thought I had seen physical perfection when Amanda Ives had come to Thorne Field, but even her flashy good looks couldn't compare. This woman was beauty personified.

"Hello. You must be Kate," the woman said in a smooth, cultured voice. "Addie was just telling me about you."

"Yes," I said, hesitantly. "And I assume you're the mysterious owner of the silver Mercedes?"

The woman smiled again, somewhat apologetically. "Guilty. I'm sorry, I should have come to the door first, but I saw Addie running into the garden, and I thought I'd stop and say hello to her before continuing into the house."

"Do you know Addie?" I asked suspiciously, tightening my grip on the little girl's hand.

"Not yet," the woman replied, and I wasn't sure I liked the tone in her voice. It was possessive and confident. Who was this person, and why did she make me so uneasy?

"Who are you?" I asked, not bothering with politeness.

I heard the disbelieving gasp from behind me before she could answer. I turned to see Tyler frozen in the middle of the garden path, his face a mask of horrified surprise.

"Camille," he breathed.

I stood there, stunned into silence, staring at my fiancé's dead wife, who, despite widespread belief, appeared to be very much alive. I could literally feel the shock emanating in waves from Tyler, and it mirrored my own astonishment exactly. How could this woman be Camille? How was that possible?

"But they—they told me you were dead." Tyler looked as though he had hit a cinder block wall at ninety miles an hour.

"I know," Camille said softly, her eyes fixed on his face. "I'm sorry. I know how much trouble it must have caused you to have to take on the responsibility of Addie. But I'm here now. I've been to hell and back, but I'm here." Her look was intense as she stared at the man I loved. "Tyler . . ." She paused as if gathering the courage to say something very important but very difficult. "I'm so sorry. For so many things. I've missed you so much."

Nobody could doubt the sincerity of the words. Everything about the woman's expression called out for Tyler. She took a few hesitant steps forward as if something were pulling her toward him, but she seemed to lose her nerve halfway there. Instead, she reached out and pulled Addie to her, placing her hands familiarly on her shoulders, as if she had known her all her life. I wanted to scream at Camille to let go of my daughter, but I knew how ridiculous it would sound. Addie was *her* daughter. The thought forced all the oxygen from my lungs. How would this affect Addie? How had this even happened?

Camille stroked Addie's cheek lovingly, her expression mesmerized as she gazed at the daughter she hadn't seen in nearly ten years.

"She's so beautiful, Tyler," she said, looking up at him. "You've done such a wonderful job raising her. I told you that you would be a great dad." She smiled, her eyes becoming distant as though she were focusing on something miles away. "Do you remember? Our fifth anniversary, when I . . . ," she trailed off and her eyes snapped back into focus. She bit her lip, and I knew she regretted bringing up the past.

Tyler said nothing, just stared fixedly at Camille, his gaze showing only stunned disbelief. He took a hesitant step toward her. His eyes fixed immovably on her face. He seemed to be studying her, looking for evidence that she might not be who she claimed to be. But I knew he wouldn't find it. I couldn't explain how, but somehow I knew Camille Thorne stood in our midst. And Tyler knew it too.

Camille allowed him to study her, but she appeared to be suffering some kind of internal struggle. She was biting her lip and blinking tears from her eyes. Finally, as though she couldn't stand it another minute, she rushed forward and threw her arms around his neck. She kissed him passionately, her hands pressed into his hair. It was a kiss of deep familiarity, one that looked comfortable and practiced. I felt compelled to look away as if I were intruding on an intensely personal moment.

At the sight of the fiery embrace, I was suddenly reminded that Camille and Tyler had been together for many years. She knew him better than I, had shared things with him that I never had, or would, now that she was back. The thought crashed into me like a tidal wave. I nearly sank to my knees in the despair that arrived in its wake.

No, no, no! my heart screamed at me. *I won't give him up! I won't!*

But I had no choice. I watched in agony as Tyler accepted his wife's kiss with no resistance. His arms went around her and I watched his eyes close. With that encouragement, Camille deepened the kiss considerably.

Through the haze of shock and dismay, it occurred to me to wonder what on earth Tyler was doing. I could understand expressions of astonishment and confusion, but shouldn't it stop there? Where was this wholehearted acceptance coming from? Was I finally seeing all of Tyler's true feelings laid out on the table? I had always suspected that he was still in love with Camille, but since she had been thought dead, the idea hadn't seemed as threatening before. But the threat was frighteningly real now. More than real. As I watched the passionate embrace, I realized that Tyler's feelings for Camille were more than a threat—they represented the death of every single one of my hopes. They would destroy it all. In the face of those feelings, I ceased to exist.

To my further dismay, I noticed tears leaking from Camille's eyes as she kissed him. In all my speculations of Tyler's first marriage, I had imagined Camille a heartless witch, a demon bent only on destroying him. But this was no demon. This was a woman who seemed broken, desperate for the man she had loved and lost through her own poor choices. Unable to watch any more of the passionate reunion, I turned and ran toward the ranch house.

As I sprinted through the back door, trying desperately to escape the nightmare behind me, I nearly collided with Charlotte, who was heading toward the office with a duster in her hand.

"Goodness, Kate!" she exclaimed, grasping my shoulders to keep her balance. Then she saw my face. "Merciful heavens, what's the matter?"

I couldn't speak. I just stood there, looking at her. I was strangely numb, as if I had been shot full of novocaine. It felt as though my heart had decided that it had had enough and had powered off. I hoped it never powered on again, because I didn't think I'd survive it.

"Kate!" Charlotte said, shaking me slightly. "What is it? Tell me! Where is Addie? Tyler? Kate, talk to me!"

Suddenly, the french doors behind us opened, and in walked Tyler with Camille's hand comfortably in his. Her face still held traces of tears, but her expression was radiantly happy. Tyler's air was still slightly bewildered, but he finally seemed to have a sense of what was going on around him. Addie was hanging on tightly to Camille's other hand. She seemed to have at last fully accepted that this beautiful woman was her mother and was looking at her worshipfully. I tore my eyes away from the scene, knowing my tentative hold on sanity couldn't take it.

Charlotte's mouth fell open. "Camille!" she gasped. "But it—it can't be! You're dead!"

Camille laughed, a light, musical sound, and shook her head. "No, Charlotte, I'm not. It's so good to see you again!"

She withdrew her hands from the grasp of husband and daughter and drew Charlotte into a hug. "You look marvelous!" She pulled away and moved familiarly down the hallway past the library and office and toward the entrance hall, the rest of us following in her wake. "This place hasn't changed a bit. Oh, the memories I have of this house . . ."

I watched with no expression as she took in the scene she knew so well. I finally turned to look at Tyler, expecting to see him staring at Camille in wonder as everyone else was. Instead I found him staring at me, his face holding a beseeching look, as if he was hoping I could somehow explain to him how this could have happened. I looked back at him with the same expressionless face; I wasn't sure I'd be able to show any kind of emotion ever again.

Camille again came to his side and put an arm around his waist, drawing Addie to them with her other arm.

"This almost seems too good to be true." She sighed, her brilliant smile seeming to light the very air around her. "To have my family back with me . . ." Her voice resonated with sincere happiness and gratitude. "I have so much to tell you." Her eyes fixed on Tyler, as if her words were meant only for him. "And so much to explain."

She didn't seem to notice that she'd rendered everyone in the room speechless. Finally, her wide brown eyes, so much like her daughter's, fell upon me. She walked forward and took both of my hands in hers. I didn't have the energy to resist.

"Kate," she said sincerely, her eyes staring steadfastly into mine. "Thank you for all you've done for my family, especially Addie. From what she's told me, it's obvious she thinks the world of you." She squeezed my hands as if to emphasize her words. "I can't tell you how much I appreciate you doing what I didn't have the courage to do. I owe you a great deal."

I felt her fingers brush the engagement ring on my left hand, and her eyes flicked downward in curiosity. When they again settled upon my face, a shadow of realization and panic danced behind them. She studied my face for a moment, then glanced in Tyler's direction. The look of pleading on his face as he looked at me was enough to allow her to connect the dots. But she didn't react. The panic disappeared, and her face again broke into a dazzling smile.

I searched desperately for some sign of deceit in that brilliance. I'm ashamed to say, I hoped I would find it. But I didn't. She appeared as genuine and grateful as she sounded.

It was then, looking into those sincere and determined eyes that I knew that I was leaving. I was going to walk away. I had to. I would leave behind everything familiar and beloved, because suddenly, I was second in line. My eyes flitted to Addie's face, and then to Tyler's. I had an inferior claim on these hearts. Someone held a lien superior to mine, and she was asserting it. The pressure on my hands as she held them was enough to convince me of that. It was a nonverbal reminder, and I fully understood it.

Besides, now, having seen firsthand Tyler's reaction to Camille's return, I finally understood the real reason for his hesitancy to ever fully accept Addie into his life. I didn't think Tyler himself even realized it. He didn't resent the little girl because she was the living proof of Camille's infidelity. It was because she was the cause of Camille's desertion—the cause of her death. Addie's conception had been the catalyst, resulting in the explosion that had left Tyler alone, devastated, emotionally bloodied. Tyler Thorne could deal with infidelity. Infidelity could be overcome. Abandonment? Death? Not so much. But the deserter had returned. The dead had been resurrected. All was right with the world.

I felt as though everything inside me was wilting and shriveling. Every spark of happiness was obliterated, and there was only emptiness. I was forever hollow.

"Mommy?" said Addie, still staring at Camille. The word shocked me from my thoughts. She seemed to be trying the term, to see how it sounded.

I shut my eyes, the agony threatening to grow so great it would override the numbness currently reigning in my midsection. *That should have been me*, I thought, and the echo reverberated throughout the empty shell I had just become. But the voice seemed to be somewhat detached from the rest of me, as if all the pieces of me were separating into different compartments where they wouldn't have to communicate with each other. My heart went in one drawer, my consciousness in another. Maybe if I locked them away tight enough, I'd never have to feel them or hear from them again. It would be so much easier just to be this vacant human sheath from now on.

"Yes, honey?" Camille said, turning from me to face her daughter.

"Do you wanna see my room?" Addie asked shyly.

"I'd love to, sweetheart," she said, tenderly taking the nine-year-old's hand and allowing Addie to lead her up the stairs. I heard their voices fade into the upstairs hallways, their giggles combining in perfect harmony.

I brought my eyes around to meet Tyler's. They were still fixed on my face.

"Kate," he began.

I shook my head silently and moved toward the hall table where I spotted my purse and keys. It was time to go. The longer I stayed, the more painful it would be. I had to leave before my brain had the chance to register fully what I was about to give up.

"Kate, wait. Please." Tyler's voice held a note of desperate pleading that made me stop. I turned to face him, my expression every bit as dead as the hope inside me.

"Just give me a second to work this out," he said, raking his hands through his hair in agitation. "Let me figure out how to handle this."

"Don't," I said, my voice flat and emotionless. "There's nothing to say. Nothing you can do. You're married to her, Tyler. She's here; she loves you. And don't try to tell me that you don't love her. I think I've always known that you did. I shouldn't have ignored it."

"I . . . I don't know," he said. He looked almost panicked, and he grabbed for my hand. "But I do know that I love you. Isn't that enough to make you stay? Don't you love me, Kate? Has everything you ever felt for me really disappeared in less than ten minutes?"

"I do love you," I said woodenly. "I always will. But you'll never hear it from me again." I tried to pull my hand from his, needing to get away from him.

Tyler's grasp tightened to the point of pain. "Wait! Don't go. We'll figure something out. We—"

"Tyler." I heard Camille's voice call from upstairs. "Come up here, you're missing this!" Laughter mingled with her words, and in them I could hear the happiness that I had a faint memory of once feeling. It seemed long ago, a time-weakened echo. Tyler's eyes followed the sound, his expression fixed on the upstairs hallway. And in that moment, I saw the longing in his face. That was where he wanted to be. The center of his universe had shifted—it was pulling him toward a past dream and away from me. I pulled my hand firmly from his grasp. His eyes shot to mine again, and his expression was once again pleading.

"Promise me," Tyler said, gripping my hand tightly again. "You won't go anywhere until we have a chance to sit down and discuss this. We'll talk later, okay?"

"Later," I repeated, refusing to make a promise I knew I would break.

He pulled me toward him as if to kiss me, then seemed to remember that he was no longer at liberty to do so. He froze within centimeters of my face, and a familiar flame began a slow burn where his fingers dug into my shoulders. Knowing what would happen if I allowed that flame to fill the echoing space in my chest, I quickly pulled away. He clenched his jaw at the abrupt action, then turned to ascend the stairs.

I watched him disappear down an upstairs hallway, memorizing every movement, knowing it was the last glimpse I would have of him. It would have to last me forever.

Finally turning away, I numbly met Charlotte's gaze. Her eyes rested on me, her expression knowing. She walked slowly to my side and kissed me warmly on the cheek.

"Take care of yourself, dear," she choked. "Be happy."

I managed a miserable smile at the ridiculousness of such a mandate. Happiness was undoubtedly beyond the realm of possibility for me. But I reached out to squeeze her hand anyway, before taking my purse from the hall table. Then, with one deep, agonizing breath, I pulled open the door and left forever the house that had been my only true home, containing every last thing that I loved.

ten

"Room available for rent. Inquire inside," the sign said straightforwardly.

I immediately pulled to the side of the road and worked up the courage to approach the white clapboard house.

It had been a difficult few weeks for me. After leaving Thorne Field, I drove aimlessly for days. I somehow found myself in Boston, not really remembering how I got there. My mind was a mass of dark despair, but thankfully, my survival instincts remained sharp. Realizing the importance to my peace of mind, as well as to the happiness of those I loved most, I sought to make it impossible for Tyler to ever find me. I buried myself as thoroughly as I knew how. Now, on the opposite side of the country, armed with new bank accounts, credit cards, and employment, all obtained using my middle name, Marie, I had done all I could to keep Tyler from locating me. Because I knew he would try.

Shaking myself back into the present, I made my way up the path toward the front door of the lovely home. It really was ideal, being only two hundred yards from the school at which I was to teach. Ringing the old-fashioned doorbell, I waited eagerly for the door to open. When it did, a tall, slender young woman with hair the color of caramel stood before me. She looked to be in her mid to late twenties, and her large, green eyes were friendly.

"Hi! Can I help you?" she said kindly, smiling at me.

"Yes," I said hesitantly. "I understand you're renting a room?"

"Yes, we are," she said, her smile deepening. "Are you looking for a place?"

"I am. I'm beginning work at Middleton Academy on Monday and I'd like to stay somewhere nearby."

"You teach?" the girl cried in unwarranted delight.

"Yes . . . ," I said, taken aback by her enthusiasm.

"We do too! My sister and I," she quickly explained. She grabbed my arm and pulled me inside, turning to yell into the recesses of the home. "Mariah! Come here!"

"What? What is it?" I heard as a shorter, plumper figure emerged from a door down the hall. Her hair was a completely different color and texture than her sister's, a beautiful, dark chestnut mass of curls. Her eyes were identical, however—large and green. Both girls were somewhat plain, but the open friendliness on their faces made them appealing at the same time.

"This is . . ." The tall, thin girl turned to look at me with expectation.

"Marie," I provided helpfully. "Marie Evans."

"Yes, Marie," said the girl, as if she had known all along. "She's going to be teaching at MA starting Monday! She's looking for a place to stay!"

"Calm down, Danielle. You're scaring her," said Mariah, laughing at the look of open surprise on my face.

Danielle turned to me and grinned. "We teach at MA—"

"Middleton Academy," Mariah interrupted, explaining the acronym needlessly.

"Yes, that," said Danielle. "We teach there too! I teach fourth grade and Mariah teaches fifth. What grade are you teaching?"

"Second," I provided. "Apparently there's a teacher going on maternity leave—"

"Jane," interrupted Danielle. "She's an ornery thing. I'm sure the kids will be glad to get rid of her—"

"It's probably due to the fact that she's as big as a house, though," added Mariah. "Watching her suffer through her pregnancy has made me realize the virtues of birth control."

"Well, if I had a husband who was anything like Jane's, it would be more a matter of complete abstinence," said Danielle.

"Danielle!" Mariah exclaimed, putting her hands to her face. She looked apologetically at me. "I promise, we're actually very nice people."

"Oh, come on, Mariah. Don't pretend you don't agree with me. Jane's husband is a troll," Danielle said, turning to me.

I snorted with laughter. I decided immediately that I liked these two.

"Well, anyway," Mariah said. "Why don't we show you the room?"

She led me up the steep staircase to the second floor and into a bright, airy room painted a light yellow. The bed was old-fashioned and hung with a white linen canopy. An old nightstand stood next to it, painted white, with chunks of wood gouged out of the sides and corners. A desk, also white, stood in the corner, holding an old-fashioned desk lamp.

"It's not much," said Mariah, following me into the room. "The furniture is ancient, but it has a certain charm, don't you think?"

"It's wonderful," I agreed fervently.

The entire house had an aged feel, but it was the kind of age reserved for classic romance novels. The hardwood floors creaked and groaned with every step and the wood furnishings looked stressed and old, but it only added to the historical ambiance of the place.

"How long have you girls lived here?" I asked.

"Oh, forever," claimed Danielle with a bit of pride tingeing her voice. "This house has been in our family for more than a century. Our great-grandmother, grandmother, and mother were all raised in it."

"When our mother died, she left the house to us," Mariah said.

"What about your father?" I asked.

"Our dad died when we were tiny," said Danielle. "I was only two, and Mariah three. We don't remember him at all."

"Mom married again when we were in high school, but she and our stepfather were killed in an accident soon after Danielle graduated," Mariah continued.

"I'm so sorry," I sympathized. "My parents are gone too. They died when I was eight." Then, realizing that I was revealing more about myself than I wanted to, I changed the subject. "So, do you think you could stand having me live with you?" I asked.

"Well, I'm sure it will be a very great trial . . . ," began Danielle.

"But we'll muddle through," finished Mariah.

I laughed. It felt wonderful.

The more I got to know Danielle and Mariah Rivers over the following days, the more I was struck by how different they were, and the more I liked them for it. Mariah was the more proper and restrained of the two, often reigning in Danielle's enthusiasm or sarcasm with a reprimand. Danielle was sweet and good, a hopeless romantic. She was also in possession of a sharp-witted tongue and often made comments that caused her sister great embarrassment, and me great amusement.

I moved into River House, as Mariah and Danielle referred to it, the morning after I met the sisters, and I was completely unpacked and situated before noon. Having few earthly possessions really was more of a blessing than a curse, I realized. The girls were busy at MA during the day, so I took the chance to explore the area a little.

Milton, the small town outside of Boston that I had chosen to be my new home, was a surprisingly historic place. In my wanderings, I found that the area had actually been settled in 1640 as part of Dorchester, Massachusetts, and Milton itself was established as an independent town in 1662. There were countless historical sites and nineteenth century homes nearby, and I was excited for the opportunity to explore them.

I returned to River House around the time that school got out and met the sisters as they walked home, both bundled heavily against the late November chill. We spoke merrily of our daily adventures, and for a moment, I could almost forget that I was actually Kate Evans, the runaway.

In the company of Danielle and Mariah, it was much easier to pretend that I had never had another life. I had informed them that I was originally from Utah but had grown up in California. When they began to probe for further details, I told them kindly that my past was behind me and I had no intention of dwelling in it. They didn't press me, immediately understanding that I was uncomfortable with personal questions.

I awoke early the Sunday before I was to start at MA. After locating the nearest LDS chapel via the Internet, I dressed quickly for church and went downstairs to breakfast. I was eager for the opportunity to encounter something familiar, even though I was nearly a continent away from home.

"You look nice," said Danielle, yawning from the table. "Where are you headed?"

"Church," I said simply, grabbing a piece of bread and shoving it in the toaster.

"Church?" asked Danielle blankly as if she'd never heard the word. "What church?"

"The Church of Jesus Christ of Latter-day Saints," I said smoothly, pouring orange juice into a glass.

"Come again?"

"The Mormon church," I sighed, knowing the reaction I was about to get.

"You're a Mormon?" Danielle was shocked. "Don't they eat their babies and have a million wives and all that?"

I turned to stare at her. "Danielle, do you consider me a reasonably intelligent human being?" I asked her.

She looked at me strangely and nodded.

"Do you honestly believe that I would belong to a church that ate babies and allowed men to have a million wives?"

"I guess not." She shrugged. "But that's what I've heard about the Mormons."

"Well, you're welcome to come with me and find out for yourself," I invited, already knowing what she would say.

"Thanks, but no thanks," she said, standing. "I have better things to do than investigate some crazy Utah religion." She winked at me to let me know she was joking and left the kitchen.

The nearest LDS chapel was in Boston, so I had roughly a fifteen-minute drive to get there. As I drove, I found myself contemplating the turn my life had taken. There was no doubt in my mind that my prayers were being answered in merciful ways, and I was truly grateful. But I couldn't help but feel a little cheated. The happiness I had expected to be experiencing at this point in my life had been snatched away from me in such a cruel manner, I wondered if maybe I was doing something wrong. Recognizing the dangerous turn of my thoughts, I inserted a Mormon Tabernacle Choir CD into the slot in the console and turned it up way too loud.

That night as Mariah, Danielle, and I sat in the living room around the fireplace, Mariah asked about my engagement ring. For some reason I couldn't identify, I had never taken it off. I supposed it was because doing so would be a little too final. As if everything that had made my life worth living one short month ago no longer existed. Pointing at the diamond sparkling on my left ring finger, Mariah inquired as to whether or not I was married. I quietly informed her that I was not and never had been, not offering any other explanation.

"Well, we'll have to introduce you to our brother, then," said Danielle with a giggle.

"He's quite a catch," agreed Mariah.

"You never mentioned a brother," I said in surprise.

"You never asked," Danielle pointed out simply. "He might be a little old for you . . . he's a few years older than Mariah."

"He turned thirty-one last April," Mariah informed me. "He's pretty cute, Marie. Successful too."

"By that she means filthy rich," Danielle said enthusiastically. "I guarantee you'd like him. We can totally hook you up."

"Oh, really?" I said, attempting to show enough interest to at least be polite. "That's nice of you, but I'm not really into the whole blind dating thing," I said softly. "But thanks, anyway."

"If you saw him you might change your mind," Danielle teased.

"Almost every woman we've ever introduced him to has fallen head over heels for him. Unfortunately he's kind of hard to please when it comes to women."

"Then I'm sure I'd be the last thing he'd want," I assured them. "Better try out your matchmaking skills on someone more worthwhile."

I rose to my feet to signal an end to the conversation. "Well, school comes early tomorrow and I want to be at the top of my game," I said. "I'll see you guys in the morning, okay? 'Night."

"Good night, Marie," said Mariah, smiling almost apologetically at me. I had a feeling she regretted ever bringing up the subject of romantic attachments.

"Sleep tight!" said Danielle, seemingly oblivious to the subtle tension in the room.

That night as I lay in bed, I had to work harder than ever to keep my thoughts away from Thorne Field Ranch. Every time I closed my eyes, I felt like my mind was frantically scrambling over the miles as fast as it could go, attempting to drag me back to my mountain home before I could stop it. But I was getting pretty good at controlling my thoughts. Expending some effort, I managed to focus on the coming day at school. I firmly turned my reflections to my lesson plans, eventually falling into a restless sleep.

My first day at MA dawned sunny and cheerful, despite the freezing temperatures. As soon as my eyes opened, I was aware of the nervous clenching in my middle, a testament to my pathetic amount of experience in the classroom. All my old insecurities began to resurface.

Who am I kidding? I thought miserably as I dressed for the day in black slacks and a red sweater. *I'm no teacher. I've only ever really taught one pupil at a time! I must have been out of my mind to have applied for this job.*

Unfortunately, I'd come to my senses a little too late.

Mariah and Danielle tried to comfort me and get me to eat some breakfast, but the very thought of food made the clenching in my stomach turn to churning.

As we walked toward the school in the freezing cold, I prayed silently for comfort and assistance, feeling more like I was going to face a firing squad than a room full of eight-year-olds.

"It's okay, Marie," said Mariah soothingly. "It's really not that bad."

"Yeah, they really are sweet kids," added Danielle. "You get them when they're still cute. By the time they come to us, they're little monsters."

I felt like I was hyperventilating, the steam issuing from my mouth coming at erratic intervals.

"Man alive, relax, will you?" said Danielle, rubbing my arm vigorously. "They won't eat you, you know."

"I know, I know," I panted. "I've just never done this before."

"You've never taught before?" asked Mariah, her eyebrows raised. "Then you must have *really* made an impression on Jerry. He never hires first-time teachers."

I thought of Jerry Haskins, the principal. When I'd met him, he'd seemed almost eager to hire someone with inferior experience. He must have been desperate. This thought did not make me feel any better.

"Oh, I've taught, just not in a classroom setting," I explained. "At least not since my student teaching days. And even then, it was never so many at once. I have no idea how to do this!"

"Aw, it's just like teaching one," said Danielle, waving my concerns away with her hand. "Only . . . with more than that."

"How profound," said Mariah dryly, rolling her eyes at her sister. "It's really not that hard, Marie. You'll get the hang of it! And the kids will love you."

"Especially after having someone like Jane for a teacher," Danielle added, winking at me.

By this time, we were at my classroom door. Danielle leaned over and gave me a quick squeeze.

"Good luck. You'll do great!" she sang and danced down the hall toward her classroom.

Mariah hung back, looking at me with concern. "Hey, it'll be fine," she said kindly. "If you run into trouble, just send one of the kids to get me, all right? I'll come save you."

I wasn't sure if she was kidding or not, but the idea that she would bail me out if I bit the dust made me feel better. I smiled wanly at her and entered my classroom.

It was a pleasant room with blue-carpeted floor spread evenly with desks and white walls with colorful hangings. I hurried to my desk and opened the folder on top, glancing over the class roll. Twenty-eight students. *Twenty-eight!* It may as well have been six hundred.

I groaned and dropped my head into my hands, wishing with all my might that the day was over. I heard a noise by the door and my head shot up. Jerry Haskins stood in the doorway, grinning at me.

"Hello, Marie!" he said cheerfully. "All ready?"

I tried to muster a confident smile, but I was sure it was more of a grimace. "Absolutely," I said, my voice pathetically weak and shaky. "All set."

"Good, good," said Jerry, his smile not faltering. I hoped that meant he hadn't noticed my nervousness. "Remember, lunch is at eleven thirty. Lunchroom is down the hall to the right and the faculty lounge is one door beyond that. Good luck!"

He waved merrily and left the room.

"So how's it going?" Danielle asked as I sat down beside her in the faculty lounge with my bagged lunch. She took a big bite of her turkey sandwich and grinned at me. "Nobody dead or anything, right? Nothing to worry about."

I grimaced at her, and she laughed.

"What's funny?" asked Mariah as she sat down on my other side. "Any disasters, Marie?"

"No," I admitted grudgingly as I unwrapped my own sandwich. "It's a lot easier than I thought. The kids are great."

"I told you!" said Danielle, smacking me playfully on the arm. "Nothing to it."

"Hey," murmured Mariah, reaching across me to nudge her sister. She nodded toward the door.

A tall, blond, bespectacled young man in a sweater and slacks had just entered the room. He was nice-looking in an academic sort of way, and I noted that Danielle immediately flushed to her fingertips.

"Who's that?" I whispered to Mariah.

She grinned, eyeing her sister. "His name is Carson Wright," she said, popping a potato chip into her mouth. "And Danielle has it *bad* for him."

"Shhhh!" shushed Danielle, glaring at her sister. "Do you want to make me the laughingstock of the faculty?"

"He's cute," I said, looking at her. "Why would liking him make you a laughingstock?"

"He's *painfully* shy," Mariah emphasized, looking at me earnestly. "Annoyingly shy, actually. Kind of has reputation for it. Only around women, though. He's lively enough in his classes."

"What grade does he teach?" I asked.

"Oh, he teaches at the high school level," said Mariah, still smiling at Danielle who was openly ogling Carson Wright. "Political science. He's very good. The kids love him."

"They're not the only ones who love him," I teased, poking Danielle in the ribs.

She barely glanced at me, and Mariah snickered.

When it became clear that as long as Carson Wright was in the room, Danielle was useless in terms of conversation, Mariah and I ignored her and discussed the town and its occupants. She shared with me the latest news, entertaining me with tales of the various quirky personalities I was likely to encounter. Once the political science teacher left the lounge, Danielle joined in enthusiastically. The lunch hour passed quickly, and the next thing I knew, it was time to fetch my students from their after-lunch recess.

"See you after school!" Danielle said, and Mariah nodded and waved as we parted ways.

December flew by in a dizzying waltz of classes, faculty meetings, and quiet nights spent with Danielle and Mariah. Most of the time, I managed to keep my mind anchored firmly in the present, but as Christmas approached, my thoughts were drawn to the past with increasing frequency.

"What are your plans for the holidays, Marie?" Danielle asked one night about a week before Christmas.

We were gathered around the fireplace at River House, each involved in a different task. Danielle sat with her watercolors, painting the scene outside the window. Mariah hunched over her crochet hook, focusing on a colorful afghan. I sat with a book in my lap, attempting to force my mind to concentrate on the words on the page instead of drifting back to snow-covered memories of Thorne Field.

"Now that school is out for Christmas, you're free to go spend it with your family, I guess," said Danielle.

"I don't have any family," I said softly, not meeting her eyes.

"Well, good!" she cried jubilantly.

"Danielle!" Mariah scolded.

"No, no!" Danielle said quickly. "I only meant that it's good she's not going anywhere, so she can spend Christmas with us!"

"I can't think of anyone I'd rather spend the holidays with," I said, smiling softly. "Are you sure, though? I don't want to intrude on family time."

"Oh, it's only us and Alex," Mariah said, frowning as she attempted to undo a large knot in her yarn. "That's all it ever is, since our parents died."

"Alex?" I asked, not recognizing the name.

"Our stepbrother, remember?" Danielle explained, looking up from her painting. "He's coming the day after tomorrow, and he'll be staying through the New Year."

"Stepbrother?" I asked. "He's not related by blood?"

"Nope," Danielle answered. "His dad married our mom."

"You'll like him," said Mariah, a wry smile on her face, although she didn't look up from her afghan.

"So you've said," I said dryly. "But I doubt he'll like me, so don't be getting any ideas. I am not eligible for romance."

"Sure, okay," said Danielle, grinning at me.

I sighed in frustration and rolled my eyes. I attempted to focus my thoughts back on my book. Immediately they flew thousands of miles away, settling on a chair in front of the library fire at Thorne Field, where a tall figure with blue eyes—

Stop! I screamed inwardly at myself. I must have flinched, because Mariah's attention was suddenly fixed on my face.

"Marie?" she asked. "Are you all right?"

"Fine," I said, but my voice sounded strained. "Just tired. I think I'll head up to bed."

"Okay," she said, but she didn't sound convinced. "Good night."

" 'Night," I said.

Danielle smiled at me as I passed, but she looked worried.

I knew my friends were getting increasingly uneasy about my mental state. I hoped having their stepbrother here would distract them from their resolve to bring me out of my shell. As far as I was concerned, despite the fact that his sisters were determined to throw him in my general direction, he couldn't come soon enough.

The day of Alex's arrival was overcast and bitterly cold. It had been snowing on and off for a few days, and Mariah and Danielle worried that his flight would be canceled. He made it on time, however, and their excitement at the appearance of a luxurious rental car in the driveway very nearly rubbed off on me.

I retreated to the back of the house as a knock sounded at the door, reasoning that the sisters would want some private time with their stepbrother. I knew that this was just an excuse, though. I was actually just anxious to avoid any attempts at matchmaking for as long as possible.

Unfortunately, Danielle and Mariah had other ideas.

"Marie! Come and meet Alex!" called Danielle from the front of the house. "We've told him all about you, and he's dying to meet you!"

I sighed and pulled myself from the chair next to the fire. I would be polite but aloof. Maybe even cold, so he would know that this match-up thing was not my idea.

I began to walk down the passage toward the entry hall, and I could hear Mariah and Danielle laughing at something the man had said. But when his laugh reverberated through the hallway, I nearly tripped. That laugh . . . there was something oddly familiar about it. Apprehensive, but not quite sure why, I emerged from the hallway. I saw immediately that my trepidation was fully justified.

Jonathan Kelly stood in the entry hall, one arm around each sister. As I appeared, he swung his gaze to me and the delighted smile froze on his face.

"Jonathan," I breathed, horror-struck. This couldn't possibly be real. What were the odds?

"Kate?!" he gasped in disbelief. "What are you doing here?"

"I . . . uh . . . ," I said, my voice weak and shaking.

"Kate? Who's Kate?" Danielle asked, looking around as if expecting to see some stranger standing in our midst.

"You two know each other?" Mariah asked, grasping the situation more quickly. "And did you just call her Kate?" She swung her gaze back to rest on her brother.

"That's her name," said Jonathan.

Mariah and Danielle turned on me, their stares accusatory.

"You told us your name was Marie!" cried Danielle. She seemed genuinely hurt, and I felt a desperate need to explain, if only to wipe the injured look from her face.

"Kathryn Marie Evans," I said. "I used to go by Kate, but I go by Marie now."

"Oh, you do, do you?" said Jonathan, sounding supremely irritated. "Marie now, is it?" His irritation was quickly shifting to full-blown anger. I winced. "Well, *Marie*, it's nice that you've finally decided to make an appearance, albeit on the opposite side of the country. I can't believe this! Kate, do you have any idea what we've been going through for the past two months, having no idea where you'd disappeared to? Tyler has been—"

"*Don't!*" I shrieked, my hands seeming to fly to my ears of their own free will. I spent most of my time actively repelling thoughts of him. And there was no way I could be successful if Jonathan talked about him. Just hearing his name was more painful than I had anticipated. My cry echoed throughout the rooms beyond and the others stood staring at me in stunned surprise.

"Please . . . ," I whimpered. "Just . . . don't."

It was as much a plea to my subconscious mind as to Jonathan. Memories that I had managed to bury months ago were suddenly rushing at me with all the force and power of a tidal wave. It was too much, and for once I couldn't fend them off. With Jonathan's face in front of me, it seemed my entire history was displayed before my eyes. I closed them tightly in an attempt to rid myself of the uninvited vision. But I could practically hear Jonathan's thoughts screaming at me from the other side of his pressed lips, and I knew it wouldn't be long before he lost control of them. Knowing I couldn't face such a thing in my frame of mind, I turned and raced up the stairs, leaving three pairs of wide eyes behind me.

eleven

Marie? Uh, Kate?" came the hesitant voice from behind the door. I opened my eyes blearily and winced as my head began to pound with a vengeance.

"Come in, Danielle," I said, my voice a rough croak.

The door opened and Danielle and Mariah entered, Mariah carrying a tray containing what looked like a bowl of soup. She set it on the nightstand next to my bed and then seated herself next to me. Danielle reached out and took one of my hands and Mariah took the other.

"Did he tell you?" I asked, not meeting their eyes.

"Oh, Alex won't tell us anything," said Danielle, sounding frustrated. "He says it's your business, and you'll tell us when you're ready."

"He's right, Dani," said Mariah with a reproving glare. "It's not our place to pry."

But I could tell they were both dying of curiosity, and I didn't see the point of leaving them in suspense any longer. Now that Jonathan was here, it wasn't as if I could escape my memories. I took a deep breath and began my story, starting with my years at the Whitman residence. I talked steadily through my entire history, finishing with

Camille's return to Thorne Field and my subsequent flight. The only thing I did not disclose was my uncomfortable relationship with Jonathan, feeling that he would prefer his sisters not know of it.

"Oh," breathed Danielle when I finished, seeming to be close to tears. "How terrible. I'm so sorry."

I didn't say anything. Mariah remained silent as well, her fingers moving absently over my knuckles as she stroked my hand.

"So . . . what are you going to do?" asked Danielle, finally breaking the long silence.

"Do?" I asked in surprise. "What do you mean?"

"Well, are you going to go back?" she asked tentatively. She bit her lip, seeming almost afraid of my response.

"No," I said immediately, almost harshly. "I will never go back."

"But, Mar—I mean, Kate, you're in love with him!" Danielle protested hotly. "You can't just—"

"Yes, Danielle, I can," I said coldly, with absolute finality. "I will never go back to Thorne Field. I will never see him again."

And then, so they couldn't see how much the harsh reality of the statement actually affected me, I turned my back on them in a childish gesture and burrowed my face into the pillow. I heard them leave the room a few seconds later, pulling the door shut softly behind them.

I lay in the dark for a long time, trying not to think. The shock of suddenly coming face-to-face with Jonathan Kelly was wearing off now, and dread was taking its place. I didn't want to walk down those stairs and answer to his accusing stare. I didn't want to explain my actions. But more than anything, I didn't want him to tell Tyler where I was.

I was suddenly propelled to my feet.

He can't tell him where I am, I thought in panic. *What if he's already called him?*

I sprinted out the door, down the stairs, and into the kitchen. Jonathan was seated at the table, a bowl of soup in front of him.

"Jonathan," I gasped, out of breath from my quick descent. "You can't tell him where I am."

"What?" he said, his face a mask of surprise and his spoon frozen halfway to his mouth.

"He can't know," I repeated. "I left for a reason; I changed my name for a reason. He can't find me."

Jonathan looked at me steadily for a moment, his face impassive. "Kate, listen—" he began, but I cut him off.

"No, don't try to reason with me," I said firmly. "There is no room for negotiation. You *must not* tell him. Promise me."

"Kate, Tyler's my best friend! I've known him since college! He's worried sick about you. I can't just—"

I walked around the table and took his face in my hands. "*Promise me*," I said emphatically. "Please. I can't tell you how important this is."

Jonathan looked into my eyes, and I could see the indecision and conflict running rampant through his mind and across his face. Tyler was his oldest and dearest friend—how could he keep something like this from him?

But I knew Jonathan liked me. A lot. As cruel and selfish as it was to take advantage of his weakness for me, I counted on it to swing his decision in my favor. And I was right.

"All right, Kate," he said, sighing unhappily. "I promise."

"Thank you," I said and pressed a kiss to his forehead. "I won't forget it."

"I know you won't," Jonathan grumbled, clearly choosing to interpret my words as a threat. He glared at his soup bowl, appearing to have lost his appetite.

Behind me, Danielle and Mariah entered the kitchen. They both stopped when they saw me standing over their brother and the mutinous look on his face.

"What's going on?" Mariah asked carefully.

"Nothing," Jonathan grouched. "Kate's just proving to me, yet again, how stubborn she is."

I laughed quietly with no trace of humor. "You probably curse the day you met me, don't you?" I said, putting a hand on his shoulder.

Jonathan looked up at me, his gaze intense. He took my hand softly in his. "No," he said seriously. "It's just a few of the days since then that I could stand to forget."

Danielle and Mariah looked back and forth between Jonathan's intense stare to my slightly apologetic one and down to our clasped hands. They glanced at each other, and something passed between them. I knew they had put two and two together. They obviously knew their brother well enough to ascertain what was going on behind that handsome face when he looked at me.

I closed my eyes in frustration. This was the last thing I needed. I firmly pulled my hand from Jonathan's grasp and turned to the girls with a determined look of nonchalance.

"So, why do you call Jonathan 'Alex'?" I asked.

They looked bewildered for a second at the sudden change of subject. Mariah was the first to recover.

"Oh, well, his middle name is Alexander," she replied. "His dad's name was Jonathan too, so our family called him Alex to differentiate. He's Jonathan everywhere else, though."

"I see," I said with feigned cheerfulness as I turned to the sink and began filling it with soapy water. "Makes sense."

I could feel the others' eyes on my back, but I ignored the sensation. I began to wash the dishes with steady hands. I wondered how I was managing to stay so calm with the trauma I had suffered in the past few hours. I didn't turn around again until all the dishes were dry and put away. By the time I did, the kitchen was mercifully empty.

I sank into the chair Jonathan had vacated and dropped my face into my hands. This had the potential to be a very uncomfortable Christmas.

"So what have you been doing with yourself since I saw you last?" Jonathan asked me the following day as I was dust-mopping the hardwood floor in the dining room.

"Nothing much," I answered vaguely, not meeting his eyes.

"Sure, Kate," he said sarcastically, leaning against the wall. "Come on, the last time I saw you, you were in Oakley, Utah, wrapped around my best friend with an engagement ring on your finger. Now you're in Boston, Massachusetts, somehow living with my sisters . . . with an engagement ring on your finger." His gaze had fallen to my left hand and his face held a puzzled expression. "Why are you still wearing it?" he asked softly.

"I don't know," I answered honestly. "I've just never taken it off."

"Don't you think that it's probably time?" Jonathan asked, his voice gentle.

I immaturely rammed the dust mop into his foot as I passed him. "Butt out, Jonathan," I said through gritted teeth.

"Look, I'm just worried about you," he said, taking me firmly by the shoulders and forcing me to let go of the dust mop. "I'm not saying that you should be completely over Tyler. I mean, I know you loved him and it's only been a couple of months, but—"

"I said, *butt out.*" My voice was venomous.

Jonathan studied my face for a moment. "Okay," he finally said with a sigh. "But just let me say this. Yes, Camille is back, and she and Tyler are trying to make a go of it as a family, but that doesn't mean that Tyler doesn't love you."

"Is that supposed to comfort me somehow?" I screeched, staring at him incredulously. "To know that he still loves me, despite the fact that he's off being a devoted husband to another woman?"

I tore myself violently from his grasp. "Thanks, Jonathan, but next time you're trying to cheer me up, why don't you just blow up my car or something?" I turned on my heel and began walking quickly away.

"He's been searching constantly for you since the day you left, you know," Jonathan called after me.

I stopped, almost against my will. Jonathan continued, encouraged.

"He called me in a panic as soon as he found out you were gone, begging me to help him find you. It was like he'd gone crazy." His voice was pained at the memory. "You should have heard him."

I closed my eyes, feeling the familiar burning behind them.

"What could he do, Kate?" Jonathan pleaded for his friend. "Tyler has known Camille for most of his life, *loved* her for most of his life. He spent more than five years as her husband. She's the mother of the little girl who has become so important to him, largely thanks to you. Despite her affair, Tyler was crushed when he thought she had died. Now that Camille's essentially come back from the dead, how could he face himself in the mirror every day if he didn't at least try to keep his family together?"

I wanted to be angry at Jonathan for appealing to my soft side. I wanted to hurl something at him for making so much sense. Instead, I just calmly turned and looked at him.

"My name is Marie," I said, and then spinning on my heel, I walked away.

At my insistence, Danielle and Mariah continued to address me as "Marie," even though they protested strongly at first to doing so. Jonathan, on the other hand, staunchly refused to use my middle name.

"Your name is Kate," he said. "And that's what I'm going to call you. I'm sorry if you don't like it, but you'll just have to live with it."

I was so irritated with him that I childishly refused to acknowledge him for nearly two days. Jonathan responded in kind by following me around from room to room, attempting to trick me into talking to him. He seemed to think it was an extremely entertaining pastime.

Finally, I grew so weary of trying to avoid his company that I relented, if only to keep him from dogging my every step. I agreed to answer to "Kate" as long as he only used the name within the confines of River House. In public, he was to address me as "Marie," or not address me at all. Surprisingly, Jonathan agreed to this condition and finally gave me some space.

On Christmas Eve, the four of us jumped in Jonathan's rented Lexus and headed toward Boston for a night out on the town. After a scrumptious dinner of Boston's famous clam chowder and French bread, we headed to the Citi Performing Arts Center to see *The Nutcracker.* Jonathan snored through almost the entire thing. I found myself nodding off a time or two as well, although my fatigue was due to too many sleepless nights instead of mere boredom.

"So why did we do that again?" asked Jonathan good-naturedly as we left the theater.

"It's culture, Alex," said Danielle, smoothing the hair at the back of his head that had been mussed from his nap. "And heaven knows, you need culture."

I snickered at Jonathan's affronted look.

"I'm from New York, for crying out loud. That city is the *definition* of culture!" he insisted.

"Well, I might agree with you, if you ever set foot outside your office when you were there," said Danielle. "But I swear, your rear end is glued to your office chair."

"You could live in the basement of the Metropolitan Museum of Art and not necessarily have culture, Alex," said Mariah, smiling. "Your proximity is not the issue; it's how often you partake."

Jonathan grumbled under his breath, something about his sisters not complaining about his lifestyle when they needed access to his bank accounts. Danielle giggled self-consciously and smacked him.

As we walked down the Boston streets toward where we had parked the car, I noticed Danielle subtly take Mariah's arm and pull her more swiftly along the sidewalk. I knew exactly what she was doing. In a matter of seconds, Danielle and Mariah were several paces ahead of Jonathan and me, and rapidly increasing the distance.

I sighed resignedly. I knew the sisters were determined to shove their stepbrother in my direction, hoping against hope that he could dispel the loneliness that Tyler's absence had created. I already knew it was a hopeless cause, but I figured I could humor them as Jonathan would only be around for another week or so.

"Have you attempted to contact your uncle while you've been here?" Jonathan asked, catching me completely off guard.

"No, I haven't," I said. "Why do you ask?"

"Well, if you are determined to avoid Tyler at all costs, you may not want to. That was the first place Tyler went when you disappeared," Jonathan explained. "You mentioned to him that your uncle owned a publishing company in Boston. With Tyler's extensive business contacts, it wasn't hard to locate your uncle."

"What happened?" I asked. "My uncle didn't even know for sure that I existed. My aunt told him she had never heard of me."

"Well, naturally, your uncle was overjoyed when Tyler contacted him and confirmed that you were alive and well. They've joined forces and have been searching for you together. So, if you contact your uncle, you'll be contacting Tyler as well."

"Frankly, with all their resources, I'm surprised they haven't been able to find me," I said.

"Well, the only roads that would lead to you are credit reports and employment records, unless you've registered your car since you've been here," Jonathan answered.

"No," I replied. "And I've canceled my credit cards. My employment records at Middleton Academy say 'Marie Evans.'"

"Well, since they're searching for a Kate Evans, that's probably why they haven't located you," said Jonathan logically. "Kate Evans is a pretty common name, and that's slowing them down. I don't think they're looking too hard in the Boston area anyway, because they figure that if you were living around here, you would have contacted your uncle by now."

"So if I want to meet my Uncle Jack, it would mean revealing my location to Tyler," I said softly, looking at the ground.

"Yes. I'm sorry," Jonathan said. His face held a sympathetic look, but I detected something steely behind his eyes. He was still upset about my insistence that he hide his knowledge of my whereabouts from his best friend. I couldn't blame him, really.

"Thank you for telling me," I said, reaching out to squeeze his hand.

I had new respect for him. It would have been easy for him to conveniently forget to impart this information to me. If he had, he would still be keeping his promise to me—since he wouldn't be telling Tyler directly where I was—and not betraying Tyler either, because I would eventually inadvertently reveal myself to him. This revelation on Jonathan's part made me that much more confident of his feelings for me. The thought was simultaneously comforting and guilt-inducing.

As we walked toward the sleek black Lexus, Jonathan gripped my hand hard, not allowing me to gently pull my fingers away. I told myself it was friendly gesture and nothing more. When I saw Danielle and Mariah's delighted smiles upon viewing the scene, however, guilt sliced through me and I yanked my hand from his. I didn't miss Jonathan's answering smile and wink to his sisters. I was in trouble.

twelve

Christmas morning was a pleasant affair, with the four of us sitting around the Christmas tree with carols playing on the stereo and a fire roaring in the fireplace. I had purchased a new set of watercolors and several canvases for Danielle. I had given Mariah a set of books by her favorite author. Not particularly imaginative presents, but Danielle and Mariah squealed as if I'd given them the moon.

The girls were thoughtful in their gifts to me. Mariah gave me a set of seasonal classroom decorations. Danielle surprised me with a beautiful drawing set with charcoal and lead pencils and thick sheets of sketch paper. I was a bit confused by the gift, since I had never proclaimed myself an artist.

"I've watched you sketch on your napkin at lunch," Danielle said, a knowing smile on her face.

"Those are just doodles," I protested, looking at the intimidating artist's collection. "I wouldn't know how to begin using any of this!"

"Just explore. Have fun," she suggested. "Your 'doodles' are actually really good, Marie."

I just shook my head but hugged her tightly. Despite my protests, I was really excited to try sketching with the new materials.

"Doesn't anybody care what *I* got them?" Jonathan grumped, gesturing to the packages in front of us. I knew he had gone shopping for my present the day before, determined to make sure he had something for everyone. I felt guilty since I had not taken the time to get him anything.

"No," Danielle answered him even as she ripped the paper enthusiastically from her large present. "Alex!" she gasped, pulling the last bits of paper away and revealing a gorgeous painting framed to perfection. "A Francis Kendall!"

"A what?" Mariah asked, her face confused.

"The painting . . . it's a Francis Kendall," explained Jonathan. He looked incredulous that neither Mariah nor I had any idea who he meant. "One of the most popular and celebrated painters in New York . . . ," he prompted. He looked back and forth between our clueless expressions and threw up his hands. "And you say *I* don't have any culture?" he cried.

His teasing was cut off as Danielle tackled him to the floor. "It's too much! This must have cost you a fortune!" she cried.

Jonathan gave her an incredulous look. "What else am I going to spend my money on, if not you?"

I watched them, smiling at Jonathan's easy and affectionate nature. I had always known he was a good man, but watching him with his sisters gave me a whole new perspective on his character.

"All right. Now you, Mariah," Jonathan said, dumping Danielle unceremoniously in her chair and returning to his own.

"Okay," said Mariah, and she began meticulously unfolding the shiny silver paper covering her gift.

Danielle rolled her eyes in disgust. "Oh come on, Mariah. Marie would like to open her gift before Memorial Day, if that's not too much trouble."

"Patience," said Mariah. "If I don't rip the paper too much I'll be able to reuse it."

Danielle grumbled under her breath but allowed her sister to unwrap the gift at a snail's pace.

When all the paper finally fell away, I heard Mariah's breath catch in her throat. In front of her stood the most beautiful wooden chest I had ever seen, made of cherry wood and polished to a shiny finish.

"Alex, it's gorgeous!" breathed Mariah.

"You told me you wanted a hope chest, so here it is," Jonathan said, his satisfaction at her response written on his face. "It's a Chippendale, so it better last you forever. I don't think I can afford to spend that kind of money twice," he joked.

Now it was Mariah's turn to tackle Jonathan. He took her gratitude good-naturedly but seemed a little self-conscious at her enthusiastic response. I didn't blame Mariah for being ecstatic. The chest was an absolutely perfect fit for River House's antique style.

Once Mariah got back to admiring her trunk and Jonathan was once again seated in his chair, he turned to me with a twinkle in his eye. "All right, Kate. It's your turn."

My gift was much smaller than Danielle's or Mariah's, but I was more than a little apprehensive about what it might contain. I picked it up, set it on my lap, and stared at it for a few seconds. I was trying to get up the courage to actually tear the paper, when Danielle decided she'd had enough suspense.

"Well, come on!" she urged. "Open it!"

I tore a small piece of wrapping paper off and found that the box underneath was generic brown cardboard. After all the paper was cleared from the box, Mariah handed me a pair of scissors so I could slit the tape holding the box closed. I wasn't sure I wanted to.

"If you don't open it, I will. Either way, you'll see what it is," warned Jonathan. He seemed to sense my hesitation and know exactly why I didn't want to know what he was giving me.

What if it revealed the true nature of his feelings for me? I wasn't sure I could handle the awkwardness it would inspire.

Finally slitting the packing tape, I opened the cardboard flaps and cleared away the tissue paper hiding the contents of the box from view. My breath caught painfully in my chest.

There, nestled in a bed of tissue paper, was the culmination of all my hopes, wishes, and dreams. That plain cardboard box held my life—my everything.

"Oh," I breathed, tears pricking my eyes. I pulled the handsomely framed picture out of the box and held it up, a smile coming unconsciously to my lips.

The enlarged photograph showed Tyler, sitting in his preferred chair in the Thorne Field library. Addie was tucked in the crook of his arm, her favorite storybook open on her lap. The beloved faces were turned toward each other, laughing. I remembered that day with perfect clarity. In fact, I had taken the picture.

The tears ran shamelessly down my cheeks as I stared at the photo. It looked almost professionally done—as if it had been staged in a studio, but with none of the triteness that staged photographs often held. It was warm and honest and beautifully sincere. It was cruel of Jonathan to give it to me, knowing I could never see its subjects again, yet I loved him for it. Rising slowly, I walked toward him, setting the picture almost reverently on a chair as I went. He was already standing, waiting for me with open arms. I hugged him tightly, my head against his chest.

"Thank you," I whimpered, the tears still coursing down my cheeks. "I don't have a gift for you. I wish I could somehow repay you for this."

"You can," said Jonathan. He pulled back, and I looked up at him. He seemed about to say something facetious, but stopped, his eyes searching mine for an indeterminable amount of time. Slowly his face descended toward mine, and our lips met. The kiss was soft and unassuming, and it immediately sent my body into throes of turmoil. While my head reasoned that I at least owed him this, my heart screamed in protest. It didn't feel right. It wasn't supposed to be like this. And yet . . .

Jonathan's arms came around me and held me to him. I didn't resist. But as his lips became more insistent, I finally tried to back away. He seemed to realize my predicament and let me go.

"Kate, I—" he said, his face stricken. "I had no right—that's not why I—I shouldn't have. I'm sorry."

"It . . . it's okay," I said, still trying to make sense of what I was feeling. My head was swimming, and it felt like every nerve in my body was tingling, but something inside me was still screaming in disapproval. What was wrong with me?

"Marie?" Danielle's voice sounded far away. "Are you okay?"

"Alex, look what you've done to her," chided Mariah, but she sounded oddly pleased.

"Kate?" Jonathan just sounded worried. "Kate, are you all right?"

"Fine," I said, shaking my head to clear it. "I'm fine." I finally met Jonathan's gaze and held it. "Thank you for the picture, Jonathan. It's absolutely perfect."

Hugging the large wooden frame to my chest, I turned and made my way shakily toward the stairs, feeling three pairs of eyes once again follow me from the room.

Once upstairs, I sat on my bed and set the framed photograph out in front of me to study it. I couldn't tear my eyes away. The picture had been taken shortly after Tyler's proposal when I had actually believed that he, Addie, and I would someday be a family. I could still remember the feeling of absolute bliss warming me as I had snapped the picture, knowing it would be one that I would always treasure. With the rush of wedding plans combined with Tyler's departure for New York, I had never transferred the digital photo to my laptop. Since the camera had been Tyler's, it had remained at Thorne Field when I left, along with the only copy of the beautiful picture. I could never repay Jonathan for giving me back one of the happiest moments of my life, even though it was only in memory.

As I continued to stare fixedly at the two dearly loved faces, my bedroom door opened and Danielle and Mariah entered. They sat on each side of me, studying the picture with great interest.

"Is that Tyler?" asked Danielle softly. "And Addie?"

"Yes," I answered. "I took this picture just a few days after he proposed to me. Actually, this was the day we found out that we could legally adopt Addie." Tears escaped the corners of my eyes as I said this. "I was so happy . . . thinking I'd finally found my family."

"He's very handsome," said Mariah.

"To me, he is," I said with a smile. "He's beautiful and wonderful and perfect. But if *he* had heard you say that, he would have laughed out loud." My own laugh ended abruptly with a strangled sob.

"Oh, Marie," said Mariah, her eyes filling with sympathy. "This must be so hard for you."

"Oh, it's not so bad," I said shakily. "I know it looks like I'm miserable, but I'm completely content here with you two. And I am so grateful to Jonathan for giving me this. It's nice to remember such happy times." I looked back down at the photograph, and I felt a genuine smile light my face. "This is how I want to remember them."

"You talk like they're dead," protested Danielle. "You don't have to do this, you know. You don't have to be separated from them!"

"Danielle," Mariah warned.

"No, listen," said Danielle passionately. "You're in love with Tyler. That much is obvious, and he must love you because he proposed to you, didn't he? So isn't your love worth fighting for? Can't you go back and force him to choose between you and Camille?"

"Danielle," I said kindly. "He *has* chosen between us. He chose Camille."

"You don't know that!" Danielle cried. "You left without giving him the chance! Maybe Tyler would have chosen *you* if you'd stayed!"

"But then what?" I asked, just as passionately. "What would have happened? How could I have kept him from a woman he had once promised a life to? The woman he loved first? How could I have kept Addie separated from a mother who wanted to know her? How could I have lived with myself if I'd done that?"

"You really think Tyler still loves Camille?" Mariah asked curiously.

"It would certainly appear that way," I said glumly. "He's with her, isn't he?"

Danielle sighed, sounding completely dejected. "I suppose you're right."

We were silent for several minutes, each of us lost in our own thoughts. Suddenly Danielle perked up considerably.

"Well, since you were forced to give your family away—to a much less-deserving woman, I might add—you can be part of ours," she said, her voice sparkling with enthusiasm.

"What?" I said, absently.

"We're adopting you," she replied, simply.

"What?" I said again.

"That's right!" said Mariah, catching the spirit of things. "You are now officially our sister. You have been adopted into the Rivers family. Congratulations!"

I smiled at them. "I'm honored."

"Of course you are," said Danielle, jumping up from her curled position on the bed. "Now, sisters, let us go downstairs to Christmas breakfast, which I'm sure Alex has generously prepared for us."

"Don't hold your breath," Mariah muttered.

"I won't," laughed Danielle, pulling both of us from the room and shutting the door behind her.

The remainder of Christmas Day passed quietly, all of us concentrating on different pastimes. Danielle, as usual, sat at the window, working on an oil painting this time, while Mariah read aloud to us from the books I had given her. I sat by the fire, attempting to sketch from my memory. It was eerie, how easily the lines seemed to flow out of my fingers and down the pencil, assembling themselves on the paper exactly how I wanted them to. Addie's face looked up at me with astounding clarity and resemblance. I was actually quite shocked as I studied the drawing.

"Is the turkey done?" came Jonathan's voice from the doorway behind me.

"People who work on Christmas Day don't get turkey," said Danielle, not looking up from her painting. "Christmas is a time for family, not stocks and investors and UFOs."

"CFOs," Jonathan corrected.

"Whatever," said Danielle. "You're not getting a bite of turkey, or anything else for that matter, until your laptop is stowed completely out of sight."

"Yes, mother," said Jonathan, quickly dodging out the door as Danielle hurled a sofa pillow at him.

"I'll go make sure the turkey is actually fit for eating," said Mariah, rising from her chair. "With Danielle, you never know."

"Oh, you want a pillow sandwich too, do you?" said Danielle, smiling teasingly at her sister.

Mariah laughed and left the room before Danielle could make good on her threat.

Danielle stretched and yawned, finally setting down her brush and palette. Wiping her hands on a rag, she rose to her feet and came to stand at my side.

"Well, let's see what you . . . ?" she began, but the words died in her throat as she stared down at my sketch of Addie.

I frantically tried to hide what I'd done, but Danielle was much too quick for me. She snatched the sketchpad from my hands and stared hard at it. She looked at me, then back to the drawing, her eyes wide in disbelief.

"You said you haven't had any training!" she said, almost angrily.

"I haven't," I defended. "I'm as surprised as you are that it turned out . . . like that."

"Marie, this is incredible!" Danielle praised, studying the sketch with a practiced eye. "It took me years to get to this level of realism. You have a gift." She handed back the sketchpad absently; she seemed to be contemplating something.

"I have an idea," she said finally.

I was instantly suspicious.

"I put together the Milton Art Show every year in early October," she began, her voice suddenly honey smooth.

I knew that voice. She turned it on whenever she wanted a gargantuan favor.

"I'm always looking for exciting new talent to feature," she said. "Especially if the artist is local. Do you think you could contribute some pieces?"

I was already shaking my head. "No way," I said. "I'm not an artist. I'm a complete novice! There's no way I'm letting you drag me into something like that—I'd only embarrass myself and you. The answer is no."

"Come on, Marie!" Danielle said, turning on the persuasive tone full force. "Look at that drawing! You're *amazing* for a beginner, and you've got plenty of time to brush up on technique. The show is almost a whole year away! It would be a tremendous help to me."

I looked into her startlingly green eyes and wavered. After all Danielle and her sister had done for me, how could I not help her out?

"Ask me in a few months," I said finally. "If I feel like I know what I'm doing by then, we'll see."

"Thank you, thank you, thank you!" Danielle cried, hugging me. "You won't regret it, I promise!"

"Hang on a second, I never—" I protested, but I was interrupted by Jonathan's voice from the hallway.

"Mariah says dinner's ready," he said, poking his head in the room. "Smells great and looks terrific, Dani. Good job."

"Don't sound so shocked," she said loftily as she walked toward him, towing me along. "Why is everyone always so surprised when one of my culinary masterpieces turns out all right?"

They continued to banter back and forth, but I didn't bother to listen.

Is my sketch really that good? I wondered. Could I really be featured in an art show with virtually no experience and no training? The thought of having something created by my clumsy hands displayed for the world to see tied my stomach in knots.

The week after Christmas was full of fun outings, compliments of Jonathan Kelly. He seemed determined to keep us out of the house and on the go as much as possible. We spent most of our time in Boston, visiting art museums, going to plays and sporting events, and trying new restaurants.

One night, Jonathan took us ice skating at Frog Pond on the Boston Common. It was a cold but gloriously starlit night as we drove from Milton into Boston. Once equipped with skates, Mariah and Danielle took off by themselves, as I knew they would, leaving Jonathan and me to skate together.

"Have you ever ice skated before?" Jonathan asked, watching me as I wobbled precariously on my skates.

"I grew up in California," I said, my voice tight with tension. "What do *you* think?"

"I'm thinking no," Jonathan said, reaching out to catch me just in time. "Well, let me give you some pointers."

For the next half hour, I skated around the rink with Jonathan's arm tucked firmly around me. I needed it to keep from face planting on the frozen surface, so I didn't protest. By the time we had skated around the rink half a dozen times, I felt reasonably sure-footed and shrugged Jonathan's arm away.

"Kate, er . . . Marie, can I ask you something?" Jonathan stuttered, remembering our deal at the last moment.

"Yes," I said, concentrating on keeping my feet underneath me.

"Do you really believe that marriages last forever? That they continue even after death?"

So unprepared was I for such a question that I took my eyes off my feet to stare at Jonathan. He had to reach out and catch me again to keep me from going down hard. Once we were back on solid footing, I could turn my attention back to him. What would cause him to ask such a thing? The question had come completely out of left field.

"Um, yes, I do," I said carefully. "As long as it takes place at the correct location."

"Meaning one of those temple things?" asked Jonathan, studying my face.

"Yes, one of those temple things." I smiled. "We believe that if a couple is married in the temple, and they keep the sacred covenants that they make there, their marriage will last beyond death and into the eternities. Why do you ask?"

"I heard Tyler talking about it once," Jonathan said carefully, as if gauging how much to say about my former fiancé.

"Oh?" I said, trying to sound nonchalant. "When?"

Jonathan wasn't fooled for a moment by my attempt at indifference. "During that month he spent in New York, when you two were engaged."

"I see," I said, the relief rushing over me. Tyler had been referring to an eternal marriage to me then, and not to Camille. The thought gave me a small measure of comfort, even though none of that mattered anymore. Since Tyler was choosing to remain married to Camille, I was sure that, provided she joined the Church, he would be sealed to her and Addie eventually. The thought made me instantly glum. I was mad at myself for the reaction. I would never again set eyes on Tyler Thorne. I had no right to be upset about his future plans.

"So how would one go about getting married in one of these temples?" Jonathan asked, interrupting my psychological scolding. His voice was now a study in practiced indifference.

"Well, you have to be a member of my church," I explained.

"Once you've been a member for a year, you are eligible for a temple recommend."

"Recommend?" Jonathan asked in confusion. "You have to get recommendations to go there? Who recommends you?"

"Your bishop and stake president," I said, smiling.

"Stake president?"

"This is going to take some explaining," I said, grinning at his confusion.

For the next twenty minutes, I related to him the organization of the church and the requirements to be a member and a worthy temple recommend holder. He listened carefully, nodding his understanding.

"Doesn't sound so hard," he said finally when I had finished. "No drinking, no smoking, no sex. Easy enough."

I looked at him carefully, reading his expression. "It's actually a lot more than that," I finally said. "We don't just live the Word of Wisdom and the law of chastity and call it good."

"What else is there?" Jonathan asked. He sounded wary.

"Well, the whole point of the temple is to make sacred covenants that enable us to return to live with God," I explained. "You have to be willing to make some pretty important promises to Someone who will immediately know if you break them. It's not something to enter into lightly."

"So is that where you'll get married?" Jonathan asked.

I looked at him sharply. "Well, I doubt I'll ever get married," I said carefully. "But if a miracle happens and I somehow manage to fall in love again, then yes, I'll get married in the temple. I won't marry anywhere else." Jonathan studied my expression steadily for a second, then looked away. We skated in silence for a few minutes. Then, in curiosity, I turned back to him.

"Jonathan, have you been investigating my church?"

He shrugged, avoiding my gaze. "No, not really," he said. "I'm just curious. I mean, I've seen Tyler practice his religion to a limited degree, and it made me wonder a little about it, but I haven't tracked down any of those missionaries you guys have running around all over the place."

"Well, that's probably a good thing," I said, watching him out of the corner of my eye. "I doubt you could handle it anyway."

He perked up, just like I knew he would. Jonathan loved a challenge.

"What makes you say that?" he asked, sounding slightly huffy.

"Well, in order to go to the temple, you have to be a full tithe payer," I said innocently. "Do you know what that means?"

"No," said Jonathan, watching my face.

"It means you'd have to cough up ten percent every time you get one of your million-dollar paychecks. Danielle and Mariah would never forgive you," I said and skated off, hearing his laugh echo behind me.

New Year's Day was the last day that Jonathan had intended to spend with us. Our original plan was to attend Milton's annual celebration, but at the last minute, Jonathan decided that wasn't good enough. He wanted to fly all of us down to New York for the First Night celebration in Times Square.

"He's just trying to impress you, Marie," said Danielle, winking at me. "He's never offered to fly us down to Manhattan for New Year's before."

"Well, I don't think I can go anyway," I said, trying desperately to think of an excuse. The truth was I didn't want to run the risk of somehow encountering Tyler Thorne on the streets of New York City. Granted, New York was a city of millions and the chances of that were slim, but the chance of running into Tyler if I stayed in Milton was virtually zero.

As usual, Jonathan saw right through me. "He won't be there, Kate. Tyler's spending the holidays at Thorne Field with Camille and Addie."

I breathed a small sigh of relief, even managing to ignore the sharp stab of pain in my chest at the reference to Tyler's new family. It was becoming more bearable every day.

"I guess I can come, then," I said quietly, not meeting anybody's eyes. I knew they were all looking at me.

"Great!" said Jonathan, but his voice held an edge of gloominess that hadn't been there before. "Our flight leaves at 11:00 a.m. on the thirty-first. That will give us plenty of time to get to my place and down to Times Square before the festivities start."

"Alex says we can stay the weekend with him, if we want," said Mariah excitedly, turning to me. "School doesn't start back up until the following Monday, so we can fly home that Sunday and be back in time for classes."

"Well, as long as—" I began, but Jonathan cut me off.

"He's not due back in New York until the fifteenth, Kate," he said. His frustrated terseness told me that his temper was reaching boiling point.

I nodded and said nothing.

I really did hate to keep bringing Tyler into the conversation, but it was still just as important to me that my whereabouts remained unknown as it had been the day I'd fled from Thorne Field. I attempted to move the conversation on to another topic to assuage Jonathan's moodiness, but his irritation didn't seem to be fading as it usually did. In a rare show of annoyance, he suddenly pinched my arm fiercely between his fingers and led me from the room, leaving his surprised sisters behind us.

"All right, Kate, you've made it abundantly clear that you want Tyler nowhere near you," Jonathan hissed once he'd deposited me unceremoniously on a chair in the dining room. "I've promised you silence against my better judgment, and I think I have a right to know why I'm doing it."

As I studied his expression, I realized he was sincerely oblivious to the reasons why I had requested that my location remain under wraps. And judging from the scowl on his face, he had been wanting to say this since I first extracted the unwilling promise from him. I struggled to come up with an appropriate response.

"I can face you, Jonathan," I finally began. "It took awhile, but now I can handle the memories that your presence brings to the surface. They're getting easier to bear, the longer I'm away from him. But actually seeing *him* again . . . I couldn't do that. You know him," I said, sincerity ringing in my tone. I leaned over and rested one hand on Jonathan's arm to emphasize my words. "You know that if he finds me, he'll want to see me—if only to make sure I'm all right. It's probably best for all concerned that that never happens. Besides, I doubt I can survive it." I swallowed hard. "I left him once, and it was the hardest thing I have ever done. I don't think I could do it a second time. I'm pretty sure it would finish me off."

Jonathan didn't look convinced. "You're head-over-heels in love with the guy, but you don't want him to know where you are because then you'll be forced to see him?"

I winced. Well, sure, it sounded insane when you said it like *that.*

"Yes," I said, attempting to inject my tone with a firmness that I no longer felt. "I know it sounds crazy, but I just can't see him. At least not right now. It would be too hard. Geez, seeing *you* nearly drove me over the edge, and you're only his friend and business partner."

"Oh, is that all I am?" said Jonathan, raising an eyebrow. He looked miffed, but I could see the hurt in the creases around his eyes as well.

"Well, by that, I mean your relationship to *him* . . . ," I began lamely. I was becoming very proficient at inadvertently injuring Jonathan. That, or he was just incredibly sensitive.

"Oh, forget it," said Jonathan in a huff. Rising quickly to his feet, he left the room.

We left for the airport around 9:00 a.m. on the thirty-first of December. Jonathan had exchanged barely six words with me since our conversation in the dining room two days before. His sisters could sense the tension between us, but they said nothing.

The flight was blissfully short, and we touched down at JFK around 12:30. The traffic was unbelievable, but in the back of Jonathan's luxurious town car (chauffeured, of course), I didn't mind the long trip. I was mesmerized by the city around me. Never before had I seen so many people in one place, not even in L.A. The buildings seemed to be built almost on top of one another. Many of them were so high that I couldn't see the crowning floors, even with my face pressed against the window.

Jonathan chuckled when he saw my wide-eyed expression. The flight and the thrill of being back in the bustling city seemed to have cooled his temper, and I was back in his good graces.

"Like nothing you've ever seen, is it, Kate?" he said.

"Marie," I corrected automatically. Here more than anywhere else it was essential that he address me by my adopted name.

Jonathan waved my concern aside with his hand. "You're going to love it here," he said. "New York is the most beautiful city in the world."

"I'm not sure about that, but it's pretty great," I said. "I can't believe all the people!"

"Just wait till tonight." Jonathan grinned. "Nearly a million people gather in Times Square for this every year."

"Oh, I can't wait!" cried Danielle.

"How often do you and Mariah come to New York?" I asked her.

"Alex usually flies us down a few times a year for a visit," answered Mariah from my other side. "But we've never been here for New Year's before."

"We mostly like to visit museums and go to Broadway shows," said Danielle. "New York is the best place to find good art."

"Oh, give me a break," said Jonathan, laughing. "When you come down to see me, you spend ninety-eight percent of your time shopping, and you know it."

Danielle giggled and turned to look out the window again.

When we walked into Jonathan's penthouse on East 59th Street, I whistled in appreciation. It was decorated in a modern style, with angular furniture in black and white. It had a masculine undertone, and I wondered if Jonathan had decorated the place himself or had it professionally done. Danielle whispered as she passed me that although it was only 2,700 square feet, the condo had cost Jonathan nearly $7 million.

I was staggered. Seven million dollars for a condo roughly twice the size of my little cabin at Thorne Field . . . how could anyone who wasn't a millionaire afford to live in New York City?

The condo had two guest bedrooms, so it was established that Mariah and Danielle would take one, and I would take the other. I settled my suitcase on the plush, black comforter of the queen-size bed and looked around appreciatively. Not even at Thorne Field had I felt surrounded by such wealth. Thorne Field was all peaceful landscapes and wide-open spaces. Jonathan's condo was so professionally upscale that it rammed the suggestion of wealth down your throat.

I heard a soft knock on the door and turned to see Jonathan leaning against the doorframe, his arms folded.

"Room okay?" he asked needlessly. "Got everything you need?"

"Jonathan, it's incredible," I breathed. "I've never seen anything like it."

"If you think this place is something, you should see Tyler's," Jonathan said. Realizing immediately that he'd said the wrong thing, he quickly changed the subject. "You hungry? Ready for lunch?"

"Starving," I answered heartily.

"Did I hear someone mention lunch?" asked Danielle as she strode confidently into the room, Mariah on her heels.

"Yep. What sounds good?" Jonathan asked his sisters. "We can eat here or go out, but I warn you, my cupboards contain a limited selection. We can choose between crackers and moldy cheese or possibly, if we're lucky, I've got a can of soup somewhere."

Danielle grimaced. "What's the point of money if you're not going to spend it on the necessities of life?"

"You would be surprised how seldom I spend my money on food." Jonathan smiled. "Most of my meals are purchased by clients. Behold, the perks of the brokerage business."

We laughed at his playful arrogance.

"So, you ready to brave the streets of New York?" Mariah asked, looking at me.

"Bring on the overwhelming crowds, pushy street vendors, and transients!" I said, jumping to my feet.

Jonathan laughed and held out an arm to me. "Come on, then. New York City awaits."

thirteen

The day was more extraordinary than almost anything I had ever experienced. Although the jostling crowds were intimidating, Jonathan kept a firm hold on my hand to keep me from getting separated from him. He said the streets were more crowded than usual, due to the holiday.

We ate lunch at one of Jonathan's favorites, a place on Third Avenue, apparently known for its steaks. The prices made me gasp several times in succession, causing Jonathan to finally snatch the menu from my hand and stow it out of reach. I kept forgetting that I was in the company of one of New York's wealthier citizens. Jonathan just didn't seem to fit the description of the millionaire business tycoon. He was too down-to-earth.

The conversation was constantly entertaining, but I felt guilty that I had so little to add. Danielle, Mariah, and Jonathan had so much history together that I found nothing to comment on. Still, they didn't seem to mind my silence, relating all kinds of hilarious stories and giving me new insight into their close relationship as siblings.

After lunch, we wandered through the New York streets aimlessly, stepping in and out of various shops and boutiques as Danielle dictated. Jonathan pointed out to me some of his favorite haunts. He had entertaining stories for each. I noticed how careful he was not to mention Tyler's name in any of his tales. He would say "my friend" or "a business associate" instead of stating specifics, but I knew exactly who he was talking about. I could clearly make out Tyler's signature on every story. I appreciated the gesture regardless.

Danielle finally yanked us into an art gallery when our directionless wanderings were too much for her. We spent two hours studying abstract paintings, which I found a little dull. Jonathan seemed to share my lack of enthusiasm. Instead of musing over the insight of the various artists, Jonathan began suggesting possible sources of inspiration behind the colorful confusion. We were laughing hysterically by the time Danielle and Mariah finally caught up to us at the end of the exhibit.

"You could at least make an effort, you know," Danielle said disapprovingly to us. "There are some truly brilliant pieces here."

"Brilliant?" Jonathan said, attempting to mold his features into a serious expression. "I guess one man's brilliance is another man's boredom. My kind of art includes a nice, neat gridiron and the musical poetry that is the crunch of an offensive lineman mowed down by a defensive tackle."

"You are so . . . so . . . so *male*," Danielle said, her tone scathing. She turned and marched toward the door of the modern gallery.

Mariah rolled her eyes and smiled at us. "If there's one thing you don't want to insult in Danielle's presence, it's art," she whispered to me. "She considers it sacrilege."

"That's what makes it so fun," said Jonathan, taking my hand comfortably and leading me toward the door. I knew I should pull away, but I didn't. The pressure on my palm felt good. Comforting. I told myself that it was the same for Jonathan, but I'm not sure I believed it.

We returned to Jonathan's condo around five that evening. I was exhausted already and the New Year festivities hadn't even started. I collapsed on the black comforter in my bedroom and let my eyes close. I was awakened by a sudden shaking sensation.

"Marie!" Danielle's voice was urgent as she shook my shoulder.

"Come on! Why are you sleeping? It's only eight o'clock, the party hasn't even started!"

"Sorry," I murmured sleepily. I pulled myself to my feet.

"Hurry up, we're all ready to go!" Danielle exclaimed as she headed toward the kitchen.

I nodded and hurried to the bathroom. After a quick teeth brushing and change of clothes, I met my three friends at the door.

Jonathan whistled as he looked me up and down. "Very nice," he said.

I blushed and rolled my eyes. "Please," I said as I wound my sky blue scarf around my neck and perched the matching hat on my head. "Don't embarrass yourself."

Jonathan laughed. "Are you ready to face more people than you've ever encountered at one time in your natural life?"

"Absolutely!" Danielle crowed. "Lemme at 'em!"

We were laughing as we emerged onto the New York streets, my hand once again firmly enclosed within Jonathan's grasp. I again rationalized, telling myself that he simply didn't want to lose me in the crowds.

It was a considerable walk to Times Square, but despite that and the freezing temperatures, I enjoyed myself immensely. The streets were crowded and noisy, and excitement was thick in the air. Fireworks were already sending brilliant bursts of color across the sky, despite the fact that midnight was still hours away. The nearer we got to Times Square, the brighter and more crowded the streets became.

Finally emerging into the huge intersection, I was suddenly hit with a solid wall of humanity. Jonathan was right. I had never seen so many people in one place in my life. I was content to stand on the outskirts of the crowd and simply study the scene, but Jonathan and Danielle wanted to be in the thick of things. Fingers wound tightly through mine, Jonathan led me straight into the heart of the crowd and toward the gigantic stage at one end of the plaza, where a recording artist I didn't recognize was hollering an annoying rap song.

For the next couple of hours, we listened to the provided entertainment, stared shamelessly at some of the more creatively attired individuals in attendance, and conversed merrily. We did quite a bit of shivering too. The temperatures were well below freezing and getting much colder as the night wore on. I felt the cold penetrating to my bones and wondered if my teeth would rattle right out of my head.

Close to midnight, Jonathan finally realized how deeply cold I was and despite my weakly delivered protests, he pulled me into his arms, my back tight against his chest. I was ashamed of myself for not pulling away, but the fact was, I was cold and Jonathan was warm. I decided to abandon my resolve to keep Jonathan at arm's length until I was in a more agreeable climate. I allowed myself to relax against him and enjoy the excitement around me, tapping my foot to the now much more pleasant music blaring from the speakers all around the huge plaza.

As the final countdown to midnight began and the square reverberated with millions of voices combining to welcome the new year, I felt Jonathan shift a little behind me. Assuming he was just moving to get more comfortable or to warm himself up a bit, I didn't think anything of it. When the ball had made its final descent and the square was echoing with the cheers of the crowd and the blasts of the colorful fireworks, I was shocked to suddenly find myself facing Jonathan, his lips descending toward mine. I didn't have time to react, and truthfully, even if I had, I wouldn't have known what to do. His lips met mine softly at first but quickly gained confidence. Finally coming to my senses I pulled quickly away, confused by the strange palpitating of my heart. It was the same disconcerting warmth I had felt when he had kissed me on Christmas Day, and I had no idea what it meant. I stared up into his eyes, uncertain of how to react. I opened my mouth, still not sure of what would come out of it, but something directly to my right caused me to stop.

A tall, dark-haired figure stood roughly ten feet away, holding a small girl with chocolate-colored corkscrew curls. They were both staring at me.

Even over the deafening roars of the crowd pressing in around us from all sides, I could have sworn I heard the gasping sound of the word as it escaped his strangely white lips.

"Kate."

I felt as if the cold had finally reached my core and frozen me in place. Tyler's eyes were locked with mine, and in them I could read all the pain and uncertainty that was reflected in my own. Although I'm sure my gaze held a healthy dose of fear as well. This was exactly what I'd been dreading when Jonathan had invited me to come to New York. My worst nightmare and yet my most desperate dream had been realized. He was standing feet from me. He was looking at me with all the love I'd thought had been eclipsed by a stronger claim on his affections.

Jonathan felt me stiffen and saw the sudden change in my expression. He pulled back, relaxing his hold on me and turned to see what had me so engrossed. His body was suddenly stricken with the same strange rigor mortis as mine when his eyes fell upon his best friend. Tyler's gaze went suddenly from longing to betrayal as he met Jonathan's eyes. I felt I could hear exactly what was running through his mind. Not only had his friend knowingly withheld my whereabouts, he was attempting to step into a role that had once been expressly Tyler's.

The bright blue eyes swung from Jonathan and fastened again on me, seeming to drink me in. Strangely, although the three of us had been locked in a staring match for at least a full minute, Tyler had yet to take one step toward us. But suddenly, he seemed to register that the woman for whom he had been searching for months was *right here.* He took a halting step toward me, and Addie, her face softening from its look of shocked surprise, suddenly broke into a wide smile.

"Kate!" she screamed over the crowd, reaching toward me.

I wanted to run to her more than anything in the world. I wanted to grab the little girl and cling to her more tightly than I'd ever clung to anything. I wanted to run into Tyler's arms, apologize for leaving him, for causing him so much trouble and so much worry.

But I didn't. I was at a crossroads; I could feel it. I'd thought that I had encountered it months ago when I'd fled Thorne Field, but I'd only been taking the road leading to it. Now I stood at the fork, gazing to the left and right, seeing clearly what would happen if I chose to move in one direction or the other.

If I ran to Tyler, buried my face in his chest and clung to him, as I was wanted to do, I wouldn't be able to tear myself away again. Already, I could feel the ties that I'd been working so hard to sever in the past months beginning to heal and reform, binding me securely to the man who stood so near to me. The bonds that had felt like rope thickly coiled around my heart, squeezing and chafing me inside, were actually something else entirely. The rope that I had been sure was beginning to unravel in my months separated from Tyler, was not rope at all. It was steel, attaching me firmly and irrevocably to him. I knew that now. I would never escape it. Yes, as I was separated from him by time and distance, the steel cable would become easier to ignore. The endurance of the sharp, steel barbs currently mutilating my heart would become a thoughtless, daily routine. But even then, I would never again be truly free and unbound.

I knew that if I allowed myself to take that step toward Tyler, to run into his arms, that cable would never cause me pain again. The barbs would disappear and the cuts would heal. That steel embrace would be every bit as comfortable then as it was painful now. Happiness was that close.

But then another figure moved into the picture. The petite brunette threaded her arm through Tyler's in an absent-minded, but still possessive sort of way. She reached up and stroked Addie's curls, pushing them behind her small ear. Finally, turning to look at what had her husband and child so engrossed, Camille's eyes met mine. First I saw confusion, then a flash of recognition, and finally a slight smile. She nodded politely, her arm still threaded through Tyler's.

The spell was suddenly broken. In that moment, I knew which fork in the road I was going to take, which destiny was mine. I allowed myself the guilty pleasure of one final glance at Tyler and Addie. I drank in the feeling of having heaven so near and took a deep breath. Tyler's face tightened, as if he knew what I was about to do. He took another halting step toward me and the arm not holding Addie made a jerking movement, as if he were about to reach toward me.

I turned and ran.

"Kate!" I actually did hear it this time. His voice rang angelically in my ears and almost caused me to falter in my steps. I felt a choking sob building in my throat and focused stubbornly on my feet to keep it from breaking free. I raced through the celebrating crowd. For the life of me, I couldn't figure out what they were so happy about. Couldn't they tell that the world was ending? Again.

As I left the noise of the crowd behind, it registered that I was hearing pounding footsteps behind me. *No!* my mind reverberated. He *could not* stop me. Staring at him was one thing, but I knew I couldn't bear to face him, to speak to him. Not when my road was so firmly fixed in my mind. A road that would never again intersect with his.

I increased my pace as much as I dared but it wasn't enough. I felt a hand close on my upper arm and yank me to a stop. I was suddenly being held against a broad chest, but it wasn't the sudden feeling of home that I was expecting. I sighed in relief and let the sobs break free of my chest, allowing Jonathan's coat to absorb them. He held me tightly, pressing my head to his chest and whispering soothing words in my ear. He apologized over and over for what had happened, blaming himself. I could hear a tangible fear in his voice, as if he were afraid I was going to break into tiny pieces in his arms.

The fear in his voice was enough to jar me from the painful haze. I firmly told myself to get a grip, and my sobs quickly abated. Once I was quiet, Jonathan pulled back to look into my face. He studied my splotchy visage for a few seconds, evaluating what he saw there.

"Are you all right?" he asked, his voice hesitant.

"Yes," I said, my voice scratchy and resigned. "I'm fine. It was just a *slight* shock." My tone rang with irony.

Jonathan smiled. "Let me walk you back to my place. You look like you could use some alone time. Heaven knows, you won't get any out here."

I smiled tiredly. "Probably not."

We walked in silence for several minutes, Jonathan continually looking behind us. I knew he was ensuring that Tyler was not following us. I allowed my thoughts to roam over the consequences of what had just happened. Tyler now knew where I was. He knew whom I was with. Suddenly my heart constricted.

"Oh, Jonathan!" I cried.

Jonathan jumped. "What?" he exclaimed, stopping to look into my face. "What's wrong?"

"I'm so sorry! He's going to be furious with you, isn't he?" I could feel the tears welling up in my eyes again.

Jonathan looked rather grim. "Yeah, he's probably not too thrilled with me at the moment."

"I've completely ruined your friendship!" I wailed. "I'm a curse! I make everyone miserable! I should just run away to some secluded place where no one can find me and where I can't hurt people."

"Kate, Thorne Field is about as secluded as you can get, and that's where this whole mess started," Jonathan reminded me. "I don't think that's the answer."

I covered my face with my hands. "You're right!" I cried. "Even in seclusion I'm a curse. Oh, I'm such a horrible person! I wouldn't blame you if you never forgave me."

"Oh, relax, Kate," Jonathan said, his voice sounding tired. "I didn't have to promise not to tell Tyler where you were. I knew this could potentially happen. Tyler and I have been friends for years, I'm sure this will blow over . . . eventually." He didn't sound particularly hopeful.

I put my hand on his arm. "I'm so sorry, Jonathan. Please tell him that I made you promise. Tell him it was all my fault. *Please.*"

"Kate, I'm not blaming you," Jonathan insisted. "I understand why you didn't want him to know. Especially now, having seen your reaction to running into him again. Will you just calm down? Everything will be fine."

He reached for my hand and held it firmly against his chest. "Speaking of your reaction to seeing Tyler, you're not going to suddenly go all ballistic on me, are you? You're not going to go into shock or have some kind of fit?"

"I'm not sure," I answered truthfully. "I feel like I've just torn open an old battle wound or something. I hurt so much I'm not sure I can remain standing for much longer. But you know something, Jonathan?"

Jonathan shook his head, looking at me curiously.

"I'll survive," I said, giving him a pained smile. "Sure, it hurts and I hate it, but I know how strong I am now. He was feet from me and I walked away. I *walked away.* Well, ran away, I guess. But even so, I'm stronger than I thought."

"You didn't think you were strong?" Jonathan sounded incredulous. "You amaze me with your strength, Kate. I've never met anyone like you, anyone so unselfish. And you wonder why he fell in love with you."

I snorted and began walking again, pulling Jonathan with me, my thoughts in turmoil. Unselfish? Hardly. I couldn't think of anything more selfish than forcing Jonathan to destroy his friendship with Tyler, just to keep me safe. I was furious with myself. Jonathan kept pace with me and said nothing for several minutes. Finally he squeezed my fingers and chuckled.

"What?" I asked.

"I guess one good thing did come out of this whole fiasco, though," Jonathan said.

"What?" I asked again curiously.

"I never have to call you Marie again," he said, letting go of my hand and pulling me into his side.

Somehow, I managed to smile.

After returning to the condo, Jonathan settled me into my guest room, refusing to leave until I was safely tucked into bed.

"I'll be back in a few," he said, running his fingers down the side of my face. "I'm going to run back to escort Danielle and Mariah back here. Don't do anything crazy or go into shock while I'm gone, okay?"

I rolled my eyes. "I'll do my best," I said, pushing him toward the door.

He laughed and waved before shutting the door behind him. After he left, I sat in bed, letting my mind run over the events of the evening. I had been having such a good time. While somewhat guilty, I had felt warm and comfortable in Jonathan's embrace while we waited for the New Year to come. I remembered the feel of Jonathan's lips on mine as he had kissed me, and the strange warmth that had accompanied the kiss. I allowed my thoughts to linger on Tyler's face as it had gone from astonishment to adoration to betrayal and back. I remembered Addie's arms reaching for me.

Finally, I remembered Camille's possessive hold on Tyler's arm. I mentally examined the gorgeous woman, remembering how, even in the extreme cold, she looked supremely comfortable and put together. I wondered if she and Tyler were happy. He had certainly seemed happy to see her when she had returned months before. I found my mind returning to that day with a clarity I hadn't allowed until now. As I remembered the events of that horrible morning, I realized that Camille had never explained her ten-year absence.

Suddenly, I sat up. Where had she been? How could the lawyer who had managed all of her affairs and who had been in possession of her child be mistaken in her death? How was that even plausible? And why had I never wondered before? I had been so focused on the reality of Camille's return that I had never pondered her absence.

When Jonathan peeked in on me an hour later, I was still sitting up in bed, thinking.

"Not asleep yet?" he said as he seated himself on the end of the bed. "You look pensive. What's up?"

"Jonathan," I began, drumming my fingers on the comforter as I thought, "how did Camille explain her absence? I mean, she was gone for ten years, and her own lawyer told Tyler she was dead. How can she justify something like that?"

Jonathan looked at me thoughtfully. "Well, naturally, 'where have you been?' was the first question that Tyler thought to ask. She told him that when Addie was born, she realized she wasn't ready to be a mother. Especially on her own. She said she was scared, afraid she would ruin Addie's life like she'd ruined her own by leaving Tyler. She knew Tyler could afford to take care of Addie and could give her a good life, but if he believed Camille were alive, he would have sent Addie back to her to raise. So she insisted that her attorney inform Tyler that she had died giving birth. Since her attorney was an old friend of her father's, he felt compelled to agree."

I gaped at him. "She wasn't ready to be a mother? *That* was her excuse?"

Jonathan nodded. "Tyler wasn't terribly impressed either, but I guess she begged for forgiveness and insisted that she had changed. She said that these last ten years had been hell for her. She missed Tyler and wanted to get to know her daughter." Jonathan's expression became one of sympathetic understanding as he looked at me. "I have to admit, she certainly seemed sincere. I was there when she explained. I believe her."

I stared down at my hands. "Apparently he believes her too."

Jonathan reached over and put his hand over mine. "Kate, you have to understand something. I'm not sure you comprehend how deeply Tyler mourned Camille when he thought she had died. Even I was surprised, and I thought I knew Tyler better than almost anyone else."

"But that's just what I don't understand!" I cried. "I know he loved her once, but how could he mourn someone who treated him like that? I mean, when I first came to Thorne Field, he could barely stand to *look* at Addie because of what she represented to him. Now Camille's shown up out of the blue and he's fallen right back in love with her?"

"Think about it," Jonathan said. "It's the ultimate example of hating the sin and loving the sinner. Tyler loved Camille. He hated what she did. Addie was the physical representation of Camille's infidelity. Can't you see why it might be difficult for him to be around her?" Jonathan looked at me earnestly. "And I don't think Tyler ever actually fell *out* of love with Camille, so he never had to fall back in love with her. When she came back, all of those feelings were just waiting for her."

It did make some kind of twisted sense. I had never thought of it quite in those terms. I wasn't through yet, however. "Well, all right, but what about that part? How could he continue to love someone who had hurt him so badly?"

Jonathan sighed. "Think about it this way. When Tyler took Camille back and broke your engagement, conceivably, it could be said that he destroyed everything you thought your life would be. Right?"

I nodded, biting my lip and wondering what he was getting at.

"What if you received news tomorrow that Tyler had been in a fatal accident? Would you mourn? Would you stop loving him?"

I flinched. Jonathan was right. Even though Tyler had hurt me more than I had ever been hurt before, if I heard tomorrow that he had died, I would feel everything inside me die along with him. I loved him with all my heart and soul, and even if I couldn't be with him, his death would destroy me too.

"You see, Kate?" Jonathan said softly. "Can you imagine the pain Tyler experienced? Camille was once the most important part of his life and he lost her . . . in more ways than one. Now he has her back.

As flimsy as her excuses may seem, it's not something Tyler can take for granted."

I nodded. "I understand," I said, looking up at Jonathan and smiling weakly. "Thanks, Jonathan. Nobody can help me understand his twisted psyche quite like you can."

"Well, it helps that I know the guy better than he knows himself." Jonathan smiled tenderly at me. He looked down at his hands for a moment and then back to my face. I felt my pulse accelerate slightly as he slowly reached up toward my face. He traced my lips with his fingertips, and a subtle yearning played on his features as he studied me. At his touch, my thoughts raced back to his kiss in the square, and I blushed.

Wait a second, I *blushed*? What was happening to me? Six months ago I would have firmly pushed his hand away and reprimanded him for the overly familiar behavior. Now I could only smile at him and squeeze his hand in my own before giving it back to him.

"Good night, Jonathan," I said.

"'Night, Kate," he answered and quietly left the room.

fourteen

The following weeks seemed dull and uneventful after the exciting holiday season. Still, I found myself enjoying my class as time went on and I got to know each and every personality. I also was warming to Milton itself, with its friendly people and small-town atmosphere.

At River House, things also began to settle into old and comfortable patterns. Jonathan called several times a week to check on us. His first call after our return from New York was answered by Danielle, who quickly passed the phone to me when she realized who it was.

"Oh, is it for me?" I asked as she shoved the phone into my hand.

"Um, sort of," she said, biting her lip.

"Sort of?" I asked, covering the mouthpiece so the caller couldn't hear our conversation. "How is it *sort of* for me? Who is it?"

I suddenly had a sinking feeling in my gut. As Tyler now knew my whereabouts, it would be easy enough to obtain my phone number. There was no way I was putting the phone to my ear if there was any chance it was Tyler on the other end.

"It's Alex," Danielle said, fighting a smile. "I just figured he'd rather talk to you than me."

I rolled my eyes and put the phone to my ear. "Jonathan?" I asked.

"Kate, is that you?" Jonathan said, his voice puzzled. "What happened to Danielle? I could have sworn she answered the phone."

"She did," I said. "She's maintaining her self-proclaimed role of matchmaker."

"Oh," Jonathan chuckled. "Well, I don't mind if you don't. How are you?"

"What does that matter?" I asked. "Have you seen Tyler yet? Does he hate you?"

Jonathan laughed. "It matters a lot to me. But it sounds to me like you're just the same as when you left, so I won't press for details. As for Tyler, no, I haven't seen him yet. He took Camille and Addie back to Oakley, and he won't be back in New York till the fifteenth."

"Oh," I said. I wasn't sure if I was upset or relieved at the news. It would do wonders for my peace of mind if Jonathan were able to tell me that Tyler had forgiven him for keeping his promise to me, but somehow I knew that that was unlikely. Tyler would probably need awhile to forgive and forget this time. The thought made me physically ill. I had never wanted to injure Jonathan and Tyler's friendship, but as I thought back to the day I had extracted the promise from Jonathan, I wondered how I could have expected anything else. I felt again that overwhelming shame for my selfishness. How could I have required Jonathan to keep something so important from his best friend? I was the world's biggest heel.

"Kate, are you still there?" Jonathan asked.

"Yes, I'm still here," I said. "Jonathan, I'm such a jerk. I'm so sorry."

"Um, okay," Jonathan said. "Not really following your train of thought here, Kate."

"I can't believe I made you promise not to tell Tyler where I was," I said miserably. "How could I have thought he would never find out? Ugh, I am such an idiot!"

"Come on, stop it," Jonathan said. "I thought you were over this. I told you I went into that promise knowing full well that this would probably happen. It will be fine. Please stop worrying about it."

"Right," I said sarcastically. I was so angry at myself that I found I didn't want to talk to him anymore. I wanted to ram my head through the kitchen wall instead. "Hey, I have some things to do, so I need to go," I said, trying to unwind my voice from where it was tightly bunched in my vocal chords. "Do you want to talk to Danielle or Mariah?"

"Oh," Jonathan said, sounding disappointed. "Um, no thanks. I'll just call in a few days. Bye, Kate."

"Bye," I sighed. I hung up the phone and stared into space for a few seconds until a hand waving in front of my face woke me up.

"Helloooo," Danielle said. "What's up with you?"

"Oh, just thinking," I answered.

"About Alex," Danielle said knowingly.

"Yes, but not in the way you're imagining," I said. "I really wish you and Mariah would get that thought out of your heads. Nothing is going to happen, you know."

"Uh-huh," Danielle said, smiling at me. "That's what you think. Oh, Marie, it's so obvious! Alex is head-over-heels in love with you. I've never seen him so whooped!"

"What?" I said, my head snapping back to look at her. "You think he's actually in love with me?"

"Of course he is," said Mariah, coming into the kitchen with a glass in her hand. "You act like this is news or something."

"He's not in love with me!" I protested. "Okay, I know he kind of likes me, but—"

"*Likes* you?" Danielle snorted. "What is this, middle school? Look, Marie, I know you've known my brother for a few months, but I've known him for years, and when I say he's in love, he's in love."

I was horrified. "Well, what am I going to do about it?" I cried.

"What do you mean?" asked Mariah. For the first time, she started to look worried. "Is it a problem?"

"Uh, yeah!" I said, my eyes wide. "Kind of a big one, actually."

"Are you saying you don't like him?" Danielle asked. She looked like she was gearing up for a good argument.

"Oh, come on. Of course I like him!" I said. "But I don't love him! Not even close!"

Danielle and Mariah shared a look. They both took a step toward me and I could hear the persuasive tone before it actually hit my eardrums.

"Marie, of course you love him!" Danielle said earnestly. "You haven't seen the way you look at him, but we have. Okay, you may not feel as strongly for Alex as you did for Tyler, but you definitely love him. There's no doubt about it."

Mariah nodded but didn't bother to verbally back up her sister's arguments.

"But I don't!" I said, but my voice didn't hold the conviction that it should. For some reason, my mind was flipping through images it had collected during the time I had spent with the man in question. Jonathan pulling me suddenly into his arms as we strolled through a garden at sundown. His adoring gaze as he told me of his hopes for the future of "us." The injured look on his face when he stumbled across Tyler's marriage proposal. Jonathan's face descending slowly toward mine on Christmas Day. His arms holding me upright on an ice rink. Laughing uproariously with him as we studied an abstract painting. And perhaps most of all, Jonathan's lips on mine in Times Square on New Years. And I couldn't pretend I hadn't felt anything. I put my hands to my face.

"Oh my," I said softly. "Oh . . . my."

"See?" said Danielle excitedly, jumping up and down. "You know exactly what we're talking about!"

I ignored them and walked out of the kitchen, my hands still held to my face in wonder. Did I love Jonathan? If I did, it certainly wasn't the all-consuming passion I felt for Tyler. Wasn't that what love was supposed to feel like? I knew I *liked* Jonathan. More than liked him. I needed him, especially now. In the few short weeks he had spent with us, I had grown to depend on him. He was truly one of my closest friends.

But did I love him? I didn't know.

I waited all day on the fifteenth of January for Jonathan to call. Finally around 10:30 p.m., I couldn't wait any longer and called him instead.

"Hello?" He sounded dead tired.

"Jonathan?" I said hesitantly.

"Kate!" All the fatigue was immediately replaced with genuine pleasure. "This is a nice surprise! How are you?"

"I'm fine, I guess," I said impatiently. "Jonathan, Tyler came back today, right?"

Silence.

"Jonathan?"

"Yes, he did." Jonathan's voice once again sounded as if he were carrying the weight of the world on his shoulders.

"And?"

"And what?"

"Oh, for crying out loud! Stop this, you know exactly why I called!" I cried. "What happened?"

"Nothing," Jonathan said simply.

"Nothing?! You mean he acted as if nothing had happened at all?" I couldn't keep the relief from seeping into my voice. "Well, that's wonderful!"

"Hang on, Kate. That's not what I said," Jonathan said quickly.

My heart sank. "What do you mean?"

"Well, he didn't blow up at me or cause a scene or anything. He actually hasn't said a word to me. But I know he's furious. We had an executive staff meeting today and he couldn't even look at me." Jonathan's voice was haggard.

I felt sick.

"So I've decided on something that may interest you," Jonathan continued. "Tyler mentioned in the meeting today that he wants a junior partner to oversee a merger in Japan and to stay on as head of the operation over there for a while. I've decided to volunteer."

"Japan?" I breathed. "Why?"

"Kate, he can't stand the sight of me," Jonathan said, the pain in his voice more pronounced now. "He would never send me away himself, so I think the best thing I can do for him is to voluntarily leave for a while. And I know he wants me to take it—"

"That's ridiculous!" I interrupted rudely. "How can you possibly know that if he hasn't spoken to you?"

"I know him," Jonathan said simply. "Every time he looks at me, all he's going to see is you and me in Times Square. Would you wish something like that on him?"

"It can't be affecting him that much," I insisted. "After all, he's the one that chose to let me go."

"That's not entirely true," Jonathan argued. "As I recall, you're the one who ran off without so much as a warning. He may be married to Camille, but that doesn't mean his love for you has just evaporated, does it? Stuff like that only happens in the movies. Real life is messy."

I scoffed, ignoring the comment. Even though I felt a morbid kind of pleasure knowing Tyler still wanted me, there was also something disturbing about it. How did Camille feel, knowing she didn't hold 100 percent of her husband's heart? Did she even realize it? I tried not to think about that part too deeply. I didn't want to feel sorry for Camille. "How long do you think it will take for him to get over this?" I asked, my voice sharper than I intended.

"I'm not sure," he said. "But this transfer is a minimum three-year commitment."

"Three years?!" I screeched. "No way am I letting you do this, Jonathan! Danielle and Mariah will kill you! And when I tell them it's actually all my fault, they'll kill me!"

I was horrified. This was even worse than I had imagined. Tyler was furious but cared about his friend too much to actually do what he wanted to do to him, which was send him as far away as possible. So Jonathan was throwing himself on the chopping block to make up for it. He was going to willingly separate himself from his family and friends. For three whole years. And it was all because of me. The thought of how Danielle and Mariah would react to the news was a like a punch in the gut from a heavyweight boxing champion.

"Jonathan, is there anything I can say to convince you not to do this?" I asked, close to tears. "I can't stand the thought of you leaving because of me."

"Oh, stop it, Kate," Jonathan said grouchily. "You're not making me feel any better by being a martyr. Look, I've got a lot on my plate right now, so I've got to go. I promise I don't blame you, all right?"

"Hang on a second. *Me*, a martyr?" I shot at him. "I'm not the one sending myself to a foreign country for three years just to ease my conscience. I promise you, Jonathan Kelly, if you go through with this, I will never forgive you."

"I've got another call, Kate," he said, but I knew he was lying. It was nearly eleven, after all. "I've got to go. I'll call soon."

"Jonathan—" I began.

He hung up.

I knew the second Jonathan had broken the news of his voluntary transfer to his sisters. He told Danielle first, and her scream probably woke the residents of the cemetery down the street.

"Mariah! Marie!" she shrieked. "Get down here! Now!"

I was down the stairs and in the kitchen in less than three seconds with Mariah on my heels.

"What is it?" Mariah cried. "What's wrong?"

"Alex . . ." Danielle couldn't seem to get the words out. She was holding the phone to her chest like it was a lifeline. I could hear Jonathan's concerned voice on the other end.

"Alex what?" pressed Mariah, sounding slightly panicked. "What's going on?"

"Alex . . . ," Danielle tried again, but trailed off for the second time.

"Oh, give me that," said Mariah, yanking the phone from Danielle's hand. "Hello? Alex, is that you?" She listened for a second. "She's in shock. What on earth did you say to her?" Pause. "What opportunity?" Another pause. "What? Japan?" she repeated faintly. "For three years?" Mariah looked like her legs might give out. I quickly led her to a chair and sat her down. I took the phone gently from her and held it to my ear.

"I told you they would react like this," I said without preamble.

"Are they okay?" Jonathan asked, his voice concerned.

"No, they're both on the verge of a coronary," I answered. "Jonathan, you can't do this. Can't you just stay out of Tyler's way for a while? Why do you have to move to the other side of the world?"

"I can't stay here and 'stay out of Tyler's way,' Kate," Jonathan said, exasperated. "Our offices are less than ten feet apart. And I'm not just going for him. I think I could use some time away. Some time to think through some things."

"What things are so pressing that you have to go to Japan to think about them?" I demanded.

Jonathan chuckled. "You'll just have to trust me on this. This is what I need to do. You won't change my mind."

"When are you leaving?" I asked, feeling the hopelessness well up inside me.

"I plan to leave a week from Thursday," he answered.

"What? So soon?" I cried. "Will we even get to see you before you go?"

"Why, Kate," Jonathan said, his voice teasing, yet sounding the slightest bit pleased. "Could it be that you are going to miss me?"

"Of course I'm going to miss you, you idiot," I snarled, sounding as if the last thing I planned to do was miss him. "Are you coming up here before you leave?"

"If you want me to, I'll come."

"Then come," I said.

Jonathan laughed. "I'll be there on Tuesday."

Jonathan arrived on Tuesday night, two days before his departure for Japan. When he arrived in the entrance hall with only two pieces of luggage, Danielle looked scandalized.

"That's all you're taking with you?" she cried. "What did you do, sell all your earthly possessions?"

Jonathan laughed. "No, Dani. I'm keeping almost everything in my condo back in New York. The firm is providing me with everything I need in Tokyo. I'm basically just taking my clothes with me." Jonathan briefly hugged his sisters and then turned to me.

"Have you forgiven me yet?" he asked with a smile.

I did not smile back. "Of course not," I huffed. "I still think you're being ridiculous and dramatic. This is not the answer."

"Kate, you have to let me do this my way," Jonathan said sternly.

"Well, your way is dumb," I snorted, turning away from him. "Why didn't you just tell him that everything was my fault and if he wants to be angry, he can be angry at me?" I could feel Danielle's and Mariah's eyes on me, no doubt wondering what I was talking about. As far as I knew, Jonathan had not informed them of the real reason for his transfer.

"We've been through this a hundred times, and I'm not going to discuss it," Jonathan answered, turning back to his sisters. "So what's for dinner? I'm starved."

The confused looks abandoned Mariah and Danielle's faces as they rushed to care for the brother that would soon be thousands of miles away from them. Within twenty minutes we were all seated at the dining room table with bowls of hot chili in front of each of us. We ate in silence for several minutes before Danielle finally spoke up.

"So, will we get to see you at all in the next three years, or are you required to stay in Japan for the duration?"

"I'll be home for the holidays," Jonathan answered with a smile. "So you'll actually get to see me in less than a year." I guess the three of us didn't look particularly mollified, because Jonathan's smile fell off his face as he looked around the table at us. "Come on, guys. It's not going to be that bad. You only see me five or six times a year anyway."

"Yes, but we know we can see you anytime," Mariah pointed out, tears filling her eyes. "Knowing that we can't see you even if we want to makes it that much harder."

Jonathan came to his feet and walked around the table to pull Mariah into a hug. Danielle rushed to join the embrace. I watched them as they stood in the middle of the dining room for several minutes, their arms wrapped around each other while Danielle and Mariah sniffed and wiped tears away. I felt like the biggest jerk in existence. It was my fault that this family was being torn apart. Jonathan kissed each of them on the cheek before letting them go back to their seats. None of us was particularly hungry anymore. Abandoning the idea of dinner, we moved our silent moodiness into the sitting room and sat around the fire, each of us absorbed in our own thoughts.

"I think I'm going to head to bed," Jonathan said after nearly an hour of silence, getting to his feet. "I'm a little tired from the drive."

He kissed Mariah and Danielle each on the cheek and then walked toward me. I held out my hand like an idiot, actually expecting him to shake it. He ignored it and bent down, brushing a soft kiss across my lips. Both my breath and my protest caught in my chest and I stared at him as he walked away, a tiny smile playing around the corners of his mouth.

Around three the following afternoon, a knock sounded on my bedroom door as I sat on my bed sketching. "Well, hi," I said as I opened the door to see Jonathan standing there. "Haven't seen you much today."

"Danielle and Mariah have been monopolizing my time," he admitted ruefully. "But I was wondering if you might be interested in taking a drive with me. I'd like to spend some time with you before I leave tomorrow."

"Sounds nice." I smiled in pleased surprise at the suggestion. Grabbing my coat from the closet, I walked down the stairs and out the door with him. We climbed into his rental car, a silver BMW this time, and made our way through the snowy streets of Milton.

"So how have you been in the past few weeks, Kate?" Jonathan asked. "Every time I've spoken to you, you've either ignored the question or given me a worthless answer."

"I'm fine," I assured him. "I've been more worried about you and Tyler than anything. Has he spoken to you yet?"

"Only the necessities. When I volunteered for the transfer, he did tell me that he had crafted the position with me in mind." He looked sideways at me with "I told you so" written all over his face. "That was all I needed to hear," he said when I ignored him.

"But that doesn't necessarily mean that he's angry with you, does it?" I said, my voice slightly high-pitched. How could Tyler be so furious as to silently encourage his best friend to move a world away? It seemed so heartless and, therefore, completely unlike him.

"Right, Kate. What else could that possibly mean, given the circumstances?"

"I know," I said, sighing. "I realize you're sick of hearing this, Jonathan, but I really am sorry."

"I know you are." He smiled. "Even if you didn't keep saying it, I would already know it. Don't worry, though. Despite the fact that I'm going to miss you and my sisters, I'm actually pretty excited. This is a great opportunity for me."

"Well, I'm glad you're excited about it. But I still feel guilty for Danielle and Mariah's sake."

"Yeah," Jonathan said, the smile on his face slipping slightly. "Well, there's not really anything we can do about that. They'll be fine. Hey," he said, quickly changing the subject and allowing a boyish smile to light up his face. "There's a place around here I'd like to show you. Is that okay?"

"Sure," I answered, grateful for the change of topic.

We drove for ten minutes in complete silence, the road winding through snowy woods. Finally, Jonathan pulled off onto a slick gravel path through the trees. He drove about fifty feet until the highway was completely concealed from our view.

"This is as far as we can drive in. Are you up for a chilly walk?" Jonathan asked.

"Why not?" I said, glad I had decided to wear a pair of heavy boots, mostly just to protect my wimpy California feet from the cold.

We walked for about ten minutes until we came upon one of the most beautiful sights I had ever seen. A frosty, glassy pond appeared in front of us, frozen solid. The snow-covered trees surrounding it made it look like the set of some 1950s Hollywood musical.

"Oh," I breathed, entranced.

"Pretty amazing, isn't it?" Jonathan said, smiling at me. "Our parents used to bring Mariah, Dani, and me ice skating here every Christmas Eve when the girls were in high school. Even though I was at Northwestern at the time, I still made sure to come each year."

"You three have gotten along that well since your parents married?"

"Well, the girls knew that their mom was lonely, since their dad had been gone for so long. So when she met my dad, they were all for it. I took a bit more convincing, since my mom had only been gone for a few years, but who can resist those big green eyes?" Jonathan smiled.

"Tell me about it," I said, thinking about Danielle's pressure to include my sketches in the Milton Art Show. "They have the power to get you to agree to things you never would ordinarily," I sighed.

Jonathan seemed to be reading my mind. "Danielle showed me your sketches. You're very talented, Kate," he said with admiration.

"I'm the beginningest of beginners," I said, laughing. "But Danielle is determined to get my drawings for that art show."

"I think it's a good opportunity. You should do it."

"We'll see," I said vaguely, ready for another subject change.

"My sisters are crazy about you, you know," Jonathan said, a strange smile on his face.

I smiled in response.

"They're not the only ones," he continued, looking at me pointedly.

"Jonathan—" I began, but he cut me off.

"Kate, I'm going to say it whether you like it or not, so you might as well just let me."

I sighed and looked away.

"You know how I feel about you. You've known it since I showed up on your cabin doorstep at Thorne Field. I'm in love with you. And what's more, I'm convinced I'm more in love with you than Tyler ever was."

I watched him, unsure of what to think. He was giving my powers of observation much more credit than they deserved. I hadn't known he was in love with me until his sisters had informed me of the fact.

"I'm not telling you this so you'll come with me," Jonathan said, taking my hand. "I'm not asking you to marry me or anything . . . at least not yet. All I want is for you to think about this while I'm gone. Three years is a long time. Maybe even long enough for you to get over Tyler. Maybe not. Either way, I just want you to consider the possibility of you and me. You seemed reluctant the last time I asked you to do that, but I think things might be a little different now."

I just stared at him, still mulling his words over in my head. He was right, they were no revelation to me—not after my conversation with Danielle and Mariah, at least—but I still wasn't sure what my reaction should be. I knew my feelings for Jonathan were sincere, but nowhere near as powerful as the fire Tyler evoked in me—yet Tyler was gone and Jonathan was here. Wasn't Jonathan the next best thing if I couldn't have what I truly wanted? Was I doomed to spend the rest of my days alone and longing for the man I could never have, or could I find happiness with someone else?

But there was another problem besides the fact that I seemed to be irrevocably tethered to someone else. Jonathan wasn't of my faith. He couldn't take me to the temple. So, at least for now, my answer had to be no, regardless.

"Jonathan, it just wouldn't—" I began, but he shook his head.

"I don't need an answer now," he said. "Just think. That's all I want, okay?"

Sighing, I nodded slowly.

"Good." Jonathan smiled in response to my hesitant nod. "Now let's get going. We need to be back in time to grab Danielle and Mariah for our last dinner together."

I allowed him to pull me back toward the car, my mind still racing through his declaration and the new path it had created for me.

The day of Jonathan's departure for Tokyo was full of half-hearted attempts to pretend that it wasn't a huge deal that he was moving thousands of miles away. We spent the morning at River House, talking and laughing, speaking of interesting things that Jonathan could conceivably encounter in that part of the world. Jonathan didn't seem nervous at all about his move to a foreign country. If anything, he seemed eager. I wasn't sure how I felt about that.

I had been thinking almost constantly about our conversation the day before, but he was acting as though it had never happened. I suspected that he was trying to tell me that he wasn't going to pressure me. I appreciated it, but unfortunately it didn't dispel any of my confusion.

As Jonathan stood in the entryway that afternoon, the three of us gathered around him, the first vestiges of nervousness and uncertainty played at the corners of his eyes and lips. I felt my heart soften just a little as I watched him hug his sisters tightly. His eyes shone, but no tears fell. When he finally turned to me, he stood looking at me as if unsure what to do. Not waiting for any kind of invitation, I rushed forward and threw my arms around his neck.

"I can't believe you're doing this," I said softly into his navy blue sweater. My voice was tight. "But even though I'm beyond irritated with you, I *am* going to miss you."

Jonathan's arms came around me in a tight embrace. "I know," he said, and I could hear the smile in his voice. I felt his lips in my hair on the top of my head. "Take care of yourself, Kate." He tightened his arms around me for a few seconds, squeezing me extra hard, and then released me abruptly. I backed away and watched as he bent to pick up his luggage.

He walked toward the door, then stopped suddenly and turned to face me. "Oh, by the way," he said with a twinkle in his eye. "I thought of another good thing that has come from all of this."

"Yeah?" I said, unconvinced. "What's that?"

"Now that Tyler knows who you've been with, he could, conceivably, come see you anytime."

I flinched. Was he trying to be funny? I could just imagine Tyler Thorne showing up on the doorstep of River House and demanding to see me, aggravating the steel-ridden scars already mutilating my insides. How was that a good thing? But Jonathan wasn't finished.

"And because he already knows where you are, he now has no reason to continue the search with your uncle." He smiled broadly at me.

Ahhh, I thought. I was beginning to understand.

"Here," Jonathan said. He reached into his pocket and pulled out a folded piece of paper. I opened it and read, "Jack Evans, Blue Heron Publishing, Boston, Mass." The paper also contained phone numbers for my uncle's office and cell, as well as his company email address.

"Where did you get this?" I gasped, holding the miraculous bit of paper to my chest.

"I've had it since you first disappeared and Tyler asked for my help," Jonathan answered, looking slightly guilty. "I decided not to give it to you. I thought the temptation to contact him might be too much for you to resist."

"It probably would have," I said softly, my eyes shining. I reached up quickly and kissed him on the cheek. He looked surprised and delighted. "Thank you," I said sincerely.

"You're welcome," he said. He grinned down at me, but the smile began to fade almost immediately. Suddenly his look became more intense, more sincere than any I had ever seen on his face.

"I love you," he said, almost fiercely. Then he turned and walked out the door, shutting it behind him.

fifteen

I didn't get up the courage to contact my uncle Jack until nearly three weeks later. Each day I would pull out that piece of paper, unfold it, and study the words written there for minutes on end, my mind racing. Then I would fold it again and return it to my pocket. I had done it so many times that small, frayed holes were beginning to appear in the creases of the thick paper.

There were several reasons I could identify for my hesitancy. Would my uncle be angry at me for waiting so long to contact him? Would he even want to see me? What if he didn't like me? What if he ended up with the same opinion of me as all my other relatives? None of them could stand to have me in the same room with them.

It was Jonathan's disappointment that finally spurred me into action. He called once a week to ask after us and let us know how he was adjusting to the culture, the work, the food, and the huge difference in time zones. It was during one of these weekly conversations that he finally brought up the topic of my uncle Jack.

It was lunchtime at school one cloudy Thursday in late February, and I was in my classroom as usual. I sat behind the desk with my feet propped up on the edge, the phone cradled between my ear and my shoulder as I shoveled yogurt into my mouth.

"So, how is Jack?" Jonathan asked, his voice registering sincere interest. "Much better I hope, now that he knows you're alive and safe."

My feet fell off the edge of the desk and yogurt splattered up out of the plastic container and all over my blue shirt. I didn't even notice.

"Ummm . . . ," I hedged. I suddenly felt a twinge of nausea. I closed my eyes, knowing exactly what Jonathan would say when I told him I hadn't summoned the courage to call my uncle yet. "Well, I haven't actually, um, gotten around to, um, calling him yet."

"You haven't gotten around to . . . wait, what?" Jonathan sounded slightly confused. "Sorry, this connection is really bad, say that again."

I sighed. "You heard me right. I said I haven't gotten around to calling him yet."

"Now wait just one second!" Jonathan said, instantly irate. "You're telling me that even though you've been dying to meet the last living relative who will claim you for more than six months, when you finally get the chance, *you don't do it*? Do you have any idea how much that man wants to get to know you?"

"Don't yell at me," I pleaded, sounding petulant. "I'm terrified, Jonathan. What am I supposed to say to him?"

"Oh, I don't know," Jonathan said. His voice was sharply sarcastic. "How about, 'Hi, Uncle Jack, it's me Kate. You know, the niece for whom you've been desperately searching for the past *ten years*. Just thought I'd drop you a line and let you know I'm not lying in a ditch somewhere.' That might work."

"You know, if you're trying to make this easier, you're not," I said scathingly. "And stop being such a drama queen. He knows I'm not dead. Tyler must have told him. After all, he just saw me a month ago."

"I wouldn't count on it. Tyler's been kind of MIA for the past month. I'm not really sure why, since he doesn't exactly confide in me anymore, but I'm guessing that you weren't the only one traumatized by the New Year's encounter. Anyway, given how little he's been around the office, I doubt he's been all that accessible to Jack."

"You really think he's still dwelling on New Year's?" I was

stunned. True, the memory of the expression on Tyler's face in Times Square was the stuff of nightmares and frequently haunted me, but if I tried hard enough, I could manage to escape it. At least for a few hours at a time. But Tyler? Tyler had always seemed so . . . unshakable. I just couldn't fathom that one unexpected meeting would affect him so deeply.

"Yeah, I do," Jonathan's matter-of-fact answer broke into my thoughts. "I don't know for sure, obviously. But something's happened to make him retreat to Thorne Field for nearly all of January and February. He's actually there right now. That's unusual, especially for this time of year. Joshua tells me that Tyler's been making appearances at the office for important meetings, but for the most part, he's doing all of his work remotely from Utah. But stop changing the subject." His voice was once again full of stern reproach. "Call your uncle. Today. As soon as you hang up. He needs to see you, and you know you need to see him."

"You're right," I said, sighing. "I'm being a coward."

"Yes, you are," Jonathan said, but his voice was much softer now. "But you've got nothing to worry about. You'll never regret getting to know Jack. He's a great guy."

"I'm sure he is," I answered, smiling into the phone. "Thanks, Jonathan."

"That's what I'm here for," he said and I could hear his answering smile. "To shame you into doing the right thing. Let me know how it goes. And have a good week, okay?"

"You too. Be safe. Tokyo's a big city. Don't go getting run over by a bus or anything."

Jonathan laughed. "I'll do my best to steer clear of the buses. I love you, Kate," he said.

He ended every call like this, and it never failed to send a pang of guilt stabbing to my core. My answering phrase was always a hesitant, "I miss you too, Jonathan." Today was no exception. But after I had delivered the practiced line, I added, "a lot." That had to count for something, right?

"Bye, Kate," he answered, and I almost didn't hear the accompanying sigh of frustration. Almost.

I sat and stared at the phone for several minutes, thinking about my uncle. I could do this. It was just a simple phone call to a relative. No sweat. No need to remember that phone calls to relatives, in my limited experience, were generally things to dread. I took a deep breath and picked up the receiver, dialed the number that I had committed to memory weeks earlier, and waited while the telephone rang on the other end of the line. I heard the click of the connection, and my breath seemed to hang strangely suspended in my chest. I couldn't remember how to exhale. All my focus was centered on the next sound reverberating across the miles of telephone wire.

"Jack Evans," came the deep, pleasant voice on the other end.

I opened my mouth to respond, but it was as if my vocal chords had vanished. No sound escaped my throat, and I sat there, my mouth gaping open and closed like some kind of demented goldfish.

"Hello?" the voice said. "Is anyone there?"

"Yes," I finally rasped desperately, afraid he would hang up and I would have to go through the whole ordeal all over again.

"Oh," Jack said and waited for me to speak. When I again couldn't seem to phrase any kind of coherent sentence, Jack cleared his throat. "Can I help you?"

"Yes," I said again. I was inwardly lecturing myself fiercely for this ridiculous show of weakness. Finally managing to get a hold on my voice, I squeaked, "Uh, hello, Mr. Evans. I got your number from Jonathan Kelly."

"Jonathan Kelly? That overpaid Wall Street guru? Why exactly is he handing out my cell phone number?" He sounded irritated. Marvelous. "Look, if you're trying to get something published, you have to submit your manuscript like anybody else, even if you *do* know Jonathan Kelly," Jack informed me coldly.

"No, no," I attempted to explain, but he rode right over me.

"Also, tell Jonathan from me that I have no interest in hearing from him, Tyler Thorne, or anyone associated with them ever again unless they can give me some concrete information on the whereabouts of my niece."

"Mr. Evans, that's why I'm calling," I said quickly before he could hang up.

"What?" he said, sounding as if he hadn't understood me at all.

That didn't surprise me as he had probably had the phone halfway hung up before I had spoken.

"I'm calling about your niece," I repeated.

"My niece? What about my niece?"

"I, uh, know where she is," I said lamely.

"What?" he gasped. "You found her? Really? How is she? Where is she? Is she okay?" Jack's voice was suddenly charged with an energy I had not anticipated.

"She's here," I said. "In Boston."

I wasn't quite sure why I was insisting on speaking in third person. But now that I'd started, I couldn't really switch over to first person and start referring to myself as "I."

"She'd like to meet you," I continued. I considered telling him that I was some kind of private detective who specialized in finding random lost relatives uninvited, but he didn't seem to care who I was.

"When can I see her?" he shouted into the phone, making my ears ring.

"You can see her whenever you'd like," I said, a soft smile lighting my face. He wanted to see me. He was *eager* to see me. In fact, it sounded as though he could hardly contain himself. I was sure I had never inspired such a response in a relative before. The relief was so sweet I could nearly taste it.

"Today? Right now?" Jack cried. "Bring her to my corporate offices! Or you can tell me where she is and I'll come get her!"

"No, that's all right," I said quickly. "She's actually working right now, but how about, say, four o'clock this afternoon?"

"Fine! Good! Perfect!" Jack said, his voice sounding light and enthused. "My offices are at 676 Liberty Way. Tell her she can come straight up. Twenty-sixth floor."

"I'll do that. Thank you, Mr. Evans," I said.

"No, thank *you*," said Jack. "I really can't thank you enough, Ms. . . . what did you say your name was?"

"Um, Rivers," I said, grabbing the first name that came to me. "Charlotte Rivers."

"Rivers. . . ." Jack was musing now. "And you say you know Jonathan? You wouldn't happen to be related to him, would you? He mentioned to me that his stepsisters are named Rivers. In fact, they live around here somewhere."

"Um, distant cousin," I fibbed. "Well, Mr. Evans, I will convey your message to your niece and she will be at your offices at four o'clock this afternoon."

"Wonderful!" he cried.

I quickly hung up and put my head down on my desk, my breathing coming a little faster than usual. Although I still felt keyed up, my heart was light. One of the dreams I had been reaching out for was finally within my grasp. It was a lifeline, and I grabbed onto it with both hands, praying that this time I would never have to let go.

That face. It was a face I hadn't seen for more than fifteen years. It was the same face that smiled up at me every day from the picture by my bed, only maybe with a few more lines around the eyes and mouth. The same face that had been growing dimmer and dimmer in my memory as the years passed. The publishing office grew somewhat hazy around me as I gaped openly at the reincarnation of my dead father.

"Kate!" the man said, his voice a delighted rasp. His eyes were shining with unshed tears as he halted in front of me and took my hands in his. He studied me silently for a long moment. "You look so much like your mother," he said finally, his voice almost reverent. He leaned forward and kissed me softly on the cheek. "I can even see a bit of Matthew in you, you poor thing." He laughed softly.

I stood stock still, staring up at him.

"I'm your uncle Jack," he said as he squeezed my hands. "Your dad's twin brother."

"T-twin?" I stuttered, unable to tear my eyes away from his face. It made complete sense since the resemblance between the two brothers was perfect, but my mind was having a hard time grasping the reality. I was staring at the last living connection to my parents, a man who obviously wanted to know me and love me. And instead of the unknown character I expected to find, his familiar appearance dispelled my fear and discomfort, replacing it immediately with trust and affection. My eyes searched his face hungrily. He had the same strong, square jaw. The same longish sandy hair and laugh lines crinkling the corners of his eyes. In some small way, it was like getting a piece of my father back—an unexpected and miraculous gift. "You're my dad's twin brother?" I verified.

"I am," Jack said, his smile dimming a little. "You didn't know? Well, I didn't expect you to know much about me, but I was sure your dad would at least have told you that."

"Um, no," I said cautiously. "No, he didn't. He actually never told me anything about you. I didn't even know you existed until about six months ago."

Jack closed his eyes and his expression was deeply pained. He squeezed my hands again, almost unconsciously. "I guess I shouldn't be surprised," he said softly.

"What do you mean?" I asked, wondering what could cause such a look of disappointment to cross my uncle's face. "Why wouldn't my dad tell me anything about you?"

Jack avoided the question. "Why don't you come and sit down, Kate? I want to hear all about you. We have twenty-three years to catch up on, you know." He took my arm and began leading me toward an overstuffed leather couch.

"Mr. Evans," I began, about to insist he tell me why he and my father had been estranged. "I—"

"Good grief!" my uncle interrupted, a good-natured smile erupting on his face. "Don't you dare call me that! I'm Jack, or Uncle Jack, if you prefer."

"Uncle Jack," I began again. "Why won't you tell me why my dad never mentioned you? Why have I never seen you before? Why did you never come to see us?"

Uncle Jack put a hand to his face. "It's ancient history, Kate," he said, his voice sounding suddenly tired. "It's better if I don't think about it."

Despite his attempt to hide it, I could see the pain pulsing in his eyes, so I didn't press him. But the fact that he didn't want to tell me just made my curiosity burn hotter. I wasn't giving up. Someday I would approach the subject again. I allowed Uncle Jack to move the conversation on to other topics. He asked me for my life story and indicated that he knew from his conversations with Tyler and

Jonathan that I had lived with the Whitmans, despite Aunt Sarah's claim that she had never heard of me. When I told of my move to the Brooks' his expression showed no surprise, so I knew Tyler had informed him of that part of my history as well. In fact, Uncle Jack showed no surprise at any part of my story. Tyler had apparently filled in all the blanks of my past. My uncle Jack already knew much more about me than I knew about him. However, as I told him of Thorne Field, and Tyler, and Mariah and Danielle, and Jonathan, his expression began to change. It flitted from surprise to angst to anger to humor and back.

As I approached the end of my story, I realized that I was leaving nothing out. I did not edit my story at all. For the first time in a very long time, I laid everything out on the table. I revealed the innermost feelings of my heart to this familiar stranger. And my Uncle Jack listened intently, his hand wrapped securely around mine.

By the time I finished, it was fully dark outside and my voice was hoarse. "And here I am," I croaked. "That's about it."

"So, you and Tyler Thorne were engaged and then when this Camille woman showed up, he dropped you like a sack of potatoes, is that it?" Jack demanded.

I flinched. "Well, not exactly like that," I said weakly.

Jack sounded furious. "He neglected to mention the part about booting you out of his house when he was filling me in on his connection to you."

"He didn't force me to leave. I just did it to make it easier on him," I defended. "And because I felt like it was necessary. My responsibility."

Jack waved a careless hand. "Never mind him. What about Jonathan Kelly?" he said, a strange look in his eye.

"What about him?" I asked, confused.

"Well?" he asked. "He's told you how he feels about you. What are you going to do about it?"

"Do?" I said, confused. "What can I do? He doesn't even live here anymore. And I don't know how I feel about him."

"He's a good man, Katie," said Uncle Jack. "Despite his unhealthy level of income. I don't pretend to know him well, but I can feel it."

I smiled, my heart warming even more to the man. As far as I could see, my uncle wasn't exactly struggling financially himself.

"I know he is," I assured him. "And I think a part of me does love him."

"But?" Uncle Jack prompted.

"But I can't," I said softly.

"You're still in love with Thorne," he said knowingly.

"Always." I sighed. "It's like my heart is refusing to open to anyone else. I wish I *could* love Jonathan. Heaven knows I'm not happy pining for a man I can never have."

"Kate, you're acting like you have no say in the matter," Jack said. "The heart you're talking about is *yours*. It's not an appendage of someone else's that just happens to reside in your chest. You dictate how your heart responds to outside forces."

"I'm not sure I do," I said. "Tyler would be so much happier without me in the picture. If I could, I would give him wholeheartedly to Camille. Then his family would be complete, and I wouldn't feel like I was constantly fighting for air."

"Would you?" Uncle Jack said, raising an eyebrow. "Would you really give him up, if you could?"

I looked at him. His face showed skepticism at my declaration, and it made me think. Was I being completely honest? If it were my choice, would I immediately bottle up all the love I had for Tyler inside me and give it away?

"No," I said resignedly. "I guess I wouldn't."

"You see what I mean?" Jack said, patting my hand. "Your heart holds on to him because you don't want to let him go. Give Jonathan a chance, Katie. You won't regret it."

I looked down at our entwined hands for a minute before speaking. "I know Tyler is gone forever, but I'm just not ready to let go yet," I said, looking up at him. "Don't worry, Uncle Jack. I won't be like this forever. I just need some time." I smiled and he smiled back at me.

"In the meantime, try to let Jonathan in a little," he said. "He'll be good for you."

"I don't think I should," I said. "Even though I wish I could."

Uncle Jack looked confused. "Why not?" he asked.

"Well, we don't really have the same beliefs," I explained.

His look of confusion did not change. "Beliefs about what?"

"Religion, mostly," I informed him. "I'm a Mormon, and—"

Jack stiffened so conspicuously that I stopped abruptly. His hand tightened painfully around mine, almost convulsively, as if he were trying to save me from something determined to pull me away from him.

"What is it?" I asked in alarm. "What's wrong?"

He appeared to be holding his breath. His jaw clenched, and he stared fixedly out the window, looking as though he were desperately trying to control his facial expression.

"Uncle Jack?" I cried in alarm. "Are you all right?"

"I . . . ," he attempted. He closed his eyes for a moment, and when they finally opened again, they were dark with disappointment. "It's nothing, really. It's just that I didn't expect—but I should have. I should have known my brother would pass that foolishness on to you. But I . . . I was so sure that it would die eventually. I hoped against hope that you would have the sense to see through it."

"What . . . what foolishness?" I breathed in alarm. "I don't understand what you mean."

"*Mormonism*," he spat coldly. "That cult that Matthew and Caroline belonged to. It's . . . I don't know, idiotic. Crazy, even."

I stared at my uncle, nonplussed. Did it even occur to him that those words might be hurtful to me? Visions were rushing unsummoned through my head. Memories of Aunt Sarah ridiculing me for my insistence that I attend church every Sunday and my cousin Elizabeth telling me how embarrassed she was to have a relative who was a Mormon. Even Uncle John's look of bewilderment and disapproval appeared for a moment before me, and I remembered when he had happened upon me reading my scriptures in the library shortly before his death. And now Uncle Jack? Was all of my family condemned to religious intolerance? I resisted the urge to put my face into my hands and cry. I had been so hopeful. Uncle Jack's manner had been so loving and so accepting. But the most important part of me he could not accept.

"Katie . . ." Uncle Jack's voice was low and controlled but icy. "You are my last living relative, and you mean a great deal to me. I have searched for you for years. I want us to be close. I want to get to know you, to spend time with you, maybe even fill my brother's shoes now that he no longer can. I will support you and be there for you always. But I will not allow you to get mixed up in that ridiculous nonsense like your parents did."

I flinched at his verbal verification of my fears. I stood quickly.

"I'm sorry, Uncle Jack, but you have no say in my religious beliefs," I said in a firm but respectful tone. I stood confidently in front of him, feeling like a tower of indignant strength. "I have been a member of this church all my life. I don't just believe that it's true. I know it with all my heart. I'm sorry you can't accept that. But I made the decision a long time ago that if I ever had to choose between my faith and something or someone else, my faith would always win."

I turned and began walking toward the door to his office, something inside me silently bleeding. I stopped with my hand on the door and looked back at him. All of the fury and rigidity was gone from his face. Instead he just looked stunned.

"I'm glad I got to meet you, Uncle Jack," I said softly. "Despite your disapproval of my dad and his beliefs, you remind me a lot of him—and not just physically."

I left the office quickly, heading for the reception area. The offices I passed were all deserted, as was the receptionist's desk. I pushed the down button for the elevator and stood waiting, still trying to grasp what had just happened. I wondered if I would ever see Uncle Jack again. Tears pricked my eyes, but I wouldn't allow them to fall. I felt the loss of another—my last—relative deeply, but I also felt something else. A warm assurance of peace and love was swelling in my chest, filling me with comfort. Everything would be all right. I just knew it.

"Hey, you," came a voice from the classroom doorway a week later, interrupting my thoughts. I looked up and saw Danielle propped against the doorframe.

"Hey," I greeted, setting the pile of workbooks I was holding on a back table. "What's up?"

"Ah, not much. Um, can I ask you a question?" She looked a little nervous.

I nodded, perplexed.

"I know you talk to Alex every week." She looked at me for

verification and I nodded again. "I think that's awesome that you talk to him so often, but . . . well, Mariah and I were wondering if you could get him to give us a call every now and then." She smiled, but I could tell she was irritated.

"I was just barely talking to him about that." I laughed, referencing a conversation we had had that morning. "He said he calls you almost every week but that you never pick up, and so he leaves you messages. Have you checked your voice mail lately?"

Danielle blushed. "I forgot my password," she admitted. "I can't check my voice mails."

"What about Mariah?" I asked. "Why doesn't she check hers?"

"I don't even think she knows how," Danielle answered, rolling her eyes. "She's not exactly tech-savvy." She pursed her lips for a second. "Why doesn't he just call during our lunch hour? He knows we pick up then," she suggested.

"I told him that," I said. "I think he's going to try to call then from now on."

"Good," Danielle said. She glanced around my classroom vaguely for a few seconds before finally looking back at me with a sly smile. "So . . . what do you and Alex talk about?"

"Nothing really," I said quickly, turning my back on her and grimacing as I walked toward my desk. I had known the interrogation was coming, but I had been hoping for more time to prepare for it.

"Oh, come on, Marie," Danielle pleaded. "Mariah and I have been dying of curiosity ever since Alex brought you home from wherever you went on his last night here. I think we've waited the appropriate amount of time before prying into your personal affairs. So, spill. Where did he take you and what did he say to you? Your face was all red and you looked dazed when you guys walked in."

"We were walking outside. It was cold," I said weakly, hoping she wouldn't pick up on the evasion of truth. I wasn't that lucky.

"Please," Danielle scoffed. "Where did he take you?"

I supposed I was safe enough in revealing that. "He took me to the pond that your parents used to take you guys to every Christmas. He just wanted to show me—" I stopped short when Danielle's ecstatic scream filled the air.

"Oh my gosh!" She cried. "Oh my gosh! Are you serious? Oh my gosh! I *knew* it! I just knew it! He proposed to you, didn't he?" She was jumping up and down in inane excitement. "You're going to be our real sister! Oh, Marie, I'm just so . . . so *thrilled*!" She shot forward and squeezed me with all her strength.

"Danielle," I gasped, trying to breathe despite her death grip. "We're—not—engaged!"

"Oh, Mariah's going to completely—" Danielle stopped midsentence and pulled back, looking at me. "Wait a second, what?"

"We're not engaged," I said, breathing deeply and massaging my ribs.

"You turned him *down*?" Danielle looked as though she was about to grab me again, this time focusing solely on my throat.

"No," I said quickly. It would probably traumatize my students for them to find their teacher dead on the floor after lunch. "He didn't propose at all; he just wanted to show me the pond."

"Just wanted to show you the pond?" Danielle repeated incredulously. "Why would he want to show you the pond? Who cares about the pond? Why would he take you there if he wasn't going to propose to you?"

I wasn't following her train of thought. "Well, it's really pretty," I said. "What if he just wanted me to enjoy the view?"

"Don't be ridiculous, Marie," Danielle said, a finger at her lips and appearing to be deep in thought. "He must be planning to propose to you, then. After all, he wouldn't take you there otherwise—"

"Danielle, stop it!" I complained. "I'm not the one being ridiculous here. Just because Jonathan took me to some frozen pond does not mean he's planning to ask me to marry him!"

"If it was just some frozen pond somewhere, it probably wouldn't," Danielle said, once again meeting my eyes. "But that particular pond is where Alex has always planned to propose to his future wife."

"Says who?" I said, still skeptical.

"Alex, of course." Danielle looked at me strangely. "See, that's where his dad proposed to his mom. After his mom died and his dad married my mom, we started going there every Christmas as a family. It was Alex's dad's way of kind of joining his two different families. So naturally, it's a very special place to Alex. I know he wouldn't take just anyone there."

"Oh," I breathed, thinking back to the conversation Jonathan and I had had while sitting at the edge of the pond.

I'm in love with you, he had said. *And what's more, I'm convinced I'm more in love with you than Tyler ever was. I'm not asking you to marry me or anything . . . at least not yet. All I want is for you to think about this while I'm gone.* It was true he hadn't proposed to me, but he had as much as said that he was planning to propose at some future date. I wasn't sure how I felt about that. A portion of me was cringing away from the thought and determinedly chanting Tyler's name, but another part was dancing an Irish jig. My reaction to this realization only confused me more. How could feelings be so conflicting and so complex?

I sighed.

Danielle was still grinning at me. "You will say yes, won't you?" she asked.

"Danielle, I—" I began, trying to keep the frustration out of my voice. "I—I don't even—I mean—how on earth am I supposed to answer that question?"

"I know," Danielle said, instantly faking a repentant attitude. "Sorry. But if you're confused or unsure about what you should say when he *does* ask you, just remember how irritated Mariah and I will be if you say no."

She smiled sweetly at my disgruntled look and left the room.

Sixteen

Hello?" I said in a determinedly cheerful voice when I picked up the phone later that night.

"Hello, I'm looking for Kate Evans," said a pleasant voice on the other end. I knew immediately who it was.

"Speaking," I said.

"Katie," my uncle said with some hesitancy. "How are you?"

"I'm fine, Uncle Jack, and you?" I said politely.

"Well, not that great, to be honest," said Jack quietly. "I'm actually quite ashamed of myself."

"Oh?" I said, trying to keep the subtle note of sarcasm out of my voice.

"You didn't deserve that treatment," Uncle Jack said. "If I come get you in an hour, will you let me make it up to you? I'd like to take you to dinner."

"I suppose so," I said. My voice was hesitant, but my stomach gave a leap. Could we really mend this? I would give anything to have at least one dream remain intact. Maybe this was it. I quickly gave him the address of River House and went to change, my spirits flying higher than they had in days.

"You'll love this place, Katie," Uncle Jack said enthusiastically as he led me by the arm into the little Italian restaurant situated on a picturesque pier. "Best pasta in Boston."

"It certainly smells good," I agreed, inhaling deeply. The décor reminded me of an Italian villa I had seen in a movie somewhere. I looked around eagerly, noticing that it had all the indications of being a very expensive restaurant. I was once again reminded that my uncle was the president and CEO of a successful publishing firm. It seemed I was constantly surrounded by the wealthy and powerful. It was one of the reasons I was so grateful for the financial equality that I enjoyed with my roommates.

"Hello, Maria," Jack said as we approached the restaurant hostess.

"Mr. Evans!" she replied with a smile on her pleasant face. "It's been a while since we've seen you."

"Yes, I haven't been dining out too often lately," my uncle said. "But tonight I have a reason to celebrate."

"Oh?" said the olive-complexioned Maria. "Does it have something to do with this young lady?" She smiled kindly at me.

"It does indeed," Jack answered. "This is my niece, Kate."

"You found her!" Maria cried in delight. "How wonderful!"

I looked at my uncle in surprise. "Do you tell everyone you meet about me?" I asked.

"Just about," he said, unabashed. "I've been looking for you for a long time, Kate. It's been my chief concern for years, so naturally my friends and acquaintances know about you."

Feeling a sudden rush of affection for the man, I threaded my arm through his and squeezed it. "I'm glad you found me," I said.

Uncle Jack leaned over and pressed his lips to my forehead. "Me too," he said.

"Well, in honor of the occasion," Maria said. "I'm going to give you our best table. Not that I don't always give it to you anyway," she added with a wink to Jack. She led us to a table in a corner of the restaurant, surrounded by windows overlooking the water. The view was magnificent.

"I'll be right back with your usual, Mr. Evans," Maria said as she slipped menus in front of us. "We save it just for you."

"Thank you," Jack said to her, and she walked away. He turned to me. "So how have you been this the past week? Anything exciting happen?"

"No, not really," I said. "I lead a very boring existence for the most part. Happy, though," I assured him.

"Well, that's all that matters, then." Jack smiled at me, but it left his face so quickly that I almost didn't catch it. "I know I apologized before, Kate, but I really am sorry that I attacked you the other day. You didn't deserve that."

"No, I didn't," I agreed straightforwardly. "I need to understand why it happened. Why are you so against my religion?"

"I really don't wish to discuss it," Uncle Jack said firmly. "I'm sorry that I spoke to you so unkindly last week, but that doesn't mean that my feelings on the matter have changed at all. I believe that the Mormon Church is errant fraud. However, I will agree not to broach the subject with you if you will promise to never bring it up with me."

"Uncle Jack," I said, as patiently as I could. "Even if I did agree to never speak to you directly about the Church, you would still be exposed to it every time you were in my company. I live it. It's part of everything I do."

"Don't be ridiculous," Uncle Jack scoffed. "Nobody lives their religion that . . . well, religiously."

Just then, Maria arrived with a bottle of wine and thus commenced what seemed like an absurdly rehearsed ritual of cork-smelling and wine tasting. When my uncle proclaimed the clear yellowish beverage drinkable, Maria poured him a glass. As she turned to do the same for me, I shook my head.

"No, thank you," I said. "I wouldn't care for any."

"Kate," Uncle Jack said soothingly, putting a hand over mine. "We're celebrating! I promise you, it's the best you'll ever taste. It's Burgundy Montrachet! It does have rather high alcohol content, but as I always restrict myself to a single glass, there's no reason to be worried about that."

"I don't drink, Uncle Jack," I said firmly, looking directly into his eyes.

"You don't what?" he asked politely, as if he didn't understand the words that had come very clearly out of my mouth.

"I don't drink," I said simply.

"Why not?" he asked. "Not even in honor of an occasion like this one?"

"No," I answered. "Not even for special occasions."

Maria withdrew from our table quietly, tossing a speculative look over her shoulder at us.

"I'm not sure I understand," Jack said, trying to maintain his tolerant smile. "Why are you refusing to toast a reunion with an uncle who has been searching for you for nearly a decade?"

I almost rolled my eyes at his attempt at a guilt trip, but I caught myself just in time. "I would love to tell you, Uncle Jack, but I'm forbidden to speak to you about it," I answered sweetly and took a drink from my water glass.

Uncle Jack's eyes hardened. "Fine then," he said, turning to look out the window and bringing his wine glass to his lips. He looked so much like a pouting toddler that I wanted to laugh.

After about two minutes of silence, he turned back to me. His petulant look had been replaced with one of determined civility. "So how do you enjoy your work? Is teaching everything you thought it would be when you decided to study elementary education in college?"

"Oh, I love teaching," I answered. "There's just something about taking young minds and making it possible for them to succeed. I feel like I make a difference every day."

"I'm sure you do," he replied, his polite smile turning warmer. "Your mother was a teacher, you know."

"She was?" I said in astonishment. "I never knew that."

"Oh, she stopped teaching about the time you were born, I believe," Jack said. "Although I can't be sure. We were no longer in contact by that point." He immediately looked sorry that he had voiced the last part. But it was the perfect lead-in for the question I had to ask.

"Why were you and Dad estranged?" I asked quickly, before he could change the subject.

"I told you, Kate—it's ancient history," Jack replied. "I don't like to think about it, and I definitely don't like to talk about it."

"But don't you think I deserve to know?" I asked, fighting to keep my voice calm.

"I don't see how it has anything to do with you," Jack countered firmly.

"It has *everything* to do with me!" I cried. "I grew up thinking I was all alone in the world after the Whitmans shrugged me off."

Jack winced. "Well, maybe it affected you, but there's no point in you knowing the reasons behind it. You can't change them now. Your father is gone, and you and I are finally together."

"But—" I started.

"No, Kate," Jack interrupted. "There's no point in asking because I won't tell you."

I sighed and slumped back in my chair in defeat. "Well, at least I know which side of the family I got my stubbornness from," I muttered.

Jack laughed.

I lay on my bed wide-awake for several hours that night. Squinting, trying to make out shapes in the dark, I let my mind run freely through the conversation I had had with Uncle Jack. My curiosity was burning hotter than ever, and I was determined to find out why my father and his brother had severed all contact so many years ago. I had a gut feeling that if I were able to find that out, I would also know the reason for my uncle's religious prejudice. I couldn't explain where this feeling had come from, but something in my mind had connected the two secrets and made them one.

Turning in frustration to my side and trying to force my mind to go to sleep, I shut my eyes tightly and focused on the blackness behind my eyelids. It didn't work. Pictures in vivid, living color raced through my brain. Most of them focused on individuals thousands of miles away from my current location. They were never far from me. It seemed like I spent 95 percent of my waking hours thinking about them, and nearly all of my sleeping ones were either moments relived or dreams unrealized.

Finally, sighing in frustration, I sat up. I flipped on the lamp next to my bed and pulled out my laptop, thinking I would go over my lesson plans for the next day, even though I already knew them cold. I waited impatiently as my computer booted up and pulled up my files as soon as the musical chime informed me that I was logged in. I had scarcely pulled up my first electronic document when I heard a small ping and a box appeared in the bottom right-hand corner of my screen.

Jonathan says: What are you doing up, you crazy person?

I smiled. It was early afternoon in Tokyo, so Jonathan must be sitting in his office. I quickly opened the chat box and typed back.

Kate says: I can't sleep.

Jonathan says: I understand. I can't sleep with a laptop open on my lap either. How are you?

Kate says: Pretty good, actually, and you?

Jonathan says: Dead tired. Too many late meetings. So, any new developments in the Jack situation?

Kate says: Yes, actually. We went to dinner tonight. He apologized for blowing his top and said as long as I didn't speak to him about my religion, he would try to pretend I was something normal. You know, like a Catholic.

Jonathan says: I can't tell if you're joking.

Kate says: Only a little.

Jonathan says: He really doesn't want you to talk about your religion at all? Does he not understand how much of yourself he's asking you to hide?

Kate says: Apparently not.

Jonathan says: His loss.

Kate says: Thanks.

Jonathan says: Have you come any closer to figuring out why he and your dad cut ties?

Kate says: No, but for some reason I have the feeling that the religion thing and their estrangement are connected.

Jonathan says: How do you figure?

Kate says: I can't explain it. Just a hunch.

Jonathan says: Have you ever considered that maybe they were estranged because of the religion thing?

I sat back against my propped-up pillows. *Kate, you're losing it,* I thought incredulously. How stupid I'd been! Having experienced my uncle's wrath firsthand, how could I not have come to the conclusion that Jonathan was suggesting? I looked back at my screen and began typing.

Kate says: I can't believe I didn't think of that.

Jonathan says: Neither can I. Now that I've said it, it seems so obvious. What's wrong with you? ☺

Kate says: I know! I wonder what the whole story is, though. I know both my parents were converts to the church, but I don't really know their conversion story.

Jonathan says: Why don't you ask Jack?

Kate says: Right. Ask Jack. That's a great idea. Especially since my religion and my parents are the two topics he loves to discuss with me the most. You've been eating too much late-night sushi.

Jonathan says: I know. What does that have to do with the price of rice in China?

I rolled my eyes and chuckled before going back to the matter at hand.

Kate says: If I could just get him to open up all the way about my parents, it would make this so much easier! Come to think of it, he DID mention my mom tonight. And I didn't even press him. He gets this soft look in his eye when he talks about her. I wonder if they were friends at one point.

Jonathan says: Sounds intriguing. You should do some research. I could use a good story.

Kate says: Research?

Jonathan says: Don't you have any of your parents' old things?

Kate says: There were a few boxes of personal belongings that were left to me. They're in a storage unit in L.A. Why?

Jonathan says: I think you're lying about not being able to sleep. You must be tired, because you're not usually this slow. Come on, Kate! Did you ever look through them?

Kate says: Not really. They've always just . . . been there. I mean, I've seen the stuff in them. Most of the things in those boxes are mementos of my baby years and stuff I made for them when I was little. You know, school projects and Mother's Day presents, that kind of thing.

Jonathan says: You should have them shipped to you. Might find some clues.

Kate says: Maybe I will.

By the time Jonathan and I said good night, I had a lot to think about. I put my laptop away and sank back into my pillow. My parents' past was never really something I'd thought a lot about. I treasured my memories of them, but I usually only thought of them in the context of being my parents, not Matthew and Caroline, the high school students or Matthew and Caroline, the newlyweds. I wondered why it had taken me so long to wonder about their early years. With my head full of thoughts of my parents, I quickly fell asleep.

Now that Jonathan had planted the idea in my head, I was anxious to get started on researching my parents' background. I called the storage facility during my lunch break the following day and arranged for them to ship my storage boxes to me. It was not cheap, but I rationalized that it would have been much more expensive to fly across the country to pick them up.

With my plans now fully set in motion, I became increasingly antsy as the days passed. Danielle and Mariah, to whom I had related my ideas in full, were also impatient for my parents' belongings to arrive. Danielle, who had a definite flair for the theatrical, seemed to regard the whole affair as a thrilling mystery. I could tell she felt she was living in one of the dramatic novels she liked to read. I had to admit, I felt the same sense of anticipation, on a much more personal level.

I received an impending delivery notification from the shipping company the day before the boxes were to arrive, and I spent the entire next day wishing I had never shared it with Danielle. She ran haphazardly into my classroom every half hour to inform me that, from her window, she had not seen the boxes arrive yet.

"Danielle," I finally said on her sixth interruption of my class. "What's the point of telling me that the boxes *aren't* here yet? If you don't have good news, don't deliver any news at all."

"But it's almost two!" she cried. "What do you think is taking them so long?"

"The email said that estimated time of delivery was four thirty, remember?" I said, rolling my eyes at her frantic fidgeting. "I appreciate that you're so concerned about the welfare of my packages, but could you please postpone any further nondelivery notifications until school is over?"

"But they might be early!" she exclaimed. "How often are those emails right? And . . . ooh!" She put her hands to her mouth as if she'd just seen a drive-by shooting occur right outside the classroom window. "What if they come early and you're not there to sign for them? The delivery guy might not leave them on the doorstep! He might leave one of those annoying 'Sorry I missed you' stickers that never seem to come off the window, and then we'll have to drive all the way to Boston to pick them up, and we won't have time for that till this weekend!" She ran frantically to the window and looked out. "Maybe one of us should get 'sick,'" she mimed quotation marks around the word, "and go home, just so we make sure we don't miss him."

"Dani, it'll be *fine*," I said in exasperation. "If anything, the delivery will be late, not early. Now will you please stay in your own classroom so I can finish my social studies lesson? You're getting my kids all riled up."

"Fine, but if we miss the delivery and we have to wait till this weekend to dig through your parents' stuff, you're making your own meals for the next six months," she said loftily and stalked out of the room.

Luckily for me and my dietary welfare, we did not miss the delivery of the boxes. My parents' belongings arrived around six that evening, at which time Danielle ceased biting her nails to shreds and began rooting frantically through the kitchen drawers for a pair of scissors to cut the packing tape. The three large boxes sat in the middle of the sitting room, looking plain and unobtrusive, but anyone looking in our windows would have thought they contained a life-saving medication required for our survival. I fidgeted wildly as I waited for Danielle to return with some kind of sharp object, and Mariah kept crawling around the boxes, examining them from every angle. She looked as though she hoped by studying them she would be able to discern what was hidden behind the brown cardboard. I could hear

Danielle banging drawers and cupboards in the kitchen, her frustrated mutterings finally turning to a cry of triumph as she located a suitable instrument. She tore into the room holding a sharp, silver letter opener high in her clenched fist.

"Okay!" she said. "We're in business! Get out of the way, Mariah." She pushed her sister aside and began to work on the packing tape with zeal.

"Careful!" Mariah cried. "You're going to damage whatever's in there!"

"I *am* being careful," Danielle insisted through clenched teeth as she sawed through the thick brown tape.

"Here," Mariah reached for the letter opener. "Let me do it."

"Mariah, I've got it! Stop nagging," Danielle complained, still through clenched teeth. She tried to shoulder Mariah's reaching hands out of the way.

"I'll do it." I interrupted their struggle by pulling the letter opener from Danielle's frantic fingers. "You're going to end up stabbing each other at this rate."

Danielle muttered darkly toward her sister as they both retreated. I made short work of the packing tape and, taking a deep breath, pulled the flaps of the first box open.

Inside was a burst of color. I recognized the preschool projects I had labored so diligently over, happily anticipating the delighted cries of my parents upon their receipt of them. There were colorful drawings, glittering Christmas ornaments, painted handprints, and even a life-size construction paper cutout of myself at age five. I laughed as I pulled each item out, memories I'd forgotten I had rushing to the forefront of my mind.

Finally, I pulled out the last item, settled in the corner at the very bottom of the box. I smiled softly as I caressed the cover of the familiar navy-blue book.

For Christmas my second grade year, I had presented my mother and father with a paperback copy of the Book of Mormon with my testimony written inside the front cover. It had been one of those primary-orchestrated gifts, where each child was given a book and told what to do. Still, having been baptized just a few months before, I put a lot of thought and heart into my written testimony. I remembered trying to convey in writing to my parents that I understood the step I had taken and that I had truly gained my own testimony of the gospel. It was the last gift my parents had ever received from me. Their car slid off the road and into a cement barricade less than two weeks later. I held the book to my chest as my mind raced through the memories of that horrible period of time with astonishing clarity. I hadn't realized the memories were so well preserved. I almost wished they weren't.

"Marie?" Mariah put a soft hand on my shoulder.

"Sorry," I said, snapping back to the present. "I was just remembering. I gave this to my parents the Christmas before they died. It was my last gift to them. They passed away just weeks later."

"Oh, how sad," Danielle said, scooting closer to me. "What is it?"

I turned the book around so they could see the title. They both recoiled a little bit. Although they knew of my religious affiliation and that I attended church in Boston every week, they had been very careful not to show the slightest interest or curiosity in my beliefs. I suspected that Danielle had informed Mariah of my church membership immediately after discovering it, and I knew both girls were somewhat uncomfortable with the topic. The LDS Church was a complete mystery to them, and I had the feeling that it was not a mystery they were anxious to solve.

"Oh, that's very nice," Mariah said somewhat vaguely as she turned toward the second box. "Now let's see what's in here."

Danielle was slower to turn away. She eyed the book cautiously for a few seconds as though waiting for it to jump out of my hands and bite her, and then she also turned to the second cardboard box. I set the book carefully on a nearby chair, wanting to read through the testimony a little later.

"Okay," I said. "Let's see what else we have here."

Mariah slid the letter opener smoothly through the tape on the second box and pulled the flaps open to reveal several leather-bound books and a lot of ancient-looking paper. As I began to pull papers out of the box, I realized what the parcel contained.

"It's genealogy!" I cried.

"Come again?" she said.

"Family history," I clarified. "My parents were doing their family history. These are my ancestors. Yes! Look, see?" I grabbed at a newspaper clipping and pointed out a printed statement. *May 2, 1923 – Son, Benjamin Henry Whitman, born to Mr. and Mrs. Josiah Adam Whitman, Santa Clara, California*, the statement read. "That's my grandfather! My mom's dad! He died before I was born."

"That's great, Marie . . ." Mariah looked a little unsure. "But why did your parents keep all this stuff? I mean, it's nice to know where you come from and all that, but . . . ," she trailed off.

"Who cares?" Danielle said, a bit more bluntly. She was perusing another typewritten page, squinting at the small print. Looking over her shoulder, I saw that it was a family tree. "Sure, it's interesting to know your grandparents' names and everything, but why do you need to know all this?"

"Temple work," I said, without thinking. I grabbed for the family tree and Danielle let it go without a fight. Both girls were looking at me in surprise.

"Temple work?" Mariah repeated. "All this stuff has something to do with those big white buildings your church has all over the place? The ones with the gold guy on top?"

"Yes," I answered, wondering if it was such a good idea to get into all this with my roommates. "We take our family history information to the temple so we can bind our families together forever. You know, one big, long family chain."

"But these people are dead!" Danielle protested. "How can you bind them to anything?"

"It's all done by proxy," I attempted to explain. "They don't have to be physically present to be sealed."

"Sealed?" Danielle asked. "What does that mean?"

I started to reply, but Mariah interrupted. "Why don't we save this conversation for another time?" she said, with forced cheerfulness. She was looking decidedly uncomfortable. "We still have one more box to look through."

Danielle opened her mouth as though she might protest but at the last minute decided to follow her sister's lead. She grabbed the letter opener and began hacking away at the packing tape on the third box, her face still showing slight consternation. When the tape had been thoroughly pulverized under Danielle's aggressive hand, the flaps were pulled open, and I gasped in delight. It was exactly what I had been waiting for.

"Yearbooks!" Danielle cried. "Now we're in business!" She grabbed the black, hardcover book on the top of the pile and started rifling through it frantically. "It says this book is from 1978! When were your parents born?" she cried.

"Um, my dad was born in 1960 and my mom in 1962," I replied, scooting closer to look over her shoulder. Mariah joined us.

"So this would be your dad's senior year, and your mom's sophomore year?" Danielle questioned, still flipping through pages at lightning speed.

"Yes," I replied breathlessly.

"There!" Mariah cried, shoving a finger between the falling pages. "He's right there!" She pointed to the picture of a young man with sandy hair, parted in the middle and combed back in the signature '70s style. *Matthew Evans.* The words below verified the picture was indeed my father. To the immediate left of the photograph was a young man with identical features. *James Evans,* the words underneath stated. I smiled at the two photos, noting the exactness of the resemblance. Down to the crinkling at the corner of the eyes, the two young men were perfect replicas of each other.

"There's an index!" Danielle cried. While I had been staring at the pictures of my father and uncle, Danielle had been attempting to examine the back pages of the book. "Let's see if we can find other pictures of them." She ran her finger down the column until she came to *Evans, Matthew,* with a short list of page numbers next to it. "Page 47!" she cried.

"That's the page we're *on*, Danielle," Mariah huffed, rolling her eyes.

"Oh, right," Danielle said, not registering her sister's scorn. "Page 114 is the next one."

I turned to the page quickly, noting that it was the page for the baseball team. "He played baseball?" I murmured to myself. My eyes ran quickly over the page and fell on the picture of two young men with their arms wrapped around each other, bright smiles on their faces. The caption below the picture read, *Twin brothers Matthew Evans, shortstop, and Jack Evans, pitcher, congratulate each other after the team's victory in the regional championships.* I grinned at the picture, happy in the knowledge that at some point, my dad and his brother had been friends.

"What's the next page?" I asked hungrily, and Danielle flipped back to the index.

"Um, page 153," she answered and we were off tearing through the pages again.

"Choir? Really?" I laughed as I took in my father's face as he beamed from the third row of the black-suited men's choir. My uncle's face appeared right next to his, again making me smile. The brothers seemed to have been more than friends; they almost appeared to be attached at the hip.

"What about my mom?" I asked. "Where are her yearbooks?"

"All the yearbooks in here are from the same high school," Danielle said, her voice somewhat muffled as she buried her head in the box, reaching down to see the books at the bottom of the pile.

"That's weird," said Mariah. "Why would your parents only save your dad's yearbooks?"

"Maybe my mom didn't—" I began, but Danielle cut me off.

"Wait, isn't this the yearbook we're looking at already?" she asked, pulling out a black book identical to the one in my hands.

"My parents went to the same high school!" I cried. "That's why there's two of them!"

"Let's see," Danielle answered, flipping back to the index at the back of the yearbook. "Caroline Whitman, right? Yes, here she is! Okay, she's on pages 86, 119, and 148!"

I turned quickly to page 86 and immediately located my mother's face. Her dark hair fell silkily around her shoulders and her large blue eyes, so like mine, smiled shyly at the camera. I found her other pictures, smiling bigger and bigger as I found that she had been involved in swimming and the art club. I was more like her than I had thought.

"All right, let's evaluate," Danielle said, clapping her hands together. "Now, did we see any sign that your parents knew each other in high school?"

"No, not really," I answered. "They were involved in completely different activities and I didn't see an entry from my mom in my dad's yearbook."

"Okay, let's keep looking, then," Mariah encouraged. We set aside the black yearbook and pulled out the next one, which was dark blue with the silver lettering "Santa Clara High 1976" embossed on the front. Over the next few hours, we steadily worked our way down through the pile of yearbooks, searching through each one in turn. We found nothing. I was starting to feel discouraged. How did my parents meet if they didn't know each other in high school? I was about to give up when suddenly Danielle screeched.

"Here!" she sang. "I found it!"

I yanked the book away from her and stared at the picture she'd found. It was a photograph taken at my mother's senior prom in 1980. My parents were standing under a canopy of balloons, their eyes fixed on each other. My father's arm was around my mother's back and they looked as though they were laughing at something. Happiness seemed to radiate from them.

"How sweet." Danielle sighed, gazing at the picture. "You can tell just by looking at them that they're in love. See the way he's staring at her? He's smitten!"

I laughed, my heart feeling light at the sight of my parents together. I turned to Mariah, wondering why she was so silent. The look on her face made me choke on my laugh.

"Mariah?" I asked. "What's wrong?"

Her face was fixed, her eyes slightly squinting as she stared down at the page. She pointed one finger to the caption below the photograph. I read it quickly, my smile falling immediately from my face. *Caroline Whitman enjoys the Senior Prom with her date, Jack Evans, celebrated former pitcher for the Santa Clara High Razorbacks, Class of 1978.*

"What?" I gasped. "Uncle Jack?"

seventeen

"How could it be Uncle Jack in that picture?" I wailed as Danielle and Mariah tried to comfort me. They weren't equipped to do a very good job, because both of them were every bit as astounded as I was.

"I don't know," Mariah said weakly. "I . . . I don't know. Maybe it's a typo?"

"A typo?" Danielle said, raising an eyebrow. "A typo that turned the word *Matthew* into the word *Jack*? Somehow I don't think so."

Mariah glared at her sister. "Well it could have been a mistake. After all, they were identical. Maybe the person who took the picture thought it was Jack when it was really Matthew."

"I guess that could have happened," I said, unconvinced. "But I really doubt it."

"Well, technically it's not *that* much of an issue anyway," Danielle insisted. "So your mom went out with your uncle before she got together with your dad. Big deal. That kind of thing happens all the time."

"But you said it yourself!" I cried. "In that picture they look so . . . smitten with each other. How did she end up with my dad after that?"

"Oh, anything could have happened! Come on." Danielle put her arm around me bracingly. "It's not like the world's ending here. In fact, this opens up a whole new realm of possibilities!"

"Sorry?" I said blankly.

"You've forgotten the end goal already?" Danielle said disapprovingly. "We only wanted this stuff so we could figure out why your dad and his brother were estranged. Doesn't it seem pretty obvious now?"

"You think the whole disagreement was over my mom?" I questioned, biting my lip and considering.

"Well, I have no idea, naturally," Danielle admitted. "But I really hope so." She sighed and collapsed back on the floor. "Wouldn't that be romantic? Like a movie."

Mariah rolled her eyes. "Danielle, we're not really interested in what you want to happen. We want to know what *actually* happened."

"I know that!" Danielle raised her head and snapped at her sister. "I'm allowed to fantasize, aren't I?"

"But what about the religion thing?" I asked, interrupting their argument. "Where does that come in? If my Uncle Jack was already estranged from my father by the time my parents joined the Church, what does that matter to him? Why would he care about them getting baptized? It would have absolutely no effect on him!"

"Who says they were already estranged when your parents joined the Mormons?" Danielle asked. "Maybe your parents signed up before they even started dating! Or maybe your mom and your uncle broke up and the three of them were all just friends, and then your mom and dad joined your church and your uncle was kind of . . . you know, booted out of the club."

"It's possible, I guess," I said, mulling it over in my head. "But do you really think that would be enough to turn my uncle completely against his brother? Just the fact that he was no longer 'in the club'?" I imitated quote marks around the words.

"It does seem kind of unlikely," Mariah commented. "Especially given that they seemed to be so close in high school."

"Well, I don't know, then!" Danielle huffed, collapsing back to lean against the couch. "If you're going to shoot down every possible explanation . . . ," she trailed off, looking annoyed.

"Well, is there anything besides yearbooks in that box?" I asked, going up on my knees to peer into the cardboard carton. "Maybe we'll find some more clues."

"Let's see!" Mariah said enthusiastically. She began pulling the hardbound books out of the box, examining each as she lifted it. We had already flipped through most of them and they were therefore set quickly aside. Finally, as she was getting near the bottom of the box, Mariah pulled out a book that looked quite different than the others we had seen so far. It had a plush cover with embroidery on the front. Mariah took one look at the words embroidered on the cover and squealed.

"Marie! Look at this!"

Danielle and I jumped simultaneously and both started crawling toward Mariah at top speed. Danielle attempted too much velocity and ended up banging her knee as she passed the coffee table. Since Danielle was incapacitated, I managed to reach Mariah first. I snatched the book from her hands.

"What? What is it?" I cried. "Oh . . . ," I breathed as I saw the words. *Our Wedding ~ Matthew and Caroline Evans, November 24, 1984* was embroidered in flowery script on the soft cover of the album.

"Well?" Danielle gasped as she rolled around the floor, holding her knee to her chest and rubbing it vigorously. "What is it?"

"It's their wedding album," I said softly. I opened the front cover, and tears immediately filled my eyes as a smiling picture of my parents came into view. They were standing on the steps of the Salt Lake Temple. My mother's head was thrown back in laughter, and my father's eyes were fixed on her. He looked mesmerized. In fact, he looked much like his brother had in a picture taken with the same young woman several years earlier. I bit my lip and pushed the thought away, wanting to focus on the happiness of the monumental day my parents married.

I turned the pages slowly, beaming more brilliantly at each photograph. However, when I arrived at the picture of my father with his groomsmen, I couldn't help but notice the absence of one face. Uncle Jack was nowhere to be found. I flipped more quickly through the pages then, searching through each photograph for some sign of my father's brother. He was not there. Uncle Jack hadn't even come to his brother's wedding? Was I to understand, then, that the brothers' estrangement had occurred prior to my parents' marriage? I supposed that made sense. I suspected that the estrangement was either a result of my parents' baptism or their marriage, and as my parents had been married in the temple, their baptisms had come at least a year before their wedding. I bit my lip, the longing to know the whole story stronger than ever.

"Well," I said, exhaling loudly. "We know a lot more now than we did before."

"What? We don't know anything!" protested Danielle. "All we *really* know is that your dad and his brother were close at one time, and that your mom dated your uncle before she married your dad."

"We also know my dad and my uncle had broken all contact before my parents married," I pointed out. "My uncle is nowhere to be found in here. He didn't even come to their wedding! That narrows things down a bit."

Danielle sighed. "I suppose, but there are the makings of a fabulous story here, and we can't do anything but speculate. I want the skinny. The details." She pouted for a few seconds, tapping her feet on the rug impatiently. "You're going to have to ask your uncle, you know," she finally pointed out.

"Ask Uncle Jack?" I repeated. "I already have. A dozen times, it feels like. You know he won't tell me anything."

"Well, now you're equipped to unload the heavy artillery," Danielle said. "You know more now than you did before. You can ask more specific questions. Instead of 'Hey, Uncle Jack, won't you please tell me why my dad never mentioned you?', you can say, 'I know you dated my mom in high school. Why did you break up?' I'll bet that would get him sweating."

"I'm sure it would," I answered. "And swearing, and throwing things, and probably disinheriting me too."

"Oh, don't be dramatic," Mariah said, pulling her knees up to her chest and propping her chin on them. "I'll bet once he realizes how much you know, he'll open right up to keep you from getting the wrong idea."

"Unless he wants me to have the wrong idea. A lot of times the truth is much worse than lies," I said, sighing. "But you're right. Now that I know this much, I have to at least ask him, if only to see his reaction."

"Good. Now that that's decided, when are you going to ask him?" Danielle pressed. "Tomorrow? Tonight? How about right now?"

"Danielle," Mariah scolded. "Give her some time to think of how to approach it. It's kind of an important conversation, you know."

"Yes, and with important conversations, it's often a good idea to jump right in with no preparation whatsoever," Danielle argued. "Just run with it. Go with the flow. It ruins the effect if the conversation is too scripted."

"No one's scripting anything," I replied, distracted. "But I do want to think about it a little. The less damage I do to the relationship, the better."

I rose vaguely to my feet, possible conversation starters running through my mind.

So, Uncle Jack, I was going through some of my parents' old stuff the other day . . . No. Any outright mention of my parents would send the conversation into an immediate tailspin.

Did I ever tell you about the boyfriend I had in high school? The one with the twin brother . . . Nope. Not only was it completely pathetic, but it was also a lie and I was not an accomplished deceiver.

What's your view on girlfriend-stealing brothers? Nice. I could just see the look on my uncle's face at that inspired opener.

I paced around the room, Mariah and Danielle watching my every move. They didn't speak, allowing me to think without interruption. They deflated as I sank onto the couch, finally admitting defeat.

"I have absolutely no idea how to broach the subject with him." I groaned. "What do I say?"

"We'll think of something," Mariah soothed. "Why don't we sleep on it?"

"Good idea," Danielle said, in a completely uncharacteristic show of capitulation. "I'm dead tired." She stretched and yawned.

Leaving the books, papers, and albums strewn about the room in complete disarray, we headed for bed.

Given the excitement of the evening, I was surprised I managed to fall asleep as quickly as I did. However, I woke up much too early and lay in bed for a full hour, trying to come up with some way to convince my uncle Jack to tell me the story I wanted so very much to hear. Finally, my frustration mounting with each increasingly desperate mental suggestion, I resolved to tell him the truth. I would hit him quickly with what I had discovered and ask for an explanation. He would be so surprised by my hitherto unsuspected knowledge that he would blurt out the entire story before he could stop himself. Maybe it could work. Regardless, I was determined to get the full story, even if it meant questioning my uncle once a day for the next twenty years. With some semblance of a plan, I leapt out of bed and headed downstairs for another get-together with my parents.

"So?" Danielle asked as she bounced down the stairs an hour or so later and settled herself on the couch next to me. I was seated on the middle cushion, my legs folded, with my parents' wedding album open on my lap. "Did you come up with anything? Any dream visitations or major epiphanies during the night?"

"Nope," I answered, turning the pages of the album with care.

"Me neither," she answered glumly.

"But I know what I'm going to do anyway," I said simply. "I'm just going to ask him."

"Seriously?" Danielle said, looking slightly put out. "Isn't that what I suggested in the first place?"

"Maybe, but somehow it sounds more reasonable when I say it." I smiled sweetly at her.

She elbowed me deliberately as she reached for the yearbook containing the photograph of my mother dancing with Uncle Jack.

"I wonder if she ever got confused," Danielle said as she studied the picture, her nose less than an inch from the page. "I would. I mean, dating two completely different guys who happen to look absolutely identical? How did she keep them straight?"

"Well, I assume she liked one and loved the other," I answered, going back to the wedding album.

"Maybe. But Jack's not the only one who looks infatuated in this picture, you know. And she dated Jack first. Do you think she ever saw your uncle Jack when she looked at your dad?" Danielle asked vaguely.

My head snapped up and I answered much too forcefully.

"*No.*"

Danielle looked over at me quickly and her expression became repentant. "No, of course she didn't. You're right. I'm sorry, Marie. That was tactless."

I ignored the apology as I considered Danielle's suggestion. Had my mother been torn between the two brothers? How had she chosen between them? Did she ever regret her choice? I settled back against the couch cushion and let my head fall back.

"Marie?" Danielle asked tentatively. "Are you okay? I really am sorry. I didn't mean to suggest that your mom didn't love your dad as much as . . . ," she trailed off. "Marie?"

"Hmmm?" I said, turning to her, distracted. "Oh, you're fine, Danielle." I patted her halfheartedly on the arm. "I'm just so confused. Everything is so much more convoluted than I thought it would be. Not that it's really a big deal now. My parents are gone. But my uncle's attitude toward my parents' memory seems to suggest that it still affects him a great deal, whatever the reason for the estrangement was."

"So what if it does?" Danielle asked. "It's not really likely to affect you. He wouldn't let any grudges against your parents carry over to you, would he?"

"I don't think he would intentionally," I answered thoughtfully. "And he seems okay with everything apart from my religion. I don't know. I'll just have to ask him and see what he says."

"Good plan," Danielle agreed. "Now . . . go ask him." She started to push me unceremoniously off the couch.

"Dani!" I laughed, crumbling to the floor.

"I'm sick of waiting for the behind-the-scenes account!" she said imperiously, running her fingers through her caramel hair. "I'm out of patience. Go call your uncle."

"Fine, but I'm not going to have this conversation over the phone. I'll call him and ask if we can talk sometime."

"Sometime *today*."

"Right, sometime today."

"Very good. Carry on." Danielle stood and headed for the kitchen, a self-satisfied smirk on her face.

At 3:25 that afternoon, I was pacing up and down the hall like a caged tiger. My attitude was feline as well. I was ready—ready to pounce on my uncle the minute he pulled in the driveway to pick me up for our impromptu meeting. Surprisingly, I wasn't even nervous to have this conversation, I was eager for it. I wanted to confront him with the information I had learned in the past twenty-four hours, wanted to hear his explanations for the things I had seen and read. I wasn't even trying to come up with a way to tactfully broach the subject. I was too impatient to be concerned with diplomacy.

I had the front door open to the chilly March weather before Uncle Jack could even ring the doorbell.

"Hi, honey," my uncle said as he pressed his lips to my forehead. He took me by the shoulders and looked into my face, studying it with a worried crease between his eyebrows. "How're you doing? You sounded a little agitated on the phone."

"I'm fine," I said reassuringly. "I just have something very important to talk to you about."

"Well, let's get going then," Jack said, leading me from the house.

As I turned to shut the door behind me, I noticed Danielle's and Mariah's heads protruding from the sitting room doorway, mouthing good luck wishes at me. I winked at them and shut the door firmly.

Let the battle commence.

"You—were—supposed—to—get—it—out—of—him!" Danielle was punching a couch pillow in frustration. It was a few hours later, and I had come home, yet again, with empty hands. Despite my verbal assault, Uncle Jack hadn't wavered the slightest bit in his resistance to my prying. He had beaten me. He was a master.

"You were supposed to come home with the full story! I'm tempted to chuck you right back out unless you can come up with a darn good replacement!" Danielle continued to torture the decorative pillow as she glared at me.

"What was I supposed to do, put a gun to his head?" I asked her. "If he won't tell me, he won't tell me!"

"Well, you're not giving up," Danielle answered haughtily. "I'm even more anxious to hear the story now than I was before. The fact that he's refusing to tell you means it must be a juicy one."

Mariah rolled her eyes. "Let's just start dinner, okay?" She headed for the kitchen, then stopped when she realized Danielle wasn't following.

"Well . . . you're welcome to start dinner, but I won't be, ah, eating with you girls tonight," Danielle said, her belligerent tone suddenly light and almost embarrassed.

"What? Why not?" I asked, noticing the subtle flush to her cheeks.

"Carson called this morning and asked if I'd like to go to dinner with him tonight," Danielle whispered, her cheeks bright red now.

"No way!" Mariah said, collapsing on a chair. "Carson? As in Carson Wright? Carson Wright the Poly Sci teacher at MA? He called you of his own free will, with no blackmail attempts, bullying, threats of disembowelment, or—"

"Oh, shut up," Danielle interrupted. "Yes, he called me, and we're going to dinner tonight. So you two enjoy your solitary macaroni and cheese with the knowledge that I'm out with the most gorgeous male in Christendom."

Mariah and I stared at each other. Carson Wright could barely look a woman in the eye, and he had managed to call Danielle, one of the most intimidating women on the planet, and actually ask her on a date? Did some kind of cosmic interference account for this?

"Well, Danielle," I said, sure my astonishment still registered on my face. "Congratulations. That's pretty awesome, considering that you've had a crush on him forever and you've never actually spoken to him before."

"I have too!" Danielle protested hotly. "I say hello every time I see him. And the fact that he hardly ever says it back is entirely beside the point!" She threw the last sentence in as soon as she saw her sister's mouth open to comment.

"Well, the way I see it," I interjected, "that just means you'll have an awful lot to talk about tonight. I'm happy for you."

"Thank you," Danielle said petulantly. "Now, if you'll excuse me, I'm going to get ready for my *date*." She emphasized the last word in Mariah's face as she passed her.

Mariah smirked as she watched Danielle climb the stairs. "Do you believe her?" she asked me.

"Well, despite the fact that pretty much everything I know about Carson defies her claim, I'd have to say that I do. It's one of those things that is just so far out there that it pretty much *has* to be true."

Mariah laughed and gestured toward the kitchen. "Macaroni and cheese, roomie?"

"Don't mind if I do."

Despite my uncle's discouraging response to my attempted assault via unjustified bluntness, I had far from given up. I continued over the following several months to attempt to get him to respond to veiled inquiries about my parents, hoping he would inadvertently reveal some tidbit that would confirm my theories.

He didn't. He was masterful at spotting and avoiding my verbal snares. Not that they were particularly stealthy. But despite his lack of response, I persevered. In the meantime, I had other, more pressing issues on my mind. I had finally agreed to contribute some pieces to the Milton Art Show when Danielle had threatened to spread the rumor that Jonathan and I were secretly engaged. That wouldn't have been too terrible, but then she promised that she would see to it that the rumor would make it to Jonathan's crowd in New York, which she knew included Tyler. I didn't doubt for a second that Danielle would do it, and not only would that have been humiliating, but also a cruel thing to do to Jonathan. So I sucked up my nervousness and my lack of confidence and agreed to display some of my sketches. I had completed several in the months since Christmas. In fact, I was shocked at the number as I spread them out before me one sunny day in July.

The summer holidays were in full swing, and I had filled up my suddenly very empty days with walks through the park. I loved watching as the different phases of life waltzed by me. Old couples with clasped hands strolled along the pathways, young families picnicked by the pond, groups of young men and women gathered to play energetic games of flag football or volleyball. I watched middle-aged women brave the weather, rain or shine, as they determinedly power-walked along the winding paths. I saw old men settled comfortably on the park benches, calmly watching the bustling activity around them. I found so many subjects for my sketches that it was difficult to choose.

I smiled as I studied the drawings I had spread out on my bed. My eyes moved to a sketch I had completed the week before. It was a small girl, perhaps two or three, squatting down in front of a bright dandelion. Her nose wrinkled adorably as she leaned forward to press it to the soft flower. It was such a sweet example of what I felt no one was wont to do anymore. With nothing but time stretching out before me, I had discovered in the months since leaving Thorne Field that finding joy in the small intricacies of life brought me a surprising amount of happiness. It seemed like such a simple principle, but one that most adults completely disregarded.

As I'd watched the precious little girl appreciate something that most would consider a nuisance, I'd been reminded of the innocent wisdom of children. Hadn't the Savior Himself said that we must become like them to be exalted? The scene had become almost a spiritual one, and I had been so moved by the spectacle that I had immediately captured it.

I picked up the drawing in question and studied it, deciding in a split second to make my contribution to the art show a collection of the pieces I'd done depicting children. Danielle had asked for five sketches that would be grouped together in my own corner of the exhibit. I had at least four that I knew I wanted to use, and I had roughly three more months to find the subject for my fifth piece and complete it. My eyes ran over the sketches spread out over my comforter and searched out the other pieces I desired: the small boy being walked by his much larger dog, the twin girls holding hands as they soared through the air on swings, and the baby clinging desperately to his mother's fingers as he struggled to take unsteady steps across the grass. I gathered up all the sketches other than the ones I planned to give to Danielle for the art show and put them aside. Setting the chosen sketches out side by side, I examined them with a critical eye.

Yes. If I had to choose art created by my amateurish fingers to display, these pieces were the right ones. There was a kind of gripping emotion in each one, despite the fact that the subject had had no idea they were being captured and immortalized. Perhaps that was the secret behind the emotion. There was no pretension, no facade. I smiled.

"Marie?" Mariah's voice startled me, and I turned to see her entering my room with a determined look on her face. She stopped when she saw the four large pieces of sketch paper spread out on my bed. "Oh, are these your drawings for the exhibit?" she exclaimed. She studied them intently and grinned. "Marie, these are fantastic!"

"Thank you," I said uncomfortably. "I still think Danielle is crazy, but better I'm humiliated over a few drawings than over a supposed engagement. It was the lesser of two evils."

Mariah laughed. "Danielle doesn't play nice when she wants something."

"No."

"So . . . speaking of engagements . . . ," Mariah trailed off and glanced at me speculatively. "How are things going between you and Alex?"

I was surprised. Prying was Danielle's forte, and Mariah generally left the meddling to her. She would just wait in anticipation for Danielle to share whatever juicy tidbits she'd discovered. It was unlike her to go for the jugular herself.

"What exactly do you mean by that?" I asked her.

"Oh, nothing," she said innocently. "But he's called you every week for more than six months now. He talks to you five times more often than he talks to either Danielle or me. We just figured that you must have arrived at some kind of decision about him. And that decision might just be that you like him," she said quickly at my thunderous gaze.

"Yes, that's it," I said, glaring at her. "I like him."

"Okay . . ." Mariah hemmed and hawed. "But how much do you like him?"

What was this, sixth grade?

"Mariah, come on," I whined. "I'm not having this conversation. What's wrong with you? I would expect a question like that to come from Danielle, not from you."

"Well, I'm just curious. I mean, you never talk about him, but you walk away from conversations with him grinning like the Cheshire Cat. I think I'm entitled to know what your intentions are." Suddenly she was the protective younger sister, hands on her hips and a steely glint in her eye.

"Oh," I said, suddenly feeling cowed. "Um, my intentions?"

"Yes, Marie, your intentions," Mariah said, really getting into her role now. She took a formidable step forward and her look grew, if possible, even more intense. "I have my brother's best interests at heart, but I'm not sure you do."

"Mariah!" I said, shocked. "You know I would never intentionally hurt Jonathan!"

"Do I?" she said, raising an eyebrow. "All I know is that my brother has been in love with you for nearly a year now and you've given him enough encouragement to keep him interested and not enough to elicit a marriage proposal. Why is that?"

"Um, I . . ." I looked frantically around me, though I wasn't sure why. I felt distinctly cornered. "I haven't intentionally been—I mean, don't get me wrong, I like Jonathan, I just—I didn't mean to—I . . . I . . . I'm sorry," I finished lamely. "Am I leading him on?" There was an almost pleading note in my voice, and I felt pathetic.

"I don't know, Marie," Mariah said coolly. "Only you can answer that. None of us are in any doubt that you like him, given your enthusiasm when he calls. But do you love him?"

"I don't know!" I cried helplessly. "I don't know. I . . . I need him. He's become a part of me, and I think if I never saw him or spoke to him again, it would be like being separated from my arm. But even knowing that doesn't help, because I just don't feel for him the way I do for Tyler! I *know* I'm in love with Tyler, because being separated from him isn't like being separated from a limb, it's like being separated from me. Like being split in two. It's as if I don't really know myself without him. There's no doubt in my mind that what I feel for Tyler is what love feels like. It's the definition of the word. But what I feel for Jonathan is just . . . different."

"But you need Jonathan. You depend on him. You . . . want him," Mariah said, watching me closely.

"I . . ." I said. *Want* him? It sounded so lustful. "No, I wouldn't say I want him. Not in the way you mean," I said, a little defensively. "It's not just physical desire, even though I'm definitely attracted to him." Who wouldn't be? The man was gorgeous. I gathered up the four sketches, just for something to do, and put them carefully inside my sketchpad. "I just . . . need him. He's my friend, Mariah. He's become a piece of me. An ingredient of Kate. A necessary part of my sanity. You know, now that Tyler is . . . not around."

"So he's your fix? Your painkiller now that the guy you really want is gone?" Mariah sounded angry, and I was sorry for that, but I couldn't deny her assertion.

"I guess so," I said meekly. "I never intended for it to happen. The last thing in the world I want to do is hurt him."

"Well, unless you can make up your mind—honestly and definitively—you will," Mariah said harshly. "I know this past year has been hard for you, Marie, but you can't keep stringing him along like this. He's hoping, you know. Hoping that at least by the time he gets back from this idiotic stint in Japan, you'll have arrived at the conclusion that he's the one for you. What are you going to say to him then?"

I looked down at my bare feet. I didn't like to think about that. I had never honestly considered the possibility of ending up with Jonathan. I couldn't anyway, given our religious differences. He knew that. I'd told him. But did he really believe I was serious about it? The thought made me pause. Maybe I hadn't been clear enough that a future involving both of us was out of the question unless he joined the Church. Regardless, the idea of ending up with anyone besides Tyler seemed laughable at this point, even though I knew I would never be with him either. So usually, I just pictured myself alone, or not at all. Maybe that was the solution. Don't think about the future. I was closer to adopting the Scarlett O'Hara–esque procrastination tendency than I cared to admit. I did seem to postpone thinking about my troubles as much as possible. It was as though I really believed that tomorrow they wouldn't seem quite so depressing.

I was jarred from my thoughts as I felt arms come around me. Mariah's face had softened and she hugged me tightly.

"I know you're confused. I'm sorry to be hard on you. I just want my brother to be happy. And believe it or not"—she pulled back and looked into my suddenly watery eyes—"I want you to be happy too."

"Thanks," I sniffed. "And you're right. I do need to make some decisions."

"Would it be easier if Jonathan were here, do you think?" Mariah asked curiously.

"I don't know," I said. "I do miss him, but I don't know that him being here would make it easier to make any long-term decisions."

"I'm not sure about that . . . ," Mariah said thoughtfully. "Sometimes we don't realize how much we love something, or someone, until they're standing right in front of us, reminding us of what we've been missing."

"I suppose," I said. "It doesn't really make any difference, though. Jonathan's visit is still six months away."

"Mmmm," Mariah said, only half-listening. "Well, anyway, give it some thought, Marie," she said. She reached out and squeezed my arm.

"I will. Thanks," I said, smiling weakly. I watched her leave the room, her eyes still far away in thought.

After my slightly strained conversation with Mariah, I was wholly expecting a full-on ambush from Danielle on the same topic. I dreaded it, since Danielle was much blunter and much less sympathetic than Mariah. So when Danielle knocked on my door two days later, I was hard-pressed to muffle my groan.

"Marie, can I talk to you?" Her voice was softer than I expected as she called through the door.

"Sure, Danielle. Come on in," I said, pushing the words reluctantly through my lips. I had been laying stomach-down on my bed, flipping through my scriptures when her knock sounded, and I marked my place and closed them as the doorknob turned.

The door opened slowly and Danielle slipped in. This in and of itself was unusual. Danielle usually charged into a room like a rampaging bull. I noticed that she had something small and dark in her hand, but she was half-concealing it behind her back. She looked self-conscious, an emotion I hardly recognized on her face.

"Danielle?" I said. "Are you okay?"

"Oh, sure," she said with a small smile. "I just need your, um, advice on something."

"Oh, okay," I answered, relieved. This didn't appear to be the conversation I had been dreading. "What's up?"

"Well, you know that Carson and I have been dating for a while," she began unexpectedly.

And how, I thought bemusedly as I nodded at her. She and our fellow MA teacher had been nearly inseparable for several months now. As their relationship had progressed, I had been amazed at the change in Carson Wright's demeanor and address. The shy teacher had come completely out of his shell. He spoke easily and frankly with everyone, male or female, and had even progressed to the point of starring in a faculty skit that we had performed in the Academy talent show at the end of the school year. I had never seen Danielle glow more brightly. And even now, despite her uncertainty, I could still feel the happiness radiating from her.

"Well, we want to get married," she said matter-of-factly.

I jumped to my feet. "Oh, Danielle!" I exclaimed. "I'm so happy for you!" I threw my arms around her and squeezed.

"Thanks," she said, almost shyly. "But that's not really what I want to talk to you about. There's something else."

"Okay . . . ," I said, completely baffled. "What is it?"

She shuffled a little from one foot to the other, then taking a deep breath, she pulled the item in her hand from behind her back and showed it to me.

My breath lodged in my chest as I recognized it. I stared up at her, bewildered.

"I'm going to be baptized," she said.

eighteen

I stared at the Book of Mormon in her hand, not quite comprehending what it was doing there.

"You . . . what?" I said, staring up at her.

"I'm going to be baptized," she repeated. "Actually, both of us are. Carson and I."

"How . . . how did this happen?" I nearly choked. "Where did you get that?"

"It's yours," she said, opening the cover and showing me the childish scrawl of my testimony inscribed on the front cover. "I took it when we were going through your parents' stuff." Suddenly she looked sheepish. "I hope that's okay. I didn't say anything to you at the time because I was afraid you'd go all convert crazy on me and the next thing I'd know, we'd have the missionaries on our front porch."

I laughed, but it sounded almost like I was wheezing. I was still completely stunned.

"Anyway, I read what you wrote on the front cover and flipped through it a few times, but that was pretty much it," Danielle said, still fidgeting with the pages of the book. "It wasn't until Carson and

I started thinking about getting married that I remembered reading this." She indicated the testimony inside the front cover.

I took the book from her and read the words I had written years earlier.

Dear Mom and Dad,

My primary teacher gave me this Book of Mormon and told me to write my testimony in it so that you would always have it. I want you to know that even though I'm little, I know that the Church is true. I'm so grateful that we are a forever family, and I can't wait to get married in the temple so that I can have my own family and be with them forever and ever. I know the scriptures are true and that the prophet tells us the things Heavenly Father wants us to know. I'm thankful for both of you and I love you a lot!

Love, Kate

"See," Danielle began when I had finished reading. She took a deep breath as if preparing to make a very weighty declaration. She sat on the edge of the bed, facing me, her legs folded beneath her. "I love Carson. A lot. More than I can really describe to you. And the thought of losing him or being separated from him is scary to me. Well, when that occurred to me, I remembered what you wrote here about being a family forever and . . . I just needed to know." She shrugged and studied her fingernails, not wanting to meet my eyes. "I did some research on the Internet," she said. "And I read what your church believes about eternal families. I want that. For me and Carson."

"What about this?" I asked, holding up the book. "Have you read it? All of it?"

"Yes," she answered, her eyes still fixed on her hands clasped in her lap. "A few times, actually."

"And?" I asked her, breathless. "What did you think?"

"I believe it," she said simply. "I knew it was true before I'd even read it through all the way the first time." She finally looked up at me. "Why didn't you tell me about it?" she asked. "You knew all the time that you had the truth and I didn't. Why didn't you say something?"

I was instantly ashamed. She was right. I should have tried harder to share the gospel with her and her sister. My sisters.

"I'm sorry," I said softly. "You're right. I should have said something. I guess I was just afraid that you'd feel I was pushing you."

She studied me for a second. "It's okay," she finally said. "I guess I understand. Knowing me, I probably would have resisted anyway."

"So, what happened with Carson?" I asked.

"When I decided that I believed what I was reading, I gave the book to him and asked him to read it. He didn't want to, but I'm persuasive." She smiled at me and winked. "It took him even less time than me to come to the same conclusion." She shrugged again and started playing with my bedspread. "We've been meeting with the missionaries for about a month. We've decided to be baptized next Saturday. I just wanted you to know."

"I'm so glad," I said, the smile on my face so big it was almost painful. "But why have I never seen you at church? If you've been meeting with the missionaries, then you'd think I would've seen you around."

"Well, I didn't want anyone to know. Especially you," Danielle answered, with a sheepish shrug. "I was afraid you'd be disappointed in me if, you know, I decided it wasn't the right thing for me. You mentioned that you were attending a singles ward, so Carson and I have been attending the family ward so we wouldn't run into you."

"Very cloak and dagger," I complimented her, laughing. "Oh, I'm so happy for you!" I sprung forward and threw my arms around her again.

"I'm happy too," she said, and I could see it shining from her eyes. They say that the eyes are the window to the soul, and I could tell that at that moment, Danielle's was brilliant.

"Have you told Mariah?" I asked. Mariah was much more logical and down-to-earth than her sister, and she wasn't easily caught up by emotion. I doubted she would be thrilled to hear of Danielle's conversion to the Church.

"No," Danielle seemed to wilt a little. "I'm not sure how to tell her. She's not big on religion."

"Well, let's think on it. We'll have to tell her before Saturday, you know."

"I know," Danielle said nervously. "She'll be furious that I decided to do it without talking to her first." She shuddered slightly. It was an unusual sight. I considered Danielle to be, by far, the more formidable of the sisters. Yet she seemed to be sincerely frightened at the thought of angering Mariah.

"Don't worry," I said. "We'll think of something. We can even tell her together."

Danielle looked relieved. "Okay," she said and, smiling, left the room.

Telling Mariah turned out to be easier than we anticipated. In fact, we didn't even have to do it. Danielle informed Jonathan of her plans to be baptized in a phone conversation later that week, and Jonathan, not realizing that Danielle had not yet told Mariah, mentioned it to his dark-haired sister. The next thing we knew, Danielle and I were seated next to each other on the couch like naughty children while Mariah paced in front of us.

"Why didn't you tell me this was going on?" Mariah asked her sister. She didn't look exactly angry, just a little shell-shocked and hurt. "Why didn't you tell me you were interested in Marie's church?"

"Because it was personal. And I was in up to my elbows before I even realized that I was 'interested.'" Danielle emphasized the words with her fingers. "It all went so fast. What with the way things were going with me and Carson, I just . . . didn't know how to tell you." She looked down at her entwined fingers sheepishly. "Are you very mad?"

"No, not really," Mariah said, slumping into a chair across from us. I wished she would look at me. I couldn't help but feel that she was purposely avoiding my eyes. Was she upset with me? Did she feel I had gone behind her back to try to convert her impetuous younger sister?

"I just wish you would have told me about it while it was going on," Mariah continued, putting a hand to her face.

"Why, so you could have stopped me?" Danielle said, indignantly. "I'm not stupid, Mariah. I know you don't have much good to say about religion, but just because you don't believe in anything doesn't mean that none of us should!"

"That's not true!" Mariah cried back. "I have nothing against religion. I just don't think it's for me. And, yes, I have to admit I'm surprised that when you felt the need to get religious, it was the Mormons you turned to!" Her eyes flicked guiltily toward me, but she didn't apologize. "I mean, come on, Danielle! The *Mormons*? You, a Mormon?"

I bit my lip to keep from protesting. Voicing my indignation would not help anything right now. I let Danielle fight this particular battle, knowing that if she truly believed, it would only strengthen her. She did not disappoint me.

"Yes," Danielle said proudly. "Me, a Mormon." She reached out and took my hand as she faced her sister bravely. "You know me better than anyone, Mariah," she said. "Do you really think I would just jump into something like this without thinking it through? Something *really* important?" she pressed, when Mariah appeared to be about to answer affirmatively. "I know this is true! I *know* it!" She squeezed my hand as if to reassure me as much as her sister. She stood and walked to Mariah's side, placing a hand on her shoulder. "I'm sorry you're disappointed in me, but I want you to know that I'm happy with my decision. It feels right for me. It is right for me." She squeezed her sister's shoulder and then left the room, leaving Mariah and me alone.

We sat in silence for several seconds. Finally, I could stand the awkwardness no longer.

"Mariah," I began but she held up her hand.

"Don't," she said, and I was astonished that her voice was steely and cold. I had never heard my warm, sweet, sensible Mariah sound anything like that before. "Don't try to talk your way out of this one, Marie. Don't say that you didn't mean to, or you didn't expect this to happen. That particular excuse is getting old." She rose to her feet and turned her back on me. "First, Alex to Japan, and now, Danielle to some weird religion. Are you determined to tear my family completely apart?" She didn't look at me but left the room at almost a dead run. I thought I heard the sound of a sob before her footsteps faded away.

I sat alone in the sitting room, wishing for a moment that I had never come to Milton.

"So, are you okay with it, then?" I asked Jonathan late that night. I had been fidgeting on my bed for the past two hours, waiting, needing to hear his assurances. As soon as I was sure he was awake and probably in his office, I had dialed his cell number. He had picked up almost immediately.

"Of course," he said, surprise evident in his tone. "Why wouldn't I be okay with it? It's Danielle's choice, not mine. And there are plenty of other much more bizarre religions she could join. I think, everything considered, she's made a pretty reasonable decision."

"Good," I said softly. "Now what am I going to do about Mariah?"

"She'll come around," Jonathan assured me. "I think she's feeling a little left behind right now. With Danielle getting married and moving on, I think Mariah feels lost. She and Danielle have been a package deal for nearly their whole lives. I don't think she was ready to lose that yet. The religion thing was probably just the straw that broke the camel's back."

"I understand," I said. "I really do. I just hate feeling like I've hurt her personally. Like I've betrayed her."

"She'll calm down in a few days. She just needs some time to get used to the idea."

"I hope you're right. So how are things going on your end?" I asked, needing a change of subject.

"Good," Jonathan replied. "Everything's settling into place here. I'm really pleased."

"I'm glad!" I said sincerely. "That speaks well of your abilities as the Big Man on Campus."

Jonathan chuckled. "I suppose so," he said, not bothering with false modesty. "I understand that you finally capitulated to my sister and are now a featured name on the Milton Art Show program. Congratulations!"

"Thanks," I said dully. "She blackmailed me into it."

"I have no doubt." Jonathan laughed. "But I think you did the right thing, agreeing to it. I only wish I could be there to see it."

"Me too," I said. "You being here would go a long way toward settling my nerves."

"I'll take that as a compliment, even though you're probably only saying that my companionship has the effect of a sedative."

I laughed. "No, you're just my lifeline, that's all. My superhero. You fly to the rescue whenever I need it, and usually when I don't," I teased. "I might start calling you Clark Kent. I hope that's not a problem."

"You know I would do anything for you, Kate." Jonathan's voice was completely serious. "I'll always be there for you, regardless of how you feel about me."

"Um, thanks, Jonathan," I said, feeling distinctly awkward. Mariah's accusations from days before were running through my head. *Don't give him false hope,* I reminded myself. "You're such a good friend," I said, and winced. It could not have been more obvious that I was attempting to take a huge emotional leap backward.

Jonathan chuckled, a harsh, grating sound. "Relax, Kate," he said. "I'm not pressuring you."

"I never thought you were!" I lied convincingly. "I meant it. You *are* a good friend. The best. *My* best."

"Well, due to the fact that my best friend can't stand the sight of me, I'd have to say that you currently hold the top spot for me too," Jonathan replied, the mirth in his voice still not managing to hide all the pain.

"He's still not speaking to you?" I said. "Really? After all these months?"

"Well, he has to speak to me—the firm would go under if he didn't—but he doesn't relish the experience. We usually only talk about business. But it's getting better. He at least begins our conference calls with asking me how I am. That's progress."

I groaned.

"Oh, it's fine," he said, and I could almost hear his eyes roll. "But speaking of conference calls, I have one in less than two minutes. I'll call you later, okay?"

"Okay. Have a good day, Jonathan."

"I will. Sleep tight, Kate. I love you."

I hung up the phone with those three little words running through my mind. Would I ever be able to say them back? Ever since Mariah's lecture, I had given the subject a lot of thought and prayer. The experience had been an illuminating one and I had made a few discoveries in the process. One, I knew that I loved Jonathan. I had at least been able to admit that much to myself. Two, I knew that although I loved him, it wasn't enough. At least not yet. It just wasn't strong enough to build a life on. Not enough to make me forget the other love I felt—the one that was so much stronger. Besides, even though I could now admit that I loved Jonathan, that didn't change the fact that he was not of my faith, and therefore, could never be more than my friend. But what if that changed someday? He certainly seemed to have an open mind when it came to my beliefs. An open mind was the first step to an accepting mind. Maybe, someday . . .

I collapsed back against my pillows and closed my eyes. *I won't think about it now,* I thought, reverting back to my default reaction of late. Tomorrow, maybe everything would make more sense.

Danielle's baptism took place at the nearest stake center, a large, brown-brick church building in downtown Boston. Carson was baptized first and then sat and watched with a peaceful smile on his face as Danielle entered the font. The moment was so beautiful and so perfect that tears gushed down my cheeks in salty rivers. Danielle's face glowed as her fiancé pulled her to him after she emerged from the changing room. Then, surrounded by the missionaries and bishopric, each was confirmed a member of The Church of Jesus Christ of Latter-day Saints. Warmth filled me as my sister of less than a year became my sister in the gospel.

Mariah had refused to come with us, so I was astonished when I saw her leaving the room after Danielle's confirmation was complete. My heart warmed further at the sight of her, even though she was walking quickly away. She knew how important her sister's baptism was, if only to Danielle, and she had taken the time to be there. That was an encouraging sign.

nineteen

The day of the Milton Art Show dawned beautifully sunny and surprisingly warm for October. My classes went smoothly despite my distracted air and several of my students and their parents expressed excitement to view my drawings at the exhibit later that night. Each time such sentiments were articulated, I could manage nothing but a slightly manic laugh and halfhearted nod.

As the day progressed, I decided that the caffeinated butterflies that had taken up residence in my middle must be breeding at an unprecedented rate. I couldn't sit still. In fact, I couldn't sit at all. Every time I tried, I was driven to my feet almost immediately with a powerful need to give my nervous energy some kind of release.

"Marie, if you're going to insist on plowing a furrow in that rug, at least put it in a place that isn't quite so visible," Mariah said in exasperation as she watched me pace back and forth in front of the fireplace in the sitting room. "For crying out loud, if you're so nervous, don't go. Your drawings will be displayed with or without you there."

I whirled to face her, my face a mask of utter joy. I was about to run and throw my arms around her in appreciation. I would have loved to skip the exhibit. My intense relief was dashed almost immediately.

"Forget it. You're going," Danielle said in a garbled voice. She was frantically attempting to pull her shoes on, brush her teeth, reapply her faded mascara, and do a final check of the evening's itinerary all at the same time. She was heading over to the exhibition hall a few hours before Mariah and me to ensure that all was ready for the evening's festivities and was finding herself a bit behind schedule.

Mariah gave me a sympathetic look. "I know you're nervous, but you'll be so glad you did this. I promise."

My look must have portrayed a pretty profound representation of the incredulity I felt, because Mariah changed tactics. "Alex called earlier. He told me to tell you good luck."

"He didn't ask to talk to me?" I said in disappointment. Talking to Jonathan would have gone a long way in calming my nerves.

"He said he was late for something." Mariah shrugged. "But he told me to tell you that he's thinking of you and he's proud of you."

I smiled softly, feeling the fluttering insects in my stomach change their flight pattern slightly. I took a deep breath, trying to get a hold of myself. What was the worst that could happen? People could hate my sketches and make snide and condescending remarks. But I could handle that, even if those people were some of the other featured artists. Sure, it would be embarrassing and uncomfortable, but it wasn't as if my drawings would ever end up in another exhibit. It was one night of humiliation. I could deal with that. Pulling air desperately into my overworked lungs, I finally sat down on the edge of the couch and clasped my hands in my lap.

"There, you see?" Danielle said as she raced through the room toward the dining room where she'd deposited her purse. "Everything's going to be fine. Now don't forget, you're expected at the exhibition hall by seven fifteen so that you're in place next to your pieces when the visitors start arriving at seven thirty."

"I know," I said a little breathlessly. "I'll be there."

"You'd better," she said as she shot back the other way toward the hallway to the front door, purse clutched in her hand. "If you're not, the whole of Milton and half of New York will believe you're engaged to my brother by eight." She gave me one meaningful look before disappearing down the hall.

"But I don't understand why I have to stand here!" I hissed at Danielle a few hours later. We were positioned in front of my five black-framed sketches, two of which were placed on decorative metal easels. The other three were displayed on the temporary wall behind, which had been painted a deep red. The color accented the stark white of the sketches magnificently, and I was pleased by the overall effect. Danielle was insisting that I remain standing close beside my drawings so I could greet the visitors to the art show as they came through. I felt like I was in a school science fair instead of in an art exhibit.

"Why can't I just enjoy the exhibit along with everyone else?" I asked desperately. People were beginning to arrive and I didn't want to be anywhere near my exhibition when they began to study it.

"Marie, you're the featured local talent!" Danielle said needlessly through clenched teeth as she motioned to the metallic plate on the wall underneath the largest sketch. *Kathryn Marie Evans, Featured Local Artist, Milton, MA* the small plaque read.

"Patrons are going to want to know where you got your inspiration, who your influences are, which ones are your favorites, et cetera," Danielle insisted.

"Oh, they are *not*," I whispered back. "The only thing they're going to do is feel obligated to express admiration they don't feel because I'm *standing* right here as they look at my stuff!" I attempted to walk away again, but Danielle's steely grip held me fast.

"Do you *want* to get engaged tonight?" she threatened.

I considered telling her to make my day, but I had no doubt that she would do it, and it really wouldn't be fair to Jonathan. Especially with so many people he knew personally from New York present at the exhibit. Sighing in exasperation, I planted my feet firmly beside my sketches and resisted the urge to stick my tongue out at her. Danielle gave me one last piercing look before turning toward the door and pasting an almost maniacal smile on her face.

I stood uncomfortably and silently by my sketches as the first patrons began to trickle in to the exhibit. When I noticed Danielle step out of the hall, I spotted my chance to escape, but a hand on my shoulder distracted me from my quest. I turned to see who was disrupting my bid for freedom.

"Uncle Jack!" I cried happily. I hadn't had much of a chance to see him since school had started up again, and he had been busy with the acquisition of another publishing firm. He had assured me he would be at the exhibit, however. "You made it!"

"I said I would be here," Jack said, looking grumpy at the idea that he would have missed such an important occasion. His eyes found my name on the plaque on the wall, and he studied the drawings displayed with great interest. "You're very talented, Katie," he said after a minute with something like awe in his voice. "These are beautiful. Astonishing, even."

"Thank you," I replied self-consciously. "But they're not nearly as good as some of the other pieces displayed here. You should see—"

"I came to see your pieces," he interrupted, not looking away from the drawings. He studied each one with great attention, noting the detail and commenting on certain parts that struck him. Finally turning to me, he surprised me by saying, "You have your father's gift."

"My father?" I said, astounded. "But my mom was the one in art classes. I saw it in her yearbook!"

"Your mother loved art," Uncle Jack agreed. "But your father was the artist. I have some of his sketches. I'll show you sometime."

I nodded dumbly, too surprised by the sudden mention of my parents to say more. Uncle Jack left me to go and congratulate Danielle on a job well done in organizing the art show.

As the evening passed, I kept reluctantly to my post, nodding to those I recognized from town and thanking those who commented on the quality of my work. Finally, the crowds began to thin as people returned to their homes, speaking enthusiastically of the inspiring art pieces, the delicious food, and the beautiful music. I was just beginning to think that the evening had actually turned out to be a virtually painless one when I heard a sound that nearly knocked me flat.

"Well, your drawings are incredible, but I have to say, I think I'd rather look at you."

I whirled around, my mouth falling open in shock.

"Jonathan!"

Jonathan stood a few feet away, his hands in his pockets and a crooked smile on his face. He was dressed casually but attractively in tan linen slacks and a white, button-down shirt open at the neck. He was breathtaking, as usual. I stared for a second before launching myself at him. He laughed as his arms closed tightly around me, and I felt his lips in my hair again and again.

"Kate," he said softly. He took my face between his hands and kissed me soundly, sending small shivers down my back. Knowing as I did that I loved him, I didn't even think about protesting, but I couldn't suppress that inevitable pang of unease either. We couldn't be together.

I've got to stop this, I thought as he pulled away.

"I have missed you so much," he said meaningfully, looking into my eyes.

"You've talked to me every week," I said, laughing. "How could you possibly miss me?"

"It was easy," he said, running his hands up and down my arms and putting his lips to my forehead. He skimmed his lips from my forehead down the side of my face to my cheekbone. My fingers clenched unconsciously on his shirt. My eyes closed involuntarily and I forgot for a second that there were other people in the room.

"Well, what a surprise," I heard from a few feet away. My eyes snapped open and I backed away from Jonathan. Uncle Jack raised an eyebrow at me before looking toward Jonathan with something akin to disapproval on his face. "I didn't know you were coming tonight, Kelly."

"It was supposed to be a surprise," said Jonathan, reaching out to shake Jack's hand. "I didn't tell anyone I was coming, though Mariah was the one who suggested that I should. Good to see you, Jack."

"And you," Uncle Jack replied, but the look on his face said otherwise. "Although I'd prefer to see you keep your hands in your pockets and off my niece when in a public venue." He sent a significant look in Jonathan's direction, and Jonathan had the grace to look ashamed. "So," Jack continued in a more civil tone. "Are you home for good or just for a visit?"

"Oh, I'm in the States just for a few days. I'm headed back to

Tokyo on Monday," he said. "Of course, I'll be home again in a couple months for the holidays."

"I see," said Uncle Jack. "So are you still thinking you'll be in Japan for the next couple of years?"

"Actually, things have moved along more swiftly than we anticipated," Jonathan answered. "I expect I'll be home much sooner than originally planned."

"Really?" I said, delighted. "That's wonderful! Have you told Danielle and Mariah?"

"I think it's probably better that we don't mention it quite yet," Jonathan said quietly. "You never know, things might blow up unexpectedly and I'll have to stay longer. I don't want to get their hopes up."

"Oh," I said, a little disappointed.

"Looks like they're not the only ones apt to get their hopes up," Uncle Jack mused, winking at me.

I rolled my eyes and threaded my arm through my uncle's, not looking at Jonathan. "No comment. So, how about we head for home and celebrate Jonathan's arrival with a little ice cream?"

"Not yet," Uncle Jack said quickly. "There are still a few pieces I'd like to see." He patted my arm and strode off toward the other end of the exhibition hall. I turned to see Jonathan staring at me with a smile on his face.

"What?" I asked, placing my hands on my hips.

"Nothing. I've just missed you," he said simply. "Come with me. I need to talk to you." He took my hand in his and pulled me toward the door, leading me out into the unseasonably warm night air. There was an ornate park bench about twenty feet from the door to the hall and Jonathan pulled me to it.

"What is it?" I asked him as we sat. I noted the nervous stiffness in his movements. "What's wrong?"

"I wasn't going to do it like this. I had something quite different planned, but I can't wait any longer." Jonathan stood and walked a few steps away, then turned to face me. He looked at me with such tenderness that I couldn't help but smile up at him. I had missed him more than I thought.

"Kate, I have something important to tell you." He sat down again by my side and took my hand. "I've never admitted it, but I . . . I've been investigating your church for quite a while now."

The news didn't surprise me as much as it should have. I think I had subconsciously suspected it all along. I smiled at him and nodded for him to go on.

"I ran into some missionaries in Japan about six months ago, and I think I was just missing home and you so much . . . it was so good to encounter something relatively familiar that I agreed to see them before I realized what I was doing." He looked down at his hands, sheepish. "It took awhile for it to make it through this thick head of mine, but I finally realized that I believe it. All of it. I was baptized last week."

"You've already been baptized?" I said, the astonishment finally hitting me.

"Yes," Jonathan said, his face radiating happiness. "I thought about telling you that I was looking into the church three months ago, when Danielle called to tell me about her plans to be baptized, but I wanted to wait and tell you in person."

"That is a surprise," I agreed. "A wonderful surprise. I'm so happy for you!" I hugged him tightly. "How do you feel?"

"Good. Wonderful, even," he said, his arms still wrapped around me. "I'm happier than I've ever been."

"The gospel does that to you." I grinned at him.

"Yes, it does, but that's not the only reason I'm happy. I've actually discovered something," Jonathan said. He took my hands in his and looked into my eyes for a long moment. I fought the urge to look away. His expression made me suddenly nervous.

"Kate, I've told you over and over that I'm in love with you. You've never said it back. I told myself that it would come eventually. That you would grow to love me like I loved you. I was sure that if I gave you enough time, one day you'd say those words back to me. But, you know, I think I was wrong. So I'm going to ask you something right now, and I want you to be completely honest—both with yourself and with me. Can you do that?"

I stared at him for a long minute before nodding slowly. Shoot. I knew exactly what he was going to ask, and there wasn't a thing I could do to stop him. I nearly winced as he opened his mouth.

"Do you love me?" he asked, and I heard his breathing stop as he waited for my reply. I knew I couldn't deny it, even though I felt like I might be doing more harm than good to admit it.

"Yes, I do, Jonathan," I said. "But—"

He didn't let me finish. He pulled me into his arms and our lips met. I resisted at first, wanting to explain further, tell him that even though I knew I was in love with him, it didn't necessarily change anything. But I didn't have quite the determination to resist Jonathan's advances as I once had. Finally, I melted into his arms and returned his kiss with enthusiasm, a spasm of tingles playing in my middle.

"I knew it," Jonathan said breathlessly when he pulled away. "I *knew* you did."

"Watch it, pal, or someone might think you've got a big head or something," I murmured with eyes closed, my face pressed against his chest.

"Kate, will you marry me?"

The question came at me completely out of left field.

"Wha—what?" I choked. I tried to scramble backwards on the bench, but Jonathan's arms held me fast.

"I love you, and you've admitted that you're in love with me," Jonathan reminded me, ". . . finally." He added the last word as an afterthought. He traced his fingers along the side of my face. "I don't think the question is an unnatural one. I want to be with you. I need to be with you. Will you marry me?"

"I . . . I . . . ," I stammered. How did I handle this? Could I marry him? As inexplicably guilty as my feelings for him made me feel, I knew I needed him too. As I had explained to Mariah, Jonathan was a part of me now.

But wait, why was the guilt still there? Up until this point, I had believed that my guilt originated from the fact that Jonathan was not of my faith. But now he was. The guilt should have dissipated as soon as Jonathan told me of his baptism. So why was it still lodged in my middle like a chronic stomachache? Why couldn't I just give in to my feelings, however understated, and try to be happy with him? If I couldn't be with Tyler . . .

As my mind began shouting the name of my former fiancé, I suddenly experienced an unexpected sense of déjà vu. I felt I was back in the big city, standing in a bright, crowded intersection in the arms of one man while another looked on, both intensely dear to me. And in that moment, I knew. I closed my eyes and groaned, the sound one of dread and fear.

"Kate?" Jonathan's voice was worried. "Kate, what is it?"

I slowly opened my eyes and turned to stare at the open doorway leading to the exhibition hall. Tyler Thorne stood framed in the light streaming from the hall, his face tense and unreadable.

twenty

Jonathan rocketed to his feet, his jaw going slack.

"Tyler!" I wasn't sure which one of us had actually said it. Maybe both of us.

Tyler didn't say a word but took a few steps toward us. I wanted to back up proportionately. He approached at a steady pace, his face coming into sharper focus as he drew nearer. So familiar. So beloved. My mind had recalled it with perfect clarity in the months we had been separated. He stopped within a few feet of the bench on which I sat dumbfounded, his eyes fixed on me. He opened his mouth and I braced myself.

"Hello, Kate," he said simply. His eyes warmed as my name escaped his mouth. He seemed to linger over it, to relish the taste and sound of it. So did I. I had to consciously keep my eyes open. They wanted to close, to drown in the sound of his voice. It had been so long since I had heard it.

"Tyler," I breathed. "What are you doing here?"

His face broke into that angelic, slightly crooked smile he saved just for me. I felt my knees go weak. "I came to see you, actually," he said. "But from the looks of things, I picked an inconvenient time."

He turned, his eyes focusing for the first time on Jonathan. I tensed, ready to spring between them if necessary, but Tyler's expression held no condemnation. In fact, to my surprise, he smiled warmly.

"It's good to see you, Jon," he said, holding out his hand to his best friend.

Jonathan looked as astonished as I felt, but he immediately grasped Tyler's hand. "And you," he replied.

"The reports from Japan are phenomenal," Tyler said conversationally. "I'm impressed with what you've accomplished over there."

"Thanks," Jonathan acknowledged. "I'm pleased with the way things are going."

I stared back and forth between them, my mouth hanging open. *Business?* Jonathan was mid-proposal, Tyler was accosting me with his presence for the first time in nearly a year, and they had come to the conclusion that the best course of action was to stand around discussing business? Didn't they realize that I was seconds away from falling to pieces? Was this some kind of corporate male bonding ritual? My hands clenched in my lap, and I tried to keep from fidgeting in discomfort.

"So what brings you up here?" Jonathan asked, the first signs of tension entering the conversation.

"I have some things I need to say to Kate," Tyler replied, seeming perfectly at ease. "We never got a chance to talk things out, you know, and I'm in need of some closure." He smiled complacently, but something about his look seemed to drive the tension in Jonathan's frame to mammoth proportions.

"Well, see, that's the thing," Jonathan said, his voice tightening further. "Although I do understand the rationale behind the choices you've made, Tyler, I'm not sure you've earned the right to closure. At least not where Kate is concerned."

I stared up at him in disbelief. This was the perfect opportunity to patch things up with his best friend and he was going to argue over trifles?

"Jonathan—" I began, but Tyler held up his hand.

"No, he's right, Kate," he said, his eyes never straying from

Jonathan's face. "I definitely haven't earned the right to any favors from you. I've hurt you, I know." His eyes finally fixed on my face. His expression was neutral, but his eyes held a hint of the pleading I remembered from the day Camille had returned.

Camille. Where was she? Did she know Tyler was here? If so, was she actually okay with it?

"But my circumstances have changed some, and I think you and I need to talk," Tyler continued, still watching me.

Changed? Changed how? The questions zinged through my brain, but my lips remained locked.

"Wait just a minute," Jonathan interjected, moving in front of me so I was blocked from Tyler's line of sight. I wasn't sure whether I was grateful or irritated at the territorial display. "Things are different now, Tyler," Jonathan said stiffly. "Kate doesn't belong to you anymore."

"And she *belongs* to you?" Tyler said, the first signs of annoyance beginning to show in his voice. "I'm not sure you know her as well as you think you do, Jonathan. Kate doesn't *belong* to anyone."

I heard Jonathan fire a retort back at Tyler, but I didn't register the actual words. I closed my eyes, wishing both of them would just go away and let me attempt to process what was going on. What was Tyler doing here? Despite the fact that he was as frequently in my thoughts as ever, I hadn't so much as laid eyes on him for nearly a year. Why had he come? Why now? A snort of disgust brought me back to the verbal barbs flying back and forth over my head.

"I would never presume to objectify her that way," Tyler was saying, the irritation turning his voice to steel. "And it's a moot point anyway. I told you, Jonathan, things are different now. I need to talk to her. I need to explain." Yes, the irritation was there, but so was the pleading.

"No," Jonathan said firmly. "You didn't see the state of her the last time she saw you, the last time you wanted to talk to her. Do you remember that, Tyler? Do you remember the look on her face? Watching her run away? I do."

Run. What I wouldn't give to run. To get away. But Jonathan was still standing in front of me, blocking my escape route. I considered vaulting over the back of the bench, but my brain couldn't seem to locate my legs.

"That's not all I remember from that night," Tyler growled, and I heard him shuffle forward menacingly. I winced, knowing he was recalling Jonathan's New Year's kiss.

"Don't even try to intimidate me," Jonathan said heatedly, his voice dripping with scorn. "You've already made your choice. You chose Camille. I've spent the past year trying to get Kate to open herself to the possibility of someone else, and it's finally paid off. We're in love, Tyler. I've asked her to marry me." I heard the note of triumph in his voice at the same moment I registered Tyler's soft grunt of surprise.

"And what did she say?" Tyler pressed. "I don't remember stumbling onto the kind of passionate scene that usually ensues when Kate accepts a marriage proposal, so I'm assuming she didn't say yes."

I winced again. His understated reference to my acceptance of his proposal was a swing far below the belt, even to my mind. I could tell from the stiffening of Jonathan's shoulders that he had understood completely.

"She never got the chance to!" Jonathan defended. "You showed up before she could answer."

"So she hasn't accepted you, then," Tyler verified, with an unfathomable expression on his face.

"Not yet, but . . . ," Jonathan trailed off, the note of triumph replaced by a note of uncertainty. He moved from his protective stance and turned to face me. He reached down and took my hands in his, his eyes staring unblinkingly into mine. "Kate?"

I looked back and forth between the two beloved faces, both staring at me with a look of expectation. Were they serious? Did they honestly expect me to just choose between them? Right there? Either way I chose, I was guaranteed to cause pain, and not just to myself or either of them. There were parties involved who were not even present for this disaster of a confrontation. My mind raced. Had it been a simple matter of choosing Tyler or Jonathan with no other factors involved, the choice would have been an obvious one. But too many people's happiness depended on this decision. Addie. Danielle. Camille. Mariah. Jonathan. Tyler. Kate. I couldn't do this!

I knew the facts of the case, and those seemed to be the only coherent thoughts my brain was able to form. The most concrete fact of them all was that I wanted Tyler more than anything else in the world. But Tyler had a family. How could I take him away from that? How could I even consider it? Based on that vein of thought, my choice really should be Jonathan. But by the same token, how could I choose Jonathan, when I so desperately wanted someone else? How was that fair to him? I couldn't do that, to him or myself. So from that perspective, my choice should be Tyler. What on earth was I supposed to do? The silence stretched on and on, and neither man moved a muscle. Finally, the uncertainty and distress became so intense that I snapped. I shot to my feet. I looked frantically between them, my voice a distressed whisper.

"I'm sorry, I . . . I . . ." Closing my eyes against the pulsing pain in my head, I raced toward the lit doorway to the exhibition hall, away from the two pairs of questioning eyes and straight into the arms of my uncle Jack.

"Come on, Katie," Uncle Jack said as he led me gently away from Jonathan and Tyler. To my surprise, he steered me away from the exhibition hall and instead guided me around the building to the picturesque fountain in front of Milton Town Hall. He seated me tenderly on the concrete edge of the trickling fixture and settled himself beside me.

"Now," he said, taking my hand between both of his. "What are we going to do about this?"

I just shook my head. I was traumatized. Jonathan's proposal had been enough to send me into orbit, but that coupled with Tyler's sudden appearance and the resulting fireworks between the two most important men in my life was enough to send me over some kind of emotional precipice. I was somersaulting through empty space now.

"Katie, this is a choice you're going to have to make sooner or later," Uncle Jack pointed out as he massaged my fingers. "You can't live your life in limbo like this."

I didn't reply. I could feel my heart rate beginning to slow. My uncle often had a calming effect on me, and luckily, tonight was no exception. I leaned into him and put my head on his shoulder.

"Oh, Uncle Jack," I groaned. "What am I going to do?"

"Only you can answer that question, honey," my uncle replied, stroking my hair. "You know, you're not the first person to face a decision like this."

"I'm not so sure about that," I moaned. "I've never heard of anyone else having to make a choice anything like this one."

"I have," Jack claimed, and I knew he was smiling even though I wasn't looking at him.

"Oh yeah?" I said. "Who?"

"Your mother," Jack said, continuing to stroke my hair, even though I had frozen solid under his fingertips. I waited, my breath shallow, for him to continue. He was silent.

"Uncle Jack?" I prompted. I heard him take a deep breath, and I knew immediately that he was about to crack. He was going to share the entire story with me. I waited, my heart pounding for an entirely different reason than it had been moments earlier.

"Your mother," he finally said, "was the absolute love of my life. My grand passion, if you will. I met her just after my graduation from high school, but I didn't convince her to go out with me until her senior year, a year and half later. She didn't like me." He chuckled, his breath stirring my hair. "Thought I was arrogant. She was right." He laughed outright now. Despite my nerves being stretched beyond breaking point, I couldn't help smiling too.

"Our first date was one of the best nights of my life. We talked and laughed like old friends. That date was just the beginning. By the time her high school graduation rolled around, we had decided to get married." He stopped here and pulled away from me.

"Go on," I encouraged before he could lose his nerve.

"About that time, she was introduced to a pair of Mormon missionaries by a school friend," Jack continued, his voice sounding dead, completely devoid of emotion. "She was intrigued and planned to attend their services one Sunday. She asked me to go with her." He was quiet for several seconds, staring off into the distance, his eyes far away. "Your dad and I were great friends then. Inseparable. His opinion was the only one that mattered to me, except for Caroline's. I didn't want to go to the Mormon meeting without some kind of ally, so I invited Matthew to come with us. That turned out to be a mistake."

"What happened?" I asked, although I probably could have guessed.

"Caroline was excited by what she heard at the Mormon services," Jack replied. "She continued to go by herself after that first week. Mormon beliefs were much too restrictive for my taste. But Caroline seemed to inhale as much information as she could get. I believed it was just a passing interest—that it would fade with time." He rubbed a weary hand over his face, as though my mother's religious sympathies were as much a burden to him now as they had been thirty years ago.

"The more time she spent with the Mormons, the more concerned I became. It felt to me as if the more involved she became with them, the less involved she was with me. We didn't jive like we used to. I wasn't associated with this new part of her life, and that scared me. I felt that the attachment we had to each other was sanctioned by God. How else could it be so powerful? Anything that could tear it apart had to be evil. Finally, I confronted her about it. She told me that she wanted to be baptized into the Mormon faith. I told her that I thought she was making a mistake. It didn't change anything. She always was feisty. Like you." Jack smiled, but it was strained.

He picked up my hand almost absentmindedly and began stroking the back of it. "I told her that if she joined the Mormons, our relationship wouldn't survive. I gave her an ultimatum. If she joined the Mormons, we were through." Jack looked down and it was several seconds before I realized that he was fighting emotion. My heart ached at the sight of it.

"She wouldn't give up her newfound faith," he said, his voice a little shaky. "I told her we were finished and left her crying on her porch." Jack was still staring at our hands, not making eye contact with me. "She chased after me and asked me to talk to Matthew. Apparently, he'd been investigating the Mormon Church in secret, knowing how I objected to it. I was furious, not only that he'd been doing it behind my back, but that Caroline knew about it when I didn't." Jack's jaw tensed and I knew he was clenching his teeth. The story seemed to be taking its toll on him. It was almost as though he were reliving it as he spoke.

"I went home and found Matthew working on his car in the garage. I confronted him with what Caroline had told me. After I pressed him a bit, he confessed that he had continued to attend church with Caroline. He said that he had felt something the first time he'd gone and had wanted to investigate further. The jealousy that had only been pricking me thus far was then stabbing me full in the gut. The only thing my brain could seem to process was that my future wife had been spending every Sunday with my twin brother and had kept it from me. I let my imagination run wild, convinced that Caroline and Matthew had been seeing each other behind my back. I flew off the handle, accusing Matthew of all kinds of ridiculous things." Jack frowned in self-disgust. "You should have seen his face when I stopped for breath. Finally, he admitted that he had indeed fallen in love with Caroline but that he had done nothing about it, and that she had given him no encouragement."

I was staring at Uncle Jack in shock. This story was much more involved than I realized, and I was receiving much more detail than I had ever expected to. I felt my heart melting as I watched the emotions play across my uncle's face.

"I wasn't mollified," Uncle Jack continued. "His confession only made me angrier. I accused him over and over again of taking Caroline from me, and suddenly, she appeared in the doorway to the garage. She had come to talk things through with me and had overheard me yelling at Matthew. She sprang to his defense, telling me that he had never betrayed my trust in any way. However, she did confess that even though she had never encouraged Matthew, she had grown to care for him. She said she was confused because although she cared for Matthew, her feelings for me hadn't changed."

He looked at me pointedly. "So you see, Kate, you're not the only one who has been required to choose between two men. Your mother had the same problem."

I smiled weakly at him. Perhaps his revelation should have made me feel better, but it didn't. I just felt slightly ill at the look of fatigue and defeat on my uncle's face. Is that what happened to the losing side? I reached over and put a hand on Jack's arm. He smiled sadly and patted my hand.

"Anyway, you can imagine how I reacted to *that* news. It was everything I'd feared. I told Caroline that she had a choice. She could be with me and have nothing to do with the Mormons, or she could be with Matthew and go to hell. I thought I knew what her decision would be. She could claim that she would never turn her back on the Mormon Church, but I really believed that eventually she would choose me over some strange, new religion."

"I guess that's not what happened," I said. "What did she say to you?"

"She told me that she wouldn't choose between Matthew and I, but she would do what God expected of her, and that was to join the Mormon Church. Then she turned and walked out. I didn't see her for weeks. It was torture." Jack shuddered, remembering. "The confidence I felt at first began to turn to fear and uncertainty. I was full-on terrified by the time she finally did show up on my doorstep." He seemed to sink within himself again.

"And?" I prompted when he took too long to continue.

"Well, she told me that she felt it was better if we didn't see each other anymore. She told me that it had nothing to do with Matthew, but I couldn't see anything but a mental picture of the girl I worshipped in my brother's arms. I told her that as far as I was concerned, she and Matthew were dead and I slammed the door in her face. I never saw her again."

"That was it?" I said incredulously. "You were in love with my mother, and you never saw her again after slamming the door in her face?" I hated to say it, but I was appalled. I had known that there was no happy ending to this story, at least from my uncle's perspective, but I hadn't expected one so thoroughly depressing.

"Trust me, you can't be more disgusted with me than I am," Jack said, rubbing a hand over his face. "I have plenty of regrets from that period of my life, but none so great as the fact that I never took the opportunity to apologize. To tell her that her happiness meant more to me than my own and if she and Matthew wanted to be together, then I was happy for them."

"So that's your story?" I said, giving him a sharp look. "That's why you and my dad didn't speak? And that's why you hate my church so much? Because my mom chose it and him over you?"

"Yes, that's my story. But my story is not the issue here, Kate. Is it?" Jack said, almost sternly. "The real issue here is the critical decision that is currently sitting in your lap. I told you your parents' history for one reason only. I think knowing that your mother had to make nearly the same decision might be helpful to you. Maybe reflecting on her decision will help you make your own."

I stared into the trees on the other side of the street, biting my lip. My mother had also had to choose between two good men. One she loved passionately but didn't share her beliefs. One she loved with lesser feeling but shared her values. But she had grown to love my father as much as she had once loved my Uncle Jack . . . hadn't she? Or had she really married a man she knew she could never love as much as another? The thought was disturbing to me. I had wanted so badly to hear the story of what had happened between my Uncle Jack and my parents, but now that I had, I almost regretted it. Almost.

"Do you think she made the right choice?" I asked my uncle hesitantly. I wasn't sure I really wanted to hear his answer.

"As difficult as it may be to believe, I do," Uncle Jack said softly. "Your mother followed her heart. Even though her choice caused me a great deal of pain, pain that took me years to recover from, she did what she believed was in accordance with God's will. And that's a concept that transcends *all* religions."

With my uncle's help, I was able to get home without again encountering Tyler or Jonathan. I needed time to think—time uninterrupted by either one of the men causing me all this turmoil.

I sat cross-legged on my bed the following morning and stared blankly at the wall opposite. I thought of my mother, tried speaking to her, tried to channel her spirit, *anything* to help me make the paralyzing decision in front of me. As I sat motionless with my eyes fixed on the pale yellow wall, I heard the phone ring in the kitchen downstairs. A few seconds later I heard soft footsteps climbing the stairs.

"Marie?" Mariah sounded hesitant. Apparently my behavior from the evening before had been made public. "The phone is for you."

"Who is it?" I asked, dreading multiple answers.

"It's Tyler," she replied, even more quietly than before. "Should I tell him you're busy?"

My heart leapt in my chest as I slowly opened the door. How strange, to be separated from him by so many obstacles the day before, and to now be putting the phone to my ear, knowing he was on the other end. Without speaking, I sank back on my bed, mentally preparing myself.

"Hello?"

"Kate," he said warmly. My entire being quivered at the sound. "How are you this morning? Jonathan and I were worried about you last night."

"I'm . . . fine," I replied hesitantly.

"Right," he said, and I could hear the smile in his voice. "That was terribly convincing."

"I'm still processing, okay?" I said defensively, and I was pleased to hear that my voice had recovered some of its spunk.

"Well, can you continue to process while we go for a drive? I'd like to talk to you."

"I'm not sure that's such a great idea, Tyler," I hedged.

"Please?" he urged. " I've been waiting nearly a year to talk to you about this, you know."

I bit my lip and clenched my fist in my lap. "I know," I said softly into the phone.

"Is that a yes?" he pressed.

"Be here in ten minutes," I replied quickly and hung up before I could change my mind.

"You really scared me, Kate, running off like you did. You shouldn't have done it," Tyler's voice was resentful as we drove down the winding road toward the Milton town park. "I had no idea where you'd gone or what had happened to you. I didn't know if you were safe. It nearly drove me insane." His face held reproach as he looked over at me.

The submissiveness that had been my first inclination for this conversation evaporated, and anger, hot and intense, flared into existence. I glared at him. He had to be kidding. He was going to start off the first conversation we'd had in ages by lecturing me about what I'd done wrong?

"Don't even get me started on the things *you* shouldn't have done," I said scathingly through clenched teeth. "You have no right to scold me."

"There are things you don't understand," Tyler defended. "I did what I had to do."

"Maybe you did, but I don't have to be happy about it. And I understand more than you think." We each glared out the windshield in silence for nearly a minute.

"Kate," Tyler finally said in exasperation, running his hand through his hair. "My wife came back. I'd spent nearly a decade believing she was dead, and just when I had finally convinced myself that I was ready to try loving someone again, she suddenly appeared out of nowhere. She said she loved me and missed me. She wanted to be a family. Her daughter was in my care. It was like everything I'd regretted for ten years was suddenly and miraculously undone. And what about Addie? Did you expect me to throw her mother out of my house and deny her the opportunity to get to know Camille? *What was I supposed to do?*" He pounded his fist on the steering wheel to emphasize his words.

The wound in my chest that had been slowly scabbing over for the past year ripped wide open at a single desperate glance from him. The blinding, searing pain that I had expected from the moment of my desertion but had only experienced in small, measured doses was now coursing through me in full force. It was like torrents of burning lava were flooding through my veins. How had I managed to keep this fiery reservoir dammed up inside me and never known it was there? How could one raw look from the man I adored be sufficient to free it from its hidden restraints? And more important, how had I allowed anyone that kind of power over me? It was unlike me to surrender so much of my free will. The thought was simultaneously disturbing and exhilarating.

"I know!" I cried. "I know that you didn't have a choice! I know that you did the only thing you could have done under those circumstances! Okay? I get it!" I said desperately. "But I didn't leave you to hurt you, Tyler. I didn't run away because I was trying to get back at you. I ran because I didn't know what else to do. I couldn't handle it. I couldn't watch myself lose everything! Can't you understand that?"

Tyler stared at me, his face uncharacteristically betraying the shock he felt. "I—I didn't mean—I didn't want—"

"I don't think even you knew what you wanted," I interrupted coldly.

"You know that's not true," Tyler defended, the blood rushing to his cheeks. His eyes brightened with fervor and his knuckles whitened on the gearshift. "Don't be ridiculous, Kate. I told you over and over how much I wanted you. You were my life. I loved you!"

"I know," I said quickly. "I know you did. But that doesn't change anything. That doesn't make you less cruel for letting me go or me less cruel for leaving you. Everything is exactly the same. Oh, why did you have to come?" I turned my face to the window. My eyes were burning with unshed tears, but I didn't want him to see.

Tyler's voice was tired when it finally reached me. "I don't want to fight with you," he said, sighing. "I just need to explain some things, and then I'll let you get back to your life without me."

That life sounded horrific, though I had been living it for nearly a year. But what choice did I have? I didn't move, just stared out the window silently.

Tyler sighed again. He drove silently for a while, appearing to gather his thoughts as he did so.

"When Camille came back, it turned everything completely upside down," he finally began. "You know that. You were there. It took several minutes of staring at her before I could even begin to believe that I wasn't somehow dreaming. Trying to absorb the reality of her while still remaining faithful to my promises to you was more than I could handle at that moment. I didn't know what to do, what to say to you. I needed to collect my thoughts, to think of what my next course of action should be." He stopped at a stop sign and turned to look at me. "You never gave me that chance, Kate."

I glanced at him but remained silent. I couldn't apologize. I had done what I felt was necessary, as he had.

"Can't you imagine the panic I felt when I discovered that, despite your promise, you'd actually left me? I was terrified," he said.

"I never promised," I insisted, unable to stay silent. "I made sure I didn't, because I knew it was a promise I would break. How could you expect me to stay, Tyler? What could possibly have been made better by my presence? How would me standing there have made anything easi—"

"You left before I had the chance to accept anything!" Tyler interrupted hotly. "You walked out on me less than *ten minutes* after

I found out my dead wife was actually alive! I needed you more that day than I'd ever needed you before, but instead of staying with me, you left. You *left*! Just like she did. It was cruelty I didn't expect from you."

"I'm sorry you feel that way," I said, a little harshly. "It certainly wasn't my intention to follow in her footsteps." I folded my arms tightly across my chest and stared glumly out the window. Why were we even talking about this? How did this help anything?

Tyler said nothing. We drove in silence for nearly ten minutes, and I barely registered anything that flew by outside my window. My mind was a tangled mess of dueling desires, disappointments, hopes, and resentments. I chewed on my lower lip to keep it from forming the many various phrases that it ached to hurl in Tyler's direction. *I love you* and *I hate you* being the two most extreme and the two most common.

Finally, Tyler pulled into the parking lot of the Milton public park and turned off the engine. He turned to me and reached out to take my hand. His touch inspired the usual reaction and fiery tingles raced up my arm. I looked warily at him, wanting him to speak and yet dreading it at the same time. He seemed to be wrestling with something internally. His face alternated between determination and uncertainty. Finally, his jaw set, he met my eyes.

"I haven't handled this very well so far," he said, sighing. "I came to Milton for one purpose only. I needed to explain why I behaved the way I did. I know I promised you an eternity, and I broke that promise when Camille came back. I didn't deserve you before I made that choice, and I deserved you even less afterward. But I chose the way I did based on what I thought God expected of me."

I stared into his eyes, wanting desperately to disagree with him. How could God have sanctioned a decision that had caused so much pain? But I suspected even more damage would have been inflicted had Tyler chosen the other way. I closed my eyes and tried to think. I knew Tyler had chosen rightly, I really always had. But how did I reconcile that knowledge with the pain of desertion I still felt?

"Do you regret it?" I asked him. "Now, having lived with the consequences of your choice and having seen how it's affected those involved? Are you glad you chose the way you did, or do you wish you'd chosen differently?" It wasn't spoken in anger or in spite. It was an honest and sincere question, and I needed to hear the answer.

"No, I have no regrets, other than the pain I've caused you," Tyler answered immediately. "I believe I did what was expected of me."

I nodded firmly. So that was the end of it. Tyler had chosen well, if only for himself and those entrusted to his care, and I would learn to live with it. The hopes that had been haunting my thoughts for the past year—namely that Tyler would return and claim me—were now dashed to pieces, but surprisingly little pain accompanied the wreckage. Although the hopes had definitely been planted somewhere within me, their roots had not been deep. Their annihilation would not annihilate me. But I did have one final question for the man that had once been my sole dream for the future.

"Are you happy?" I asked him.

He stared back at me, seeming momentarily stunned by the question. "I . . . am not unhappy," he finally responded. "I'm perfectly content with the way things have turned out."

It was not exactly the answer I had been hoping for, but contentment was far better than misery. And if he could escape the grief I had suffered, then what more could I ask for?

"I'm glad," I said honestly. "If you're content with your life, then I have nothing to complain about." I turned my hand in his and squeezed his fingers momentarily and then released them.

"We'd probably better head back to River House," I said calmly. "I'm sure they're wondering where we are."

"They, or just Jonathan?" Tyler said quietly as he once again started the engine of the luxurious car. He glanced at me before speaking again, and I noticed that he looked pensive. "Kate, I think I owe you another apology," Tyler said as he steered the car back onto the road.

"Oh?" I said, looking back at his face. "What for?"

"For Jonathan's relocation," Tyler said. "I know he means a great deal to you, and I also know that he volunteered for the position in Tokyo because he knew I wanted him to go."

"So you really did intend for him to take it?" I asked with an eyebrow raised.

"Yes," Tyler said, sounding slightly ashamed. "I needed him gone for a while. I'm not proud of it, but I had a hard time even looking at him after stumbling upon you two on New Year's."

"He knew you did," I said with a small smile. "But I don't think that was the only reason he volunteered. He was excited for the opportunity. I think he probably would have gone anyway."

"You're both more forgiving than I deserve." Tyler smiled at me, and my heart fluttered. It would take awhile to master these reflex reactions. Hopefully once he had left for good, they would subside.

We arrived at River House shortly thereafter, and I wasn't surprised to immediately run into Jonathan. It appeared that he had been watching for our return, because he met me in the entryway.

"Are you okay?" he asked in concern, running his hands from my shoulders to my elbows. "I've been trying to call Tyler, but he turned his phone off."

"Why? Is something wrong?" I asked, alarmed.

"No, everything's fine. I just . . ." Jonathan looked suddenly sheepish. "I was just worried about you. Tyler had no right to just spirit you away like that."

"Oh, it was fine," I said quickly. "We had a nice little chat." I smiled vaguely at Tyler as he brushed by me, ignoring Jonathan's marked glare in his direction.

"Did you?" Jonathan said, watching Tyler's back as it disappeared into the sitting room. "*How* nice?"

"Nice enough that I no longer feel an incapacitating sense of loss every time I think of him," I answered, not quite truthfully. Someday, though, that statement would be absolute fact, I was determined.

Jonathan didn't look particularly comforted by my words. "Did you come to any kind of understanding?"

"Yes," I said. "Tyler is returning home, as he should, and I am staying here, as I should."

Jonathan looked taken aback. "Tyler's going back to Thorne Field?"

"Yes," I answered firmly. "Or New York. And I will stay here."

"Are you sure?" Jonathan asked, watching my face closely. "You're sure that's what you want?"

"What I want isn't important," I said. "It's what's right."

Jonathan watched me steadily for a few seconds before looking away. He seemed perplexed, as if he wasn't sure what to make of my words. I didn't blame him. After my years of obsession with Tyler Thorne, this sudden change of attitude must seem completely bizarre to him.

He took my hand gently in his own and led me distractedly toward the staircase. "You look exhausted," he said finally. "That must have been a rough conversation for you. Why don't you go lie down for awhile?"

"Thanks, Jonathan. I think I will," I said and kissed him quickly on his cheek. "It's so good to have you home."

Jonathan smiled and returned my sentiments by kissing me softly on the lips before heading toward the kitchen. I felt the familiar faint fluttering in my middle, and I smiled. Maybe there was hope after all.

twenty-one

I felt Jonathan's hands on my shoulders as I stood next to his rented SUV the next day. Sighing, I turned to face him. He didn't seem to care that three pairs of eyes were watching us as his arms closed around me. Mariah and Danielle observed from the door to the house, and Tyler stood next to the driver-side door of the SUV, eyeing us with a slightly pained look. I took a deep breath and tried to ignore it, but I could feel those eyes boring into me. The pull I felt toward Tyler had not faded in the slightest despite our conversation the day before, but I hadn't really expected it to. Still, I had to try. I willed those strange steel bands that bound me so securely to Tyler Thorne to loosen, to drop off. If I could manage that, perhaps I could attempt to weld them to the man currently enfolding me in his arms. So far they were proving maddeningly resilient, however. What could I do? Gritting my teeth, I stared determinedly into Jonathan's handsome face. He didn't seem to notice my expression of extreme focus.

"You never answered me, you know," he said softly, without preface. His comment didn't require one.

"I know," I said, looking away.

"Are you planning on ever doing so?" he asked, turning my chin with his finger. "I'd really appreciate it if you would."

"I know that too," I said, and sighed. "Jonathan, I just can't give you an answer right now. I'm not sure I'm ready to marry you. I promise to think and to pray about it, but beyond that, I can't promise you anything."

"Well, I guess I can't ask more than that," Jonathan said, and he smiled, but his smile was not a particularly happy one. He took my face softly between his hands and lowered his lips to mine.

It was a bizarre sensation, brushing my lips against his with Tyler standing scarcely twenty feet away, waiting rigidly for the embrace to end. I felt strangely unfaithful. I clenched my teeth in determination and fists balled at my sides. I would overcome this. The familiar faint warmth stirred in my stomach as Jonathan's arms held me close to him. I willed the feeling to be stronger. I commanded it to expand into the passionate, burning, driving need I knew I was capable of feeling. It refused to obey me, and no miraculous change took place.

I wanted to cry. Yes, the warmth was pleasant, but it was so tame compared to what I longed to feel. What I did feel . . . for someone else. Despairing, I pulled back. It was so unfair to Jonathan. I stood in his arms, but at least for now, I didn't belong to him.

Jonathan looked down at me in consternation.

"What is it?" he asked as he noticed my distressed expression.

I shook my head, not wanting to discuss it with so many people watching and waiting. "Bye, Jonathan," I said.

He watched me steadily for a minute, then nodded in understanding. "Bye, Kate," he said. I smiled apologetically up at him, soaking in the last moments of my dear friend's presence. "See you in a couple of months. Good luck with your various corporate ventures."

"Thanks." He rolled his eyes, but his face quickly morphed into seriousness. "Please think, okay? You hold my whole happiness in your hands, you know that?"

This did not help me. "I will think," I promised. Then, with a teasing smile to lighten the serious mood, I pushed Jonathan toward the waiting vehicle. "Now, go on; get out of here. You'll miss your flight."

Jonathan squeezed me one last time and then strode to the SUV, taking the time to wave to his sisters and shake Tyler's hand warmly before climbing in. It appeared, temporarily at least, that they had reached a truce.

Tyler and I watched silently as the SUV disappeared down the road.

"He'll be back soon," Tyler said in a comforting tone. "And I don't think he'll be spending as much time in Japan as we originally thought."

"That's good news," I said. "Danielle and Mariah will be thrilled about that."

"It must be difficult for you, to watch him go."

"Sure," I said, shrugging. "I'm always sad to see him leave, but I'm pretty used to living without him, you know."

Tyler looked at me closely but said nothing.

"Well, shall we go in?" I said with false brightness. I turned around and started walking toward the house.

"Well, actually, Kate, I'm taking off too," Tyler said quickly, catching me by the arm. I stopped and stared at him.

"You're leaving?" I said, trying to keep the distress out of my voice. "Already?"

"I think it's probably best," Tyler said. "I got up early and packed my car, so I'm all ready to get out of your hair."

"But my hair's just fine with you in it!" I cried without thinking. I bit my lip in dismay. So far the Tyler Emotional Release campaign wasn't progressing very well.

Tyler smiled at me, his eyes crinkling at the corners. "It does look pretty good," he said, reaching out to brush some of the flyaway strands from my face. He studied me for a moment without speaking. Suddenly he reached out and pulled me firmly against his chest. I felt his lips on the top of my head as he wrapped his arms around me, his hands pressing into my back. "Take care of yourself, all right?"

My voice was lodged somewhere in my rib cage, so I just nodded mutely. Fire was building at every point of contact that connected us and the ferocity of the flames licked at my insides. My heart had begun to pound and my lungs constricted as though they had suddenly turned to concrete. It was impossible to breathe, let alone speak. I wanted to scream in frustration. How was I supposed to overcome this? It was like some bizarre chemical resided in his skin that reacted violently when in contact with mine. How could simple physical contact with him melt all my defenses and determination so easily? I pulled away abruptly, afraid of what I would do if he remained touching me for much longer.

Tyler let me go but reached out with a single hand to slide his fingertips across my face. Then, without a word, he turned and walked to his car and got in. I watched his car disappear with an acute sense of loss that I couldn't help but notice had been strangely absent at the moment Jonathan had driven away. Sighing, I turned and walked toward the house.

The next couple of months flew by with surprising speed, now that the dreaded art show was over. I continued to speak with Jonathan on a weekly basis, determined to keep our relationship as it had been before. He did not press me to answer his proposal, and I was grateful. Although nearly everyone that knew of it had determined that my marrying Jonathan was pretty much inevitable, I couldn't bring myself to commit to it. That probably should have been a significant warning sign to me, but I was so busy with my classes and Danielle's hurried wedding plans, and trying to eradicate all traces of Tyler from inside my head and heart, that I wasn't terribly focused on warning signs.

"Hurry, hurry, hurry!" Mariah called to Danielle and me as she rushed through the sitting room, arms full of sheets and towels she had just pulled from the dryer. "You two are *still* straightening this room? They'll be here any minute!"

I ignored her rebuke as I sprinted around the room plumping every pillow and cushion in sight.

Danielle did not follow my example. "Mariah," she said resentfully as she tried to get a fire started in the grated fireplace. "Don't rush us. Do you know what you end up with when you rush fire-lighting and pillow-plumping? A pile of charred rubble that used to be a house, that's what. Besides, Alex needs a bed with sheets on it more than he needs a roaring fire, and guess who was assigned *that* chore?"

Mariah muttered something that sounded like an insult under her breath as she raced up the stairs, but I didn't catch it.

"There!" Danielle said in triumph a few minutes later. The flames began to snap and pop as they consumed the logs placed attractively in the grate, and Danielle sat back on her feet. "Not bad," she congratulated herself as she took in the pine-decorated mantelpiece, complete with stockings and Christmas lights. "I should just abandon the teaching thing and go into interior decorating."

"It looks great," I agreed enthusiastically. The room was cozy and festive, and the brightly colored tree in the corner made it worthy of a Christmas card. My admiration was cut short by the sound of the doorbell. Danielle beamed at me before shooting to her feet and racing down the hall toward the entryway.

"Alex!" I heard her cry at the same time I heard the door creak open. As I emerged from the hallway, I beheld a scene that was similar to the year before, when I had been astonished to find Jonathan standing in the entryway of my new home. Now I was just pleased to see him there. He smiled at me over his sister's shoulder and reached out a hand to grasp mine.

As soon as Danielle saw fit to release him, he enfolded me in his arms and pressed a kiss to my forehead. "You look wonderful," he whispered, before releasing me.

I smiled at him, but my attention was snatched away by the sight of Danielle's enthusiastic reception of her fiancé, Carson, who had arrived right behind Jonathan. I tried not to snicker as she wholeheartedly plastered his face with kisses, causing him to laugh and blush.

"What are you all doing standing in the entryway?" Mariah's voice came from the doorway to the sitting room. "Come on in and sit down! You have just enough time to warm up before dinner is ready."

The next few days were a whirlwind of activity. While Danielle and I had managed to get the Christmas decorations up in the sitting room, the other rooms in the house were sadly lacking any kind of holiday cheer. Jonathan, eager for employment, had undertaken the responsibility, much to the amusement of the household. We watched him hang twinkle lights and sleigh bells with abandon, making sure to compliment his work copiously. Admittedly, the compliments were given simply so he would keep doing it and spare the rest of us the job.

"So, what do you think?" he asked after he finished hanging the pine garlands on nails around the dining room. "Looks pretty good, doesn't it?"

"You have a gift," I agreed, smiling.

"Well, obviously," he said teasingly. He winked at me and headed toward the stairs to hang a sadly bedraggled wreath. My heart warmed as I watched his boyish excitement.

"He would be such a wonderful father," I heard from behind me. I turned to see Mariah standing there, a gentle smile on her face as she watched her brother. "It's such a waste."

"I'm sure he will be a father, someday," I comforted her.

Mariah eyed me speculatively. "Oh?" she questioned. "You think so?" I caught a glimpse of a sly smile, but she hid it quickly.

Uh-oh. I could see where *this* was going. "I'm not going to have this conversation," I said loftily.

"What conversation?" she said innocently, but I wasn't fooled. Noting my uncompromising look, she capitulated.

"Look, I know you said you weren't ready to marry him. But if you don't mind me asking"—Mariah looked at me pointedly—"why aren't you ready? I mean, Alex is the kind of man most women would dream of marrying. What's holding you back? Tyler is back with his wife, right?"

"Yes." I sighed. "I know what you're thinking. Since there's no chance I'll ever get to be with Tyler again, why can't I just settle down with Jonathan and be happy?" I sighed again. "I really wish I could, but I just can't agree to marry him in good conscience when I'm still so attached to someone else. When my feelings for Tyler begin to fade, I'll feel better about agreeing to marry Jonathan."

"So you're just going to let him wait?" Mariah looked disapproving, reminding me of the last time we had discussed this topic. "Really? You're just going torture him like that? That's not you."

Torture? I stared at her, and I could feel the dismay that her words inspired climbing northward from my gut to finally settle on my face. "You think I'm being selfish," I said. "Maybe you're right. But do you really think it would be even worse to make Jonathan wait than to just marry him with the knowledge that I feel differently for him than I did for Tyler?" I studied her face for a second, then groaned and put my head in my hands. "Oh, what's wrong with me? Why is everything so complicated?"

"It's because you're trying so hard to make the decision that's best for everyone else that you're not considering the possibility that the decision that's best for you might actually be what's best for everyone," Mariah counseled, rubbing my back gently. "You're trying so hard to be unselfish that you've come full circle and you're being selfish anyway. So . . . I can't believe I'm saying this, but . . . why not change your strategy? Try being selfish."

My head snapped up in surprise. "What?" I asked in confusion.

"Go ahead, be selfish," she repeated. "Maybe you'll actually end up making the decision you want to make instead of the one you think you're supposed to make. And maybe it will actually turn out to be the right one. Besides, why not think of yourself? This is your life, after all. So . . . what do you want?"

I looked at her and said nothing. What did I want? As I sat and contemplated, it occurred to me that the room had become very quiet. I could no longer hear the evidence of Jonathan's decorating frenzy. I glanced toward the staircase and saw him leaning against the wall, watching us speculatively. I blushed, wondering how much he'd heard. Smiling softly at me, he turned and left the room.

"Remember, Marie," Mariah said softly to me as we watched Jonathan go, "God put us on this earth to be happy. He knows what He's doing. If you make the decision that's in accordance with His will, you'll ultimately end up happy, and so will everybody else. You won't be able to help it. Because that's the way God planned it."

It was so interesting to me that some of the most profound concepts I had learned about the Lord had been taught to me by people who didn't share my religious beliefs. First Uncle Jack and now Mariah, individuals with decidedly different ideas and views about God and religion, had both emphasized to me the importance of making decisions in accordance with the will of the Lord. And despite our differences of opinion on spiritual matters, I was listening to them. Because somehow, I knew that He was trying to tell me something.

"Kate, can I talk to you for a second?" Jonathan approached me right after dinner later that evening with a determined look on his face.

"Sure, just let me clear these dishes," I said, rolling up my sleeves and reaching for the plates on the newly vacated table.

"I'll get them," Mariah said, snatching them before I could reach them. "You go ahead."

Jonathan didn't need to be told twice. He grasped my arm and led me firmly from the room.

"Ow," I complained when he had deposited me on a chair in the living room. "What's with the death grip? What's going on?"

"I need some . . . clarification, shall we say," Jonathan said. His expression was strange to me, one I hadn't seen before. It was a mixture of emotions. Determination, fear, hope, resignation, and resolve were a few I could identify as I searched it.

"Okay . . ." I prompted. "Clarification about what?"

"When Tyler was here a couple months back," he began and my middle clenched. I really didn't want to talk about Tyler with Jonathan. I always seemed to say something to hurt him when we did that. "You decided that it was best if you went your separate ways. I guess I'm a little curious as to why. I mean, I know how you feel about him. Why did you let him go?"

"Jonathan!" I cried in dismay. "I'm surprised you have to ask. How could you think I would encourage him to leave his family? You know me better than that. Yes, I love Tyler. I'm pretty sure I always will, but I would never have him abandon Camille and Addie! As much as I wish it were otherwise, he belongs with them."

"So you let him go so he could go back to Camille?" Jonathan clarified. "The only reason you agreed to go your separate ways was so he could return to his wife? If she had been taken completely out of the equation, you would have gone with him?"

"What are you talking about?" I said. His expression had changed, focused into a pinpoint of fierce energy that was burning into my eyes.

"He never even gave me that option. It never even was an option. He didn't come here to take me anywhere; he came to explain himself. What's going on? Why are you asking me these questions?"

"Kate." Jonathan sat next to me and took my hand in his. He appeared to be steeling himself to say something he desperately didn't want to say. "Camille left Tyler three months ago. They're not together anymore."

I felt as though every muscle in my body had turned to granite. I stared at Jonathan, dumbfounded. "She . . . she's gone?" I asked. "She left him? Again?" I remembered the look on Tyler's face years earlier when he had told me of Camille's first abandonment. It had been an expression of agony that could only be described as profound. And he was suffering it again? He had been feeling that same pain when he had been here, in Milton, and I had never known. My heart seared for him.

"She's gone," Jonathan confirmed. His face had finally decided on an emotion. A knowing sadness filled those eyes and his fingers gently stroked mine.

"Why didn't he *tell* me?" I breathed. "He knew I thought that he and Camille were still together, and he let me go on thinking it! Why didn't he tell me?"

"That's what I asked him today," Jonathan said. He looked down at our hands momentarily and then back at me. "I overheard you talking to Mariah this morning. I heard what you said about him returning to his wife. I didn't realize that Tyler had never told you about Camille leaving. When I overheard you today, I called Tyler. I wanted to make sure I understood what had happened. I asked him why he had never told you. He told me that when he had stumbled upon my proposal to you in October, he thought that you had moved on, fallen in love with me. He had originally come to tell you that he was no longer married, but when he saw us together, he thought he was too late. He told me today that he didn't want to complicate your life by throwing himself into the mix again. So he just let you continue in your assumption that he was still married."

I was chewing the inside of my lip so determinedly that I was surprised I hadn't chewed right through. Jonathan sensed my agitation and continued, "But I knew that Camille had left him. He told me the night he came back, the night of the art show. I never mentioned it to you because, one, I thought you knew already, and, two, I didn't want to emphasize the fact that Tyler was available. Ultimately, I thought the situation was that he had told you and you had chosen to let him go anyway. I have to admit, I was confused. I didn't understand why you didn't go with him when you so obviously wanted him so much. That's why I haven't pressed you to give me an answer to my proposal." Jonathan looked out the window, his eyes searching the trees along the road in front of the house. "I'll also admit that I was even a little bit flattered. I thought you were torn between us. I thought that maybe you had even come to realize that you loved me more. I should have known better than that. I never did quite measure up to him, did I?" He looked back at me again, and I saw the edge of pain, which as soon as I recognized it, transferred immediately to me. It hurt so much more knowing I had caused it.

"Today, when I heard you talking to Mariah, I knew I had been wrong. You weren't here with me because you loved me most. You were here because you believed the man you loved more than me belonged to someone else." Jonathan stared fixedly at me, his eyes roaming over my face as he spoke. "Most people would probably call me crazy for telling you this. After all, I am the next in line." He laughed ruefully. "But I love you enough to let you have the choice you want. And I suspect it isn't me."

"Jonathan, I . . . ," I began, but couldn't finish. He was such a good man. I almost hated myself for not being able to love him as he deserved.

"I really could have been second best, Kate," he said, his voice a little choked. "If everything had stayed the same, if Camille had never left and Tyler had been honestly devoted to her, I could have been happy being your husband, knowing I was second to him in your affections. I always knew I would be. I knew that even if you married me, you would never love me as you had loved him. And I had reconciled myself to that. Honestly, I accepted it. But I can't accept being your husband when there is a better, happier option for you. I couldn't do that to you . . . or him."

Jonathan reached into his pocket and pulled out a folded envelope. He handed it to me without another word. I unfolded it silently and pulled out a single airline ticket to Salt Lake City, Utah. The tears that had been threatening were now overflowing. I didn't even try to hide them. I threw my arms around Jonathan's neck and pressed my lips to his cheek.

"I love you, Jonathan," I said.

"I know you do," Jonathan said, smoothing my hair as his eyes searched mine. "And I also know that it would never have been enough. And that's okay." He smiled, a sad, but genuine smile, and kissed me quickly on the forehead. "Now get going. Don't worry about my sisters. I'll explain it to them. If you hurry, you just might make it to Thorne Field for Christmas."

I gave him one last squeeze and jumped to my feet. I raced upstairs and packed the bare essentials for a trip to Utah in the dead of winter and, within ten minutes, was on my way to the airport, my ticket home clutched in my hand.

twenty-two

The long plane ride to Utah was a horribly uncomfortable experience. My emotions were about as calm as a blizzard, hurricane, and tornado all rolled into one. I experienced exhilarating bliss one moment and sank into a horrible depression the next. My thoughts seemed to bounce off the walls of the metal tube in which I sat, showing me first Tyler's face and then Jonathan's. One held an imagined look of joy, the other, a remembered expression of devastation. Everything was so uncertain, and I prayed for peace, some kind of assurance that what I was doing was right. But I felt nothing but the disorderly emotions that had plagued me since takeoff. I sat back in my seat and breathed deeply, hoping to calm the fluttering and battering in my stomach.

"Feeling sick?" said a voice next to me. "It's just a little turbulence. It will pass."

I looked over and met the kindly eyes of the aged gentleman sitting next to me.

"I hope so," I said, speaking of a completely different kind of turbulence.

"Don't worry," he said, chuckling. "It feels worse than it is. Going home for Christmas?"

"Yes," I answered, and I couldn't stop the tears from pricking my eyes. "I'm going home."

Suddenly the screens on the ceiling of the aircraft descended and an announcement was made that the flight attendant was beginning the in-flight movie. The first scene opened on a panoramic view of a New England autumn. I was suddenly confronted with a vision. I was driving down a dirt lane in late September sunshine toward a massive structure. I remembered comparing the fiery mountain brilliance around me to fall in New England. A self-deprecating smile had appeared on my face at the comparison as I considered the fact that I had never actually seen a New England autumn at that point.

Well, now I had. Twice. It seemed so long since I had driven down that dirt road. The memory felt faded and almost from a different life, as did everything in my life before Tyler, despite the fact that the experience had taken place only two years previously. How much had changed since then! Turning my head toward the small window, I stared into winter sunshine winking brightly above the clouds. I closed my eyes and did something I had not done willingly for a very long time. I allowed my mind to travel back. Totally, completely, and thoroughly back. I breathed deeply as the memories washed over me. I saw Addie and Charlotte as they had been on the day I had arrived at Thorne Field. Addie with her long dark curls and chocolate eyes. Charlotte, her smile warm and friendly. I remembered the day I had first encountered Tyler, nearly meeting my death under the wheels of his monstrous truck. I remembered his furious expression as he approached me in the snow. I remembered my initial dislike of him, nearly laughing out loud at how I ever could have hated such an extraordinary man. I savored each memory, letting them all slip through my consciousness one at a time, reliving them in turn. From our first words to each other to our last, the recollections were as perfect as the day they were made. I sighed in contentment as I allowed my mind to focus on every detail and nuance that I had suppressed in the past year. I had no further need for restraint. I could allow the memories to flow freely, unhindered by fear of pain and sadness. Instead there was only hope, and the memories were like a salve instead of the serrated knife they'd been before. I burrowed more deeply into them, slowing them down in my mind, and studying Tyler's every expression and feature.

I recalled every moment, those of joy and those of pain. I watched the scenes play out in my head like the movie playing on the screen above me. I touched Tyler's arm softly as he related the story of his past. I watched him sweep me up into his arms the day I had rescued Addie from an oncoming car. I saw him, bright eyed and laughing, his arms tightly wrapped around Amanda Ives. I stood beside him at the window on the second floor landing of the ranch house, watching the moonlight spill onto the flower beds. I felt his arms fold around me as they had the night he had finally confessed that he was in love with me. I watched him kneel before me in the garden and ask me to become his wife. I saw the fear and uncertainty in his eyes the day Camille had returned. I felt his firm grip on my shoulders as he begged me not to leave him. And even more clearly, I saw the noble acceptance in his face, though I hadn't recognized it at the time, as he chose to sacrifice his happiness for mine, leaving me behind with Jonathan. I felt all the emotions of each experience as if I were experiencing them for the first time. Tears rolled down my cheeks and a smile touched my lips in turn.

And I could *feel* it. Every sting, every joyful leap. Finally, I had found the heart that had disappeared into its drawer on the day Camille had reappeared at Thorne Field. The novocaine that had paralyzed it for the past year had, at last, been flushed away by faith, leaving it as fully exposed to pain as I'd feared. But it was also open to joy and to love and to life and to the Spirit. And finally, with gratitude streaming down my cheeks, I found peace.

I drove through Oakley around 9:00 p.m., and the night was pitch black. I squinted through the darkness, searching for the turnoff to Thorne Field Ranch. It was easier to find than I expected. It was almost as though I felt it rather than saw it. I drove slowly up the familiar mountain road, as much to savor the experience as for safety reasons. Despite the yearlong absence, every turn, every bump in that road was familiar to me. I couldn't stop myself from smiling as I bounced and jolted along.

I bit my lip in excitement as I approached the last curve in the road before it straightened out and I would see Thorne Field. Throwing caution to the wind, I gunned the engine as I rounded the bend. My headlights caught the outline of a hunched figure wading through the deep snow at the side of the road just as the rented jeep began to slide. I spun the wheel, frantically trying to miss the lone hiker and stay on the road at the same time. I saw the figure dive to the left, and the jeep continued to slide as if braking were a completely unfamiliar concept. It lurched hard to the right along the icy embankment. I realized then that my eyes were closed. Opening them only when I was absolutely certain that the jeep had come to a full and complete halt, I stared through the windshield and my eyes widened in shock. I was less than six inches away from the trunk of an enormous tree. I shuddered to think of what would have happened to the jeep and to me if we had made contact.

Suddenly, I recalled the lone figure I had seen just as my jeep had made its bid for freedom. I leapt out of the small SUV and crunched through the deep snow, searching for the shape I knew was lying somewhere in the whiteness surrounding me.

"Hello?" I called a little uncertainly. "Is somebody there? Are you all right?" I squinted into the dark, trying to make out any shape that looked remotely human. The jeep's headlights were no help at all, since they faced the opposite direction. "Hello?" I called again.

I heard the sound of crunching snow off to my left. I turned instinctively toward it and saw the shadow of a hulking figure rising from where it had fallen.

"Are you all right?" I asked again.

"I'm fine," said the figure in a voice so familiar that my heart immediately flew into a frantic rage of palpitations.

"Are you sure?" I asked, and I saw the shadowy head suddenly snap up. Even though I couldn't see them, I knew those blue eyes were fixed on my shape. I also knew, because the jeep's headlights were behind me, he couldn't see my face.

"Who is that?" he said. I couldn't help but smile at the sudden eagerness in his voice. "Say something!" he demanded. His tone was harsh and forceful, but not angry.

"Tyler?" I said, my voice shaking pathetically with a mixture of excitement, fear, and impatience. I wanted to run to him, but my legs felt rooted into the snow beneath me. I just stood there, staring at the tall shadow, barely breathing.

In response to my question, I heard the crunch of a halting footstep. It echoed somewhere in front of me, but it stopped much too soon. The distance between us seemed like miles, and each moment he stood staring at my outline was agony. Finally, a sound came from the darkness in front of me.

"Kate?" I heard him whisper. It wasn't meant for my ears, but I recognized the tone of it anyway. It was a soft exclamation of shock, tinged with disbelief. I heard another halting footstep, and his outline became slightly clearer as he moved another foot in my direction. I wanted to groan in frustration at his deliberate advance. Were his joints frozen? What was taking him so long? To remedy the situation, I yanked up my imaginary roots and took a stumbling step of my own toward him.

"Hang on," he said, and I saw the shadow put up a restraining hand to stop my movement. "Just . . . give me a second." I recognized the timbre of his voice. He was deliberating, allowing the information to process in that dark head of his.

"What are you doing here?" he finally said softly. He had a hard time getting the words past his lips, as though he wasn't quite sure if he really wanted to hear the answer. I still couldn't see his face, but I could imagine it. I had no doubt that his voice exactly mirrored his facial expression. Shock, hope, fear, desire, impatience . . . all the very same emotions that danced in my middle and raced through my extremities.

"Jonathan told me," was all I said. I fully expected him to understand what was meant in those three words. In them lay the final outcome of the most difficult decision I had ever had to make. In those words was the proof of Jonathan's goodness as a man and as a friend. They restored everything that had been previously taken away from both of us. But more important, the meaning of those three little words paralleled the meaning of another set of three little words, as proven by my presence on his property. I expected Tyler to know that, but he seemed to need verification.

"And?" he said.

"And here I am," I replied simply.

"Well, why did you come?"

That stopped me cold. What? Why did he think I'd come?

"Because . . . because I . . . ," I stuttered. What should I say? It should have been so easy, but suddenly my mind was blank.

"Because you felt sorry for me," he said with a hard finality.

"Sorry for you?" I repeated dumbly. Well, yeah, I felt sorry for him. His wife had just left him for the second time. But that had been the last thing on my mind as I'd jettisoned across the country. I had come because I needed him, loved him so deeply that the thought of not being with him was unthinkable. My reasons for coming had been 100 percent selfish.

"I don't need your pity," he said, his voice icy.

"I know you don't!" I shot back. "I don't remember offering you any!"

Tyler took several determined steps in my direction. We were only a few feet apart. I could now make out his expression, and I was dismayed at how unfriendly it appeared.

"Why did you have to come back?" he said. His voice was still cold but had softened slightly with something like despair. "Why couldn't you have just stayed away? I'd almost come to terms with it. I had almost accepted things the way they were. Now it's all over. Now I have to start again." He stood motionless in the snow, one hand in the pocket of his jeans, the other rubbing his furrowed forehead.

"I see," I said softly. "So, you want me to leave then?"

"It will be easier for me if you go now rather than later," he replied. The words sounded dead in his throat. "The longer you stay, the more difficult it will be for me to watch you leave. Besides, I'm sure Jonathan doesn't love the fact that you came at all. Let's not make things harder on him than they have to be."

Suddenly everything about his stiff and hesitant reception clicked into place. Tyler believed I was with Jonathan! He thought I had come just to make sure he was all right after Camille's desertion, and that I would be leaving him to return to Jonathan afterward. The relief was nearly tangible, and I almost laughed out loud.

"What if," I said, smothering my smile as I began to close the distance between us, "I didn't have to go back?"

Tyler's fingers stopped their kneading of his temples, and he looked up. "What do you mean?" he demanded.

"What if I wanted to stay with you?" I said, taking another step toward him. I was inches from him now, and I reached forward and began playing with the zipper on his tan jacket.

"Stay with me?" Tyler repeated, and I could hear his breath come faster as he watched my fingers slide their way up his chest toward his face. I put a hand to his cheek and looked him in the eye.

"Why, of course. Thank you for asking," I teased as I slid my hand around the back of his head. Tyler stopped breathing altogether as I pulled myself closer to him. Finally, his arm came slowly around me as his face descended toward mine, but just before our lips touched, he stopped. He stared fixedly into my eyes, one hand cradling my cheek, for several seconds.

"I love you," he said with a conviction that made me ache inside.

Our lips met and the instant they touched, my newly rediscovered heart pounded in furious joy, providing me with irrefutable proof of its resurrection. My skin exploded in tingles and fireworks, and every feeling that I had ever experienced in Tyler's arms rippled throughout my frame, compounded a million times. The slow burn flared again into existence in the center of my chest. The feeling was old and familiar—the sense of being lit from within. I could have sworn that we were glowing, lighting the night around us. I felt Tyler's tongue lightly trace the top of my bottom lip and I shivered and gasped, fire ripping through my middle at the sensation. I gripped the front of his coat and pulled him closer, my knees weakening. Tyler seemed to sense that my poor, shaking legs were about to give out, and he pulled away. He seemed a little unsteady himself, but my vision was so blurred I couldn't be sure.

"You came back to me," he said after a moment. His freezing cold fingers searched my face blindly, hungry to see the features his eyes couldn't clearly make out.

"Of course I did," I replied, closing my eyes at his touch.

"I thought you had fallen in love with Jonathan," he said, his voice warm and steady. "I didn't tell you about Camille because I believed you had made your choice, and I didn't want to complicate things."

"I know. I understand," I said, smoothing the worried lines from his forehead with my fingertips.

"I thought for a while it might kill me," Tyler said with a wan smile. "But I kept my mouth shut. I believed that for once I was doing the right thing by you. It was the worst possible thing for me, but as long as you were happy, I could live with it. But I don't think what I've been doing for the past two months qualifies as living."

"I think I can comprehend that idea," I said softly, thinking of what my life had been the first few months after I had left him.

"Are you really going to stay with me?" he asked. His voice contained almost a childlike hope, and I smiled.

"As long as you want me," I answered, pressing a kiss to his thumb as he traced it over my lips.

"I hope you're not afraid of forever, then," he said softly as he pulled me once more into his arms.

Ten minutes later, we were driving across the small valley toward Thorne Field Ranch, Tyler at the wheel. I saw the lights of the house shining ahead and my heart began to pound. Inside that house slept two of the people I loved most in the world.

"How's Addie?" I asked, turning eagerly to Tyler. "And Charlotte?"

"They're both fine." He smiled at me. "Much better now than they were a few months ago."

"What happened?" I asked. As I knew he would, Tyler understood that I was actually asking for the whole story, and he started at the beginning.

"After you left, I wasn't really sure which way was up for a while. Naturally, I asked Camille where she had been for the past ten years, expecting to hear the story of some kind of terrible misunderstanding between Camille's doctors and her lawyer. But instead Camille explained to me that she had instructed her lawyer to tell me that she was dead so that I wouldn't try to send Addie back to her. She told me that when Addie was born, she panicked, convinced that she could never be the kind of mother Addie deserved. She decided that the best thing for Addie was to send her to me, where hopefully money would make up for Camille's maternal failings." I heard the disgust in Tyler's voice as he said it, and I knew he was referring to more than what he had just imparted to me. I was more eager than ever to hear the entire story.

"I didn't think much of her excuse, but I was still so thrown over you disappearing without a trace that I didn't really challenge it. Camille was surprisingly patient with my depression at first, and she didn't even object to the fact that I was actively trying to find you. I think the reason for it was because she was afraid that if I snapped out of it too soon, I might give her more substantial grief for pretending to be dead all those years. She put on an incredibly convincing show of sincerity, and I found myself believing her when she said she regretted what she'd done. I was so shell-shocked, though, that convincing me of anything wasn't particularly difficult. I had a hard time focusing on anything except how much I missed you." At this point, he reached over and intertwined his fingers with mine, as if reassuring himself that I was actually seated next to him.

"I think it finally got to her after awhile, though," he continued. "Especially after we ran into you and Jonathan in Times Square. When she saw how much it affected me to see you with Jonathan, she confronted me about it. She told me she was sorry that her coming back had caused me so much misery, and maybe it would have been better if she really had died. I felt guilty then, because I had found myself wishing, just now and then, that she really had. At least you never would have left."

"Why did she come back?" I asked, interrupting his story. "She stayed away for ten years! What made her suddenly decide to return to you?"

"I asked her that question, but I never really got a great answer," Tyler replied. "She told me that her main reason was regret. She regretted giving up our marriage and especially her chance to know her daughter. That's what she said. But I'm inclined to think her reasons for coming back were purely monetary. I got the sense that her financial situation was pretty miserable. But I have to admit, if it's true she was motivated by greed, I'm glad. It made her dedication to staying much weaker than if she had truly missed me. And I don't think either Camille or I was happy with our situation."

"Really?" I asked, raising my eyebrows and grinning mischievously. "You seemed happy enough to see her from where I was standing."

Tyler shot me a stern look. "Well, you didn't see much but the initial shock, now did you?" he said. "Anyway, by the time she finally confronted me about my feelings for you, sometime after New Year's, I was already beginning to suspect we were in trouble. I had figured out by that point that the attachment I had felt for her since her abandonment was actually guilt. I think that deep down I'd always believed that if I had gone after her and convinced her to stay with me, she wouldn't have died. I spent those ten years after she disappeared feeling like I shared some responsibility in her death. Finding out that Camille was actually alive and well woke me up to that realization, and it cured me of a lot of the misplaced affection. Anyway, regardless of the weakness of my feelings for her compared to you, she was my wife, and I owed her the responsibility of being a good husband. So I did my best. It was easy to be a father to Addie, because I had grown to love her so much, thanks to you. And it was actually pretty easy to be a husband to Camille at first, because she was trying so hard to be the perfect wife." Tyler's mouth took on a grim tightness at this point and his fingers flexed around mine.

"About six months after you left, I noticed that Camille was getting restless. She spent less and less time with us, especially with Addie. She never spent much time with her anyway, but soon she was flat out avoiding her. And me. I wasn't really surprised. Despite the fact that she was sweet and affectionate all the time, I knew by then she didn't really love me. I think it was because I knew that you did. I could see the difference." Tyler glanced over at me, a serene smile on his lips. The jeep passed under the archway proclaiming "Thorne Field Ranch" and my stomach leapt, as much with excitement as in response to Tyler's smile. I was almost home.

"By the time September rolled around, our sixteenth wedding anniversary, mind you," Tyler added sarcastically, "life was miserable. It was like we were playing one monstrous game of charades, pretending we were happily married. Both of us knew that whatever we had, or thought we had, was over. Camille was talking about sending Addie to a boarding school in Maryland. I knew that was her way of telling me that she had no interest in being a mother."

Tyler's lip curled at the memory, and his clear indignation on Addie's behalf endeared him to me even more, although I, too, had clenched my teeth. Anyone who really knew Addie would have realized that sending her away to school would crush her, spirit and all.

"So what happened?" I said through gritted teeth.

"Well, by that time, I had come to the conclusion that our marriage probably wasn't going to survive, but I wasn't willing to be the one to end it. I felt like I had an obligation to try to make things work, even though the thought of living with Camille seemed more like a life sentence than a blessing." Tyler grinned sardonically at me as he pulled up in front of the ranch house and came to a stop. He put the jeep in park and turned toward me.

"So life continued on in its general falseness until one day in early October, I woke to find Camille's side of the bed empty," he continued. "She had placed a letter on her pillow, informing me that she'd realized it had been a mistake to come back. She said we'd both changed too much, and we were too incompatible to make a successful marriage. She told me that divorce was the only solution she was comfortable with, and that her lawyer would be in touch. She also wrote that because she knew how much I loved Addie, she was giving me custody. She gave up all rights and privileges. She didn't even want visitation."

"Good," I muttered.

"Yeah." Tyler agreed with a smile. "All in all, I feel like things turned out rather well. Especially now." He squeezed my hand. "Anyway, as soon as I read the letter, I immediately picked up the phone to call your uncle."

"Uncle Jack?" I said in surprise.

"Yes," he said. "I understood from my limited communication with Jonathan that you were in contact with Jack, so I figured that he must know where you were. He confirmed that you were in Milton with Jonathan's family, as I suspected, and he told me about the art show that would be featuring your work. He pointed out that it would be the perfect time to reintroduce myself into your life, since Jonathan was in Japan and couldn't, to use Jack's phrase, 'screw things up.'"

I turned in my seat to face him, snorting with laughter. "Uncle Jack said that?" I asked. "He always seemed to be rooting for Jonathan."

"Well, he definitely likes Jonathan better than he likes me, but I think he suspected that you were more attached to me than you were to Jonathan," Tyler speculated. "He loves you. He knows that your preference is more important than his."

I smiled, thinking of my Uncle Jack. He had had good intentions, even if he had encouraged Tyler to "reintroduce himself" into my life at exactly the same time that Jonathan had surprised me with a visit and a marriage proposal. The situation that had once seemed so distressing now struck me as very funny. "Things didn't turn out exactly how you planned, did they?" I laughed.

"Not really." Tyler smiled. "Luckily, Jack saw me enter the exhibit and warned me that Jonathan was there, but I still wasn't expecting to find him wrapped around you, again, when I walked through that door that night." He looked out the window behind me and his mouth twisted in an ironic smile as he remembered.

"You did have a habit of interrupting our romantic interludes," I teased.

Tyler grimaced. "Believe me, both scenes I could have happily gone a lifetime without seeing. Now I'll never be able to get them out of my head."

"Well, you have to understand that neither of us was expecting to see you walk through that door, either," I reminded him. "You surprised us as much as we surprised you. And," I added pointedly, "don't even get me started on the many scenes involving you and various gorgeous women that *I'll* never be able to get out of *my* head."

Tyler laughed and opened his car door. He ran around to open mine for me, stopping to kiss me as I exited the vehicle.

"You have no idea how much I've missed that," he said, pulling me close to his side as we walked toward the front door of the ranch house.

Tyler led me into the library, where a magnificent pine tree stood in the corner, decorated in bright red and gold. Colorfully wrapped gifts lay piled underneath, waiting for a curly-haired ten-year-old to open them.

"Looks like you're all ready," I said. "Operation Santa was successful."

"Yeah, I put them all under the tree as soon as I knew she was asleep," Tyler said. "I usually take a walk right before bed nowadays. It helps me sleep. That's what I was doing when you nearly ran me down."

"What goes around . . . ," I reminded him with a smile.

He laughed and pulled me onto his lap in his favorite chair.

I smiled and cuddled closer to him as I looked around the room, drinking in the familiar atmosphere. Snuggling back into his arms, I felt as though, at last, I'd truly come home.

We didn't sleep that night. We spent the hours until dawn reminiscing, talking, and laughing, relishing the feeling of being suddenly together after so long.

Around seven the next morning, I heard the sound of little feet descending the stairs. I pressed a finger to Tyler's lips to silence him, as I jumped to my feet and pushed him into a corner of the library. I, myself, went and sat at the foot of the tree next to Addie's brightly wrapped presents. I waited with bated breath for her to appear, my eyes hungering for the sight of her.

She entered the room at a dead run, her dark curls flailing wildly around her head. She stopped so fast she almost fell backward when she saw me. She stood there staring for a good five seconds in complete silence. Finally she took a step forward and said in awe, "He *found* you!"

I looked at her in confusion, thrown off by the unexpected reaction. "Found me? Who? What are you talking about?"

"Santa," Addie answered as she took another step toward me. She seemed a little unsure about whether or not I was actually there. "I prayed last night that Heavenly Father would help Santa to bring you back, and he found you! He brought you to me for Christmas!" she exclaimed in wonder.

My eyes swelled with tears. Despite the fact that we had no blood relationship, there was no doubt in my mind that Addie was supposed to be my daughter. No one had ever loved a child more. I held out my arms to her and she launched herself into them, nearly knocking the breath from me.

I hugged her to me, feeling the sense of peace and rightness that only the Spirit can bring permeate the room. Tyler, his face stretched in a smile so wide it looked almost painful, settled himself next to us and pulled us both into the circle of his arms. Surrounded by family, I smiled up at him, joy overflowing from my eyes and streaming down my cheeks. All was right with the world.

epilogue

To borrow a phrase from a favorite book of mine, "Reader, I married him." Tyler and I were sealed to each other and to Addie for time and all eternity the following February in the Salt Lake Temple.

Danielle and Carson also eventually made it to the temple to be sealed. They were married in an LDS chapel in Boston three days after my miraculous Christmas reunion. Tyler, Addie, and I all flew out for the occasion. The ceremony was beautiful, and all who attended left feeling uplifted. Danielle and Carson were sealed to each other and to a brand-new baby girl one year later in the Boston Temple. They bought a small house down the street from River House and live there still.

As for Mariah, she remained the mistress of River House, following in the footsteps of her mother and grandmother. While she never married or joined the Church, she grew to respect the beliefs of her brother and sister and became quite an authority on gospel doctrine and Latter-day Saint history. She even went so far as to cover the Mormon pioneers in a history unit in one of her classes.

Uncle Jack remained in Boston, where he continues to this day to rule his publishing dynasty. He does often fly out to Utah to spend time with our family and he is always a welcome, if somewhat grumpy, addition to our family dinners. However, since his introduction to Charlotte Fairview, he has become a bit more mild-mannered, and she blushes like a teenager asked to her first dance whenever he enters the room.

As for Jonathan Kelly, he went back to Japan. He returned a year later to New York, where he eventually obtained the eternal family he asked about on an ice skating rink so many years ago. Jonathan turned out to be every bit the wonderful father that Mariah and I suspected. It is a comforting thought to me to know that Jonathan is as happy now as he has always deserved to be.

Tyler and I have now been married for nearly ten years. We are truly committed to each other, and fall more deeply in love each day. Though life isn't perfect, our happiness is rich and full, and we live each moment thankful for the blessing of spending it together.

discussion questions

1. When Camille suddenly returns to Thorne Field, how could improved communication have made Kate's predicament easier to bear? Do you think it would have changed the outcome?

2. How does the theme of independence versus interdependence play throughout the story? Which results in greater strength?

3. In what ways is Kate more prepared to be in a lasting relationship subsequent to her running away to Boston? Why?

4. Kate spends a great deal of time and energy trying to smother her feelings to avoid feeling pain. Is this the best way to deal with heartbreak? Have you experienced a similar situation?

5. Was it ethical of Jonathan to pursue Kate when he knew Kate's feelings for Tyler and Tyler's feelings for Kate?

6. Do you think Jonathan was justified in concealing Kate's location from his best friend? How could he have handled the situation differently? Was Kate justified in asking him to conceal her whereabouts?

7. Was Kate right to return to Tyler? Should she have chosen Jonathan instead? Why? Have you ever had to make a choice between two equally appealing options?

about the author

Lauren Winder Farnsworth was born and raised in Salt Lake City, Utah. She is an avid reader, a chocolate enthusiast, a musicophile and a CPA . . . who somehow also finds time to indulge in her real obsession—writing. She obtained bachelor's and master's degrees in accounting from the University of Utah, and the only entity that holds more of her heart than her alma mater is her husband, Bryan. Lauren currently lives in South Jordan, Utah, where she spends entirely too much time watching *Gilmore Girls* and looking for excuses not to clean. You can visit her at LaurenWinderFarnsworth.com.